a SHREWDNESS *of* SWINDLERS

DEANNA KNIPPLING

WONDERLAND PRESS

FREE EBOOK

Get a free ebook and sign up for the Wonderland Press-Herald at https://wonderlandpress.com/free-ebook/.

CONTENTS

The Liar's Table

The Honeybee's Sting was a speakeasy back in Prohibition days, in a big brick Lincoln Park building in Chicago. The main floor was a Chinese laundry. Upstairs was Madame Ixnay's, a house of what you might call ill repute, with eight working girls.

It was a classy joint, as far as those things went.

The bribes it took to keep that place open flowed like the Chicago River into Lake Michigan—polluted and thick.

The Boss was a big man, broad in the shoulders, with a big bushy mustache and dark hair. He had impeccable taste in suits and a knack for getting supplies of decent liquor, sometimes even with the right labels on the outside. He was connected to at least two crime families but somehow managed to stay independent. Everyone knew the Boss was bringing in the liquor via the laundry carts, but as long as the bottles weren't sticking out from under the piles of towels and bedsheets, the cops pretended not to notice.

The Honeybee's Sting was down in the basement. The outside of the building was plain brick, nothing fancy. You'd get there by car. The driver would pull up to a door in the alleyway, a huge double steel door stenciled with the words *KNOCK FOR SERVICE.*

You'd get out of the car, dressed to the nines, and knock on the door with whatever the secret code was that week, and either the door would open or it wouldn't.

That door was never wrong. There was a lock on it but we never used it. It was just that the door would open...or it wouldn't.

Like magic.

You'd go inside through a plain brick landing stacked with empty laundry carts, then down some cement stairs to the basement, where there was another heavy door, oak this time. You'd knock the code on the door again, and someone would have to swing it open to let you in.

Light and sound would come spilling out, and the smell of alcohol and perfume and men in heavy coats sweating like pigs, the sound of Black men playing jazz or an octoroon crooning, voices chattering, the sound of glass smashing, of women laughing.

You stepped inside that door and the temperature went up at least twenty degrees. The door slammed behind you, and you were in.

Back then, speakeasies couldn't afford to be all that fancy, unless they were run directly by the mob. You had to be ready for the cops to seize whatever they could get their hands on. The patrons weren't too gentle on things, either.

So the Honeybee's Sting wasn't all that much to look at in 1929. After Prohibition ended, we fancied it up, but that was later.

In 1929, the walls were open brickwork and the floors were bare cement. A high oak table served as the bar and there were high, round tables around the edges of the room. One corner was cleared for the musicians, and the center of the room was cleared out for dancing. Silk palm trees stood in pots in the corner, half-hiding the spittoons. Bare bulbs hung from overhead on cords.

Behind the bar was a door that led to a reinforced smuggler's closet that was hidden behind a second door at the back of a shallow safe—not a place you wanted to get locked up in at night, but it did mean that the cops couldn't get at the liquor stores during a raid.

Opposite the safe was a door to the back room, which used to be the coal cellar. The coal furnace had been replaced a few years ago with a gas furnace that worked more efficiently, and didn't require stoking.

At least, that's what everyone said had happened. But I never saw where that gas furnace was in that basement, or anywhere else for that matter. We had radiators for heat and no end to the amount of hot water for the ladies to wash clothes in, but I never saw a hot-water tank, either. Dom told me not to worry about it.

If the Boss was big, Dom, the bartender, was bigger.

Dom was his own favorite bouncer. If it was busy, the Boss might send one or two guys over to help him, but mostly what they did was answer the door and pour drinks for the girls. I never saw a one of those other guys have to lift a finger against a customer. Dom took it as a point of pride to handle things personally. Word got around. Dom would let loose on some scumbag about once every six months. There was one time Dom cut a guy's pinky finger off, right in the bar. I put it in a jar of milk to help keep it fresh while he saw if a doctor could sew it back on again.

Dom had an on-again, off-again middle-European accent. He used to talk to the bar itself, and that's when the accent would come out. "Tair tair," he'd tell the bar while wiping it. "Is only scratch, noboty means bat. Only scratch." Then he'd turn around and, in a pure Chicago nasal accent that went straight through your eardrums, would yell, "Hey mister, you gonna get yer fat ass offa that tabletop, or yam I gonna have ta come over and remove it?"

The tables were small, the Black jazz musicians were all right when you could hear them, the girls serving drinks were pretty and had sharpened fingernails, and I washed dishes, mopped floors, swept out spiderwebs, and served as general dogsbody.

They called me Kid. I started working there in 1927 and stayed after Prohibition ended, all the way to 1949 when it closed. Some new folks re-opened the bar in 1993. It wasn't the same. Whether that was a good thing or a bad thing, I couldn't tell you. Just different.

The Honeybee's Sting had a number of incidents worth telling stories about, but one in particular sticks in my mind.

The date was December 29th. Two nights later, it would be one of the busiest days of the year, with everyone out looking to celebrate the change from one decade to another. But the twenty-ninth was a cold Sunday night, cold enough to freeze your spit before it hit the ground, a night so cold it couldn't snow. It was windy as hell, though, and what snow there was on the ground whipped around like knives.

In short, it was a slow night, even for the girls upstairs. Nobody wanted to go anywhere. Even the jazz trio, always desperate for tips, hadn't showed up.

And yet that night, the back room had been reserved for special guests.

The back room was darker and damper than the main room and had a low ceiling, just high enough that I didn't hit my head. Two walls were nothing but rough brick, and the far wall had an old coal chute that had been rebuilt as a back exit against police raids.

When I had come in for the night, Dom had told me, "The Boss wants you to serve the special guests tonight, so the girls can go home."

I said I was game, and the girls left gratefully. I even got a kiss on the cheek from one of them. Problem was, I was so shy I could barely stutter out my own name, let alone make witty banter. I hoped I wouldn't have to say much. Maybe the whole thing would be cancelled due to weather.

I finished up my chores early, then sat at a table, reading an old back issue of *Black Mask* that I had in my back pocket. I reread one of the Continental Op stories, and waited.

The first of the special guests to come in was a dame, a real flapper type, the kind of woman who normally only appears on the arm of some guy wearing a pinstriped monkey suit. (She was the kind of gal that the Boss liked to show off.) I heard her before I saw her. She clomped noisily down the stairs, loud as a cow, then banged on the oak door at the bottom.

From behind the bar, Dom yelled, "Who da hell comes into a joint on a night like this?"

He stomped over to the door, threw it open, and burst into a smile. He said the dame's name and she snuggled up to him, giving him a big fat kiss on the cheek, kicking up one heel and standing on tiptoe on the other. She was wearing a shiny otter-fur coat and a slinky green dress underneath, kitten heels and a Marcel wave in her copper hair, dark red bow-shaped lips drawn in with pencil and lipstick, in two different colors.

I'm sure you won't mind if I just call her "the Dame." It's not like there were two of her.

Dom showed her into the back room, and I folded up my magazine and stuffed it into my back pocket. I ducked through the doorway and stuck my head in.

"Need anything, Dom? F-for the lady?"

The Dame looked at me and lifted her eyebrows, which were penciled-in arches. In a little-girl voice she exclaimed, "Oh, my! Aren't you the tall one?"

"Y-yes," I said. And blushed.

She laughed. "Oh, *Dom*. Can I keep him?"

"No," Dom said in his middle-European accent, "Da kid belongs to da bar. You can only borrow him."

The Dame laughed, throaty and deep, then in the little-girl voice said, "Dom'll bring me something in a minute, sweetie."

"T-take your coat?"

"Ooh, it's chilly down here tonight," she said. "Ask me later, when the room fills up."

"Okay, miss."

She blew me a kiss, and I excused myself right back out the door. Dom bustled in and out, bringing her a drink.

The next special guest was Madame Ixnay herself, from upstairs.

She had olive skin and black eyes and smooth black hair in a bob, a patch of silver strands at one temple. I couldn't have told you her age. She could have been twenty-five; she could have been sixty. Under a dark wool coat, she was dressed in an ivory silk dress with a long white bow. She looked like a statue of Venus or an Egyptian goddess, something you'd have to go to a museum to see.

"Hello, kid," she said. She had a deep voice, mannish, that always ruffled up the hairs on the back of my neck.

"Madame," I said, trying to give her a little bow. Dom was out of sight in the other room. "Are you here for the back room?"

She nodded.

I said, "Cold night out," while she handed me her dark wool coat.

"A good night for intimate whispers."

I didn't know what to say to that, so I shut my mouth, suddenly reminded how little I knew of what was going on. I started to lead her toward the back room.

"Still reading the magazines?" she asked, slipping the copy of *Black Mask* out of my back pocket in a way that was more suggestive than any double-entendre delivered by one of her girls.

"Y-yeah."

"You going to write for them one day?"

I felt a hot line of embarrassment ripple straight up my spine. "N-no."

"You should. Use the stories from this place! Just change the names so the Boss doesn't find out." She winked at me, then disappeared into the room. I hung up her coat on a rack by the door. The coat was dry and not even cold. She must have walked straight down from upstairs.

She had left my copy of *Black Mask* on the bar, so I picked it up, trying to decide on whether to keep reading or hide it away for the rest of the night. It wasn't like I hadn't read the stories before.

A heavy set of footsteps began coming down the stairs.

I walked over to the coat rack and tucked the magazine into my winter coat, then went to do the door to answer it.

I recognized him at first sight, of course—I had read every story of his from the pulps I could find. I was tempted to get my copy of *Black Mask* back out of my coat and get him to sign it, but he scowled at me with his wild black eyebrows and I changed my mind.

What he was doing in Chicago, I didn't know. Unlike Madame Ixnay's, his coat was cold and sparkling with melting snowflakes.

He handed me his hat and coat.

"Sir," I said, too awed to say anything else.

"I'm here for a private gathering," he said, his voice sounding thin. Then he started coughing, a terrible noise. I took a step toward him, but he held out one hand and gestured me to wait while he coughed into a red print handkerchief.

"The room's b-back here, sir," I said, when he had finished.

"Thank you, son."

I led him to the back room, where he was warmly greeted by the ladies, and by a solemn nod from Dom. I hung around for a second. It's not every day that you meet one of your heroes.

The Detective-turned-writer said, "Shouldn't you-know-who be here already?"

Dom said, "He hadta run an errand. He'll get here when he gets here."

"Does he have it?"

Dom put his hand on his chest. "I swear on the twisted oak over my grandmudder's grave, in da old country. He has it. I seen it."

The Detective's shoulders relaxed. "And he'll give it to me?"

Dom shrugged. "It's the prize for tonight. Whoever wins da contest, gets the prize. You got a good story, yah?"

At that, my ears pricked up.

But before the Detective could answer, Dom turned to me and said, "I think I hear another one," and I had to duck out before I heard the Detective's answer.

This time, it wasn't just one person coming down the stairs, but two. They moved at what seemed like a crawl. I heard an extra thump on the stairs here and there: a cane. The knock at the door was a thin tapping noise. I opened up.

The gent was both elderly and tall—although not as tall as I was. He was pale, so pale that his skin almost seemed like marble. He had thin, colorless lips and flat, deep-set eyes. Eyes without a soul.

I recognized him from the newspapers. He was a rich, rich man. And a very old one.

I was surprised he'd been able to make it down the stairs, with or without the help of the young woman beside him.

Her I recognized, too. She was an actress from the West Coast, Chinese by birth. Not a leading lady—they didn't let Chinese women lead anything, not then and hardly not now—but someone you'd recognize from her alluring, deep eyes.

The old man I'm going to call the Vampire. That's what he was, an old bloodsucker. The Actress I'll just call the Actress. Neither one of them gave me much of a once-over. They both seemed preoccupied by something, and barely saw me as I took their coats, which were both only lightly sprinkled with snowflakes.

"If you would follow me?" I asked. It was a lot easier to sound confident around a millionaire and a famous actress than it was to sound that way in front of one of your inspirations.

Slowly, we worked our way over to the open door of the back room. The Actress went in first and was greeted politely, but not warmly, although there was a certain look that passed between her and the Detective.

When the Vampire followed her, everyone went dead silent. The hostility was so thick I could feel it prickling over my skin.

Dom said, "Sit, sit."

The Vampire said, in an ancient voice, "I see that I have been forgiven for last time."

The Detective said, "More or less. As long as I get what I came here for."

"That, sir, is up to you."

The two scowled at each other.

Dom turned to me. "Kid, put the kettle on, wouldja? For tea. And open a bottle of white wine for this gentleman here. The good stuff."

"Yes, sir."

I hung up the coats. We had a little electric hot plate wired up on the wood shelves along the back wall behind the bar, and I got it started. It took me a while to find the tea. It was in the liquor storage closet, inside the safe. We made hot toddies all year long, what with weather in Chicago being what it is, but hardly anybody ever requested actual tea. Then I went through what bottles of white wine we had, and took one of the bottles out of Dom's separate reserve. I showed it to him and he nodded. I brought a glass of it out to the Vampire.

The tea kettle whistled on the hot plate and I ran back out to take it off.

By then someone else was already knocking at the door.

The new guest was in a tan wool suit with a Nehru-collared shirt. He wore small, round eyeglasses, was bald, and had a bushy moustache and eyebrows to match. He flashed me a friendly smile as I came in, and I decided I liked him.

He was definitely a tea guy. I showed him to the table and went back out to brew the tea without being asked. From inside the room I heard him speaking in a British accent.

I ran him the tea and heard more steps coming down the stairs, slow and heavy. Footsteps bringing someone who didn't much want to be there, that night.

I ducked back out to answer the door. It was a man I'd seen before, a doctor who sometimes visited the girls at Madame Ixnay's, or who attended a customer of the Honeybee's Sting when one was needed. He was so discreet that I didn't know his name. Everyone just called him "the Good Doctor." He was a colored man, not dark but not light enough to pass.

I offered to take his coat, but he shook his head. "It shall have to be hung separately. It's rather stained."

I took a second look at him. He was dressed in an evening suit with a long wool coat buttoned up in front, all deep black, like he was mourning. He had been outside long enough to put a cold, wet shine on his skin, and his coat looked damp, even across the front, like he'd been splashed with something. I wondered if the cabs had refused to pick him up.

But it wasn't until he unbuttoned his coat and took it off, draping it over a table, that I understood what he meant. His shirt cuffs were stained with blood.

I said, "Let me warm up some water for you to wash in. I can try to do something about the coat before it sets in. Dab it with rags, anyway, sir."

He blinked at me, and said, "If you would. I thank you."

I nodded. "If you'll follow me, the others are back here."

"I thank you," he repeated.

I led him into the back room, and Dom showed him to a seat.

Without greeting the others, the Good Doctor said, "I have an announcement. The last member of our party will not be arriving. He has had an accident."

The Dame gasped with an almost comic over-reaction, but nobody else looked much surprised.

The Good Doctor continued, "He was killed near here a few minutes ago, presumably while traveling to meet with the rest of us. I was called to try to save him, but was unable to do so."

Dom stood next to me and murmured, "Lock the downstairs door, wouldja? Everyone that's coming is already here, and we don't want to be interrupted."

I locked the downstairs door, poured the rest of the boiled water into a bucket and laid out some soap, set more water on to boil, then started working on the Good Doctor's coat. I did what I could, but the dark wool was clotted and sodden with blood. I wondered if I should suggest the Good Doctor leave the coat with the ladies upstairs to clean, and borrow something else for the night.

From inside the room I heard them arguing about what had happened. To my surprise, it sounded like they were accusing each other of having done it, despite the fact that everyone in the room other than the Good Doctor had been downstairs at the time of the man's death.

The Good Doctor dealt out the accusations.

"You," he said, possibly to the Vampire, "being a Temperance man, have a great deal of money and no love of rum-runners. And you—" I thought this was directed toward the Dame— "Have had a grudge against the man since 1922, when he dropped you for another woman. You," he might have told the Detective, "crossed paths with him before you left the Pinkertons, and old grudges run deep. While you," I think he told Dom, "stand most to profit from his death."

At that, goosebumps rose up on my flesh. The only death that Dom might stand to profit from was the Boss's, and if the Boss had just been gunned down, that could be bad news for the employment of yours truly.

But the Good Doctor wasn't done yet. "You are in the man's debt," he said, and I wasn't sure who he was talking to, until Madame Ixnay said, "I did not—" and the Good Doctor snapped at her with a "We can get into denials in a moment, *madame*," then continued with, "And who knows what *you* have been sent here by George to do."

The only George who had been in the papers lately was King George of Great Britain. I guessed that the last statement had been addressed to the British gentleman with the mustache—which might make the Brit a spy.

The Actress said, "And what about me? What motive would I have had?"

"You're friends with a couple of other people at the table," the Good Doctor said. "And that's enough for me."

The Actress gave a little snort.

I kept dabbing away at the coat, quiet as a mouse in church.

Dom said, "All right, all right. There is no proof that he was murdered by any of us here at the table, and he had plenty of other enemies who could have done it. Can we not call a truce for the night?"

The Good Doctor said, "What if *he* wasn't the only one who was targeted? None of us can trust anyone else in this room. And what about that boy? What if he betrays us? What if he's already gone upstairs to talk?"

A chair scraped, and Dom's face appeared in the doorway. I had a rag and was scrubbing, wide-eyed, at the Good Doctor's coat.

"I won't talk," I squeaked out.

"You are a good kid," Dom said. "But you have dose big ears." He turned back to the room. "I trust him."

Madame Ixnay's voice said, "He wants to be a writer, though."

The Spy said, "Writers *can* be discreet..."

The Detective agreed with him.

But the Vampire said, "If he's trustworthy, then let him sit with us. Since our ninth is missing tonight, he may sit in."

Dom stuck his head back out and waved me toward the room.

I protested. "Sit in? Is this a card game? But what if I don't know how to play!"

That got a laugh. Dom grabbed me by the ear, hissing, "Just do what I tell you," and pushed me inside the room.

The Vampire was getting up from his seat along the side of the table. He hobbled with his cane to the head seat, with the Actress standing quickly to help him get seated.

"I will play the Host," announced the Vampire, as he sat. "Unless there are objections."

There weren't any. What any of it meant, I had no idea. I was shivering with terror.

The table was set out as follows: Dom had the bottom of the table, the seat nearest the door. At the far end—the head of the table, with his back toward the old coal chute—the Vampire was seated. To the left of the Vampire—my right, that is—was the Actress; to the right was the Dame. Next to the Actress was the Spy, and then, next to Dom on Dom's right, was the Good Doctor. On the opposite side of the table were the Dame, the Detective next to her, and then Madame Ixnay beside him, at Dom's left.

Dom picked up a spare chair and set it at the corner, between him and Madame Ixnay.

"Have a seat, kid," Dom said.

I shook my head. Whatever was going on, I wasn't sure I wanted in.

But Dom pointed forcefully to the chair. His European accent got real thick: "*Haff seat.*"

I sat, uncomfortably aware of Madame Ixnay to my left. She smelled like soap and lavender and, well, Madame Ixnay.

The Vampire leaned his elbows on the table and steepled his fingers together, while looking from face to face. He was old, but, like the nickname I'd given him, he seemed to have far more vitality than he should have. His cold blue eyes finally rested on me last of all, and lingered.

"We have lost a member; we have found a member. We have lost a treasure... Yes?"

The Good Doctor cleared his throat. "We didn't lose the treasure."

"You were able to obtain it?" asked the Vampire. "From the body?"

The Detective said bitterly, "So he could keep it for himself."

The Good Doctor said, "A man died in my arms. I simply forgot." He reached into his pocket, then frowned and reached into a different pocket. "I seem to have—" He twisted around in his seat to the door of the room.

I jumped up and said, "I'll bring your coat." While I had been cleaning the coat, I had felt a couple of lumps here and there, but when you work for a boss like mine, you don't go sticking your hands into other people's pockets.

I was back in a flash, holding the coat out for the Good Doctor to search through. He dipped a hand into a pocket and pulled out a blue velvet box, the kind you get from a jewelry store. The box had blood soaked into it. It was too big for a ring or a pair of diamond cufflinks, but too small for a big necklace, and it had a brass hinge at the back and a little brass clip to make sure it didn't pop open. I didn't hear anything rattle or slide around within it as he took it out of an inner coat pocket, and put it down on the table.

He slid it across the table, a bead of sweat at his temple.

The Dame reached for the case, took it, and peeked inside. The others watched her closely. Then she closed the little clasp again and put the case back where it had been. "It's in there."

The Detective demanded, "The real thing?"

The Dame said, "It's the real one, all right. I can hear it scratching from inside."

Nobody argued with her, or asked for a look.

The Vampire said, "If *that* is settled, then...?" and looked around the table. No further comments were made. "Then we shall continue. We have the treasure to be won, a tidy number of members, and as many hours as we need in which to determine who shall be declared the victor. Our contest may begin."

As soon as the Vampire declared that the contest—whatever it was—could begin, everyone else in the room seemed to sink back in their chairs a little, as if they'd been on tenterhooks about the possibility that whatever it was, wasn't going to happen. The Actress even smiled, kind of lop-sided.

The Spy lifted his tea. "To the contest."

Everyone else lifted their glasses, except me. "To the contest."

I looked down at my lap.

Dom said, "Kid, go get yourself something to drink. It's on me. Don't worry about it."

I said, in a small voice, "Dom? What's going on?"

He laughed. "You don't know what any of this is about, but you're game, eh, kid?" He put a heavy hand on my shoulder, making me lose my balance in the chair. I grabbed for the table, accidentally putting an elbow in Madame Ixnay's soft, silken side.

I squeaked in apology, which made just about everyone laugh at me. I felt tears coming to my eyes and put my head down on the table, which only made everyone laugh the louder.

Dom said, "I will bring you something. Don't move."

Madame Ixnay seemed to catch her breath first. "Don't worry about it, darling boy. We all have to start somewhere. Even that old vampire at the end of the table had a first time attending—didn't you?"

The Vampire chuckled with a dry voice. "I did. Back in eighteen eighty-nine. December twenty-ninth that year, a Sunday. An old friend invited me, who has since passed." He paused to lick his lips. "It was his dearest wish."

The Detective said, "You're awful old to be hanging around so long. Haven't you ever won?"

"Perhaps I enjoy the event more than the prize," the Vampire said.

"Maybe you don't need it," the Detective parried.

What they were arguing about, I didn't know. A diamond?

Dom reappeared with something golden in a pint beer glass. I sniffed at it, then sipped: it was a Jack Rose cocktail, made with applejack brandy, lemon juice, and grenadine. I think Dom knew the man who distilled the applejack, from somewhere in Wisconsin. I sipped. A warmth spread through me, just enough to keep my insides from freezing, a hint of late fall and cinnamon. I vowed not to drink too much of it or too quickly.

"Thank you," I said.

Dom thumped his chest twice with a fist, then stretched out one arm dramatically toward the table and said: "You wish to know what we do here tonight? We are playing a game, a game that has been played since nobody knows when. The gods themselves played it when the world was young. At the end of every decade, a group of liars, cheats, and thieves meets, and on that night, they compete for a stolen treasure of great worth. Whoever wins the contest holds the treasure for the next ten years—but can never play again. Sometimes there are more than twenty players; sometimes, only three.

"And the game," Dom paused dramatically, "is to tell the best lie."

"He means the best *story*," Madame Ixnay murmured in my ear. "He's just being melodramatic."

"What?" I said. All of the words that I heard all made sense individually; it was just when they were all put together that I struggled.

Madame Ixnay sighed. "They always make it out to be a bigger deal than it is. A bunch of bullshitters get together once a decade and tell tales, with a trinket to go along with it at the end of the night to whoever takes first prize. It's just an old tradition."

"Oh," I said, not sure whether I believed her. "And...and *I* have to tell a story?"

"Yeah," she said. "But don't worry if it's bad. It's your first time. Last time was my first time, and I was terrible. I survived it. Just go with it. It's kinda fun."

"You're all a bunch of liars and thieves?" I asked.

"And cheats," Madame Ixnay said.

"And...what am I?"

"You're a liar," the Dame interjected suddenly. "They said you was a writer, didn't they?"

"I want to be one," I said. "But—"

"But nuthin'," quipped the Dame in her chirpy voice. "You wanna be a writer? Then start lyin'."

The Spy cleared his throat and said, "It really is the only way to become a writer, to simply begin."

Helplessly, I looked at the Detective to get his opinion. He nodded.

In a strangled voice, I said, "I'm in...but *please* don't pick me to go first."

They all laughed.

It was time to begin.

The Vampire said, "First to tell his tale this night...will be the Bartender."

I squeaked out, "Please don't make me go second, either!"

And everyone laughed again.

When the laughter had died down, Dom said, "I don't have real high hopes of winning the prize, but I ain't gonna come in last place, either. But first, everybody check your drinks. I wouldn't want to have to break off my story, just because some Brit ran out of tea."

The Spy chuckled at that one, and turned over his cup: only a drop fell out. "I admit I was prepared to put a brave face upon the matter, if necessary."

Dom sent me off to make up more of that bad old tea. I boiled the whole kettle and found a heavy teapot, thick with dust and mouse droppings, on a back shelf. A little spit and polish, and it was clean and ready to go, immaculate and white. I poured the water and a bunch of tea leaves in, hoping I wasn't doing it too wrong, then brought it in for the Spy to keep in front of him. I even wrapped it up in a towel to help keep it hot.

Meanwhile, Dom had made up all the rest of the drinks, and when I came back to the table, my glass was completely full again, almost too full to pick up.

I took my journal out of my coat pocket and brought it with me to the table. As soon as I was sitting down, I started flipping through journal pages, looking for ideas.

Dom gave everyone a moment to settle in, and said, "This is an epic story to rival the Odyssey *or* Ivanhoe. *It addresses a matter more important than anything in the Bible or Beowulf. It's about..." He stared at us all from under eyebrows to rival an Old Testament saint. "...running a bar."*

Several people groaned.

In a higher-pitched voice—after a moment, I realized that big Dom was trying to tell the story as a woman, one with an accent even thicker than the Dame's—he began:

When Pigs Fly
The Bartender's Tale

So I'm just a working girl in Cedar Rapids, Iowa, and at the end of 1925, there were two competing wire stores in town. A wire store is a place where you can set up a con job involving a so-called telegraph operator, a guy who thinks he's betting on horses without the inconvenience of losing money at it, and someone to bring those two people together—a roper. Also there are a number of side characters, the kind that flesh out the crowd so a guy doesn't feel so lonely while he's getting fleeced.

The general idea is that your "telegraph operator" gets the race results from Western Union, calls them over to the guy who doesn't like to lose money—the mark, that is—so he can put a bet in, and then, like two minutes later, sends the results to everybody else. The mark, no dummy, can put a last-second bet on the race winner before everyone else finds out about it.

So it doesn't look like he's getting something for nothing, the mark has to agree to give the telegraph operator a cut of the winnings.

A big one.

This works out great for the mark the first time around. First you gotta give him a taste of winning if you want him to come back for more. After that it's up to the team of cons to take as much money off the guy as possible, sometimes more than once. A real good wire store can leave it so the mark thinks that it was all just stinking bad luck that the deal didn't go through. Leaving him literally begging for another chance to get ripped off again.

A couple of rules of thumb here.

First, don't have two wire stores in one town.

One of the things you gotta do with any kind of store, be it a wire or payoff store, or even one of the old fight and foot-race stores, is put the fix in—that is, to pay off the cops. If you got two stores in the same town (aside from big places like New York or Chicago), that means that the price of the fix goes up. And not just a little bit, either—you never know when the other guys are going to screw you over and hire the cops to bust you. So you're constantly outbidding each other, which means you gotta take bigger risks during the cons. People get real emotional. People who get real emotional take stupid risks. Everything spirals outta control. It's no good.

Second, don't take a mark from his own hometown.

That one should be self-explanatory. When you're outta town and somewhere new, it kinda feels like you're in a foreign country. If you see something strange, you chalk it up to local customs. Which makes it easier for the cons to cover if somebody makes a mistake.

And nobody wants a sucker hanging around after the game is over. Some people fool so hard you couldn't scrape 'em off with a stick.

⚬

The two competing wire stores in Cedar Rapids in 1925 were run by a pair of Polish guys, which was less of a coincidence than you might think.

The first store was run by Reggie Skurski, who'd come over to Chicago in the 1880s as a kid, learned the trade, and moved to Cedar Rapids in 1904. It's not so far from Chicago to Cedar Rapids. You can make it in about seven hours if you have to, by touring car. Call it five hours in a speedster if you feel like outrunning the local cops. It was handy for trains, too. Lots of cattle started going through Cedar Rapids after the Sinclair meatpacking company set up shop in 1871. The only reason I mention this is that cattlemen make for good marks—they're used to taking risks and losing their shirts, then doing it all over again. (I grew up on a cattle ranch but that's neither here nor there.)

The second store was run by Dan Zanarowski, who was a second-generation immigrant and dressed like a Chicago mobster. He was young, about thirty-five or forty years old, and handsome. Had a wolfish look to him. Mothers would cross themselves and hide their daughters when Zanarowski went by. Shop owners would count the money in their cash drawers. You always had the sense that he was just about to pull a fast one on you. The scary part was the suspicion that he might make you like it.

Reggie Skurski was the first to come to Cedar Rapids. He was the one I worked for. Zanarowski was a Johnny-come-lately, but a good one. He'd had a store in Chicago but had been chased out by the Italians.

I never did hear the real story. Just rumors.

When Zanarowski came to town, word was that he told Reggie he was taking over the store, just like that. As if the rest of us would just hop from one owner to the other without a by-your-leave. There might have been a suitcase of money involved. There might have been a pistol involved. It was hard to keep things straight about those two guys, especially when they started shouting Polish at each other. Anyway there were insults and threats, that much was clear. And the result was that Zanarowski set up shop not three blocks away from Reggie's store.

Reggie's store was in the basement of a drugstore-soda shop. During the day the basement was a wire store; at night it was a speakeasy. The basement was almost as pretty as the upstairs, all brass and colored tile and a white marble top. If Reggie was feeling fine, he might have someone bring down ice cream from upstairs and serve it up with bootleg booze poured over it. You'd stir it up and make it a milkshake. Reggie's place had the best booze and the best music, too. He kept a rooming-house for Black travelers, which meant that a lot of good jazz musicians and singers came through. The place had a good reputation in either capacity. Some of Reggie's marks, he got Christmas cards from. That's how good he was. A real gentleman.

At first Zanarowski wasn't much of a problem. Nobody would work with him unless he brought them over from Chicago. The cops stayed bought. His store was in an honest-to-god Western Union office. How he worked that setup, I ain't got a clue. Seemed sloppy to me.

Then, little by little, things started to change. One or two guys changed sides. The cops started to waver. The price on the fix went up. Reggie started pushing for more customers, really laying it on us ropers to bring the goods in double-quick. Anyone caught taking a mark over to Zanarowski's place was dead to Reggie.

We started sending Zanarowski marks, the kind that could get him in trouble—Ku Klux Klan, Mafiosi, a couple of Chinese guys looking to set up a laundry with a little too much cash in their pockets, that kind of thing. Chicago cops' second cousins. Any fish that stank landed on Zanarowski's door. He had some close calls but stayed afloat, getting madder and madder at Reggie every time.

We crossed our fingers and waited.

Zanarowski was gonna make a mistake that money couldn't fix. We all knew it.

⸻ ◆ ⸻

My favorite spot to work was the cafeteria at the Union Station. I had a number of short tricks, not even cons really, that I could work while I was waiting to hook a fish. Card tricks including the three-card monte, cigarette tricks, sleight of hand, dice, you name it—I was even known to go home with a gent or two, or even a lady if she asked right, so it didn't look too suspicious when I found the big marks and disappeared with them. I used one under-the-table profession to cover the other. I stayed friendly with the train station staff. If they thought I was no better than I should be, then at least they didn't think I was worse than I was. If a passenger wanted to know where they could have a fun time in Cedar Rapids, the cafeteria girls sent them to me and I flashed my dimples.

So there I was. It was two days before New Year's Eve and I didn't have nobody to keep me warm—or to buy me a gin, neither. The snow was already thick on the ground. The day after Christmas there had been a real flour-paste kind of storm, the kind that knocks down trees and freezes the river so fast you can see fish stuck in the ice. Even though I was inside, I was shivering. The big open area of the train station was all marble and brass, big black-and-white floor tiles that were slick with all the snow getting tracked over them. It felt like all that fancy stonework was sucking the heat out of the air. I was holding a cold cup of coffee between my mitts and it still felt like the warmest thing in the room. I was almost ready to go home for the day. It was maybe three in the afternoon—still light out—and I told myself, if I didn't catch anything after the Chicago train came in, I was headed home.

Three thirty-five, the Chicago train rolled in and passengers started pouring out. One second the janitors were mopping the floor, the next the whole station was jam-packed with damp wool and chaos. My nose had started to run. I thought about picking a couple of pockets and skipping out.

Just then an old guy stepped into the cafeteria and got in line for the girls at the counter. He was dressed in a smoke-gray suit with a fine gold watch chain. It was so thin that it wouldn't have been any trouble to snap it off without him blinking an eye. He had a bowler hat, a mustache, and spectacles so round they looked like crystal balls. A green silk tie, polished black shoes, and a walking cane that looked like it had a fancified claw hammer on top finished the outfit. I recognized the cane. Reggie had one of 'em too. Reggie said they were used by noblemen back in old Poland. It looked like you could beat someone's brains out with it.

The man patiently worked his way to the front of the line, leaned forward to the girls at the counter, and whispered to them. One of them stood on tiptoe and jerked her head toward me.

I was on.

The gent brought a pair of steaming coffee cups with him over to my table, sat down with his cane tucked between his knees, looked around the room without really seeming to, and pulled a flask out of his coat. He added a dollop of caramel liquid to both cups and said, "So I hear that you know of a good place to get a drink."

My eyes musta been bulging out of my head to see him do it out in the open like that. He said, "My name is Robert Allgood. You have heard of me?"

He had an Eastern European accent; I was pretty sure that the name that his mamma called him wasn't anything like Robert Allgood. But yeah, I'd heard of him.

He was a millionaire. Maybe even a billionaire by then—I wasn't keeping track of the guy's bank book at the time. He owned most of the cattle trade up in Chicago. Cattle coming in, meat going out. Aha, I said to myself, here's a guy looking to buy up Sinclair's. He was supposed to be a real eccentric, too. He traveled all over the world looking for the lost treasure of Sir Richard Francis Drake, which was supposed to be somewhere off the coast of Panama or something. He'd searched for Atlantis, Hy-Brasil, Hyperborea, Thule, even lost Avalon.

It was like someone was sending me a belated Christmas present.

"Of course I heard of you," I said, giving him a little bat of my eyes. I took a sip of the coffee. The bourbon was about a hundred times better than it had a right to be. I closed my eyes and sipped again. Then I got back to business. "You're a cattleman, right? From Chicago. You were in the newspapers the other day. The business pages."

He lifted an eyebrow like he was surprised I could read. "The girls say that you know where a man can get a drink in this town."

"I do, Mister Allgood. But if you're expecting something this good, you're gonna be sadly disappointed."

He chuckled under his breath.

"But we do have better tunes than this," I said. The only music in the station was the march of booted feet marching through the open area, and not in time neither. "Bix Biederbecke's in town for sure, and I heard Bessie Smith might show tonight or tomorrow."

He nodded. "That is good."

I couldn't believe my good luck, and it made me kinda sloppy. "Whatcha doing today?"

"Looking for company."

I put my cold hand on his sleeve. "My boyfriend dumped me and I got fired on Christmas Eve, mister. I'm bored and I'm lonely and I gotta start looking for a typist job in a couple of days, or else I'm gonna have to go back to my ma's to live. If you're looking for a good time till New Year's Day, I'm all yours. After that I gotta start lookin' for work."

⸺◆⸺

That night we went to the speakeasy under Reggie's drugstore.

By then I had heard the reason Allgood was in town. Sure, he was there to check out Sinclair's, but...well, I'll get to that. If I had heard that kind of story from anyone else, I wouldn't have believed it. Even so it had struck me funny and I still wasn't too sure about it.

Reggie was behind the counter with three girls in paper hats and tight dresses to come and pick up drinks. He gave me the eyeball as I came in, trying to see whether the guy with me was a sucker or one of my other type of clients.

The place wasn't full, despite it being the holiday season. Word was that Zanarowski had taken over one of the other big speakeasies in Cedar Rapids, a place underneath the local bowling alley. At night the pin boys went home and the cigarette girls came out. I might have brought in a fish but as far as Reggie was concerned it wasn't going to put him in any kind of good mood or anything.

I expected him to change his tune once he heard how big a fish it was, though.

The biggest.

The bouncer, Cecil Dykstra, had let us in on my signal. I'd given the name Jenkins, which was a false password that meant, "Possible wire-store sucker." One of the girls whispered in Reggie's ear. He broke out in a grin.

"Hello, Genevra. Nice to see you in. What happened to Myron?"

"He's a heel and he can go to hell," I said. Myron was the mythical ex-boyfriend; me and Reggie had the whole routine already worked out.

Reggie had already laid out a Bee's Knees for me. I tossed it back, then lifted the empty glass and upended it onto the bar top with a clomp. "To Myron."

Reggie laughed. "And who's this gentleman?"

"My apologies," I said. Allgood had kept silent throughout that whole exchange, not even cracking a smile. "This here's Robert Allgood, the Chicago cattleman. He's fresh into town and needs a drink."

"What would you like?" Reggie asked him.

"Bourbon," Allgood said.

"All right." Reggie dipped low and pulled out his bottle of the good stuff—as good as we could get back then. It wasn't as good as what Allgood had served me from his flask earlier, I already knew that. "First one's on the house, Mr. Allgood, on account of you coming in with an old friend."

Allgood lifted the drink towards Reggie as if he were making a toast. He took a sip without making a face.

There wasn't any music yet and I was starting to get concerned that Zanarowski had done something to sabotage that, too. I said, "Who's playing tonight?"

"Bix Biederbecke."

"Any sign of Bessie Smith?"

Reggie made a face. "Not yet."

The story went like this:

Robert Allgood was really in town to race his pig.

Like I said, I wouldn't have believed it coming from someone else. Racing pigs. Racing pigs! Who woulda believed it, then or now? But there it was. Robert Allgood had brought with him, all the way from a farm outside of Chicago, one of his famous racing pigs. I say famous because he called them famous, not because I ever heard of them.

He wanted to race them, not against other pigs, but against men. The fastest runner that could be found in Cedar Rapids.

I kept a straight face all through his explanation. It was tough but I made it through. At the end I said, "Is this some kinda practical joke, like hunting snipe?"

He looked deeply offended and for a second I thought I'd lost him. Oh well, I thought to myself, I'd pocket his watch on the way out.

"Pigs are smarter than dogs, and they race dogs," he said, puffing out his chest and straightening up a little. He was staying in the Hotel Roosevelt, which had just opened, and we were down in the restaurant getting a bite to eat: shrimp cocktails, salami sausage slices, herring salad, anchovy canapes, blue point oyster cocktail, olives, tomato soup, chicken consommé with rice, broiled whitefish, slices of roast turkey with cranberry sauce, roast goose with apple sauce, ham with champagne sauce, filet mignon with truffle sauce, green peas that looked so fresh they had to be out of a hothouse, sweet potatoes, mashed potatoes, green salad, about a dozen cakes and pies, and I don't know what else. I could have stuffed myself silly but I didn't. There was no hurry. You get a sense when the fish is hooked.

"Yeah?" I asked, picking at my filet mignon with truffle sauce. "It sounds like, I don't know. Some kind of con job."

"From me?"

He had a point there: what need did a multi-millionaire need of swindling people out of their cash with something as unlikely as a pig race? In the middle of winter?

"You hafta admit that it sounds less than likely."

He shook his head. "The ancient Romans raced pigs. Everyone talks about the gladiators, but they had other games, too. Chariot racing, horseback racing, dog racing, pig racing, beast hunts of tigers, panthers, lions, bulls, rhinoceroses, elephants..." He broke into a smile. It lit up his face and took twenty years off his age. "Ah! You grew up on a farm, didn't you?"

"Yeah," I said. "What of it?"

"These are not..." He waved a hand. "Farm pigs, big and pink and fleshy and covered with mud. Racing pigs are black with fur, they have tusks like this," he made hooks with his fingers and held them at his mouth, looking like a vampire in a movie, "and they run fast, fast, fast! As fast as a man—perhaps a little faster. But it has to be a short race, you see, because always the men can run for longer than any animal, if he runs long enough. The man, he is a magnificent animal who can run for twenty-six miles, the length of a marathon, yes?"

"What about lions?" I said.

"They can run faster than a man, but for not as long."

"A horse?"

"Oh, the horses that are run now, they are bred for running very fast over very short distances. Two or three miles at most. But a horse bred to run long distances can run a marathon, and less time than a man could, too. There have been races where a horse has run a hundred miles over twenty-four hours, after which they have collapsed. But I have seen a man run over one hundred and fifty miles in twenty-four hours. One hundred and fifty miles! I was in Africa, where they have made a study of such things…"

The conversation, and the meal, went on for hours. The only thing missing was wine, specifically French Champagne. There was something about being able to share a tipple during a good conversation that made it special. I could see why the old guy wasn't content to just drink his fine bourbon alone in his room—he liked having an audience.

By the end of the meal, he had me convinced: he was a nut, but he was a sweet old nut, and he was here to race his damn racing pig—excuse me, his wild boar—against any takers. It was his current lunatic hobby, something to pass the time while he bought up another piece to add to his empire.

I was almost gonna feel bad about taking the guy for a ride.

I showed Allgood a good time that night. Not only that but I told him that I'd ask around for a fast runner who'd take the contest seriously. It was five hundred dollars if the runner—the human one, that was—won. I was pretty sure someone would volunteer. Where we could get a track in the middle of winter, though, that was a problem. Nobody would want a good indoor track torn up by pig trotters. And who even knew if Cedar Rapids had an indoor track? I sure didn't. Reggie would know.

The thing was, it was even odds, which might put a damper on things on Reggie's side. And five hundred bucks? Peanuts. Not worth Reggie's time. Still, I hoped he would. I wanted to see the old guy get something out of this.

I had to admit, though. After the story I heard, I couldn't help but think that the pig was going to win. Allgood was too specific about the distance: five hundred yards, no more, no less. I couldn't help but think that there was some kinda magic distance where his wild boar—which was named

Zeus, by the way—could outdistance a man every time. There was some trick to it; I just couldn't see it yet.

But Reggie said he was bored and wanted to try to get it set up. He asked me if I wanted in on the five hundred, I told him no, I was out.

"But you roped him, clean as anything," he said. "Like a cowgirl with a lasso."

I rolled my eyes. "Then give me a hundred bucks," I said. "Or nothing."

"Not a cut?"

"Not a cut," I said. "You're gonna get skinned on this somehow and I don't want you blaming me later."

"How? What do you know?"

"I don't know nothing. I just feel…" I shrugged. I just felt like this was all going down just a little too smooth.

Reggie decided it was just nerves on my part.

Sure enough, Reggie did know a place that would agree to run a race of man versus beast, as long as Allgood agreed to put down a deposit against any damages. It was a big horse-training barn out of town to the south, near North Liberty.

The runner was named Harvey Callow and he was a world-class sprinter. He had almost got into the 1924 Olympics but had come down with adult whooping cough. He had recovered and was in good shape, and was training to run in 1928. He lived in Des Moines. Reggie had him run over to Cedar Rapids by train.

A group of us drove down to the horse barn with Reggie, Allgood, and the pig in his big cage. They had to load the cage into a big truck, covered with a tarp to help keep out the wind and cold.

Reggie, Allgood, Allgood's secretary and I arrived at the horse barn in a car hired from the Roosevelt. Everyone else had to ride in another car. The guy who was driving the pig was a regular at the speakeasy, someone Reggie trusted with everything from getaway driving to delivering baby chicks. He wasn't taking any chances.

I didn't get a look at Zeus before we left Cedar Rapids—they loaded him and covered him up too quick, but I sure saw him when we arrived.

He was four feet tall at the shoulder—came up to my chest. I don't know how much he weighed, but it was enough that the steel ramp that he was led down bounced with every step. He had some stink to him, and his muscles looked like craggy boulders under the skin. I gave Allgood a look.

He winked.

But I knew better.

I had roped for enough cons by then that I knew what was coming next: Harvey Callow was going to lose. He'd pull ahead at first, then either have an accident or just...not be fast enough. Unless that pig had a heart attack and fell dead on its knees, it was gonna win.

The first time, that was. As part of Reggie's plan.

Of course, after Zeus won the first time, the general idea was to send Allgood back to the bank for more money, up the stakes, and then run the race again. This time, Harvey Callow would pull ahead, then sink back, then pull ahead just a little bit further—he'd win by a head. Something small but indisputable. And Allgood would lose his money.

Then either Allgood would walk away from the race or he'd suggest best of three. Callow would keep it close again—he'd never let on what he could do when he ran all-out. Reggie would never again let Allgood get ahead again, after that first run.

It was an old con, the "fight or foot-race store." Either you'd set up your professional bantamweight against a local guy twice his size and let the professional clean the floor with the giant, or you'd do the same thing with a pair of racers. The takes weren't as big as you could get with a wire store, but they could probably get Allgood up to a thousand or so. I think Reggie had a soft spot for the old foot-race stores, and it delighted him to be the inside man on one, one last time.

Against a pig, no less.

The racers stood at the starting line, which was powdered white chalk laid down over hard-packed dirt. The race course was laid out with white-washed sawhorses all around the outer edge. A second set of sawhorses circled the inside of the track. There were stands along one wall and an announcer's booth along the opposite side. I stayed in the stands with the rest of our guys who came to see the race, but Allgood, Reggie, the owner of the horse barn, and Allgood's secretary walked to the inner ring of sawhorses. (I woulda gone too but I didn't want to ruin my shoes.)

Allgood's secretary was a snooty-looking swain named Morton Fritz who had the kind of high-arched nostrils that remind you of bridge arches. If he'd plucked a few nose hairs he might have got a date sometime.

The pig trainer, I forget his name, held a gun filled with blanks at his side—a real starting pistol. Fritz held a brass stopwatch. The barn owner was drinking out of his flask. Reggie was leaning against the white boards with interest, and Allgood had a big, smug grin on his face.

The trainer said, "On your mark," and I swear, the pig dropped into a runner's crouch right alongside Harvey Callow. I cracked up.

"Get set..."

The trainer lifted the gun.

But before he could fire there was a banging on the door to the outside. "Police! Open up!"

Legally speaking, we were betting on an illegal race—and someone had ratted us out.

—◆—

The race was broken up with a minimum of fuss, helped out by the fact that the cops were willing to take a hundred bucks off both Reggie and Allgood to make up for the trouble of having to come all the way out to the horse barn to bust up the race. On the way back I was about spitting nails. I didn't know who had ratted us out exactly, but I did know who was behind it: Zanarowski. Out of the kindness of his heart, he had decided to stop us from ripping off a guy and his pig.

I was mad. I had tangled with Zanarowski a few times before. He wanted me to come work for him—but not as a roper, if you get my drift. He was real insistent. One time he left me with a necklace of bruises shaped like a pair of hands around my neck.

Allgood didn't need to know all that, though. When he asked me what the matter was, I said that I was upset that the race had been called off. Reggie apologized to me—and to Allgood—saying that he hadn't thought to put the fix in, because they were only going to be there one day.

I gave him a look and he gave me back a little puzzled shrug, which probably meant that he *had* put the fix in, and it just hadn't stuck—but Allgood didn't need to know that, either.

We met up again at the speakeasy that night to discuss when and where to run the race again. Allgood said that he planned to wrap up his business deals after the New Year and would probably be back on the train to Chicago again by the third of January, so if we wanted to run the race at all, it was gonna have to be soon. Reggie said he'd set something up.

The next day was New Year's Eve, which was one of Reggie's biggest days of the year. He invited Allgood to come to the party—he made a special point of it, said he'd save the best table for us. Bessie Smith was gonna be in town that night, and she was gonna come sing.

"What happened to Bix Biederbeckc?" I asked.

Reggie shook his head. "He was in some kinda hot water, I heard, and made a beeline for St. Louis this morning."

"What for?"

"Nobody knows."

I didn't like it. I tried to remember if I'd seen Bix the night before. Maybe it was him who'd ratted on us. I *thought* I remembered him hanging around when we'd been setting up the details on the race earlier, but I wasn't sure.

Maybe it was just spite, my memory putting him into a scene where he hadn't been. But maybe I was just prepared to believe the worst.

———◦◦◦———

New Year's Eve came around and I got dolled up in a black and silver beaded dress, the kind that's so heavy it drags over your skin when you slip out of it. It had no back to it, no arms, and no legs. If the place hadn't been packed I woulda froze to death. As it was I was sweating just like everybody else. There was a feathery kind of silver pattern on the top half of the dress. Shimmy in that thing and you'd light up the dark.

And shimmy I did. I mostly danced with Allgood, who wasn't so bad for an old guy. I made sure that I only danced a couple of dances with younger guys, the kind that weren't so fast on their feet. Get stepped on a couple of times by a rube and you'd throw yourself into a millionaire's arms, too. Bessie Smith came in and did some numbers with the house band. I couldn't dance then, I just stood there gripping onto Allgood's hand, the two of us listening so hard the ice melted in our drinks.

Midnight approached and we all started to count it down, with Reggie standing on top of the bar and calling the numbers off his wristwatch—the official timepiece.

Ten...nine...eight...seven...six...

I gave Allgood a fond look. One way or another, this was all going to wrap up soon, and I had almost grown to like the crazy old guy.

...two...one...Happy New Year!

We cheered, all seventy of us crammed into that little basement.

For a few seconds, nobody heard the banging at the back door, the one that led down into the speakeasy, bypassing the drugstore upstairs. But then a hush spread over the crowd.

"Open up! Police!"

I gritted my teeth. They were on to us again. Damn Zanarowski! It had to be him. Couldn't he leave us alone for one night?

The cops took us all in to the hoosegow, letting nobody loose but Allgood and his secretary. They let the rest of us out the next day—it was too much trouble to keep everybody locked up in such tight quarters. Also they must have made up their quota for the new year in payoffs. It was one second shoved up in the women's holding cell, and the next out on the street.

Allgood's secretary was waiting for me when we got out. He was holding a fur coat, kind of reddish brown. Fox or something. I melted into it—it was already warm.

"If you would accompany me, miss?"

I gave Reggie a look as he loaded up into his own car. He made a face, then nodded. If I had to guess, I'd say he was thinking, *I don't know what's going on but see what you can find out.*

I let the secretary, Fritz, hand me into the back seat of the car that Allgood had rented from the Roosevelt. He even tucked a blanket over my knees after I got in.

A quick trip back to my apartment to pick up a few things, change clothes, and powder my nose, and I was back in Allgood's rooms at the Roosevelt.

He was pacing back and forth with his hands behind his back and his jaw clenched. I watched him a second or two and guessed that whatever he was mad about, it wasn't about me. (Otherwise, why send a fur coat?) He said, "I trust that you are well?"

"Sure," I said. "They didn't even charge us."

"Good. It was unfortunate that they did not release you earlier—I paid them enough."

"You gotta be careful with those guys. They're too used to..." I almost blew the deal about having two wire stores in one town. I chalked it up to needing a drink. "...to all the graft in this town. They don't always stay bought."

"Dishonest policemen distress me," he said.

"That's just how it is in America."

"In Poland, too." He glanced at his cane, which was hanging off the back of the bedroom door handle. Then he frowned at me, sizing me up. "I have found a place to hold the pig race."

"Yeah?"

"It was unfortunate that Mr. Skurski was not available. Something has come up in Chicago. I have to leave tonight—there is no hope of staying any later."

I thought about what he was saying. "You set up a race with someone else."

"That is true."

It turned out the race was gonna be in the same place, that same horse barn, even the same runner, Harvey Callow—but this time, the guy putting up the money was Zanarowski.

I tried not to break out into a smile.

— ◆ —

Me and Allgood and Fritz the secretary took the Roosevelt car out again, with Fritz driving and me and Allgood in the back seat. I was imagining Reggie's face. He musta been about ready to give himself a heart attack. I was sure he'd heard about the race already.

The truck with the pig followed behind us, but this time the driver was somebody else—one of Zanarowski's men. We were accompanied by what looked like an entire caravan of spectators, cars and cars full of local guys. Everyone was in suits and they'd brought a bunch of girls with them, a little hung over but still dressed to kill.

When we made it out to the barn, Reggie was there, along with a bunch of our guys.

It gave me a shiver. This was gonna be big, whatever it was.

Reggie gave me a scowl but I didn't take it serious; he was the one who had given me the nod earlier. I was just playing along.

We all got out, including the pig, who was none too happy about being driven around by Zanarowski's driver, who wasn't as good as ours. His breath steamed in the cold air and he pawed the snow, looking for someone to charge. His trainer had a big leather harness on him and was holding something that looked almost like a riding crop with a thin metal plate in it. He slapped it on the snow and told Zeus to get moving.

When Zeus passed the driver he gave him a hot, nasty look that made the driver back up against the side of the truck. That pig had death in his eye. He knew what was what.

Zanarowski met us at the door. He had a girl on either arm, a cigar in his mouth, and one eyebrow lifted. He greeted Mr. Allgood and his secretary with all courtesy, then said to me, "Genevra Valentine. I see you've found the fattest pocketbook in the tri-state area once again. My congratulations. You should be working for me."

You see how he was. Didn't have the sense to shut his mouth in front of the guy he was trying to butter up.

"I'd work for you but as it turns out I don't like your idea of a choker," I said. "So why don't you go to hell instead?"

Zanarowski cleared his throat but his expression didn't change. He looked at Allgood. "The race track and my runner are ready. But what about your pig?"

"My Zeus always is ready to run."

Zanarowski shook the girls off his arms and grabbed Allgood's hand, pumping it up and down. "Twenty thousand dollars, even money."

I almost whistled out loud before I remembered to keep a straight face. Not the biggest amount I'd ever heard of being taken off a mark, but lots bigger than any foot-race store I ever heard of.

Reggie had made it to the door by then. Zanarowski broke into a grin. Reggie crossed his arms over his chest.

"And something else that's worth more than money," Zanarowski said. "Isn't that right, Skurski?"

Reggie answered something in Polish.

Allgood grimaced.

Reggie said, "I apologize. What I said just now was an insult to pigs."

Zanarowski said, "Gentlemen, gentlemen. Let's settle this on the track, shall we?" And then he went inside.

I hung back and grabbed Reggie by the arm. "What are you doing, boss?"

"I threw my dice," he said, and stomped into the barn without me.

Allgood held out his arm for me, and I took it.

"If Zeus loses, then Mr. Skurski will retire," Allgood said in a low voice.

"What?" I was shocked.

"I was there when they negotiated, yes," he said, nodding. Fritz was waiting for us to go in; Allgood gave him a little wave to send him inside ahead of us. The rest of the guys must have gone in by side doors, because we were the only two still outside. What a way to spend New Year's Day, out in the snow waiting to watch a pig race.

Allgood lowered his voice. "They asked me to make sure the negotiations did not turn violent. It seems Mr. Zanarowski was behind the police raid last night. He was demonstrating that he had bought them, yes?"

"Yeah," I agreed.

It had to come down to a showdown sooner or later. I knew it; everybody knew it. But over a pig race? On New Year's Day? Sponsored by a millionaire?

That was just crazy.

"Look," I whispered. "Are you and Reggie in on some kinda deal together? Or is it you and Zanarowski?"

His eyes opened in shock. "My dear girl! Not on your life."

"Then you oughta know that Callow runs like a maniac. He's gonna beat that pig. Excuse me, he's gonna beat Zeus. He's an Olympic runner, you know."

"Yes, I know," Allgood said. "But Zeus can run faster than his fastest time."

"He holds back," I said. I scrunched my eyes up. I felt like I was gonna start cryin'. "It's a swindle, from start to finish. Reggie's a con man and so is Zanarowski. Both of 'em. They've been trying to take each other down for years. And you and Zeus are gonna get stuck in between 'em, and you're gonna lose that twenty thousand dollars, sure as anything."

He patted my shoulder through the fur coat he'd given me. "There, there," he said. "If I lose twenty thousand dollars, then I lose it while racing my Zeus. I have not lost as much as I usually do the past year. Fritz has not shouted at me as much as usual."

I stared into the doorway of the barn. "I don't wanna work for Zanarowski," I said. "If Reggie retires, all of us go to that bastard. That guy, it's like working for a jackhammer. He ain't got no subtlety. He's up to something. We're gonna lose and lose bad. We're gonna lose stakes we didn't even know were on the table. He could take you down, too."

As you can tell, all my sophistication was going out the window. I was singing like a canary.

Allgood took it like a champ. He just patted me on the arm again. "There, there. Come inside. The wind is blowing harder, and the snow is stinging my eyes."

His eyes were dry; it was mine that were starting to run. I took the excuse to pat at them with a handkerchief outta my purse. I straightened up and put my best foot forward.

If me and Reggie and all the rest of us were going down, I wasn't going to let Zanarowski see me turn a hair. Not one single hair.

Allgood said, "You look like a princess."

"Out of a fairy tale?"

"No," he said. "Like Grażyna, the chieftainess from the story who fought the Crusaders. A warrior."

What else could I do? I kissed him on the cheek and went inside, hanging off his arm and my eyes shooting daggers at Zanarowski.

I took the same place in the stands that I had last time. This time there were more people sitting with me. The trainer led Zeus out to the track. It was easy to see that Zeus was still mad at that driver—he snorted and pawed and tossed his head at the stands. The driver was making faces at him, sticking out his tongue and leaning over the railing at him.

Harvey Callow looked a bit nervy, standing next to that pig. Whether that meant he'd run faster or not, I had no idea. Even in the chill of the barn he was dressed in a singlet and shorts, for freedom of movement, I guess. You could see the goosebumps all over his arms and legs.

I clasped my hands together in my lap, my cold hands gripping each other tight. One of Reggie's boys had put down a handkerchief under my bum, to help protect the coat from anything on the seats.

I gave him a smile.

He said, "You all right, Miss Valentine?"

"Nervous," I said.

"Me too," he admitted. "All of us."

Reggie, Zanarowski, Allgood, Fritz, and the barn owner had crossed over to the center ring. The barn owner looked like he thought it was the biggest lark of the century. Zanarowski puffed up big clouds of smoke with his cigar. Fritz had his timepiece out again.

Reggie had his arms crossed over his chest. As I looked at him, my eyes were starting to fill up with tears again. This was going to kill him, just kill him. Six months after he put down the racing charts and bar rags for good, he was gonna die of a heart attack. You know the kind of guy I'm talking about. As soon as they retire, they completely fall apart. There's just nothing left to 'em. Their lives are in their work.

When he spotted me, he *sneered* at me. I hunched down in my sumptuous fur coat like it could make me invisible. Zanarowski got this little grin that made me want to peel it off him with a knife.

It was time for the race. Zeus and Callow were ready to go. Sparks were in the air. Now Reggie had changed his foul looks over to Zanarowski instead.

You could have cut the suspense with a knife.

The trainer said, "On your mark."

Once again, both Callow and the pig dropped into a runner's crouch.

"Get set..."

The trainer raised his starting pistol.

There came a pounding at the door.

This time, the trainer fired.

And then all hell broke loose.

The doors burst open and what seemed like a hundred men in dark suits poured onto the big barn floor. Their chests showed the eagle-topped badges of Bureau of Investigation agents. The Feds! Whistles blew and shouts filled the room.

The runners had already started.

They had both burst out of their places when the gun went off.

They rounded the far end of the track and started toward the crowd of agents.

Neither man nor beast hesitated.

To this day, I would swear in front of a court of law that I saw them glance at each other, then push harder forward.

If Harvey Callow had been holding back at all from the start of the race, he was pushing all out by then. His skin glistened in the lights overhead.

The agents had blocked the sides of the stands. We couldn't move.

"Robert Allgood! Harvey Callow! Put your hands up! You and everyone in this building are under arrest!"

Allgood gave Fritz a look and the two of them shoved past the line of sawhorses and started to run for the far end of the building, where a small door had only a pair of guards.

"Get them!" someone shouted.

By then, both Callow and Zeus had rounded the far corner.

The agents at that end of the building didn't seem to think that grabbing a full-grown wild boar running at full speed was such a good idea.

The two racers passed the starting mark and kept going.

The track being the size it was, they were going to have to run around it twice in order to make up the distance they needed. Callow knew that; Reggie had told him the first time.

How the pig knew that, I couldn't say. But he knew it all right.

Callow and Zeus ran straight at Allgood and Fritz.

Fritz had pulled ahead of Allgood, being a far younger man, while waving a pistol at the two agents by the door and yelling like a madman.

And leaving his boss behind.

"No!" I shouted.

But it was too late.

Allgood went down. Tripped or something.

Callow, having pulled ahead an inch or two, swerved around him and kept running.

Zeus flew over top of him, then turned around the corner, head down and legs a blur.

I held my breath, waiting to see if Allgood would get up.

He didn't move.

The agents at the other end of the track grabbed Callow as he went past. In two shakes of a lamb's tail he was wearing a pair of handcuffs. The agents swarmed around the center ring of sawhorses and started arresting Reggie, Zanarowski, and the barn owner. They took those of us in the stands away. Even Fritz had been caught. They had knocked him down into the dirt. One man was kneeling on his back and the other was wrestling the pistol away from him.

The only one left was the pig trainer, who stood at the edge of the track with tears in his eyes.

Zeus was still running. He'd passed Allgood on the ground and was rounding the other end of the track again.

One of the agents shook his fist in the trainer's face. The trainer was pointing to the starting pistol, which the agent now held, then to Zeus, and back again. Zeus was going to round the far end and start on his way back any second.

Finally the agent held the starting pistol up and fired it toward the ceiling.

Zeus came to a stop as quick as anything. He stopped so fast that he threw up a cloud of dust off that dry dirt floor. He stopped and looked around like he'd just woke up from sleepwalking. I saw him shudder as he spotted Allgood in the dirt on the ground.

Slowly, Zeus walked toward his master, step by jerky step.

When he reached Allgood he nudged him with his nose.

Allgood didn't move.

Zeus shuddered all over again, then sniffed Allgood all over. He nudged him over and over with his nose.

One of the agents started to walk toward him—to see how Allgood was doing—and the pig bellowed at him. The agent put up his hands and took a few steps backward.

They dragged the rest of us all out of there and threw us in wagons. Which told me that they knew about how many of us to expect. Reggie's and Zanarowski's boys and girls got all mixed up together. A couple of fistfights broke out.

I got a black eye and a set of bloody knuckles out of it.

Zanarowski, who had the bad luck to get locked in the same wagon as I was, lost a coupla teeth and got a busted nose.

He shouldn't have laughed at Allgood if he hadn't wanted me to hit him in the face.

He shouldn't have *kept* laughing if he'd wanted me to stop.

Somehow or other, I ended up back on the street within the hour. The whole incident just disappeared, as far as the law was concerned.

I guess if a story about the Bureau letting a millionaire getting killed got out, it might look bad or something.

⋯⊙⋯

It was all over the papers: Allgood was dead, killed by a heart attack and his own racing pig.

That first night, we met up at Reggie's speakeasy. It was just us chickens—no outsiders. Reggie brought out the best booze he had and poured everyone a shot.

When it was all set up, he lifted his own glass and said, "To Allgood!"

I lifted mine and shouted, "To Allgood!"

Much to my surprise, my voice was drowned out. I looked around. The faces that had been serious a few seconds later had now broken into broad grins.

Reggie raised a hand. "Keep your faces on. We still got one thing left to do."

The grins disappeared.

A few seconds later, the back door opened a slam and a lash of cold air from outside. A bunch of boots started coming down the stairs.

It was Zanarowski.

He'd left the girls behind. It was just him and the toughest of his tough guys.

Reggie said, "What do you want, Zanarowski?"

"I'm just here to let you know there are no hard feelings, old man," said Zanarowski. "But the time has come for you to get out of the business anyway. It's a new year. Time for a new start."

"Yeah?" Reggie said, in a challenging tone. "You're here to buy me out?"

Zanarowski took a brown-paper package out from under his coat and slapped it down on the bar.

"Twenty thousand dollars," he said.

Reggie swept the money off the bar and stowed it out of sight. "That's for Allgood," he said.

"What are you talking about?"

"Well," Reggie said, eying Zanarowski, "his pig won the race, didn't he?"

"Nobody won the race. The Bureau stopped it."

"No," I said. Every hair on my head was standing on end. "Zeus finished the race. They arrested Callow, but Zeus kept on going until the starting pistol fired again. We all saw it. Even your men saw it."

"He was dead by then."

Reggie leaned forward and put his elbows on the bar. "I'll make sure his heirs get it."

"No," Zanarowski said.

He wasn't referring to the money. His face had gone pure white. Twenty grand was a lot of dough, but it wouldn't knock him out or anything.

He was thinking about the rest of his wager.

The one where he'd have to sell out to Reggie and get outta town.

Reggie reached under the bar and pulled out a plain white envelope, the kind that you write letters home to your ma with. If there was money in it, it wasn't no twenty thousand dollars.

He dropped it onto the bar.

"You know what's in here?" he said.

"No," Zanarowski said.

"I think you do," Reggie said. "And I bet there's a few people who'd like to see it, too. A couple of people, say, in Chicago." He looked upward. "I think I can remember the address. It's 1701 North Astor Street—"

Zanarowski started to shake. "You couldn't possibly—"

"I've been hanging on to this a long time," Reggie said. "Woman named Kitten gave it to me."

You could have heard a pin drop.

Zanarowski reached over put his hand on top of the envelope, and said, "This is the only copy?"

"Swear on my mother's grave."

"Then I'll take it, you bastard."

They stared at each other for a second, the short old guy with the bald head and a double chin and the tall dapper man with the nice suit.

"Why didn't you use it before?" Zanarowski asked finally.

"I was saving it for something good."

Zanarowski made the envelope disappear into his pocket, turned around, pushed his way through his men, and left.

I never did find out what was in that envelope.

———◆———

That woulda been the end of the story, except that the papers had got ahead of themselves. Allgood wasn't dead; he was in one of the big Chicago hospitals (with a suspicious lack of injuries, I might add—he hadn't had a heart attack and Zeus had jumped clean over him). The Bureau had been sicced on him for some kind of Mann Act violation; he'd been accused of transporting girls across state lines along with some of his cattle. It turned out that he hadn't been involved; it was a ring organized by some of the drivers, who may or may not have had connections to the Chicago mob. Someone staying at the Roosevelt had called in an anonymous tip that girls were being sold at auction at the barn where the race was held. Understandably, the Bureau took it pretty seriously, but it turned out that nobody at the race that day was directly involved.

Harvey Callow had been specifically fingered as one of the buyers. That's why the agents had grabbed him. At least, that's the reason that I heard.

Me? I was supposed to be one of the girls getting sold.

Reggie took over Zanarowski's businesses, although all the liquid assets had disappeared from Zanarowski's safes and bank accounts. About half the guys from Chicago went back home. Things settled down. About the only people who were disappointed with the state of things were the police, who now had to keep their greed under control.

Reggie started cutting back on the wire store, and finally dropped it completely. Wire stores were getting replaced by the next big thing in big cons, the payoff store, the details of which he said made his head spin. He decided to settle down and become an honest bootlegger. After fighting tooth and nail against Zanarowski for so long, he let a couple of guys from Chicago move in and set up their store without protest. They were real respectful when I met 'em, even shook my hand.

I thought about the scheme for a long time and finally asked Reggie flat out whether he and Allgood had been in cahoots or if they'd just taken advantage of each other's plans—his to get rid of Zanarowski and Allgood to race his pig. Was it some kind of Polish conspiracy? Friends from the old country? Allies from Chicago?

All I got out of that was a smile.

As for me, I got hitched.

You mighta called it a May-December romance. I'd met him in December after all.

I warned him that I was going to wear his ticker out early and take him for everything he was worth.

That was all right by him, he said.

He'd started out with the racing pig gag back in the old country, and lived long enough to see his latest, finest pig swindle a Chicago con man with the inadvertent help of the Bureau of Investigations. That, he said, should be enough for any man.

We were out in his private barn at the time.

I leaned forward and scratched Zeus between the ears. He'd taken a shine to me, and I liked to think we had an arrangement. We were gonna take care of Allgood as long as he'd let us. After that, we'd see—but I'd promised him that there wasn't gonna be any bacon in his future, or chops or sausages or anything else. I knew a farm or two in Iowa that could use a good breeder pig, though.

He leaned into my hand and I scratched harder.

"Good pig," I said. "Good pig."

———◆———

(Note: The Roosevelt Hotel didn't open until 1927.)

———◆———

When Dom had finished telling his tale, everyone sort of sat back and exchanged looks. Madame Ixnay happened to give a little snort, almost under her breath. When I looked at her, she was rolling her eyes.

"He's such an old softie," she murmured to me.

The Vampire said, "That was well enough told, although I doubt you're going to take the prize with it."

"That's all right," Dom said stretching out an arm to indicate the bar. *"What do I need with prizes, anyway? I got a good life here, in Chicago."*

The Spy said, "And where before that, if you don't mind my asking? Poland? I'm trying to locate your accent. It is curious."

"Da Ukraine," Dom said proudly, thumping his chest. *"Da breadbasket of Europe."*

The Dame said, "The backwater farm country of Europe, ya mean. The Iowa of Europe!"

That busted everyone up.

The Vampire let it go on for a minute, then said, "It is time for the next tale. Does anyone need any refreshments?"

The Dame said, "I gotta use the little girl's room—nah, don't bother showing me where it is," she told me as I started to get up. *"I know this place. And when I get back, I'm gonna tell the next story."*

"You are?" the Vampire asked archly. *"And how was this decided?"*

"It was decided by yours truly," the Dame said, blowing him a little kiss. *"As in, I don't want to let the stories get too far along before I get my knocks in. Like Dom said, it ain't gonna be the worst of stories, but it ain't gonna be the best of stories, neither, and I don't want my audience fallin' asleep while I tell it."*

With the way the Dame explained it, I was starting to regret my pleas to not go first. Would it have been better to have gotten the story over with right away? Was I just drawing out the humiliation?

But I hadn't picked a story to tell, let alone decided on how to tell it.

The Vampire said, "Very well. I had planned to tell the next story myself, for a similar reason, but I yield to your impolite and childish demands."

"Thank you," the Dame said smugly, and elbowed her way behind the chairs on our side of the table, giving a lock of my hair a tug as she went by.

After she had left, the Spy looked at the Good Doctor and said, "I understand that you were quite upset when you first arrived. But I would like a clearer description of the matter regarding the gentleman in question, the one who was just murdered."

The Good Doctor held out his hands in front of him, palm down, to see if they were shaking—they were, but only a little.

He said, "I was near Belden and Fremont Street making my way here, when I heard the shot ring out. I startled the way a horse startles, then looked all about me to determine whether it was I myself who had been shot at. By then the first shot had been followed by several additional ones, and I was able to determine that the shots had come from Belden to the east.

"It is an unkindly night, with ice slowly forming over every surface, and I could not run as quickly as I would have liked. I slipped and stumbled forward until I had reached Halstead Street, where I saw the gentleman in question lying in the doorway of one of the townhouses along the north-east corner. He was dressed in evening wear, a pearl-handled cane lying next to him. The treasure, in its case, was half-hidden under a bit of shrubbery. It looked to have been knocked aside. I tucked it into my coat to conceal it.

"I attempted to stop the bleeding, but was unable to do so. I did not call for help, or remain to answer the questions of the police, for reasons you may imagine for yourself." He lifted his chin.

What he meant was, a colored man being found next to a wealthy man's body was going to lead the police to jump to conclusions, simply due to the color of his skin. I couldn't blame him for having run.

The Spy said, "Did you see anything of the shooting? Flashes of light from the gunshots, perhaps?"

The Good Doctor answered, "I saw little. It was dark and the air was heavy with freezing mist."

The Spy nodded.

The Actress said, "Did you hear an auto?"

The Good Doctor frowned. "Perhaps I did. I seemed to hear the growl of an animal. In the darkness..." He shook his head. "If I tell you what I imagined I saw and heard, please do not take it as factual. I only give the information in the interest of determining what I actually saw."

"What did you see?" the Actress asked.

The Good Doctor said, "I heard a growl and saw a large, dark shape dash around the corner, a sort of beast. A...a sort of demon, partially shaped like a man, but partially...not."

"That doesn't sound like any auto I ever heard of," the Detective commented.

The Actress said, "And you say the gentleman in question was killed by bullet wounds? Is that definitely so?"

"No," the Good Doctor said. "It was, as I said, dark, and I did not linger. I can claim nothing with confidence."

⚬

The Dame returned from refreshing herself. This time as she passed me, she ran her fingers through my hair. The hair stood up on the back of my neck as I felt the sharp points of her fingernails on my scalp.

She noticed, and giggled, and sat, and said, "We all ready? We are, I bet. Nobody's drink is empty or cold...leastwise, it ain't now that I got sat down."

The Dame began to speak.

Myrna and the Thirteen-Year Witch

The Dame's Tale

My husband and I were always just on the edge of setting the house-fae free. But there was always something, you know? It was after the Great War, when so many of the fae came over the ocean. Immigrants, only not human ones. Mythological immigrants.

Our house-fae, Ala and Elias, weren't the pretty ones that you see in woodcuts in fairy-tale books, tall and elegant with long, wispy hair. I don't know if those kind actually exist. I never seen any, anyhow. The house-fae *we* had were small, and gray, and wrinkled, and kinda ugly. But cute. I hadta stop myself from pinching their cheeks, when they first arrived. It woulda been rude.

I got them for a literal song, a sweet lullaby that I useta sing to our son, before he was killed in a car accident with Timothy's parents. I don't remember the song anymore. It was just the most ridiculous song, I remember that. Did you know you can buy house-fae for a song? But that if you do, you lose the song forever? Two house-fae, one song, and now I can't remember the song. It's just gone. I was joking around at the time. Timothy and I were slumming in Little Tokyo, going to clubs, when we stumbled across the two of them begging for work. They looked so sad and lonely that I just started singing to them. It was an impulse. I hadn't exactly meant to pick up a pair of house-fae, and Timothy and I had *words* over the incident. But they moved in, and here we are.

A few years passed. There was this whole underground economy in fae already, who knew? A black market of magic, which always makes me think that there's a cave under the new HOLLYWOODLAND sign where dark deeds are done and creatures bought, sold, and enchanted. But my neighbors went to The Broadway-Hollywood department store to pick up their house-fae, though, and paid for him with a check, which strikes me as an insult, really, because who *buys* their help these days? They had him configured into a dishwasher, a big hollow lump of a thing. They removed one of the cabinets and ran a hose into one ear and out the other, down the drain. He, the house-fae, could unhook himself and lumber through the kitchen like a large box with short little cat-feet. He would put himself out at night, then knock with one tiny, stubby arm to be let in again, in the mornings. I could hardly stand it. They were talking about getting another one, to clean toilets. With its *tongue*.

The husband was one of those men who fuss over film accounts. He had ways of concealing the accounts that the movie bigwigs spent on strong drink and other vices, which made him popular with all the producers and directors. I swear, the film business runs on bathtub gin and cocaine.

This guy knew I was uncomfortable about him having a configured fae in his house. He'd make fun of me about it. "Hey, toots," he'd say, "At least it ain't been turned into a conveyor belt that carries automobile parts for Henry Ford, or a mechanical armature in a tuna-packing plant, or a wheeled picker out in the fields. A dishwasher? Practically a vacation."

There are some people who can make a quick rebuttal to that kind of argument, but I've never been one of them. I couldn't think of what to say.

Ala and Elias are just about the sweetest people you could imagine. They can't have children together, which is a shame. They wanted us to have children so they could take care of them for us. They didn't understand why we didn't. They understood about making films. Acting, singing, painting, any kind of art, they understood all that. But to say, "Oh, I can't have any more children! I work in Hollywood now!" was something they could never understand. That I could be married to Timothy but not be allowed to have more children for the sake of my career, they could not comprehend. It was beyond them. "But, Miss Myrna, we will take care of your little ones for you."

I tell you, there were teary nights when I couldn't understand, either. Sooner or later, I knew I was going to give up film and try to become a mother again. It tore at me, the split between wanting to be on the silver screen and wanting to dandle a fat baby on my knee. But I wanted to *be* someone. You probably wouldn't think of it to look at me now, but I was dull when I was a girl. No one would look twice at me, let alone think to speak to me. Then I blossomed, and there I was, tall, thin, elegant, and, with the assistance of a little makeup, maybe even beautiful. When the Twenties arrived, I was *à la mode* in my jet-beaded dresses and feathered boas. I had glamor.

And I thought, *I had better make something of myself before I go back to being that dull girl I once was.* I wanted to stand out, not to impress anyone else, but to prove to myself that I was really made of something. So I went to California to try to be in the pictures, and here I am.

Timothy is a dear about it. "You lack self-confidence," he says, and presents me to all his friends that way. "This is my wife, Myrna, yes, *that* Myrna, and she lacks self-confidence."

He's serious about it, but half-kidding, too. He's hoping getting laughed at will knock me out of my "funk," as he calls it. These were the same parties where, if you tried to make a conversation about anything other than the latest picture, everyone would look at you like you were an idiot. It made me wonder what they really thought of us actors. Were we all just so many house-fae to them, with our signed contracts with the studios? Something to be taken advantage of?

Something to be configured?

Probably better not to ask.

It started to come to a head in 1923, when that woman in Fresno killed her entire family and blamed it on her house-fae. People wanted to believe it and there were riots San Francisco, although it never came to anything in L.A.

Then it came out that she'd killed six other husbands back in Armenia before coming to America. Ala and Elias told me, before the newspaper even. I asked if they knew the woman back in the old country, and they told me that my geography was lacking a little. I blushed, and then we all went looking at the set of World Book encyclopedias that I'd bought from a salesman for improving myself. Armenia is kinda a long way from their old home in Poland, as it turns out.

But they knew women like her, dark witches who gained their powers from killing. Seven husbands for immortality, they said. One every thirteen years. Dark witches like to work by sevens and thirteens.

But immortality was not the same as being invincible against all dangers, though. The way Ala explained it, having immortality meant a witch would never get cancer or get much older than she was already. In the case of the woman in Fresno, she wasn't that young and definitely wasn't that pretty. I saw her pictures in the paper. But witches can still die from things like the 'flu. That one died when she was found hanged in her cell, a suicide. I've always suspected, and Timothy agrees, that she was killed to save having anything about her black magic coming out in court.

Then 1924 came along, and not only did they stop letting any new Japanese people immigrate, but they closed the doors to any new fae. Never mind that everyone who was anyone already had a couple or a dozen around the house, and of course every industry had about a thousand of them tucked back in among the machinery. "Built-ins," they called them.

"Let the humans keep to the humans," was the saying. But of course people didn't mean, "Let the humans do their own housework." That would have been crazy talk!

What they really meant was, "Let the humans run everything."

There had been talk about making the fae neighborhood, New Storyville, an official neighborhood and cleaning it up for the tourists, but after 1924 that stopped. A few years later, by the time the first talkie, *The Jazz Singer*, came out, a lot of buildings in that neighborhood were broken into and the fae who lived there attacked or killed. Sometimes they would be found configured in the strangest ways. They would have film cameras growing out of their heads, or be turned into fences or palm trees and things. And a lot of them would be just plain missing.

Where were they taken? Was some kind of kidnapping ring going on? Did some of them just run away? Were they safe? Ala and Elias didn't know, or said they didn't, and if they *did* know, I couldn't blame them for not telling me, really, because, well, it's sad but there it is: Timothy and I were human, and if it came down to a choice between justice and convenience, well, we hadn't freed them yet, had we?

I wouldn't have trusted us, either.

⸺⬥⸺

They called 1929 the height of the Jazz Age. Really it was the height of the Fae Age, because it was the fae that made Americans rich enough to afford their jazz. But both were coming to an end. There were signs that it was all a house of cards, but nobody paid attention. You know how it is, like one of those dolls who says that her boyfriend only beats her when he's drunk but he's a swell guy the rest of the time. Nobody wanted to see the writing on the wall.

Around Inglewood there were signs posted saying, *Caucasians Only—No Fae!* Groups of the KKK went from house to house, and if you were found harboring a fae or a queer or someone of a different race, oh, anyone who was even a little bit different—you would get a fine. In a couple of cases, the "offenders" were dragged out into the street and stripped naked, and the whole house set on fire with the built-ins still in it.

And there was worse, but I don't want to get into it. It was a bad time.

A lot of my friends in the movie industry tried to pretend that everything was fine. By then there were fae-autos, long and beautiful automobiles that were really configured fae. I had a friend who fell in love with hers. Then one day she went out for a drive and vanished, who knows where, probably killed and her body stuffed in the trunk and both of them driven off a cliff, is what I think.

I never rode in one. I had a friend who tried to fool me into getting into one, but as soon as I put my hand on the side of the car, warm like skin, I knew the car for what it was and burst into tears. Meanwhile, the fae that worked in the fields and the factories were being rounded up and put into camps. The fields were rotting and production of normal automobiles and things had come to a standstill. The fae were packed into big vans and driven across the border at Tijuana. They hadn't come from Mexico, of course, but that was what people were claiming at the time—that the fae were illegal immigrants from Mexico.

Everybody pretended like it wasn't happening. Even me.

It was in early October that year when someone contacted Ala and Elias from the old country. I got a letter in the mail for them, tucked inside an envelope addressed to Mrs. Timothy Smith. I gave it to them. There was a spot of blood on the flap of the letter, pressed in like a wax seal. You could see the marks of a fingerprint.

They opened it right in front of me, standing together. Elias pulled the letter out, and Ala held his gnarled gray hand. They're only two feet high, with this heavy gray skin that sags like the most wonderfully supple leather. They have delicate bat's ears and squinting, tiny eyes, and the kinds of noses that some moles have, with the little tiny tentacles, which were the only things that aren't gray about them, but pink. Their hands and feet have heavy claws and their shoulders are wider than their hips. Very stocky. I had given them some pretty silver earrings to wear, tiny little hoops that they loved of mine and that I had bought more of so they each had about a dozen along the edges of their ears, and silver rings for their toes as well.

They both shivered at the same time, their earrings making a delicate noise like the world's smallest windchimes.

Elias looked at Ala, and Ala looked at me. "Miss Myrna, there will be trouble."

"What's the matter? Is it bad news?"

"Very bad news."

"What is it? Did someone pass away, back in the old country? Is it about money? If that's all it is—" I was starting to babble. My skin prickled like it was covered with pepper.

"There is a..." Ala looked at Elias, trying to find the word.

"Witch," Elias said.

"There is a witch who owned us, back in the old country," Ala said. "A very strong witch. Our cousin says that she has found out where we are. And she is coming for us."

"What will happen if she finds you?"

"When she finds us," Ala said carefully, "she will come into the house if she can and take us back. If you and Mr. Timothy are here, she will kill you. You must go away now, and not come back until the police call you to tell you that your house has been broken into, and we are either dead or gone."

"Dead or gone?" I said stupidly. "Why don't you just run away?"

"She will still come here, and she will still kill you," Ala said.

"Why don't we all run away, then?"

"Because then she will follow us. We will still be captured, and she will still kill you. But we both thank you for your kind thought," she added after a beat.

I shook my head. "I don't see how this works. Why is she after you?"

To my surprise, it was Elias who answered. He tends to be the shyer of the two, not often speaking to me, although he will sometimes talk to Timothy.

"We belong to her," he said. "We were born to be her servants. See?" And then he vanished, so that only his hands remained, floating in the air. I just so shocked to see it happen that I couldn't believe it.

"Wow!" I said. "That's some trick!"

"We are nothing to her but slaves," Ala said. "Pairs of hands. She does not wish to see any more of us than that."

"This witch sounds like a terrible person," I said. "And kind of crazy? I mean, following the two of you all the way from Europe? Because she thinks she owns you?"

"We have appreciated our time here," Ala said firmly. "But you must not argue about it, Miss Myrna. You are used to having things your way, and when things are not your way, you only give a little shrug and wait until tomorrow, because something else will come to you, and you will get your way then. The witch is not like this. She will not give up, and she will not go away."

"I believe you," I said, but looking back I have to think that I was lucky that Ala didn't shake me for how ignorant I was. "But we need to at least talk about a plan that could keep you safe. What would I do without you? You belong here. Or at least you don't belong with that witch."

— ◆ —

Ala patiently explained to me what would happen when the witch arrived. In great detail.

First, the witch would arrive in a traveling house or hut. It could be on walking chicken legs, or it could appear down the street, hidden amongst the other houses. I would know the witch's house by the bones, Ala said.

Either the house would be made out of bones, or it would be decorated with bones. Sometimes the bones would be disguised, and sometimes they would be made up with strings, sticks, and hollowed-out, painted eggs into a kind of windchime that witches used for casting spells.

Second, she would have bony legs. All witches, Ala asserted, had bony legs. If someone accused of being a witch had fat legs, well, that person wasn't a witch. They could have a fat middle, even a fat face and fat arms, but their legs would be like sticks.

Third, a witch will always give you the chance, if you ask, to do three tasks for her. If you are asking her a favor, three tasks. If you are trying to escape her wrath, three tasks. The tasks are always impossible. The only way to win is not to play. Or you can cheat. In fact, the only times that Ala and Elias had heard of someone getting anything out of a witch was by tricking her somehow. Say a witch asked someone to bring her the moon. You would cup your hands full of water dyed with ink, so that the ink would shine like a mirror. And then you would stand under the moon and say, "I brought you the moon, now you only have to take it."

I immediately thought about hiring a lawyer. This witch stuff sounded like lawyer-talk to me. But they said no, a lawyer wasn't going to help.

If you complete the three tasks, they said, then the witch has to do whatever you asked of her. You can't make her a slave or anything. But you could ask her to kill someone, or give you a magical trinket that would make your fortune, or turn you beautiful, or let you go, or whatever you wanted. If you didn't, though, she would eat you.

Eat *me*, that was, if I dared helped Ala and Elias get out of their servitude.

When I jokingly asked why this witch was in such a grumpy mood, they told me that every time someone asked a favor of the witch and got it, she got thirteen years older. "And she can only live for three hundred years," Ala said. "So she has to make it impossible to get a favor from her." I asked how old she was, and Elias whispered to himself, counting on his fingers for the longest time. "Two hundred and eighty-nine," he said finally.

The only way to reverse her age, Ala said, was by drinking a tea made from blue roses. The kind that you made by putting a white rose into blue ink didn't count. Silk roses? No good either.

There are no such things as natural blue roses. They're even less common than a natural blonde, apparently.

Finally they were done. They both looked at me kind of expectantly. I knew I was supposed to back down gracefully. But I didn't.

"So how do you know what she's going to ask you to do? The three things?"

"You don't," they said.

"Come on," I said. "She's a powerful witch who can do things that people would give their right eye teeth over. And you're trying to tell me she doesn't get a hundred people on her case every year? Dear witchy, make me immortal. Make me famous. Make me beautiful. Make me rich. Give me an endless supply of cocaine. Surely you have some kind of idea about what she wants in return by now."

They looked at each other, and that look wasn't too hard to interpret. It said, *Humans are crazy.* I said, "I work in the movies, darlings. I know enough about people to know that there's always something you want more than life itself, that you'll burn down everything for, if only you could get it."

Elias asked me shyly, "What would you wish for?"

I was surprised to hear him speak at all. He had a look of rapt fascination on his face, not like he was all that curious about what I would go for, but like he had something specific on *his* mind.

"Nunya business," I said primly. "Anyhow, I already got what I want in this life, my face larger than an automobile, shown on the silver screen. And Timothy. I got the man I want, the money I want, and the life I want. What more could I want?"

Ala and Elias looked at each other, then held each other's hands. Suddenly I knew what it was that Elias wanted. He wanted children of his own. My heart seized up in my chest and it burned up inside me.

I had everything I wanted, it was true. Except the one thing I couldn't dare let myself want.

But what did I need a witch for? All I had to do was make up my mind and give up everything I had, in order to get it.

◆

I told them that I would leave on the week-end and only come back after the coast was clear. It was Wednesday and I had filming on the studio lot for the next few days. Timothy was out on location, somewhere outside of Leeds in the U.K., some ruined abbey he described as being muddy and cold, so he was out of the way. They didn't like that I wanted to stay until Friday, but I wouldn't let them talk me into going any earlier. I had filming to do—what were they trying to do, put me out of a job?

Saturday morning, I planned to get into my pretty new Daimler Double-Six, which was made by a company that had never used configured fae, and drive to San Francisco to stay with a girlfriend of mine.

But before that, I was gonna go look for that witch.

I pretended I wasn't going to and that I didn't care. "If she could appear and disappear like *that*," I snapped my fingers, "then it would have already been too late for all of us, darlings. You have nothing to worry about."

She might already *be* here, they told me. I laughed, put on a hat, and said that I would be out in the garden, keeping an eye out.

They begged me not to go outside. I smiled and asked them if they would mix me a martini. Prohibition being on, it was illegal, and we didn't have a drop of liquor in the house. Timothy and I had drunk it all up before he had left for the airport. I try not to keep liquor in the house when he's not home.

They tried to convince me to have a nice ginger-ale instead.

But I really dug in my heels: drinks or nothing. Finally, Ala decided to try to get some. She had a friend of a friend who was a domovoi, or house-fae from Russia, in Glendale who was sure to have some vodka. I reminded her that I preferred gin, but that of course I would get stinko on whatever I could get.

That left me alone with Elias.

I started in on him. "So what do we need to do?"

"Do?" he asked nervously.

"To keep the witch out of the house."

He burst into tears.

I said, "If there's no way to keep her out, then I'll just have to go looking for her. Toot suite."

That wasn't what he wanted to hear. We circled around the subject for a few minutes. I knew that every second I delayed, I was running out of time. Finally, he admitted that a hag stone might help, although he doubted it. A hag stone is a stone with a hole in it. Also that any birds who tried to land on the windowsills and look inside should be chased away. A French-style hairpin should be tucked into the lining of all coats to help ward off the evil eye. And whistling in the house? Right out. You were supposed to put red slipknots on all your clothes for protection. And I needed to start wearing an amulet with the number 102 embroidered on it, and putting my right foot on the floor first when I woke up, and never going outside bareheaded, and to hold my thumbs instead of crossing my fingers. In short, a lot of nonsense good-luck charms.

I said that if that was all he had to tell me, then I was going outside.

He yelped and ran to the curiosity cabinet, where Timothy and I keep all kinds of knickknacks from slumming around the world. I did have a couple of what you might consider hag stones in there, from a trip up along the coast on Highway 101 when it opened up the year before. They were dull gray basalt rocks with holes in, that was all. Nothing magical about them.

But he hung one on a piece of red silk embroidery floss and made me put it on before he'd let me go outside. I put a hat on and stepped over the threshold with my right foot forward, too, just like he'd asked.

I got in the car and started driving around the neighborhood. I wasn't sure how I was going to spot a witch's house, but I had to do something. Fortunately, it didn't take me too long to find.

The witch was already here.

I drove around the block, which, in that neighborhood, was something of a production. Up one hill, down a winding back road past a half-dozen mansions, down through a hillside full of orange trees, then a left past a produce stand and back onto my street. Timothy and I didn't have a mansion, but we had a nice place, Spanish style with clay roof tiles and whitewashed walls. The upstairs bedrooms had little wrought-iron balconies and a round tower with the formal entryway, a carved oak door with an iron knocker. It was a classy place, the kind of place where sometimes I just hugged myself for being able to live there. I grew up on a farm in Nebraska, if you know what I mean.

It was on the way back down my street that I spotted the witch's place.

It was pretty obvious. Not because it was made of bones, but because it hadn't been there before. If you think a Nebraska girl hasn't driven around a neighborhood to look at all the ritzy houses glamorizing her neighborhood a time or two, you have another think coming.

It was tucked between two houses I recognized, a Tudor and a place that looked kinda like a nunnery, a heavy stone three-story building behind a stone wall. The Tudor belonged to the accountant neighbor with the configured fae dishwasher. The witch's house was stealing his yard. He must have been steamed.

Aside from there being a house there that shouldn't have been, the reason that I recognized it right away was that the witch's house—*the whole house*—was a configured fae.

The outside was made to look like a golden stucco with a shingled roof and a brick chimney. There were stairs leading up the side of the hill, and a garage at the bottom. A French door let out onto a patio in the front, and a pair of windows with flowered window boxes looked down from some dormers.

The eyes looked out from under those windows. I saw one of the window boxes blink. The French door was the poor baby's nostrils, and the garage door at the bottom was the mouth.

I felt so bad. I couldn't let the witch have my house-fae. She might do something like *this* to them.

I chewed on a nail, which I'm not supposed to do, my makeup girls all hate it, and drove away in order to give myself time to think. What to do, what to do? Stop and ask her for a cup of sugar? Threaten to set the house on fire? Invite her over for tea and put rat poison in her cup? I wasn't coming up with anything clever.

Suddenly it came to me.

I would try to get my song back.

⸻◆⸻

I didn't stop at the house. I was afraid that Ala would already have returned with the alcohol and would try to talk me out of a confrontation with the witch. I drove around the block again instead. I was all nerves and maybe I wasn't driving the safest. I may have driven a little too fast and taken the corners on those winding roads a little too close to the edge.

But finally I made it back to the witch's house. I pulled into the driveway, which wasn't much of anything, just a short stretch of asphalt leading up to the garage. The house really wasn't elaborate enough for the neighborhood, and it hadn't been able to steal a lot of room from the houses on either side of it, so it looked a little cramped. How it was keeping the owners from calling the police on it, I don't know. "Hello, officer, I'd like to report a squatter on my property." "Oh, who is it? A hobo?" "No, it's an entire house." "Right, lady. Whatever you say."

I parked the Daimler and got out, standing next to the door for a moment before I reached back in, grabbed my handbag, and slammed the door shut. With determination I pulled my hand down over my ears and stepped up to the gate.

The whole fence was made of bones. I was at the right place.

I opened the gate and marched up the winding stairs to the front door and rang the bell.

Ding dong.

The house shuddered.

Then footsteps began to approach the door. I rested the back of my hand against the doorframe. I could feel the house twitch with every step. The doorframe didn't feel like wood, but like warm, leathery skin. I hoped I wasn't being too personal-like.

The door opened onto the sight of a nice place with a kind of old-world feel. Lots of oak paneling and brass fixtures and Arabian-Nights style carpets underfoot, the kind that have a lot of red in them. A set of narrow steps led up toward a simple stained-glass window with a white eagle and a red border to it.

A woman was coming down those steps.

She had a real look to her, with half-lidded eyes that looked like they had been drawn in with ink. Pale blue eyes that almost disappeared into the whites. A long nose with wide nostrils, not ugly, but the kind that can give your face a real snobbish look. Short, dark brown hair parted straight down the middle with a Marcel wave. A few curls had been teased out onto her face, the expression of which made me think of that old poem:

There was a little girl,

Who had a little curl,

Right in the middle of her forehead.

When she was good,

She was very good indeed,

But when she was bad she was horrid.

Spoiled wasn't the half of it. She had a look on her face like Nero playing the violin while Rome burned. You could have charged people just to come and look at her face. It was a silent picture all by itself, no dialogue cards necessary.

"Hello?" she said in a vampy voice. "Who are you? And what do you want?"

"Oh, you know who I am already," I said, waving one hand dismissively. "And you know what I want."

She stopped on the stairs, one hand hesitating on the railing. Her nails were done in a French manicure but the knuckles had some real wrinkles to them. I suddenly remembered that I should have taken a look at her gams to see if she had bony legs, but she was wearing a floor-length dress that puddled up around the feathered toes of her slippers, so I couldn't get a glimpse.

"I do," she said. I don't think she was telling the truth, actually, but who was I to argue? "But why don't you come inside and tell me all about it?"

I stepped over the threshold, right foot forward and that hag-stone under the front of my dress.

She descended the rest of the stairs and held out her hand to me. "My name is Magdalena Dauksza."

"I'm just little old Myrna Smith, as I'm sure you already know. And I'm here to get a song back."

"A song?"

"Yeah. It got stolen from me by a couple of fairies from the old country, as it were. I heard you were the kind of person to see about that."

"Who did you hear that from?"

Without skipping a beat, I gave her the name of my neighbor, the one who with the configured house-fae dishwasher in his house. I couldn't think of a better guy to drag down with me if something went wrong, you know?

Magdalena nodded.

"You can read my mind, can't you?" I asked her. "That's how you know all this stuff."

I gave her my best wide-eyed stare, the kind that all the directors like to see in their pictures.

"I can see many things," she said, noncommittally, but she looked a little smug when she said it. "But I wish for you to describe what happened completely, so that I can get the clearest picture."

"Sure!" I said. She waved me down the hallway and we sat in a little parlor, the kind that your grandmother is always telling you to stay out of. I half-expected the chairs to have covers on them, but they were nice. They had these delicate crocheted doilies on the back of the seats to protect the cloth from hair-oil and everything.

We both sat down and about two seconds later, a tap came at the door and a house-fae backed in with a tea tray, piping hot tea and two little plates with rolls of cake, slices of flaky pastry stuffed with poppyseeds and tied with gold strings.

I took the cup and the plate and set them on the table in front of me. I let my feet tap on the floor like I was too excited to hold still, which I was. "Mrs. Dauksza—"

"It's Miss Dauksza," she said quickly, then added, "Call me Magdalena, pet."

"Miss Magdalena," I said, "can you help me? Oh, please, tell me that I can get my song back."

"Who did you give it to?"

"A couple of house-fae. I was down in Little Tokyo with my husband, we had gone out dancing and drinking for the night, and there was a pair of house-fae coming down the street, and I was singing a little song that I had made up, it was just a little bit of nothing, you know? But I used to sing it to my baby son, who was killed in a car accident, and the two house-fae stopped me and asked if I was using that song, the lady just came out and asked it, *Are you using that song?* and I explained that it was just a little song that I used to sing to my son but he had died in a car accident, would I sing it again she asked, so I did, and they both looked at it and said that it was a fair exchange and they would be at the house by midnight, and I had no idea what they were talking about but then they showed up at our house at midnight which was more than a little surprising, and it was all the bee's knees until we found out that all the house-fae were going to get deported, and ours won't go because they have some kind of deal with us and they won't break it and we're going to get arrested for hiding them in our house and I don't think that's fair, is it? for a deal I didn't exactly agree to in the first place and I want my song back even if it doesn't get them out of the house but I hope it does, so we don't get arrested."

The witch's eyes sparkled. If she was supposed to be just about three hundred years old, she didn't look like it. "There will be a price," she said.

"Well, I wasn't expecting to get anything for free," I said. I had on a silver and rose-diamond necklace that was made out of paste. I pulled it over my head and handed it to her. "My husband gave this to me for my birthday. It oughta be worth something."

She pretended to look it over, turning it this way, then that way, letting the little bit of light from the lace-covered window catch it and toss sparkles over the ceiling. She gave me a sharp look to see if I knew about the necklace being a fake. I kept my best naïve face on, which is, you have to admit if you've ever seen one of my pictures, something truly special.

"Yes, this is certainly worth something," she said finally.

"Enough to get my song back?" I asked hopefully.

"You will have to promise not to tell the government about your house-fae," the witch said, acting like she had the best interests of Ala and Elias at heart.

"I kind of like 'em," I admitted sheepishly. "I don't want to see them get into any trouble with the Feds. I just don't want them in my house, you know?"

She nodded, still turning the necklace back and forth. Then she brought up the three tasks, which were the real price of her favor: "There are some things you will have to bring me, in order for me to break the contract that you have with them."

"What?"

"A blue rose, a doll that belonged to you as a child, and a silver needle."

I wasn't sure what the doll and the silver needle were for, probably nothing good. But that she asked for a blue rose didn't surprise me at all.

I gave her a sad look. "I ain't never seen a blue rose, and I didn't keep any of my dolls. What am I going to do?"

"Do you have a silver needle?"

"I don't think so? I can get one at a department store."

"Don't you sew?" the witch asked, like it was inconceivable that a modern girl with a career might not spend a Saturday night with a cup of cocoa and a basket of her husband's socks to darn.

"No, the house-fae do that," I said.

Incredulously, the witch asked, "What will you do when they're gone?"

I shrugged. "I don't know. Hire somebody to take care of me?"

"So you won't try to get me anything that I ask for."

"Nope! I mean, I won't promise you something I'm not gonna be able to get. That wouldn't be fair at all."

The witch frowned at me. "I'm not sure how you thought this was going to work."

I let myself look a little hurt. "I guess I thought I could just pay you? Somehow? And hopefully my husband wouldn't find out?"

"Why didn't you just ask the house-fae what it would take to get them to leave?"

I put the palms of my hands out. "Oh, I couldn't do that! I don't wanna hurt their feelings!"

The witch gave me a look. I thought she was ready to strangle me. We Hollywood actress types, we don't know much about anything. We're famous for it.

I sighed. Even though the witch hadn't caught me yet, I had to admit to myself that *my* big swindle wasn't going anywhere, either. It was time to go home.

I said, "Sorry, Miss Magdalena. I just can't see any way through this."

"You could work for me for thirteen years...?" the witch suggested.

I laughed and stood up. "I can't, Miss Magdalena, I got my career to think of. I made a lot of sacrifices to get where I am, and if I have to give up thirteen years of my life, well, I ain't gonna stay young forever! I guess I'll just have to pay the fine if they catch me. You won't snitch on me, will you?"

"Won't you stay for tea?" she asked, almost desperately.

"That's sweet, but I don't want to impose on you any more than I already have, and I have to get back before the house-fae find me out. I guess I'm stuck with them forever, right?"

"Unless they already have a deal with someone else. Then that would take precedence."

I perked up. "Another deal? How would I find out about that?"

The witch sighed. "The previous owner would have to come and claim them."

"So all I hafta do is find the previous owner and say, 'I have your house-fae, come and get 'em? That's it?"

The witch made a face. For a second, I saw through the glamor that she had put up. It was like her makeup cracked or something. Three hundred years old all right, give or take a decade.

She said, "If you did, the previous owner would be required to give you a gift."

"What kind of gift?"

"Thirteen years' service," the witch said, through gritted teeth.

I laughed, one of those tinkly little-girl laughs that gets under your skin and makes your ears hurt unless you're a handsome man and then somehow it seems charming, then took a card out of my purse and handed it to her.

She frowned, holding the card in her hand.

"Here you go," I said, "In case you ever want to come see me and my house-fae, Ala and Elias."

She looked up at me slowly. Her face was like a mask. Then, underfoot, the whole house shivered.

I said, "Thanks for your time, Miss Magdalena, but I gotta be going now. Maybe you can come over for tea and cookies sometime."

She didn't bother telling me goodbye.

When I stepped over the threshold and back out of the house, I stepped over it with my right foot first. Then I touched my lucky hag-stone. I dunno whether it helped or not, but boy oh boy I was glad I had it!

As I was pulling out of the stubby little stolen driveway, a light in one of the windows flickered at me.

I checked the road behind me to make sure there was nobody coming.

Then I winked back.

Like I said, we were always on the edge of setting the house-fae free, but there was always something. I told Ala and Elias all about it. Ala started to give Elias a talking-to for telling me things he shouldn't have. I told her to can it—unless she'd rather go back to that old witch, of course.

It turned out that I had guessed right. The second that the witch acted like she knew that Ala and Elias were the house-fae that she was looking for, she would owe me thirteen years' service, which had to have worked out to be longer than she had left on the old ticker anyhow.

So she was left knowing exactly where they were and not being able to do a thing about it.

I walked around the house a little wobbly for a couple of weeks. It had been a close shave, all right, and it was only pure dumb luck and Hollywood actress naïveté that had saved the day.

The witch's house disappeared, leaving a brown patch on my neighbor's lawn. He got busted for harboring a configured fae for some reason. I think someone must have called the Feds on him, just to be petty.

And I swear it wasn't me!

When Timothy came back, I told him all about it. And then I had to tell him a couple more things that he maybe wasn't going to take so well.

First, that I was expecting. There was nothing to see yet, but it must have been that we had timed it wrong while we were saying our goodbyes before he went off to the U.K. for filming. There wasn't anything to see yet, but he put his head on my belly anyway, claiming that he could hear a piano player in there, pounding away at some dramatic music. He made me laugh.

The other thing was that Ala and Elias were gone.

"Gone?" he said. "After all that? I thought they were really stuck with us now."

"They talked it over. As long as I don't tell the witch where they are, she can't get at them. I mean, they still work for us."

"They do?"

"I told them that they had to go find us filming locations, somewhere that the fae would be safe, because someday we want to film a movie there, one of our own. You'll be the director and I'll write the jokes."

He gave me a kiss right on the cheek. "My clever little duck," he called me.

"Are you sure about this?" he asked. "They're not gonna hire you at the studios if you're a mother again."

"Sure as sure, baby. You know what I learned from that witch?"

"What's that, sweetcakes?"

"Life is short...and some deals ain't worth it."

But some are. I get postcards from all over the world now. We're gonna go to Tijuana in November after the baby is born, so Elias can hold that sweet bundle of joy.

The world's a mess, honey, but what can you do? All I know is, all you have to do to really be somebody worth knowing is to be kind and try to have a good time.

———◆———

The story the Dame told wasn't anything like what I'd expected her to tell. When she was done with it, I had to sit back and roll the story around in my head a little. I was reminded, too, of what the Good Doctor had said that he'd seen out in the dark: a shadow that might have been a car, or might have been a monster. Now I was wondering if what he had seen might have been a little of both.

The Vampire said, "That was well enough told," to the Dame. He seemed a little stiff about it, like she had annoyed him somehow. Maybe she had—maybe he knew his story wouldn't top hers.

The others started talking to each other about the story, and I wanted to stay and join in, but Dom gave me a jerk of his chin, and he and I got up to refill everyone's drinks.

By the time we came back, it seemed like the Good Doctor had decided that he had definitely not seen a monster out there in the dark, but only a car. He even claimed he must have seen taillights—but was unable to describe them well enough for anyone to identify the model.

"Who did you think did it?"

The question was inevitable. Someone would have had to have asked it. In any case, it was the Detective who actually did so.

The Dame interrupted the Good Detective's answer. "I thought you was the one who did it, to tell you the truth."

The Detective said, "We all had a motive—but none of us but the Good Doctor had the opportunity."

The Dame shrugged. "Anybody can buy a hit these days. You just have to know the right people. And I gotta think that we all do. I mean, a friend of a friend of a friend can take you halfway around the world, and we ain't talking about Timbuktu."

"I didn't do it," said the Detective.

"I wasn't saying I thought you would admit to it," said the Dame. "I just thought you was the one who did it."

"And?"

"And do I still think you did it? I ain't so sure."

The Spy said, "If we all had a motive, and we all had the same relatively untraceable opportunity—that is, but for the Kid, whose shoes have been dry all evening, and who certainly couldn't afford to hire a surrogate—then it may be pointless to try to determine the culprit on our own, and we should rely upon the authorities to do so."

Nobody responded to that statement. The silence drew on, feeling like an over-tightened valve on a steam engine.

Suddenly an idea got hold of me, an idea I didn't know how to get rid of. It really had me in its grip.

I burst out with, "If you all had a motive to want him dead and someone suddenly had to put a hit on him to do it, then that means that he wasn't killed because of whatever the original motive was. I think. Maybe? Maybe not?"

Everyone looked at me like I was an idiot. I couldn't blame them. But my mind was spinning a mile a minute. I couldn't talk straight, I was thinking too hard.

I said, "I mean, whatever each person's obvious motive was, it doesn't matter. All of you had ten years to find him and have him killed. Whatever it was, was recent. Something new."

Another pause. Some of the faces frowned at me, some of them nodded thoughtfully. The Spy raised an eyebrow.

The Actress said, "And it wasn't to steal the treasure, because the treasure was left behind."

The Detective said, "Kid, I don't know if you're right, but you're not wrong."

My stomach lurched. It was almost worse to have one of my heroes say something kind to me because I said something halfway smart, than to make a complete fool of myself in front of him.

"That is as the case may be," The Vampire said. "But the next tale is mine, and I shall tell it now. It may prove to be a lengthy one." He coughed delicately into a white silk handkerchief, then smiled, showing off an old man's long, white teeth. "Pray, do not sleep."

THE MAGICIAN'S GRIFT
THE VAMPIRE'S TALE

1. The Shadow of the Tower

When I first met Professor Zuber, he told me he was the greatest magician of all time.

At first I didn't believe him. Now? I'm not sure.

It was 1929 in Minneapolis. The whole world was just about to get its heart and soul and back broke over the Black Friday stock market crash. Things had been getting bad before that, but it wasn't until the crash of 1929 that the people who mattered started to notice. When the have-nots don't have anything, that's the normal state of business. When the haves start to become have-nots, people get worried.

After the crash, it was so bad that the haves were starting to wonder if there would ever *be* haves again. And things changed, for a while at least.

Before the crash, though, we were all living in a kind of shadow. We knew *something* was going to happen. We just didn't quite know what. We were trying to carry on in the face of the unknown and the hidden. That was the real spirit of the times, you know? Everyone had a secret or two that they hid in order to get by. I know I did.

I had a good job as a lawyer's secretary. I had a steady beau but we weren't engaged. I mean, we had an agreement, but because of the economy we were putting off getting engaged and even the more serious kinds of hanky-panky. This was because I knew as soon as I announced that I was engaged I was gonna get fired. That's how I got my job. My boss, Mr. Kumpke, had let his old secretary go the week after she told him she was getting hitched. He gave her a fifty-dollar bonus to help outfit her kitchen, which was nice but it wasn't a job. It was like he had a horror of marriage and he was worried about it rubbing off on him.

Mr. Kumpke was the kind of lawyer with an unfortunately regretful face, as in, no matter what his mood was, he looked like he was just about to say, *Unfortunately I regret to inform you...* His eyelids drooped. He had jowls and thin, almost lipless lips, a long nose, and eyebrows that were two gray spots above his watery green eyes. In short he looked like a Basset hound.

"Miss Malmquist," he'd sigh. "Don't ever get married. You're the best secretary I've ever had. I'd hate to lose you."

What he was really saying was, *Nice job you have there, Miss Malmquist. I'd hate to see anything happen to it.*

So that was the situation the morning that I met Professor Zuber. I had just gone to the bank to withdraw my savings. I had a bad feeling about that bank. Every time I walked into it, I felt like I was being hypnotized or something, and lately I'd been feeling like something nasty was crawling over my skin on top of that. I only had an account in the first place because one of my father's cousins had pretended to be an uncle, and vouched for me. Let me tell you, when I tried to withdraw that money, I got a real talking-to from a bank manager about how I was helping to destroy the economy. In the end they wouldn't let me take out all of it, just twenty dollars so I could "buy myself something nice." They tried to make it look like they were doing me a favor.

I stormed back to Mr. Kumpke's office, mad as a wet hen. Me and my Robert were determined to get married and move to Iowa—near our families, but not *too* near, if you know what I mean, and I needed those savings the way I needed a wedding ring.

Anyhow I started crossing Marquette, about as steamed as an industrial laundry service.

But I didn't make it all the way across. I stopped dead in the street—traffic or no traffic.

There was a shadow across the pavement, a shadow so dark I couldn't bear to put a single foot into it. It was like looking into tar. You couldn't see anything. Nobody walking, no cars, not even the glint from a windowpane. It was like the air had been filled up with oil or ink.

I took a deep breath and started to walk forward into it, thinking that if I blinked enough my eyes would clear.

Then someone grabbed my arm and pulled me back onto the sidewalk. A white Dodge Fast Four swept in front of me about an inch from my nose, laying the horn on thick.

I twisted around to try to see who had a hold of me. It was a big hulking shape, a white man in an oilcloth greatcoat, wearing a wide-brimmed leather hat.

"Thanks, mister," I said.

"Don't mention it," he said. "Let us find a cup of coffee and make sure you're all right."

My hands shaking and my stomach sick with how close I'd come to stepping into that shadow, I said, "Sorry, mister. I gotta get back to work."

He shook his head sadly. "But if your path lies within that shadow...I cannot promise that you will be unharmed," he said. "However, if you wait another half hour, the shadow will have moved and you can proceed safely. Do come with me, Miss Malmquist, and have a cup of coffee."

Of course I hadn't told him my name. I went with him because of that.

But then I've always had more curiosity than sense.

———◆———

The little coffee shop was one that I must have passed a thousand times but never gone into. For some reason I had it in my head that it wasn't a coffee shop there, but a hat shop. And, as a matter of fact, as we started to walk up to the door, for a second the big plate-glass window out front seemed to shimmer with hats like a heat mirage.

I gave the storefront a hard look but didn't say anything. I glanced over at the gent who had my hand on his arm. He had placed his enormous hand over mine, like a beau saying *this one's mine*. I bristled, but a fella saves your life, you cut him some slack.

He was about six-foot-five or -six and built like a train. Under his oilcloth coat, his wool suit looked expensive. He had a walking stick hung over one arm.

He led me into the coffee shop. As I walked in the door I got another eyefull of shimmering hats. Black ones, gray ones, tan ones, brown ones. All men's hats. I squeezed my eyes shut for a second, then opened them again. When I did, it was a coffee shop again. About a dozen people sat around the tables, and another two at the counter, both wearing sailor suits.

"Good ta see ya, Professor Zuber," said one of the sailors.

"Greetings, gentlemen," said my escort.

The guy behind the counter said, "Morning, Zuber" with a voice like gravel pouring out of a cup.

Still keeping my hand pinned to his arm, Zuber led me toward the counter. "I have here a young lady who felt herself quite oppressed by that shadow coming from the Foshay Tower. If you look, you can see it still."

We all turned toward the front windows. The darkness was still there, although it had pulled back so only half the street was covered by it. Nobody but us seemed to notice as they disappeared into it—or appeared out of it.

I shuddered.

"Dang," said one of the sailors. "That's a big one. Wonder who cursed the place like that. Probably revenge for screwing somebody outta their life savings."

The other sailor said, "Unless they cursed themselves, to make Zuber think they weren't worth ripping off!"

Both men laughed uproariously.

Zuber cleared his throat.

"I'd like some coffee for the lady and myself, and, hmm, let us say, croissants. Hot and fresh, if you please, with butter, and as many of them as you can mound up on one of your large plates."

"Sure, yeah, whatever," was the counterman's only response. There were no croissants in the display case at the front. Or at least I don't think so. To my eye, it looked the display case was filled with hats. Little ones, the size of your fist, and buzzing around like bees.

I blinked and they disappeared, replaced by an empty case.

Zuber led us toward a booth along the wall. Then he made a big production of taking off his hat and coat and hanging them with his cane on a coat hook. He waved me toward a seat.

In about a second the counterman brought two cups of coffee and a plate of big fluffy croissants in front of us, steaming hot, and a big crock of butter.

"I brought you some honey butter," he said. "Honey *and* butter."

Zuber snorted through his nose. "You might bring me what I asked for. Or is that too much to ask?"

"Try it. The witches have a sale on honey butter this month. You might like it."

"I shall do no such thing. Who knows where those witches have been?"

I grabbed a croissant off the top of the heap, pulled it open, and slathered it with honey butter using the butter knife jabbed into the crock. I have a particular fondness for croissants, and these ones smelled like heaven. I tucked my napkin carefully into my dress, then took a bite.

I closed my eyes in bliss.

"*She* likes the honey butter," noted the counterman.

"Some ladies have peculiar tastes," Zuber said crossly. "Now amscray. Can't you see I have something to say to the young woman?"

The counterman marched stiffly off, muttering something like *stubborn old bastard* under his breath. Meanwhile I kept my eyes on Zuber, who frowned at the steaming hot croissants, then picked one up and laboriously split it with the butter knife and spread the honey butter in the middle without complaint.

"Would you like another?" he asked.

"I shouldn't," I said. "I hafta watch my figure."

Zuber ate his croissant slowly, one bite at a time, slurping his coffee loudly and holding the cup with one pinky sticking out.

I sipped quietly at mine. I swear I drank about two cups of coffee without having to refill the cup, and it was just as full when I pushed it away from me as when I first picked it up.

Finally Zuber finished. He set down the smooth white cup on the table and said, "I suppose you want to know why I brought you here. I am a magician, the greatest magician of all time."

"And I'm the Queen Mary."

Zuber's eyebrows lifted, but he kept talking without otherwise acknowledging that I'd said anything at all.

"I have brought you here because you reacted to the curse on Foshay Tower, which, by the way, is not of my doing. And, if I observed correctly, you seemed quite irritated by the illusion set over the door to this café. Both facts, I think, are telling."

He paused theatrically. I waited for him to lay some story down on me about how I better give him twenty bucks in order to lift the curse on Foshay Tower—or whatever grift he was up to. The skin on the back of my hands was prickling. I hate liars, although admittedly I feel no compunction about lying to one.

"Yeah? So?" I said.

"You...are a potential magician!" he declared, making a grand gesture with one hand that almost knocked over his coffee.

After a second or two, I said, "Really? Why don't you pull the other leg while you're at it?"

Zuber blinked at me. The two sailors broke out into laughter. Big whoops and guffaws.

"She's got you there," one of them said.

Zuber slapped one huge palm on the tabletop. "That's enough nonsense! Can none of you see that there are worse problems than the curse on Foshay Tower? There is a curse in this country, one that spreads all across the world, spread by the greed of evil men and evil magicians. We are no saints, none of us, but *we need all the magicians on our side we can get.* Even untrained ones like Miss Malmquist." He turned to me. "At the very least, I forbid you to step in the shadow of that building, *or your fortunes will sink like the Titanic!*"

I winced. Zuber was nuts, that was all, and everybody was in on the joke but him. I felt bad for the guy.

I reached across and patted his hand. "Look, okay. I won't step into the shadow if I can help it. But I gotta be back at work already, or I'm gonna get fired. You know how it is. Thanks for the coffee and the croissant."

I took a sip to finish off my coffee—I had grown up like that, never leave anything on your plate or your cup or you're likely to get whupped—but it was just as hot and full as it had been when the counterman brought it out. After a couple of gulps, I gave up trying to finish it off.

"The shadow," Zuber said.

"I'll stay out of it," I promised.

He nodded, then reached inside his suitcoat pocket and pulled out a card. It was on good linen paper stock with green ink. The border was a knotwork of vines.

"I am Professor Zuber," he said, as if his name hadn't been thrown around half a dozen times already. "And if you are in any need, call me immediately."

The words *Professor Zuber – Instructor of the Arcane and Obscure, Financial Prognostications a Specialty* were written on the card, but neither on the front nor the back was a phone number.

I looked up and started to say as much, but...

The coffee shop was gone. There were hats all around me, not on racks but flying through the air, swooping around like a room full of bats.

I kicked the base of the booth hard, hard enough to make silverware rattle on china and coffee slosh in the cup. I felt around me and found my purse. I wasn't sure what Zuber had done to me, maybe slipped something in my coffee. Or maybe I had a brain tumor. Who knew? It was that kind of day.

Taking my purse with me, I made my way to the door, waving aside hats as I went.

I did hang onto the card, though. And I took the long way back to Mr. Kumpke's office, even though it made me late.

That shadow.

I couldn't bring myself to walk through it. It still looked thick as tar, but people walked in and out of it without a second thought. I told myself that my Robert, who was the most practical, and least magical, man I knew, had to be safe, even though he worked inside the tower.

After all, if it *wasn't* safe, wouldn't the pedestrians be dropping like flies?

— ◦ —

I didn't get fired that day. I told Mr. Kumpke about the bank and that I'd been so mad afterwards that I'd stopped for a cup of coffee and a croissant at a diner. Croissants being what they are, flaky, a crumb or two had landed on my dress, backing up that part of the story.

Mr. Kumpke picked the crumb off with his fingernails, which were just a little bit longer than was pleasant. "It was illegal for the bank to withhold your savings. But I must ask: what made you want to withdraw them? It's not that you're getting engaged and transferring your funds to your future husband's accounts? You aren't planning to leave me?"

I lied and reassured him that it was just that I'd been reading his copy of the paper over my lunch break, and I couldn't see how the country's financial situation could keep on going the way it was, and that between getting a little more interest on my money today and losing my shirt tomorrow, then maybe I'd rather have those greenbacks under the mattress where my grandma always said they belonged.

I wasn't lying, exactly. It was just that the fact that I was planning to quit my job and head south before Christmas didn't need to be shared at that exact moment, that was all.

Mr. Kumpke nodded and said that he agreed with me in principle, but not in practice. *He* was in possession of a stock-market wizard who had come upon a foolproof scheme to increase his investors' money. If I *were* able to withdraw the funds in question from my rather disreputable bank, yet wished to see some real profit out of them, then of course he would be ready and willing to oblige. He would add my funds to his; it would be the simplest of tasks. And within six months I would see a two-hundred-percent growth on my investment, at a minimum.

Well, that's too good to be true, I said to myself. And then the other shoe dropped.

"You wouldn't be talking about investing in that Mr. Wilbur B. Foshay's special, uh, fund, would it?" I asked.

Word was, Mr. Foshay couldn't pay for the expenses of building the Foshay Tower, or for the huge party that he'd thrown at its opening last month in September—or for the musical march that he'd had John Philip Sousa write for it. Lately Foshay had started raising money, supposedly to invest in the stock market, but likely to cover his debts. And yet you could still see him running around town, still dressed in tailored suits and showing up in the society pages of the local papers, smiling and shaking hands.

"Why, yes it is!" Mr. Kumpke smiled, which gave his face a ghoulish appearance.

If I'd been his mother, I'd have slapped the grin right off him. At least when he was looking regretfully unfortunate the hair wasn't standing upright on the back of my neck.

I promised him I'd think about it. I would, too. I had a bad feeling about anything having to do with Wilbur Foshay or Foshay Tower, and it wasn't just because of Professor Zuber and his damned coffee shop.

After work, first checking that the coast was clear, I visited my Robert at a café. Then I went home to my apartment, which I shared with a girl named Betty Krohn, who had the kind of white-blonde hair and glassy blue eyes that might remind you of Carole Lombard. Betty didn't have the kind of discipline you needed to become a Hollywood starlet, though. She was about five feet tall and a size sixteen. Her size kept her out of the movies but not out of the hearts of about three different swains at any one time. She tended to get headaches and squint a lot, but was too vain to get a pair of glasses. She was a legal secretary. We'd met each other at a training college. She worked for another law office, one that handled family estates. I was trying to figure out how to break it to her about Robert and the move. Her boss had a cousin who was a lawyer in Des Moines, and I was hoping that she'd give me a reference.

It was Betty's turn to cook, which meant that we had big, thick noodles with about a pound of butter, lemon, and garlic, and some chicken. It was useless to try to talk to her about her weight; say a word about it and she'd grab a piece of candy and shove it in her mouth just to spite you. I liked her quite a bit.

"How's it going, sweet cheeks?"

"None of your business."

"Here, have a cigarette, ya dumb Dora."

"Don't mind if I do, ya quiff."

The apartment was in a small brick building called the Spanish Armada Hotel, with a super who treated us girls like he was paying us instead of the other way around. He didn't do any of the work himself; he just shoved an envelope with a piece of cheap paper and a room key under the door when he wanted work done. The rent was real cheap, though, and we girls were loyal to each other, which made it worth it. We taught each other how to fix plumbing, replace cracked windows, and brew up some nice gin from plain grain alcohol in the vacant apartments. New girls were carefully taken to the side and explained what was what.

I got out of my work dress, hung it up, and slipped into something more comfortable, which was long silky pants and an angora-wool pullover top, not much better than pajamas. Neither one of us had plans that night, which was a Tuesday.

After supper we got out a bottle of gin, some tonic water, and some limes. It was a habit with us. You didn't bring out the gin if you didn't mean to talk some kind of serious business.

I told her about the bank, and then about Mr. Kumpke and his suggestion and what I thought about his investments with Mr. Foshay. If he hadn't been my boss, we both coulda had a good laugh about it. As it was, I couldn't stop myself from thinking about what would happen if Wilbur Foshay lost his shirt. Or got arrested for whatever kind of scheme he was running. If Mr. Foshay tumbled, he would take a lot of people with him.

I intended to be out of Minneapolis before that happened, but...

Betty said, "All right, ya bug-eyed broad. Tell me what *really* happened today. You're holding back. You know I can tell."

I bit my lip, wondering if I were brave enough to tell her about Robert, finally. I wasn't. "I met a magician," I blurted out instead. "Or at least that's what he said he was."

"A stage magician?"

"No..."

I told her about Professor Zuber, the shadow of the Foshay Tower, and the coffee shop. She worked out where it was on the street—we both agreed about the shops on either side of it—and she declared that she'd always thought it was a jeweler's shop, all flashy diamonds and no taste.

She laughed and waved her left hand in front of her face. "The last place *I'd* ever walk into."

"Look," I said. "Are you saying that you believe me? That there is such a thing as magic?"

"Sounds like it."

"But how could anyone keep a secret that big?"

Betty laughed, looking at me from half-lowered eyelids. I blushed. All right, maybe we both had a few secrets that we were hiding in plain sight. People didn't see what they didn't expect to see. As long as you didn't get caught, who did it hurt?

I said, "So let's say there *is* magic, at least of some kind, but maybe not the kind where you have to dress up in a robe and pointed hat and chant stuff in Latin like Merlin. Maybe you can't change lead into gold but you can make a coffee shop look like the last place anyone would ever think to go into."

"Maybe you can put a finger on things and change them just enough to sway them in your favor, or to sway things against your enemies," Betty added. "I've known lawyers like that."

I nodded. We both knew lawyers like that.

"So why the curse on the tower now?" I asked. "Things were already looking not so great for Mr. Foshay."

"Maybe it's a lien enchantment," Betty said. "He made some magician mad at him, and now he's cursed until he pays up."

We both frowned at each other. It was a neat idea but it sounded wrong, although neither of us could put a finger on why.

"What, then?" I asked. "They can't have cursed themselves, can they? Made it look like they were being cursed?"

"Why would anyone do that?" Betty asked.

I snorted. "For one thing, you couldn't have a run on the bank by a bunch of magic-sensitive folks if they don't dare go into the shadow."

"Good point. But how many magic-sensitive folks could there be? No, I think it's something else."

"But what?"

Neither of us had any good answers, so we refreshed our drinks.

I went to my purse and pulled out the card that Professor Zuber had given to me. There was still no phone number on the card, front or back. We tried holding the card in front of a hot lightbulb and rubbing over it with a piece of pencil. Unless a telephone number had been written on the card with magic, there wasn't any secret message there, waiting to be found.

<hr>

2. It Worked Like Magic

I woke up the next morning with a hangover and an idea, which was how drinking gin usually works on me. The idea was this: I would get Mr. Kumpke to take his money out of the Foshay scheme before it was too late. And I'd make him think it was his idea. Then my job would be safe—for the little while longer I wanted it, anyway.

I couldn't do it alone, that was clear. Not only did I need someone else to take on the role of persuading Mr. Kumpke (because he would never believe financial advice coming from me), but the whole scheme involved a kind of expertise that I didn't have.

I needed to con Mr. Kumpke out of his money in such a way that he didn't know he was being conned, and then give it back to him in such a way that he wasn't tempted to go out and make the same mistake a second time.

Was I a con artist?

No way, no how. Like I said, it was just an idea I got the next morning, hung over as hell.

And it was Wednesday.

Which meant I had to go to work.

I showed up and did the job. Mr. Kumpke was stiff with me, which meant that he was annoyed at me for not being as sweet with him as I normally was. I made his coffee too strong, then didn't put enough cream in it. But that was on purpose. I made sure everything I did, I did just a little bit wrong. When I went out of the room I didn't back through the door while smiling at him, the way I normally do.

Finally, when it came time for lunch, I said, "Mr. Kumpke, I've been thinking hard about what you said yesterday."

His face lit up and he gave me that ghoulish grin again. I swear, his teeth came to points when he smiled. "Excellent! I wondered why you have been so distracted this morning. I hope you've come to a favorable conclusion."

"I think I have. I'm going to go down to my bank and withdraw my savings and bring them here to you to invest with Mr. Foshay. I'm not going to let them give me no for an answer. Is it all right if I take a little bit longer over lunch?"

"Perfect, my dear girl, perfect. Trust me, I shan't let you down."

"I'm sorry if I've been a bit short with you today, Mr. Kumpke. It's been a lot to think about."

He had already forgiven me, I could tell. People do that, when you're doing what they want.

I went to the bank all right, being careful to avoid the shadow of the Foshay Tower. It being around noon, however, there wasn't too much danger. Noon's a good time to go out for a walk when the only shadow you want to step on is your own.

On the way back I stopped at the coffee shop. The shop front had shrunk to about half as wide as it had been previously, but it had more or less given up on pretending to be a hat shop, at least for me. I could see three hats on stands in the front window, but they were blurry and thin, more like sketches of hats than hats themselves. I went up to the door and yanked it open, passing quickly through the illusion of flying hats. This time they looked a bit frowsy, the bands faded and the feathers limp.

The counterman looked up at me and said, "Hello, Miss Honey Butter. Cuppa coffee?"

"Hello," I agreed. "But that's not what I'm here for. I need to contact Professor Zuber. He gave me his card, but—" I showed it to him. The number still hadn't shown up.

The counterman shook his head slowly. "There's only one Zuber. And he's in da phone book."

I slapped myself in the forehead. "Well, in case he comes in before I can call him, tell him that Miss Malmquist is looking for him. I need his assistance with something."

"With magic?"

Even with his rough, gravelly voice, he sounded doubtful.

I got the impression that he was about to try to explain that Zuber was all talk and not much magic—but I was already shaking my head.

"I don't need a magician. I need a smooth talker. It sounds like my boss, who is a lawyer, is getting himself involved in that stock fiasco involving Wilbur Foshay. I need to scare some sense into him."

"Scare sense into a lawyer?" the counterman asked.

Coming from him, it did sound sort of implausible.

"Right or wrong, I don't like to give up on people without trying to help them first," I said. "If this doesn't work out, I'll see what else comes up."

The counterman nodded. He held out a hand, and I shook it. "Call me Al."

"Miss Elizabeth Malmquist. Don't call me Betty, that's my roommate's name. Call me Eliza."

"Cuppa or not?"

"No, thank you. I have to get back to my office. I have all my savings in my purse. From the bank."

Al slowly raised one thick, blocky eyebrow. "How'd you get them to cough it up?"

I said, "I may have threatened to scream and start a run on the bank. It worked...like magic."

—◦—

I called Zuber's number in the phone book, but whatdya know, it was disconnected. I *may* have snarled out loud that Zuber was going to miss out on a perfectly legitimate con job because he couldn't pay his phone bill and slammed down the receiver.

The next day, Thursday, without consulting me whatsoever, Professor Zuber showed up at the Kumpke Law Office demanding to see Mr. Kumpke.

He arrived to the sound of thunder.

We had an elevator in the building, but it was on the fritz. Sometimes it worked, and sometimes it didn't. I was in the habit of walking up the six flights of stairs to Mr. Kumpke's office every morning, and down them again every night.

I had taken the elevator exactly once, a few weeks after I had first started working in the office. Mr. Kumpke had given me a set of keys to all the rooms except his own office, so I could let myself in before he got there in the mornings. I would come in early, about seven-thirty, and make some coffee and tidy things up before Mr. Kumpke arrived. At the time I was trying to butter him up so I could ask for a raise. It was turning into a kind of game. He would fuss about his worries that I would run off and get married just like his previous secretary, and I would bend over backwards to be helpful. That might sound more like I was knuckling under, but believe me, when I choose to make someone notice how helpful I am it makes them want to scream. Anyhow I had been coming in earlier and earlier every morning, and being just a little bit more bright and cheerful when I greeted my employer each day. I might have been pitching my voice just a little bit higher and louder, wondering just how long it would take before it hit a shriek. But one day while I was carrying out this plan of subversion, I ran late, or rather was not as early as usual, and I thought, well, I'll just take the elevator for once. And miracle of miracles, it wasn't marked "out of order." There was no operator, but I already knew how to operate an elevator anyhow, so that wasn't any trouble. I got in and closed the door, then pulled the lever to the sixth-floor mark. I made it up to the sixth floor smoothly and pretty quietly, got out, left the elevator there, and let myself quietly into the front room of the law office. I was still early.

Mr. Kumpke's door was open; he was sleeping at his desk.

Whenever someone walked up the stairs, it echoed throughout the stairwell, the door of which was next to the office. Any time someone came up the stairs, the whole building got a notice. That day I hadn't given him one. I watched him for a couple of minutes and realized he wasn't breathing. I was just about to walk over to him and check for a pulse when he licked his lips...with a tongue that looked dead and gray as a fish at the market.

I took the elevator downstairs and walked all the way back up, trying to make noise like I usually did, only I couldn't exactly remember how much that was. My heart was hammering in my chest.

Just as I reached the sixth floor, I remembered that I'd forgotten to lock the outer door as I left.

When I reached the door and turned the knob. It was locked. I screwed up my face. *All right, Malmquist, you've goofed again. Pack your things now, it'll be quicker.*

And safer.

I wasn't sure what I'd seen...but I knew I wasn't supposed to have seen it. People in that position sometimes wind up missing, you know?

I let myself in the office and went about my normal routines, pretending he wasn't in yet. I was shivering and sweating at the same time, thinking, *I need the money. We need the money.* Not a sound came from the inner office. I started worrying that the old lawyer had died after all.

But then, about half an hour later, Mr. Kumpke walked in the outer door of the office and gave me the unfortunately regretful look that I had already come to recognize as his regular expression.

"Good morning, Miss Malmquist," he said. "How are things on the marital front?"

I swallowed. "Dire," I said, my voice hoarse. "I had a date last night and the guy broke it off with me. I'm starting over at square one tonight, and not a single prospect."

He nodded. "That is pleasant news." He unlocked his office door and let himself in, closing the door behind him. In about two seconds the lights went on. It was a south-facing room, and he always kept the shades down, the curtains pulled, and the lights on—even in the heat of summer.

I sighed with relief. I hadn't lost my job, or worse!

But I kept my eyes open.

As far as I could tell, Mr. Kumpke slept in his office *every* night. I got in the habit of climbing six flights of stairs and not saying anything when I noticed that things had been moved since the night before. How he got past me in order to get in the outer door every morning wasn't a matter that I looked into. I was pretty sure I wouldn't have liked the answer if I had.

At any rate, the day that I managed to claw my savings away from the bank, I heard someone coming up the stairs to the office, really shaking the staircase all the way up, and obviously taking the stairs two or three at a time. The sound echoed through the building like Kaiser Wilhelm's soldiers marching on the attack.

I knew who it was...I just knew.

Through the frosted glass of the office door, I saw a huge, shadowy shape appear. A fist pounded on the door frame. The glass rattled loudly but didn't break.

I got up and opened the door. It was Zuber.

"Yes, sir?" I asked.

"Don't play games with me, Eliza Malmquist," he roared. "What would your father say?"

Then he winked.

I hadn't even spoken to the man other than to curse at him through an out-of-service phone number. Nevertheless, he had found out the details of what I wanted done, and apparently he was in on the con. The game was afoot, and I had better keep up.

I looked down, trying to keep the flush from rushing across my face. I sniffed hard. "Is this about the money?"

"Of course it's about the money! And I want to speak to your employer this minute. That scoundrel!"

I stepped out of the way. Today Professor Zuber was dressed in a charcoal-gray suit of the same cut as the one he'd worn the previous day, although it looked even more expensively tailored than the brown one. He had upgraded from a Homburg to a fedora; the feather in the band was silver-gray with a larger black feather behind it. He carried a black leather attaché case with the initials *H R Z* set in silver on the front.

Zuber swept through the reception area toward Mr. Kumpke's office like an arrow shot from a bow. Mr. Kumpke's door opened just as Zuber raised a fist to bang on it.

"What is the meaning of this?" Mr. Kumpke asked, in a chilling voice, standing on the other side of the doorway.

Zuber blinked at him, then lowered his fist. "I have come to extricate my niece's finances from your devilish grip."

"Your niece, sir?"

"A tie of familial affection rather than of blood. But nonetheless binding."

Mr. Kumpke's jaw clenched, then relaxed. "I see. Miss Malmquist, is this true?"

I spread my hands. "I didn't *ask* him to come here. I didn't speak with him about this at all. I swear."

Mr. Kumpke said, "Come now, you can tell me the truth. You were worried that my investments would drag yours under, leaving your finances destitute and unlikely to attract a husband."

I shook my head. "Why would I be worried? Whatever happened to my money would happen to yours...and you wouldn't put yourself in a bad position. At least, not on purpose." I paused. "I may have mentioned that I had hopes of sending a windfall to my mother, though." I had told Mr. Kumpke that my father had passed, leaving my mother a small pension that was barely enough to live on, which was more or less true.

"I see," said Mr. Kumpke, still unperturbably calm in the face of Zuber's fuming.

Mr. Kumpke turned his eyes from mine and looked at Zuber, searching his face.

Zuber towered over Mr. Kumpke by at least a full foot.

Mr. Kumpke's nostrils flared. "And you wish to join us in this scheme, is that it? Is that the reason for all this drama? Am I to convince you that your niece has tapped into a goldmine with her employer, and then you will hand over a sum of money *that you already have in your case* to invest in the same area? I must say that there are easier ways of securing an invitation."

Zuber's face turned red. "I have come to liberate my niece from your schemes!"

"Professor," I said. "Please stop making a scene! We can have supper tonight and talk this over. There's no need to frighten Mr. Kumpke like this. He's done nothing but good for me."

Zuber shook his head. "He's dragged you into ruin, if only you knew it."

"Ruin? Don't be so melodramatic. It's just..." I waved a hand.

"Dishonest?" Zuber roared. "You girls are so naïve! I'll tell you how it is. Mr. Foshay spent all his money on the building of that cursed tower, did he not? And yet now he has an extravagant amount of funds. Where did they come from? And why has he not yet paid his debts?"

"He got money from investors," I said, annoyed.

"How?"

"By..." I glanced over at Mr. Kumpke.

"By selling stocks," Mr. Kumpke said.

"By selling his own stock...stock with no worth whatsoever!" Zuber exclaimed.

Mr. Kumpke responded calmly, "He has purchased a number of stocks from other companies, ones that have a great deal of value in their businesses—if nothing else, their equipment, buildings, stocks, and land value—but that have lost a great deal of their resources on paper. He buys stocks whose value will increase tenfold when the market recovers."

"*Does he?*" Zuber roared. No doubt everyone in the building could hear him. "*Does he?* If those stocks were being sold, the share volume would reflect it! I have been studying Mr. Foshay's little scheme for some time. Do you know where those stocks come from? Do you? I will tell you! They come from themselves! You are receiving worthless certificates printed up by Mr. Foshay himself, and profits derived from investors who enter this scheme after you do! At any moment, Mr. Foshay will be caught—his hidden investment empire will crumble—you will lose everything, everything! And my niece will fall with you."

My heart sank like a stone. I couldn't let Mr. Kumpke lose his shirt over this, especially as I was intending to leave him so soon. Plus, I *had* given him my savings, to the tune of five hundred dollars, which were currently locked up in his safe.

Mr. Kumpke was always pale; now he grew even paler. "What proof do you have?"

"Let us go into your office, close the door, and discuss this like gentlemen where we shall not worry our darling Eliza unduly."

I bit the inside of my cheek where Mr. Kumpke couldn't see it, and stared at my feet.

"Very well," said Mr. Kumpke. A moment later, the door of Mr. Kumpke's office closed. I heard the creak of the wood chairs from the other room as the two men sat. I also heard the sounds of the buckles on Zuber's attaché case being loosened, and the slide of paper across the desk. I couldn't take it anymore; I went down to the street for a walk.

When I came back, Zuber was gone and Kumpke was shaken. "I've been a fool, an absolute fool," he said.

He slumped onto his desktop with his hands folded in front of him. He was so limp in his chair that his chin lay on top of his knuckles.

I said, "Mr. Kumpke, can I get you a cup of coffee?"

His eyes looked up at me, reminding me of a hound dog lying dejectedly on the floor. "No, thank you," he said. "I shall be going out in a moment."

"What for?" I caught myself a moment too late. "I'm sorry. It's probably none of my business."

He shook his head, still not lifting it in the slightest. "I'm afraid it is. You see, I've given your savings as well as a large chunk of the liquid funds I had on hand to your uncle, to invest in stocks that—"

It was at that point that I broke down. I said, "That charlatan? You gave *my* savings to *that* charlatan?"

I closed my mouth with a clap.

Mr. Kumpke's eyes seemed to fly with a spark of anger for a moment—that then extinguished itself.

Oh well, I thought. *There goes my job.*

Which now I couldn't afford to lose. Because my savings had flown the coop along with Professor Zuber.

Mr. Kumpke said, "I was not aware that your uncle was a charlatan."

I was tempted to tell him the truth. But not *sorely* tempted. The man would be writing me a reference, after all, which I now needed more than ever. I sighed and rolled my head around on my neck. "Mr. Kumpke, have you ever heard the phrase, 'set a thief to catch a thief'? If that fund smelled fishy to my uncle, then you can take it as a guarantee that it was. We might have lost our money all over again, but at least he wasn't lying about the Foshay investments."

Mr. Kumpke closed his eyes. "Then I have been an even bigger fool than I thought. My dear girl, you would think that a man as old as I am would have been able to sniff out dishonesty by now."

I tried to reassure him that he wasn't that old, but he wasn't having it. He was so down that he didn't even preen under the buttering up I gave him.

Finally he sighed and heaved himself away from his desk.

"Watch the office, tell any callers that I shall return on the morrow, and if that rapscallion returns to fleece either of us again—a technique that I have been assured is not all that uncommon among thieves—then set him on his ear."

"I'd like to get my hands on him so I can get our money back," I said.

"I fear those funds are long gone," Kumpke said, "and if you have a shred of decency in your unwed heart, mention it to no one. One might lose one's investments in a stock-market scheme without shame, but if it gets about that I allowed myself to be swindled, it would be the ruination of my business."

He took his large felt hat and dark coat off the rack and escorted me out of his inner office, locking the door behind him.

"I must go," he said. "You are a sweet child, to think that you might be able to recover the money on your own. But such a swindler knows no limits, no family ties, no honor. It is gone, and we must strive to make do, until the tides of fortune carry us in the other direction."

He left the office, and I heard him walking down the stairs, all six flights of 'em.

I let myself into his inner office and opened the drawer where he keeps his receipts. (I may have mentioned that he hadn't given me keys to the office—but that didn't mean I didn't have any.)

On top of the pile was a receipt from Zuber for thirty-five hundred dollars. Next to it was a check stub for three thousand dollars.

From an account at the same bank I'd just withdrawn all my savings from.

⸺◆⸺

3. Before the Fall

The offices of Edwin Kumpke, Attorney at Law, were shortly thereafter closed for the afternoon. I don't think anybody noticed.

I tried to check for Zuber at the bank, but the guards had been instructed to be remove me on sight; they might have been worried that I would try to call a run on the bank or something. After all the threats I had made earlier that day, I guess I shouldn't have been surprised. I did get inside long enough to see that Zuber wasn't waiting in line to cash the check.

Then I checked the hat shop that was really a café. It was even easier to get into this time, with only a brief flutter of hatbands as I crossed the threshold. The facade had vanished entirely, leaving a plain window.

But Zuber wasn't at the café, either.

I marched right up to Al the counterman and said, "Zuber's got my money and my boss's money. He swindled us right up, and I need that money back. If you see Zuber," and I could feel every ear in the place pointing toward my back, "tell him to give that money back before I cause him more problems than he can handle."

"He will not give the money back," the counterman said sadly. He put a cup of coffee in front of me.

"I know," I said. Oh, I was angry, so angry that the counter and making the cup rattle in its saucer. "But at least if you tell him, he won't be able to say later that he wasn't warned."

The next step was to obtain myself some calm. I returned to the Spanish Armada and checked around the apartment, hoping for some last hideout bottle of gin hiding behind the can of olive oil in the cupboard, but as it turned out, we were all out. My best efforts to beg, borrow, steal, or make some calm resulted in one smashed flower-vase full of flowers that one of Betty's admirers had sent her, one startled neighbor who came to check on my shouting, and more cookies than a neighborhood Christmas party. I had to go knocking around the floor to get enough sugar to finish the last batch. I had a feeling that I would be calling in some favors soon.

Thursday was Betty's night to go to the pictures with one of her admirers, I forget which. Not the one whose flower vase I had just broken, fortunately. She walked into the apartment, took one sniff, and said, "If you needed me to cancel with Pat tonight, all you had to do was say so."

"I'm going to kill that man!"

"Who, Mr. Kumpke?"

"No, Professor Zuber!"

The whole story came out. At first the story was not completely truthful—I was embarrassed about getting swindled—but soon enough the details came flowing out of me, in direct proportion to the number of gin and tonics that Betty plied me with, her having run downstairs to a neighbor to beg a bottle or two.

At the end of it, Betty said, "Why don't you do some magic to *him*? Get some revenge?"

I denied my ability to do such a thing vigorously. All *I* could do was see through illusions, apparently, and then only at the cost of making myself dizzy and sick.

Betty said, "Don't give me that. Every time I get a cold, I drink some of your broth and it cures me right up. Your cooking makes me *lose* weight, no matter how much of it I eat. And those cookies are delicious enough that everyone on the floor drools for them—you can make anyone do anything you want for another one, once they've had a taste. You've had magic your whole life. Just because you didn't know what it was didn't mean you weren't hustling it right and left, either."

She made a face and raised her hand as I tried to deny it.

"And, to be perfectly honest, *that's* why Kumpke keeps trying to keep you from getting married to Robert. That old vampire!"

I shook my head. "Mr. Kumpke is a—"

A new voice cleared its throat from behind us.

"He's a terrible old man who takes advantage of you, my dear."

We both spun around. Zuber stood on the other side of the doorway, so big that he was wider than the door was wide, and taller than the door was tall. He carried a leather bag on one arm, and his cane over the other. His hat was in his hands.

"If you would but invite me in, I might explain..."

I was in no mood to believe anything Zuber said. Not a single word of it. Nevertheless I invited the man in. He ducked under the frame, edging in sideways. I closed the door tight behind him.

"All right, give me my money," I said, holding out my hand.

Zuber glanced around the front room, taking it in, from the lace curtains to the worn old drop-leaf table to the second-hand armchairs and settee in the living room. From top to bottom, the entire apartment was a study in two young women trying to make do and still set some by for hard times later. I hoped he was ashamed of himself for stealing from me.

"May I sit?"

"I don't recommend the chairs at the dining table," Betty said, sitting in one of the armchairs as cool as you please. "With your frame? They'd snap like kindling. Use the settee. It can take some weight."

I led him over to our settee, tugged the crocheted blanket on the back to cover a worn spot, and offered him a drink.

"Coffee? Tea? Gin and tonic?"

"The last of those three, if you please."

Cursing his lying tongue under my breath, I mixed him up one, extra-strong. "There's no ice," I said stubbornly.

He drank it off in a single gulp, then asked for another. I refused him at first, just to watch him beg a little for the next one, but finally handed over another.

Having attacked the first glass like a commander who senses the imminent escape of his foe, he laid siege to the second more slowly, wearing down its defenses with frowning sips.

"Homemade, I assume," he said. "It's quite lovely, all things considered. Much like yourself."

I rolled my eyes and held out my hand again, palm up.

Zuber had kept his leather bag between his feet, securely clamped between his shoes. Now he opened the top of it. It was stuffed with money, with a small piece of notepaper on top. He withdrew that, adjusted his glasses, and cleared his throat.

He reached into the bag and counted out a thousand dollars.

"For your assistance, my dear. I understand from my scrying that you are in need of a nest egg in order to—"

I grabbed the money and counted through it, rubbing the bills between my fingers to make sure the ink didn't rub off or the paper feel strange. The leather case was still filled with money.

"I didn't hand Mr. Kumpke no thousand dollars," I said. "And what are you planning to do with the rest of it?"

"That is none of your business," said Zuber, with all the appearance of dignity. The man had no shame whatsoever.

"He's my boss," I said. "If I get my savings back and he doesn't…"

"You are welcome to tell him that I have returned your funds but not his, if you like," Zuber said. "But I rather suggest that you do not. He is quite wealthy. He has no need of this money. Consider it my fee for recovering that which he took from you."

I was tempted, that is true. But I shoved the money back toward him, all thousand dollars of it.

"I don't want it."

"Don't be ridiculous." He pushed my hand away.

I tossed the money at him. The bills fluttered to the worn rug on the floor. "Ill-gotten gains will always come back to haunt you."

Zuber sniffed. "I feel singularly unhaunted. And you are a fool if you think Kumpke has your best interests at heart."

"I didn't say I did."

Zuber shook his head, then closed the bag. Betty snorted. I could tell what she was thinking: two stubborn fools, the pair of us.

Professor Zuber walked toward the door of the apartment with as much gravity as he could muster. His eyes lingered on the racks of cookies cooling in the kitchen.

"Good day," he said.

"Wait a minute," I said. "I just have one thing to ask you."

He turned to face me and made a grand gesture toward the kitchen. "Ask away. The only price is that you give me a few of those cookies as payment."

"Done," I said. "One cookie per question."

He *hmmm*ed in the back of his throat. I took that as an agreement.

I said, "Is it you who's going after the Foshay Tower? Who set that black curse on the tower?"

He made a face. "No. It is not."

I realized I had left him a loophole. I asked again, "Is it your curse?"

Another face.

"It is not."

I glanced over at Betty. She rubbed her fingers together.

"Have you found a way to take advantage of the situation at the Foshay Tower financially or in any other manner?"

Zuber walked into the kitchen and picked up three cookies. Stuffing one of them into his mouth, he mumbled an answer.

An answer that sounded awfully like *yes*.

When he had swallowed, I said, "*How* do you plan to take advantage of the situation at the Foshay Tower?"

He made a fist with one hand and thumped it on the wood tabletop, making our sugar bowl jump.

"I am not required to answer your questions!"

"Aren't you?" I asked.

Zuber's face darkened. His lips trembled.

He clapped a hand over his mouth, muttering behind it. His eyes bulged as he glared furiously at me.

Purring sweetly in a throaty voice, Betty cooed, "You should know, mister, that Eliza's been telling me all about you. And I know you told her you're a magician. Well, unlike you, Eliza's got *real* magic. There's no other explanation. Whenever she wants to change the world, she makes something to eat. Or to drink. And what's in that bathtub gin she just gave you is the urge to tell the truth. And what's in those cookies is a desire to please...to do whatever it takes to get another one of them." She smiled slyly, her red lips shimmering as they caught the light. "I should know. I've used them on my conquests before. So think about that as you try to fight the hold she's got on you, and whether you truly want to lie to the woman."

Zuber's jaw worked as he tried to choke his answer back.

Slowly and deliberately, I asked, "I repeat the question. *How* do you plan to take advantage of the situation at the Foshay Tower?"

All those years, I thought I was just plying my feminine wiles when I cooked for folks. I was going to have to think a little bit harder about how I used my domestic skills, I could tell—and how *Betty* used them. There's one good way and a thousand bad ways to do everything, and I suspected I might have inadvertently wandered into a few of the latter.

Zuber gurgled, his face turning green.

"Don't make her ask again," Betty said. "It upsets the stomach."

He shook his head, nearly breathing fire out his nose.

I took a breath. "How do you plan—"

His throat convulsed, and he raised one hand. I cut myself off. He turned toward the sink and bent over it, panting.

He gasped, "Buying up debts from his creditors...pennies on the dollar...when he goes bankrupt...first in line for his company assets...a group of us..."

Professor Gruber's financial "magic" was nothing more sophisticated than a short sale. A bear raid.

"That's enough," I said. "I get the picture. I'm tempted to march you over to Kumpke's office and make you tell him the truth."

I was disgusted at him. The man was nothing more than a con artist, giving nothing to the world, just preying around the edges like a vulture. Worse: I could see some excuse for the existence of actual vultures.

Zuber had stood up and was wiping his face with a handkerchief. "Mademoiselle, your hospitality is the most expensive I have ever known. We live in a world where each of us has secrets that we would rather not tell, do we not?"

I wrinkled my nose at him.

Zuber made a grand gesture. "Compared to those whose whims control this city, we are but frail moths swirling about a window in the darkness, looking in at the folk inside who sit at the table. Why should we not take advantage of those folk at the table, when we can?"

Betty said, "He has a point."

I thought about it.

Zuber might not be that powerful when it came to magic, but I could feel the power of his honeyed tongue working at me, just as my cookies and gin had been working at him. I suspected that, all things considered, I might be a little bit more powerful than he was—but I *knew* that he had more experience at using what little he had than I did, consciously at least.

I blinked.

Zuber might be more experienced than I was at making a lot out of a little, but I was no slouch, either. And I thought I could see just the way to use that to get Mr. Kumpke's money back.

All of it.

I said, "Professor Zuber, I have an offer for you. Something that will bring you a great deal of money...but it's going to be real tricky. It might not work and we all might have to make a run for it to keep from getting arrested if it doesn't. What do you think?"

He swept up a handful of cookies and started munching on another one. To be honest I had lost count of how many I "owed" him. And if I got what I wanted, he could have all he wanted.

He sighed a dramatic sigh, then picked up another from the pan.

"I think, mademoiselle, that if I don't agree to participate in your scheme, then I will be cursed to a serious bout of indigestion."

***

4. The Magician's Grift

In the tiny front room of our tiny working-girl apartment in a small and shoddy-but-not-too-shoddy building in Minneapolis, drawing out the details with a pencil on one of Betty's leftover cocktail napkins, I told Zuber the plan, which I was more or less making up on the spot. He wasn't too enthusiastic about his role in it at first; you'll see why later.

"I will do it," he said, his hand darting out to take another of the cookies, "but only under duress."

I slapped his hand as it sneaked toward the pocket of his expensive wool suit. "You'll stain your suit! Here, take this." I handed him another cocktail napkin. "Duress my Aunt Fanny. I ain't twisting your arm."

The cookie, and several others, disappeared into the napkin, then into his pocket. "Are you trying to claim that you have not enchanted me?"

I shook my head and started to speak but he held up a finger.

"I will do this thing," he announced with a dramatic sigh, "but I don't do it of my own free will."

Betty rolled her eyes. "You're such a fraud."

Zuber grimaced, this time looking a little less than confident as his act slipped a little. "Have the two of you not understood that the men who have cursed this tower must be more powerful than you can possibly imagine?"

I leaned against our tiny table. "Have you considered the possibility that the curse on that tower might not be exactly what it seems?"

Zuber's green eyes bulged. "What are you implying? That I cannot judge the strength of a magical working?"

Well, I *was* implying that. But I took a deep breath. "So, this afternoon?"

"Yes?"

"When you were talking to Mr. Kumpke alone in his office? I went out for a walk."

"I believe your footsteps echoed resoundingly down several flights of stairs, yes. What of it?"

"I walked somewhere in particular. Which was to the corner of Ninth and Marquette."

"Into the shadow…!" he exclaimed.

"That's right. I walked right into the shadow. And right through the illusion. I figured if Foshay Tower really was cursed that it couldn't be as bad as all that, or the people who worked there would be suffering from some kind of ill effects."

Zuber made a face, then idly stuffed another cookie in his mouth.

I moved into the kitchenette. "Coffee? Tea?" I asked. We didn't have a separate percolator.

"Better make it tea for me," Betty said.

Zuber added, "Coffee. Unless it will have some sort of ill-natured magical effect upon me, such as binding my soul to your service or forcing me to dance in red-hot shoes until I fall down dead."

I looked around the end of the kitchenette and into the front room at Betty. I had no idea what any of my magic did—if it *was* magic.

She tapped her fingers against her cheek. "*Her* coffee clears your head and keeps you from falling asleep, makes complicated things look simpler. The tea is good for heartbreak and impatience."

"You don't seem to be the least bit heartbroken, mademoiselle," Zuber said.

"Not today I ain't. But if Kumpke loses his money, then Eliza loses her job. And if Eliza loses her job, I lose my roommate. And if I lose my roommate, I lose my apartment. And so on, you know?"

"I suspect that I do." He turned toward me. "What did you *see*, my dear girl? Once you stepped past the illusion?"

I lit the burner on the stove. "At the time, I didn't think much of it. I saw a Ford Model-A delivery van with an advertisement for seed corn on the side, and two men in black suits in the front seat. A third man in a suit walked up to the van with a briefcase and got into the back. The van started up and drove away…and then, not half a minute later, another delivery van advertising soap pulled up and took its place. But that's not all."

"Oh?"

"I went up to the second van and brushed against it, to see if there was an illusion on it. When my shoulder touched it, the soap advertising disappeared. It was just a regular Ford delivery van. But I also got an image in my mind…that of an eagle on top of a badge with the Lady Justice on it."

Which was the badge for the Bureau of Investigations.

Foshay hadn't cursed the tower to protect himself, which was what I believe both Zuber and I had assumed. No, it was far more likely that the B.O.I. had done it, to cover up the fact that they were investigating.

It was then that I really started to believe in magic, I guess.

At any rate, I had no doubt that Zuber would know the best way to take advantage of such a situation.

Zuber perked up like a little boy on Christmas. "Are you sure?"

"If I hadn't been sure I would have said so."

"That is indeed most interesting…"

◆

In order for my plan to work, first we had to get Mr. Kumpke on our side.

I offered Zuber a flask full of my apparently truth-inducing gin in order to ease the process of admitting to Mr. Kumpke what he had done, but he waved it off. "My dear," he said, "I may find it opportune to tell a few lies mingled up in that truth, whether to Mr. Kumpke or to some other soul, and I wish to keep my options open."

Professor Zuber being a man who could lie using nothing but the truth, I doubted my truth-telling gin was going to hold him back in the slightest. And of course my best inspirations and insights always come when I'm in a particularly truthful mood myself, but I wasn't about to force my precious homemade gin down his throat if he didn't want any!

On Friday morning, I arrived bright and early as usual, made a pot of coffee, and drank a cup at my desk, keeping an ear out for footsteps on the stairs. My eyes closed as I reviewed my plans and found them good. I even let myself relax a little.

The door opened and Mr. Kumpke walked in without warning.

He wasn't alone.

Using one arm and what didn't look like much effort, Mr. Kumpke dragged the unconscious form of Professor Zuber across the threshold and dropped him on the floor in front of my desk.

Zuber's normally florid face had gone quite pale.

Worse yet, Zuber did *not* have his bag with him—the one with all the money, that was. Whether that meant he had hidden it elsewhere or that Kumpke had left it behind out of ignorance, I did not yet know.

"I have caught him," Mr. Kumpke said with satisfaction.

"I see that," I said. "But what about the bag with all the money in it?"

"The bag with all the...?" he asked.

"He was supposed to be bringing it back to you this morning..."

Mr. Kumpke gave me a thoughtful look. "You must have caught up with him before I did."

I put the coffee cup down on my blotter and sighed. So much for all my plans. "You might say that. Although it doesn't seem to have stuck."

"I found him in the alley behind the building earlier," he said. "I did not remember seeing any bag. My child, I suspect him of taking advantage, once again, of your good intentions."

I made a face and looked over Zuber's form on the floor. He was wearing the same gray suit that he had been wearing yesterday, which seemed out of character. Something occurred to me.

"*When* did you see him this morning?" I asked.

Mr. Kumpke shrugged. "Yesterday in the evening."

In other words, on Zuber's way home from my flat.

What had Mr. Kumpke been doing to Zuber the whole time since then? I decided not to ask.

I stood and said, "I'll go check the alley for the bag. Coffee's on...I hope you don't mind me not sticking around to serve it. Please don't hurt him if you can help it, Mr. Kumpke. Because I might need him later."

Mr. Kumpke *hmph*'d in the back of his throat, then dragged Professor Zuber into his office, out of sight.

I went down the stairs, my footfalls a drum roll as I ran down them.

The alley behind our building was still in shadow, two brick walls along a narrow corridor, just wide enough for a garbage truck and a single row of trash cans side by side. At ground level was about three feet of stone foundation above the street, with small half-circle air vents set into the brick. A few safety ladders hung overhead, well out of reach.

No bag.

I clenched my fists. The money was gone, then. But I had to check. I started walking the alley slowly...looking carefully in each of the trash cans to see if the bag might be there, even though I was sure in my heart of hearts that it wouldn't be.

I was just closing the lid on the fifth one when I heard a voice above me.

"Whatcha doing there, little girl?"

"Looking for my uncle's bag," I said. I couldn't move a muscle.

"Your uncle's bag," the voice said. "It wouldn't be this one, would it?"

I looked up. It was like the muscles in my neck had been unlocked so I could.

A tall, slender man in a pinstripe suit was standing on the safety ladder above me, holding Professor Zuber's bag in his hand.

"You better not have taken anything out of that," I said.

He had a pencil-thin mustache. "Or what?"

"Or I'll tell Mr. Kumpke," I said.

The man on the ladder dropped off it, landing elegantly on his feet, like a cat. He walked toward me, holding the bag.

I was unable to move a muscle but those I needed to follow him with my eyes.

"Mr. Kumpke is an interesting case," he said. "Old...yet naïve. Easily taken in by the crassest of schemes."

"I've never noticed it," I said.

"You must be easily fooled, too," he said. "I suppose you're the secretary he talks so much about."

I didn't answer. The man was walking toward me, and I was feeling a bit like a mouse being stalked by a cat.

"You seem a particularly useless creature," the man said. He dropped the leather bag beside me and leaned in, reaching up to cup my chin. "But don't worry. I've never been one to waste—"

His forehead knocked into mine hard enough to make me see stars.

I stumbled backward and started to fall.

Fortunately I was caught by one arm and heaved back onto my feet. The man in the pinstriped suit collapsed. Professor Zuber stood behind him. Next to me was Mr. Kumpke, holding my arm and wearing his hat, buttoned-up coat, and gloves.

"My apologies," Zuber said. "I hit him a little harder than I intended."

"Leave him," Mr. Kumpke announced. To Zuber, he said, "This was the one who said I sent him?"

"That's him, all right."

"No wonder you were so easily taken. He can be *very* convincing."

Zuber stumbled around the body, then leaned against the alley wall.

"I don't think I can make it back up those stairs," he wheezed.

"Meet us at Rademacher's in half an hour," Mr. Kumpke said. "If you are not there, I shall assume that you have truly betrayed Miss Malmquist this time and will act accordingly."

"I'll be there," Zuber said, by his voice exhausted. He touched his forehead. "Mademoiselle." He stumbled out of the alley.

Mr. Kumpke looked me up and down. I wasn't sure what to say, or how much.

He pursed his lips. "I have heard briefly of your plan to recover my funds from the Mr. Foshay's stock-market scheme...*very* briefly." He paused. "Tell me, why didn't you take Professor Zuber up on his initial offer? I know that you and your sweetheart Robert plan to wed soon and leave me."

I sighed. "I was hoping that you didn't know about Robert."

Mr. Kumpke sniffed slightly.

"Why I didn't just take the money was...I just couldn't," I said. "I mean, I could have, but I didn't want to start a fresh life that way, with dirty money. *Your* dirty money. That's even worse."

He gave me a long, narrow-eyed look. "But you don't mind stealing from Mr. Foshay?"

When he put it that way... I felt my face get hot. "Maybe it doesn't make sense to you, Mr. Kumpke. But I figure once someone starts lying to folks, it's all right for folks to lie back."

"I see." He coughed into a black glove. "While I do not generally like to step aside from a path of probity and consistency with the facts, I, too, have faced challenges where darker actions are required. Very well. Your plan is in place, and we must follow it, lest we all be ruined."

Then I asked him how far into the Foshay stocks he was invested. The total was higher than the three thousand I knew about. It nearly staggered me, and it wasn't even my money. Getting that much out of Foshay was going to be a challenge.

I sighed. "We better get back inside, Mr. Kumpke." The morning was starting to brighten.

Mr. Kumpke studied me for a moment, and then the sky. He bent over, pulled the jacket off the man in the alleyway, the man's body flopping around like a doll's as he shook the man easily out of it, and stuffed it into a trash can at the alley's mouth. "He works for your bank, can you imagine?"

I had always known that bankers were vampires—of a sort, at least—but I kept a straight face. The two of us walked around the corner and into a side door on the north side of the building.

A couple of hours later, I was walking into the Foshay building, and unless Zuber had betrayed us again, everyone should have been in place. The bruise on my forehead was covered up a hat, and I was holding the leather bag in my hand. I had an awful headache, half due to getting my skull knocked around, and half due to walking into the shadow of the Foshay Tower. Black ooze had swirled in my eyes for a couple of seconds when I stepped into the shadow. Not as bad as the last time, but still not an enjoyable experience.

The Bureau of Investigations truck was still parked along the curb. To an eye without any sensitity to magic, it would look like one of the endless delivery trucks that passed through the area. Magicians would avoid the unpleasant black shadow if they could, and hurry past without looking around if they couldn't.

That B.O.I. truck made me nervous.

The bag I was carrying wasn't full of money this time, but full of gin.

I passed the truck. The man in the passenger seat, reading a newspaper, glanced up and gave me a whistle. I blushed and hurried on by, stepping in through the doors of the Foshay Tower.

It was luxurious, to say the least.

But as solid as it looked, it was still just a house of cards.

The lobby was all terrazzo floors, crystal chandeliers, Italian marble on the walls, mahogany counters and doorframes, brass fixtures, all of it paid with investor capital and not profits. The last little thing went wrong, and it would all come falling down.

I walked up to the long banker-style desk that faced the entrance and said, "I need to see Mr. Foshay, Mr. Wilbur Foshay."

The man behind the desk said, "Welcome to W.B. Foshay Company. Do you have an appointment?"

"I do not."

"Mr. Foshay is a very busy man."

"I know that. But I suspect he is not too busy to look at the papers I have brought."

"What might those be?"

"Tell him they are papers from Mr. Edwin Kumpke of the Kumpke Law Office down the street. Mr. Kumpke has stocks invested with Mr. Foshay."

"I shall speak to his personal secretary."

The man at the desk picked up a candlestick receiver, spoke two words to the operator, then paused. He murmured a few times, then hung up with a thoughtful look on his face.

"Mr. Foshay's personal secretary will see you," he said. "I can't promise that you'll receive an appointment with Mr. Foshay himself. He is a *very* busy man."

"I understand."

I was shown to the elevators and conducted upstairs by the elevator operator, who had to use a key to let me up to the correct floor. He noted that Mr. Foshay had been in an unpleasant mood all day and gave me the sincerest best wishes that our business together could be conducted profitably and in a timely fashion. I took a leather portfolio out of the bag, then "accidentally" left the bag on the floor.

The elevator operator winked at me.

At the twenty-seventh floor, I was met by Mr. Foshay's personal secretary, a pleasant-looking man of middle years who reminded me of a waxwork figure. He wore small circular glasses.

"You work for Mr. Kumpke," he said. "As his secretary."

"I do."

"May I see the papers in question?"

We walked to his desk, and I handed him the leather portfolio. I let my hand brush his; for a moment I saw that the man had terrible pox scars all over his face. Then they vanished.

He must be Foshay's magician.

The secretary led me to a little receiving area with a group of overstuffed chairs. He sat in one and waved me toward another. He skimmed over the papers once, then got up and walked in through a pair of closed double doors to a second receiving area, not bothering to close the doors behind him.

The second area has a large desk covered with paperwork and folders, stacked up so that I could only see the top of a telephone, the kind with the speaker separate from the receiver on a cord. Through a closed, small side door came the muffled sound of typing. A second set of double doors—this pair in mahogany—led to an inner room. I could hear voices coming from that direction, angry ones.

The man sat at the large desk, took a pair of reading glasses out of a drawer, and read the papers more fully. I took a chair across from him at the desk. The area around the desk was stacked with filing boxes, many with the labels torn off. Papers lay askew on top of and between the boxes.

Finally, he said, "If I am reading these papers correctly, Mr. Kumpke is being forced to file for bankruptcy and needs to turn over his shares of Foshay stock to the court immediately…or to receive a hundred thousand dollars in exchange."

"Yes," I said.

"And you're his secretary," the man repeated. "His *lady* secretary?"

That set my teeth on edge but I tried not to show it. "I am. If you would like, I can sign against the notarized signatures on the second page."

"If you would, please."

I signed on a blank piece of paper, and he compared the two signatures for a much longer time than was necessary.

He said, "I'll take this in to Mr. Foshay. It may be a moment; he's with a client." And with that, he tapped on one of the big mahogany doors. The angry voices stopped, and he let himself in.

I tiptoed out to the elevator and pressed the button. The operator was waiting for me a floor down. He arrived quickly, then handed me my leather bag: "You forgot this, miss," he said. "I been holding on to it for you."

I thanked him and returned to my seat. And proceeded to wait.

After a few minutes, the elevator returned to the floor. The elevator operator emerged, pushing a catering cart with a covered ice bucket and a tablecloth draped over something that rattled as he walked. He passed me, knocked on the mahogany doors, and entered the main office without waiting for a reply. I heard voices speaking within. They sounded hushed. Possibly afraid.

A few minutes later, the operator emerged from the office and gave me a nod.

Now it was my turn.

— ◆ —

Three men looked up as I opened the door of Foshay's office and slipped inside.

Big windows over looked the city. Wood paneling rose up toward high ceilings lit with electric lights, recessed crystal chandeliers, gold trim running along the tops of the walls, steel panels with peacock-feather patterns, leather couches, and silk Persian rugs in gold and blue.

Two men sat at an enormous desk on the far side of the room. The secretary stood behind one of the men, who was reading papers. The other one was twisting a leather satchel so hard I thought he would about tear it in half. He wore a natty tailored suit in a subtle plum color, double-breasted, with an emerald silk pocket square, and was built larger than life but not quite as natural.

That is to say, the client was none other than Zuber himself.

Wilbur Foshay, the third man, wasn't handsome. He was fifty and had cold eyes and smooth skin around his eyes where you'd expect smile lines to show. No frown lines either, as if he were wearing a mask or covered with an illusion. As for expression, he didn't have much of one, only a gentle, interested look. He wore a modest suit with a bow tie.

If he had just been shouting at the man across from him—which he had—you wouldn't have known it. Butter wouldn't have melted in that mouth.

Foshay and his client each had a drink in his hand. Mr. Foshay had a gin-and-tonic while his client, having learned his lesson about the consequences of drinking my gin, was drinking a whiskey, neat.

Foshay's face stayed blank as I stepped inside the room. "Excuse me? Who are you?"

I said, "I am Mr. Kumpke's secretary."

"Unfortunately I am not ready to see you or to pay what your employer is demanding. You see that I have a client with me."

Giving Zuber only a glance, I said, "If I were your client, I might be interested in what Mr. Kumpke's secretary has to say."

Zuber snorted, not a glint of recognition in his eyes. "And what is that?"

Trying not to show how terrified I felt, I quipped, "That the stocks that Mr. Foshay is attempting to convince you to purchase aren't worth the paper they're printed on."

Zuber's eyebrows rose. "My dear girl, whoever you are, that is a *most* serious accusation."

He had carefully coached me earlier. All I had to do was remember what to say.

I cleared my throat. "Mr. Foshay's publicly traded stocks haven't gone up in volume," I said. "As anyone who follows the stock market can plainly see."

The client rolled his green eyes and said, "Your expertise is evident, Mademoiselle Secretary."

"Ask Mr. Foshay what these stocks are trading on, then, if it's not his utility company."

Zuber tilted his head slightly and faced Mr. Foshay, who had frozen with his gin and tonic half-finished, halfway to his lips.

By now the gin would have started to take effect.

Zuber asked lightly, "What *are* the stocks trading on, Wilbur?"

Foshay opened his mouth, then snapped it closed. "We haven't time for this. Melman, please escort this girl out of my office."

The secretary walked toward me and took my arm. I tried to shake his hand off, but not too hard.

Zuber said, more seriously now, "Before she goes, I should like to have her question answered."

Mr. Foshay turned toward Zuber with a harassed look on his face. He was willing to entertain a man handing over a few thousands of dollars with a drink and his usual spiel, but he wasn't willing to be *questioned* by such small fry.

"Really, I think that should be obvious," he said.

"It is obvious," I said. "Because it's really nothing that those stocks are trading on. Nothing but a pile of debt."

"Do you deny it?" Zuber asked coldly.

"I cannot believe that I am being—"

Zuber raised his voice. "I said, sir, do you deny it? A straight answer, at once! Are the stocks which you are attempting to sell to me backed by anything other than empty promises? Come now!"

Foshay's smooth face had turned red.

"I refuse to answer such an impertinent question!"

"Then return my check at once!" Zuber held out his hand.

In the silence that followed, I dropped another carefully coached statement: "Another question that you might want to get answered real quick, Mister. Why are men from the Bureau of Investigation parked along the street in a van, watching Mr. Foshay's every move?"

The secretary dropped my arm and walked over to the window. "I don't know what you're talking about. It's impossible that..." He looked down. "That's a cigarette delivery truck."

Foshay followed him over to the glass. "That's no cigarette truck, it's a baker's..." Foshay choked as the truth came to him. "The advertisement's an illusion! It melts away when I look at it! Can't you see it? You're the damned powerful magician!"

Melman's eyes widened, then squinted tight as he tried to see what his boss was seeing. "How...?"

"I want you to go down there and check it personally...tell them to get off my sidewalk. Now!"

I put Melman's chances of being taken by the investigators at about fifty-fifty if he did so. The investigators had to have him on their list of people they'd like to talk to.

"Yes, Mr. Foshay," Melman said. He left through the double doors, back straight. I figured him to head out a back door, stop at the bank, and buzz off to Canada before anyone could say "boo."

When the door closed, Zuber said, "My check, if you please."

Foshay handed it over to him without a second thought. It was chump change, as far as he was concerned.

"And now give the young lady what she asked for," Zuber said.

"What?"

Zuber withdrew a pistol from within his tailored jacket.

"I say, *give the young lady what she asked for.* In fact, double it."

Foshay blinked at him.

Zuber slowly cocked the pistol.

I said, "Look, mister, are you sure that's the right thing to do?"

Zuber looked Foshay straight in the eye and said, "Men like you are a disgrace to the name of swindler, Mr. Foshay. Either write that check or I will shoot you down like the dog you are...which would be a mercy in your case."

"You can't—"

Foshay cut himself off as he realized that what Zuber said was the truth. My gin works like that. It doesn't just force you to speak the truth—it forces you to see it. In vino veritas, as it were.

Zuber's eyebrows twitched.

In about a minute, I had a check for two hundred thousand dollars in my purse.

❖

The typewriters in the other room had gone quiet. At the secretary's desk, one of the file boxes had gone missing from the stack nearest the desk. More papers lay on the floor, scattered. *There went a man who was thinking about turning evidence...*

I stepped out past the second set of double doors and crossed the floor to the elevator. The attendant was waiting for me.

I asked, "Didn't the secretary just come out of here? How'd you get back here so soon?"

"I advised him to take the stairs. There's a couple of men watching the elevator doors down below."

I stepped into the elevator and the attendant closed the gate and turned the lever. We started descending.

Then me and the elevator operator kissed.

Robert said, "Mr. Kumpke owes you big-time."

"That he does. But I don't know if it's enough to make him accept that I'm just going to have to get married."

"And soon," Robert murmured.

"And soon," I promised.

Zuber waited in Mr. Foshay's office for half an hour, by which point I had deposited the check into Mr. Kumpke's account and he had withdrawn it all in cash a few moments later, an operation much expedited by the fact that it was the same bank that Mr. Foshay used and by the additional fact that Mr. Foshay gave permission over the telephone, when called.

Then Zuber pulled an amscray and disappeared.

When questioned, the elevator operator swore he had brought Zuber up like normal, but had never taken him back down or seen him take the stairs.

In fact, Robert had taken Zuber down a floor, put him on the service elevator, then come back up before Foshay had untied himself and come charging out of the room. It had been a risk, but one that Robert had agreed to take.

We met back at Mr. Kumpke's office later, me and Robert and Zuber. I received, in total, twenty thousand, five hundred dollars. In cash. Zuber took home thirty grand, and Mr. Kumpke walked off with the rest—and the gun he'd loaned Zuber.

A tidy profit, all around.

Mr. Kumpke wished Robert and me the best of luck in our lives ahead of us in Iowa. But it was October twenty-second, and I have to admit that our plans soon changed when the stock market crashed: we never did make it to Iowa and points south, except to bring my momma up from Missouri.

Betty and I swapped jobs; I couldn't work for Mr. Kumpke anymore, being very shortly thereafter married and in the family way, but Betty never did have that problem. Mr. Kumpke stayed in business for another ten years, then left the firm to his nephew, who took over right where Mr.

Kumpke left off, and who happened to know all of Mr. Kumpke's clients just as well as old Mr. Kumpke had himself. Al's café remained an oasis for those as could find it.

Mr. Foshay was arrested shortly after the crash for exactly the scheme that Professor Zuber had accused him of. He'd lost everything. Even his check to John Philip Sousa for twenty thousand dollars, for a march that Sousa had written for the tower's dedication ceremony, bounced.

I felt bad about fleecing the man until the next time I fixed myself a gin and tonic. Then I felt bad for those who had trusted him instead.

Professor Zuber disappeared for about a year, coming back with trouble in his wake, which I'm sure is a shocking circumstance, what with Zuber being such a reliable gentleman and all...

In short, we all did what we had to do to get by. But that's another story.

———◦◦◦———

The Vampire brought his tale to an end, and I gave a start. For a time, I had heard nothing of the old man's weak and whispery voice, but only the sound of a young woman speaking—or I had thought I had. I felt as though I had been literally hypnotized.

Maybe I had been.

The Spy cleared his throat. He looked uncomfortable, very stiff-upper-lip-ish. "And that is why you sent me that telegram, then. Regarding the collapse."

The Vampire said, "And did you deliver my recommendation as I requested?"

The Spy said, "I did, but I do not know what was done with that information. I...took certain steps of my own, with regard to a few others. Will the world never recover, then?"

I blinked. They were talking about the crash that had just happened on Wall Street, the one that had all those men in New York jumping out of tall buildings. I was all ears.

We all were. People were losing their jobs left and right.

The Vampire shook his head. "The world never recover? Hardly. All but a few of the wealthy will, of course, discover ways in which to profit from the situation. War, Famine, Disease, and Death herself—the four Horsemen of the Apocalypse—are such tools as fortunes are made of. As you well know."

The Spy harrumphed to himself, as if admitted that much were true. "But...what will fall? How long will it remain fallen?"

The Vampire's expression softened. His hand twitched, as if he were about to extend it—then he pressed his lips together. "You know my thoughts about things that should have long since fallen. Empires, for example."

The Spy sighed. "I do know your thoughts on the matter."

Out of nowhere, the Actress interrupted. "I've been thinking..."

The Vampire patted her hand and said, "I would rather you were listening, my dear."

Her lips twitched. "Oh, I've been listening. But I've been thinking that the kid is right. The gentleman in question was killed because of something that happened recently. I think he was about to tell a story that would have said something damaging about someone else."

The Vampire had lifted his eyebrows. "And what might that story have been?"

The Actress shook her head. "I have no idea. But that's the shape of it, isn't it? Either something happened recently...or he found out something recently."

There was a pause. I raised my hand. Everybody looked at me.

Blushing at the attention, I said, "Or someone found out something about him recently."

Dom narrowed his eyes at me. "Wot makes you say dat?"

I shrugged. "I dunno. It's just a possibility. In a mystery, it's a bad sign when you get locked into an idea about what happened, uh, in advance of the facts."

The Brit flashed a grin at me. I was quoting Sherlock Holmes. With his back as straight as a poker, he said, "Yes, by all means. Let us consider the possibilities before we eliminate them. What else do we know? Or can we surmise?"

Nobody said anything.

Finally, Madame Ixnay stretched her head this way, then that, until the bones popped. She said, "I want the next story."

The Detective snapped back: "No, I want it."

Madame Ixnay batted her eyes at him. "Ladies first."

The Detective sneered at her. "If you were a lady, you wouldn't have said that."

Madame Ixnay riposted: "If you were a gentleman, I wouldn't have had to."

"Then I want the story after that," the Detective said.

"Of course," Madame Ixnay purred.

They both looked at the Vampire, who shrugged. "As you wish."

Madame Ixnay said, "My story is a prediction. A tale of the future."

I murmured to her, "That's called science fiction now."

She said, "Is it? I like that. Yes. It is a tale of science fiction."

The Spy said, "Is it a prognostication of what will happen after the crash?"

She said, "No. Yes. Sort of. Not really. It's further in the future than that. About a lot of rich people, doing what they do best."

The Vampire asked coldly, "And what might that be?"

"Getting whatever they want, and stabbing each other in the back to make sure no one else gets it," Madame Ixnay said.

The Vampire frowned but didn't say anything.

As far as I knew, the Vampire—if I had pegged him right—was the wealthiest person in the room. Had that been an accusation on Madame Ixnay's part?

The Detective said, "Whatever. Get started, why don't you?"

Madame Ixnay gave him a smile, and not a nice one. She took a slight breath, and exhaled with a little puff of what might have been steam. I suddenly realized how cold it was, down in the back room, and how strange it was, that nobody had taken out a cigarette or a cigar to smoke.

All the Retros at the New Cotton Club

Madame Ixnay's Tale

The top of the bar was solid Brazilian mahogany, the kind that looks like it's made out of bourbon-colored smoke. The wood underneath the projected illusions of the New Cotton Club was real but it was the far less expensive oak.

The dame at the bar looked vaguely familiar, like Charlie had seen her before but never at the bar—like it had been a while. He slid her a gin rickey in an Old Fashioned glass and she rolled him a virtual coin across the bar. He closed his hand around it and made it disappear. She started stirring the ice cubes in her Old Fashioned glass with the tip of her finger. She had the whole getup on—Marcel wave, cigarette in a long black holder, and a black-and-gold striped dress that ended at her knees in black fringe. Voices chattered and forks rattled on china plates. On the stage at the other end of the hall a trumpet player in a penguin suit was using a tinny mute at the end of his horn to good effect. The trombone and clarinet players were trying to keep up.

Out of the corners of Charlie's eyes the room looked like it was swirling with smoke, but it was just the rendering overlay. Tonight there was a heavy retro presence in the room and it was causing the servers some headaches. Over the last hour there had been about a hundred minor virus warnings. Somebody was infected. The system was trying to track down the source but it seemed to be coming from every direction. At any rate, some of the finer details up around the ceiling looked cheap and misty but otherwise there was no sign of the heavy server load. The floor was packed and the balconies were filled to the brim. A quick glance showed that the other bartenders were in the weeds but not so bad that they needed to break character. Just another Friday night at the club.

Later, when the diners finished eating and the amateurs left for the night, they'd clear a space in the center of the room for dancing. Miss Alice and the rest of the swing band would come up on stage and dancers doing the Charleston would take over.

Charlie mixed up a tray of cocktails for one of Dolores's tables: a Mary Pickford, a Corpse Reviver, a retro Hanky Panky, and a bourbon on the rocks. Whoever ordered the bourbon was going to regret it. The stuff was authentically terrible. It didn't contain anything that could kill you like it could have in Prohibition times—then as now, bad for business—but it was about as tasty as drinking an ashtray.

The dame at the bar said, "Charlie, I'm in trouble."

He didn't know her; it was just that all the bartenders were called Charlie at the New cotton. He just happened to be Charlie off-duty as well as on.

"Yes, miss?"

"Bad trouble."

"Anything we can do to help?"

"I don't know, Charlie, can you do anything about ghosts?"

Saying that word, here at the New Cotton Club, could be touchy. Some people liked to call the virtual presence of A.I.s "ghosts." Some people liked to be rude. The more acceptable term was "retros." Retros weren't exactly legal—some idiots in Congress had used a bunch of scare tactics to make the retros seem like they were trying to tear down mortal society, and now A.I.s were supposed to be strictly modeled after a few safe "strains" and monitored closely.

Although when it came to rich people, of course the laws went out the window. The New Cotton Club was literally underground but it wasn't exactly a secret. It was a place for retros and mortals to socialize. They even had rooms upstairs for more intimate activities. Charlie had taken a couple of retro girls upstairs a few times. With the lights off and the retro jacked directly into your nervous system, it was hard to tell the difference.

Charlie rubbed a lemon half around a bowl-shaped cocktail glass and sugared the rim. He iced the glass, then started assembling ice, triple sec, lemon juice, and French cognac in a French shaker. The metal went icy in his hands.

"Don't know about ghosts, miss. Just spirits."

The side of her mouth curled, showing of a dimple and a few lines around the eyes. She took a sip of the gin rickey in front of her.

"Let me tell you about it," she said. "And you tell me what you think. Don't worry. I won't interrupt your mixology or whatever they called it in the Roaring Twenties."

"Bartending, miss."

She laughed again.

One of his waitresses, Dolores, had been keeping an eye on him; she swept in to pick up the etched silver tray just as he put the sidecar down on it and tapped the bell. She was moving at ninety miles an hour but the levels in the glasses barely rippled.

"Two French 75s," she called over her shoulder. "One vee, one real."

"Wait your turn, toots."

She sneered at him and he started on a tray of drinks for the new girl, Yvette, who was waggling around the bar like a bee coming back to the hive.

"It all started when my husband died," the dame at the bar said. "Or maybe it started before that. It's hard to say. But I'm going to start it with Bobby, because that's where it started for *me*. And I'm the important one, you know."

He nodded. Three sidecars and a sympathetic ear coming right up.

She took another sip at her drink. "The god-damned center of the universe, as a matter of fact. Bobby was older than me. A lot older. But he was a good apple, a real peach. He got the full fountain of youth treatments when they first came out. If he maybe didn't have the stamina of some of the younger boys, he made up for it with class. He was the kind of guy who paid attention. I didn't deserve him."

She stared off into the distance. Charlie kept working. Three sidecars in a row was a cake walk; he was done in jiff. Charlie hit the bell and Yvette made the sidecars disappear while blowing him a kiss with her bow-painted lips.

Next up a tray for Marie. His hands hesitated, though. He hadn't seen Marie in a couple of minutes—he scanned the room for her.

The waitresses were dressed in short gold dresses covered with sequins that flipped from bright gold to tarnish depending on the direction they were flipped. Hard to miss them as they floated through the room. And hard to miss the signs of someone mussing their sequins. If you grabbed one of 'em you left a handprint of upside-down sequins for everyone to see. Charlie added an extra drink to the customer's bar tab when he saw it.

Marie was leaning against the wall beside the stage with her hand over her face.

He sent a message over to Marie. *UOK?*

The dame at the bar said, "When he died I got a nice chunk of his money. His first wife and kids got most of it—got the mansion in upstate New York, too, although who wanted such a big old rattletrap of a place, I don't know. I got a little brick place here along Willow Street and enough money to keep myself warm for a good long while."

Willow Street in Chicago, a street where a one-room shack could go for over a million. Not that there were any one-room shacks on Willow Street. "But—?"

Leave it alone for once would you Charlie. My boyfriend left me this morning okay? I'll pick up my drinks when they're ready.

He nodded and started on the pair of French 75s for Dolores. He could afford to give Marie a minute or two. She'd been dating a retro guy for a couple of months. Trying to keep up the appearance of being a normal

couple had finally sucked the charm out of the relationship—it took someone desperate or saintlike to make something like that work. Or both.

Charlie started cutting long, thin strips of lemon peel. Most people used
a lemon stripper but he liked doing it with a knife. The lemon oil got up
in his nose, fresh and bright.

A horn honked outside like a macho guy whining. A door slammed, and
two deep voices started shouting.

Across his retinal display a yellow icon flashed. He opened the alert.
Situation at the door, two mortals and one retro demanding entrance after
being blocked, threatening to call police. *All retro alert, yellow level. Server
resources shifted to alert status. Stay in character.*

The mists around the edges of the room thickened and the framerates
dropped; the retros stayed as solid as ever, though—paying customers
almost always got what they paid for at the New Cotton. Conversations
dampened but the trio kept playing.

The dame said, "But there was a condition. I had to agree to let him
haunt me for three years."

Even though he was distracted by the alert, Charlie's eyebrow rose. It
was one thing for the dead to upload their personalities and memories
online and become retros; it was another thing for them to haunt the living.
Retros who got themselves installed directly onto a mortal tended to creep
out both the retros and the living.

Charlie set up one champagne glass to chill, set the retro drink to copy
the first—which the customers had long since decided was fair, since a
bartender might make two identical real drinks at the same time if it was
busy—then shook the gin, lemon juice, and simple syrup in the cocktail
shaker along with some ice. The gin was ice-cold. He poured the first 75
into the real glass, then flicked the switch to retro on the bottom of the
shaker and mimed filling the second.

They'd said to stay in character.

"That doesn't sound too bad," Charlie said cautiously. "You liked him, you said."

"I did. I loved him and I didn't deserve him." She stared at the pair of French 75s and frowned. She glanced up at him. She had dark circles under her pretty violet eyes.

Dolores was swooping in, Marie was dabbing at her face with a napkin, Yvette was standing too close to a customer and he was slipping a business card into her garter, and the sound of shouting upstairs had stopped. The yellow alert shifted to green and the muted conversations across the floor burst into relieved laughter.

"Ah. So having him so close was harder than it sounds."

"I hadn't been strictly faithful to him while he was alive, Charlie. Him being dead wasn't gonna make it any easier..."

⸻ ◆ ⸻

Her name was Bernice.

The house was narrow but long, like a townhouse but not pressed up cheek to jowl with the neighbors on either side. The bricks had been erected in 1886 but the conveniences were all modern. The tile in the foyer was black and white in a crazy snowflake pattern that looked like the tile version of jazz.

The rest of the house was wood floors, white furniture, and marble counter tops. It had the kind of kitchen that begged for a gourmet chef—too bad Bernice had about as much talent in the kitchen as a eunuch had in bed. One of the bedrooms had been turned into a master bath upstairs, with a shower so big it was practically a three-seater. The walk-in closet looked like some kind of museum archives with all the drawers and shelves.

The top floor had skylights and the staircase was open so you could stand at the top and look all the way down, an M.C. Escher view of stairs and railings and hardwood floors. The back yard was a postage stamp of the most perfect green Kentucky bluegrass that you could imagine. A couple of lilac bushes accented the back fence, which was made of enamelled steel.

She liked the place. It was killer for parties and lovely for inviting men over. It was even good for solitude.

Three years. She could play the good girl for three years, out of respect for Bobby's memory. A respect that maybe she hadn't treated so respectfully while she was alive. She sat in front of the white marble fireplace in the front room and drank a glass of champagne. The bandage behind her ear itched. She wanted to scratch it like a dog.

Bobby would "wake up" when he "woke up," the black market doctor had said. It might take a couple of hours or a couple of months for his software to integrate with her wetware—that was the thing about a ghost. It didn't just upload itself into a living person's hardware. It could read their memories, use their senses, and even project itself onto their retinas, eardrums, and tactile nerve endings. Ghosts could touch you; they could even make you feel their breath on the back of their necks. Only things they couldn't do were make you taste or smell them. The technology just wasn't that evolved yet.

Bobby wouldn't hurt her. She knew that. But it was still creepy.

Three years—and then she'd be able to have his hardware chips removed. Bobby-the-ghost would get uploaded onto a server, and then he and Bobby-the-regular-A.I. would negotiate what memories they kept, what they deleted, and to what extent they merged before Bobby-the-ghost was deleted. None of this would affect the will. As long as she showed up for the removal in three years she would be set for the rest of her life.

She refilled her champagne and touched the rim of the glass on the other flute sitting on the glass-and-steel table in front of her. "Cheers," she said. Bobby had died of a cancer that finally had outwitted the doctors, something that started in his pancreas and spread until it had seemed like there was more cancer than Bobby at the end.

She loved him but the last six months had been rough. She'd wanted at least a couple of weeks to mourn, but no—she had to have the chip put in the day after he died, or nothing.

Were you always this demanding and I just didn't know it?

No answer.

She sipped her champagne and waited.

———————— ⋄ ————————

It didn't happen for a few weeks. She was almost ready to go back to the doctor and have him check. She'd started to worry. She'd made it through the funeral, feeling self-conscious in front of Bobby's first wife and his two sons. The first wife, Mary, had been decent, but the two sons were assholes, one skinny smart one (Robert) and one beefy bland one (Ted). They'd demanded to know when she was leaving the big house (she'd already left it) and when they could have the keys to the house on Willow Street (they couldn't; it was hers and they knew that). They'd found out about the chip somehow and demanded that she have it removed (she'd removed the bandages but the dissolvable stitching was still in place, a delicate Frankenstein detail that nobody could see unless she wore her hair up) and that they be able to speak to their father (who wasn't speaking to anyone). By the time it was over she was exhausted. Mary leaned over and took her arm in the funeral home. "Just block them."

"I can't do that. They're grieving."

"So are you."

Bernice dabbed at her face with a handkerchief that one of the funeral directors had given her. "I don't feel like I have the right to grieve."

"Because you're...so young?" Mary gave her a look of almost prurient interest and Bernice had to force herself not to flinch.

"Because of the chip."

"Ah. I'm sure you must be…proud. To carry it for him. He carries some extremely valuable information in that mind of his. A financial genius."

Bernice didn't answer. The sons sniggered.

Mary shot the two sons a look that suggested that it was backed up with a nasty message or two via a short-range network and they backed off. She turned back to Bernice with a look of genuine interest on her face.

"Would you like to come to the reception?"

Bernice pressed her lips together. The message *Are you nuts?* appeared on her retinal display, almost of its own accord. She deleted the message and shook her head. "I'm going to have a gathering at the house for a couple of friends that we had in common. If you'd like to come?"

Mary shuddered. She was almost ninety and had chosen for a less intense fountain of youth treatment than Bobby had; Bobby had always laughed at her fears that the full treatment would do something bad to her genetically. The doctors had assured Bernice that Bobby's cancer had nothing to do with his youth treatments, but…

"Goodness, no." Mary chuckled. "You're all right, but *some* of the people he'd been spending time with. Just no."

Bernice had lifted an eyebrow. But by then the service was wrapping up; it was almost time for the family to file out of the room and follow the casket to the grave site. Bobby had always intended to die young and leave a pretty corpse. In a sense he'd achieved neither—but it wasn't for lack of trying.

⸻⸻◆⸻⸻

Bobby woke up while Bernice was in the middle of taking a bubble bath. She was pacing herself now that the funeral was over: one bottle of champagne a day. If Bobby didn't show by eleven in the evening, she'd drink the bottle and go to bed.

The tub looked as fragile as a teacup but was made of some kind of super-insulating polymer. She'd put the open champagne bottle on a small table next to the tub and had turned on some music—some of Bobby's favorites, old-time jazz and swing. He'd been a fan of the Roaring Twenties and had had all kinds of old movies and music uploaded to her hardware.

She was lonely. She'd almost picked up a guy at a club earlier in the evening in an effort to bring Bobby back faster—on the theory that it always rains right after you wash the car—but had chickened out. Or rather grieved out.

Bobby. I miss you like crazy, babe.

At first she hadn't liked the idea of hosting his ghost for three years. Now she was terrified that she wouldn't be able to.

The trumpet playing in her eardrum sounded like it was about a hundred years ago and a half a block away. She sank into the bubbles and imagined that outside the house, down the block was a street party going on, a couple of hundred people out in the street barbecuing and dancing on the asphalt, carrying drinks in one hand and paper plates with cake on the other.

A waltz started. She imagined Bobby working his way out of the crowd and holding out his hand to her. She wiggled her feet in time with the music.

Hey doll.

Her heart stopped. "Bobby?"

You're in a maudlin mood. I expected you to be throwing a party or something.

She felt a ghostly feather against her forehead. A kiss.

She smiled, tears pricking her eyes. "I tried. It was a bust."

Pick anyone up yet?

"Also a bust. Hanging around without you, Bobby. It's depressing."

Come on, that's not the girl I married. You're about as sentimental as a hammer.

"Having your partner in crime die on you puts a damper on things."

She couldn't stop the tears rolling down the sides of her face but then again she couldn't stop smiling, either.

They chatted for a while; he declined to make a visual appearance. From his perspective he'd just died of cancer a few minutes ago. He was having a hell of a time getting the hang of his new lifestyle. A few days and he'd be more confident. Some people were naturals—he wasn't one of them.

I'll practice while you're asleep.

"Great, give me nightmares."

While you're dreaming is my downtime, he said. Reboots, software patches, virus programs...

"You can get a virus?"

Of course I can. The chip uses the same networks that you do.

She shook her head. "That sucks."

She felt a caress along her arm, then the side of her neck. She raised her lips for a kiss and distinctly felt his finger brush along them from one side to the other.

Them's the breaks, kiddo. So tell me about my funeral. Were the boys complete and utter shits?

"Mary was an angel..."

———◆———

Then one day she got a call from the funeral home, long after Bobby's body was interred. They left a message—there must be something that they forgot to gouge her for. The funeral had cost a bundle but all she had had to do was sign off on the expenses, thank God. The funeral director had handled the setup with the black market chip and doctor; she'd paid him under the table in cash for the parts of the agreement that were less than legal.

Earlier that day she had been riding the streets in one of the red-and-black self-driving trolleys that the city was spending so much money advertising. There had almost been an accident. A toddler had run out in front of the trolley. It had swerved at the last second, making its passengers scream—but leaving the little guy untouched. The reaction had been so fast and so nicely calculated that a human driver couldn't have done it. The kid was scooped up by its sobbing mother.

On the way home in the trolley she and Bobby had gotten into their first post-death argument. She needed something to do with her life. Bobby kept telling her to wait for the end of the three years. She told him she was too bored to wait that long. He told her that it was time for her to live it up, not act like an old woman. The argument went on for miles. She probably looked crazy, talking to herself. First on the trolley and then the few blocks back to the house.

She ended the argument at home by breaking off to return the funeral home's call across a secure connection.

"Hello, Ms. Stimac, thank you for returning the call. This is William Codere, the director."

"Hello, Mr. Codere. Is there an issue with my late husband's funeral that I need to address?"

"Not with his funeral, no..."

Mr. Codere explained that Bobby's A.I. transfer had failed to reboot itself. Normally, the main A.I. was set up with all sorts of backups and failsafes, but a bunch of things had failed and—in short—the only viable copy of her late husband was the one residing behind her ear. He'd gladly refund the money—

She cupped a hand around the chip protectively. "You *lost* my husband?" she asked.

Not lost him so much as...yes. They'd lost him. Could she come in and have him uploaded again? It wouldn't be much trouble, the process would take about four hours and...

"Of course," she said. "Please let me know when—"

Bobby appeared in front of her. He'd been flickering in and out lately; now he showed up, dressed in a pinstripe suit with pencil-thin legs and a white pocket square. He had his hands on his hips and an over-serious pout on his face.

No.

"How about the eighteenth?" Mr. Codere said.

"Hang on, he's talking to me," Bernice said. "His ghost is, I mean."

"I'll wait."

I'm fine here, Bobby said. I'll just transfer in three years like we planned. No sense on you wasting time on something like this.

"But what about your business?" she said. An A.I. couldn't exactly take the business he'd built as a living guy with him, but he could build a new one on the other side. Lately, Bobby had been complaining that his sons were screwing up the business he'd created as a living man. She'd told him to get over it. His position was that they were making stupid mistakes; her position was that not everybody could be a financial wizard.

My business can wait. Or I can manage the transactions while you sleep.

"What if I die before the end of the three years is up? What then?"

Then they'll get us both from our chips. If you want to be a retro, that is—I know you haven't done your will yet, but it's time to make up your mind.

She sighed. "Are you sure?"

Yes.

"You better send them a certified message, then. I mean, if I were them, I wouldn't believe someone who talks to herself on the phone."

...It's done. Don't worry, doll. I'll be safe here.

"Just don't leave me," she said.

His image, which had flickered in and out of view and had finally frozen in place, started to blow her a kiss and locked up again. She caught it and ate it.

Then she turned her attention back to the phone. "Mr. Codere? He says he doesn't want to and that he's going to send you a certified message to back that up."

Mr. Codere paused. "Did he say why?"

She was surprised that he seemed so accepting of her word; if she was him she would have waited until she saw the proof before she believed that the young widow wasn't trying to pull a fast one.

"Not exactly. He said I shouldn't waste time on it but I doubt that's all there is to it."

I'm right here, Bobby said. To remind her of this, he began drumming his fingers on her thigh.

Mr. Codere sighed and she agreed with him. Bobby was that kind of guy, even in death.

Mr. Codere said, "I got into this business so that I could make the transition from life to death easier, not more complex and harrowing."

Mr. Codere had seemed fairly young to her, but that didn't mean much these days. "Bobby doesn't mean to inconvenience people, usually," she said. "It's just that he doesn't think that aspect through."

I'm still right here, doll. Bobby sounded amused. He began nibbling on her ear; she grinned and tried to brush him away—not that it did any good.

"The transition has changed," Mr. Codere said. "But the essence of what I do has not. It makes me profoundly uncomfortable not to have some sort of backup of his A.I."

"I understand," she said. "But Bobby's going to do whatever he's set his mind to do."

"Indeed. Thank you for your time, and I hope to remain in contact with you over the next three years in order to..."

"Make sure that Bobby's okay. I get it, Mr. Codere. I'll check in once in a while and let you know how he's doing. Right now he's a bit flickery and a bit stubborn, but that's nothing new."

Doll...! He pinched her. She hung up and squealed. She had to carry herself up to the bedroom, but otherwise it was just like old times.

———◆———

Two years passed in a blur. She was bored and didn't know what to do with herself, and Bobby increasingly needed more time to get his business up and running during her waking hours, so she started learning the ropes. She'd always resented it when business had taken him from her when he was alive—she got it and she didn't put up a fuss, although it always brought her down—but now that she was watching over his shoulder, she could see what the fun was.

Money was one big, long, complicated game when you had enough of it to matter. Being a player was different than being a pawn or even a queen—moving pieces around instead of getting moved. Money wasn't just something you used to buy things with. Buying things was incidental. Money was so weird that it was close to magic. She liked it. She was never going to be as good at it as Bobby was, but he helped her set up a few accounts that she could play around with. To keep her sharp he set up phantom financial accounts reflecting the probable amounts and decisions that his two sons were using, and dared her to try to top them.

Sometimes she won, mostly she lost—but she was getting closer. And that, he said, was a good sign.

Bobby finally told her the truth about the A.I.: He didn't feel safe with another copy of him floating around. His sons were always trying to find ways to hack into his accounts or get his will invalidated—they wanted him deleted.

"Oh, Bobby," she said.

Watch out for people with stuff that looks like guns. They're developing these things called disruptors that can shoot an electronics-filled canister that can fry a hologram into static—and then, when the servers try to recompile the image, cause all the encryption on the data to disappear for a few seconds. They might be able to record everything I know from that.

"How does that work?"

When I project myself so other people can see me, it's not just an image. Part of me is really there.

He ran his fingers across her skin and she sighed. "Be here for me, Bobby..."

━━◆━━

She took up with a lover, a pretty blonde girl from Des Moines who was delighted at everything that Bernice showed her, in and out of bed. She'd tried to keep Bobby a secret but Jasmine found out anyway. She didn't seem bothered to have been invited to a virtual threesome. In fact she begged to have a retro chip installed so she could see Bobby, too, and feel his touch.

"That one's going to be trouble," Bobby warned her. "She's going to scam us, one way or another."

"How can you tell?"

"She's got that greedy look. The way that she's never satisfied with something for long—she always wants to move on to the next big thing. And it has to be bigger and better and more shocking than before. She's a thrill-seeker. Whatever she does, don't let her get a retro chip installed. She could make your life hell for decades, if not centuries."

Bernice eventually gave the woman kiss-off money and launched her out of the house on Willow Street, then blocked her after Jasmine burned through all the money Bernice had given her and begged for more. A minor scandal cropped up on the news media, a flash in the pan—then gone. The only surprising thing was that the fact of Bobby's haunting her never went public.

After that, she started going to retro clubs. Half virtual, half real—only people who'd been fitted with retro chips could go. About a tenth of the people who filled the clubs were retros. Because all the guests and most of the staff possessed retro chips, it was almost like the bodiless could have bodies again. They could flirt, drink virtual drinks, and even rent a room upstairs where the line between the virtual and real was even fuzzier (and sweatier) than it already was.

The clubs, like the retros themselves, weren't exactly legal, but as long as everyone stayed discreet it all worked.

At first she was charmed. She could even dance with Bobby again, as long as it wasn't a waltz or something that required a partner's kinetic energy. He'd order their drinks. They could dine together. They even held business meetings where she could meet potential business partners who were also incorporeal. It was a gas.

And then—

<hr>

The dame swirled the ice around in her empty glass. The cubes had melted together so that the ice no longer clinked as it moved. The yellow alert had disappeared. Everything had gone back to normal—or had it?

The rendering was still thick with smoke and object framing. Charlie stayed on alert status.

"And then it was time for him to go," she said. "For him to move out of my brain and into servertown or wherever it is that A.I.s of powerful men go."

"And?"

"And at first it just about damn near killed me..."

The loss of Bobby had come as a shock. She had drunk herself insensible the night before, then drank more in the cab on the way over to the doctor's office. She wanted to renege but she knew that Bobby wouldn't put up with it. By then he was impatient to get out of her head and into the more updated, expanded hardware that he'd purchased somewhere in the Bahamas.

They argued in the cab.

"Don't leave me," she said.

Don't think of me as leaving, just as scouting out the next location. You'll be with me once you decide to shuffle off the mortal coil.

"I don't like it. Can't you leave a copy of yourself behind to keep me company?"

You know how much I hate that. One of me. There can only be one of me.

She had had her suspicions that Bobby had sabotaged the main copy of the A.I. but she'd never brought it up. "Are you saying that two of you would be too many?" There were tears streaming down her face. The cab driver kept giving her looks.

Yes. We'd kill each other.

She shook her head. "Just give me the one with no ambition...oh, what am I *saying*, Bobby? I would hate that. I would hate it with a passion."

You see what I mean?

"What am I going to do with myself? It's going to take years and years before I can...we can..."

She sobbed. She felt his arm around her, squeezing her shoulders. *It's not forever.*

The appointment at the doctor's office went smoothly. The doc gave her crap for showing up drunk but in the end it didn't matter: four hours later she was alone in her skull again. She had the receptionist call her another taxi to take her home. She couldn't think of anywhere else to go.

She'd always been a cheerful girl. She cried at movies but that was about it. She'd made Bobby a good companion, always in a good mood and ready for action, whether it was dancing, gambling, traveling, or in bed.

But now she felt a black curtain drop over her. She'd been on a stage and now the play was over. She might as well knock back a couple of lead antidepressants and get herself uploaded into the virtual world right now.

She opened the drawer by her bed where she kept a pistol, a little holdout revolver. She spun the chamber around a couple of times, then got caught up in cleaning it.

Bobby would be pissed at her if she shot herself in order to get an early release from this prison she called life. She could almost hear his voice, disgusted—still loving her, but disgusted.

She raised the barrel to her mouth and put it in for a moment, then closed her eyes.

No. She wouldn't do it—for Bobby's sake. She didn't want him to be disappointed in her.

She slid the handgun back in the drawer and made herself forget about it. Instead she told herself that Bobby's chip hadn't been removed—it had been broken and they'd replaced it. All she had to do was wait for him to come back.

She got out a bottle of champagne and two glasses and settled in to wait.

—◦—

The days and nights passed. She kept up with her investing practice. Soon she was outstripping the virtual accounts kept by Bobby's two sons easily. She could almost predict their mistakes before the market did.

Bobby was right. They were idiots.

She drank a bottle of champagne most nights. When she did, she always set out two glasses. One of them stayed empty—but it made a real sound when she clinked the flutes together at the rims.

She traveled. She showed up for charity boards and fundraisers and found some favorite causes. She played with her money. She felt increasing hollow...thin. Blurry. She began to see movement out of the corners of her eyes, shapes that disappeared when she looked at them straight on. Like ghosts.

Then one day she got a call from Bobby.

Or not a call, exactly.

Another haunting.

She was back in the bathtub, shrouded with bubbles and a hot towel over her face so she wouldn't be distracted by movement out of the corners of her eyes. The open bottle of champagne rested on the small table next to her, two champagne flutes as always. She was almost ready to fall asleep.

Hey doll, he said.

Her heart squeezed in her chest and her eyes flooded so quickly with tears that they started to run down her cheeks faster than the hot, damp towel could absorb them.

"Bobby."

She took the towel off her face and struggled to sit up. She'd drunk most of the bottle; just the flat little dregs were left.

He stood in front of her, looking more solid than he ever had before. He flickered a little, but it was more like the effect of an old-time silent picture than the lagginess of a bad network connection.

Miss me?

"You know I do."

I have a business proposition for you.

"Are you in my head? Or are you…"

I hacked your network.

She nodded.

I need you to hold a package for me.

"Of course."

Don't you want to know what it is?

She shook her head. "It's you, Bobby. It doesn't matter what it is, I'll take it."

It's not a material package. It's a virtual one.

"What is it?" She grinned at him. "I don't need to know. Now I'm just curious."

He shrugged. He'd grown a mustache; he tugged at the end of it. *It's better if you don't know.*

She waved one hand. "It doesn't matter. You know I've got your back, Bobby. Can you load it over the network or…?"

No networks. It's on a chip.

"I'm assuming you don't want anyone to know that I've got it."

Bingo.

She'd been keeping an eye out for another black market doctor willing to do underground chip implants—not that she'd known that Bobby would want her to get another one, but because she was almost to the point where she wanted…she craved…something she would *never* tell Bobby about.

She'd been looking for a way to have his kid. A retro kid. It was sick and wrong. For a retro kid to grow up without direct contact to the retro world would be like being raised by wolves. The only contact they'd ever have would be with *her*. And that wasn't fair. Or good for anybody.

At least, that's what she kept telling herself.

"How do you want to set it up?"

I know a guy…

The guy that he knew was the same black market doctor they'd used before, Dr. Wiltsey—Bobby's idea of a joke. The real deception was happening on the digital level. The doc was told he was implanting her with a chip that would help treat her for depression. It was new technology built on new hardware, which necessitated the implant—and so far, tests were showing that it was better for the treatment to be on a chip separated from her intracranial system. Depression was a powerful disease. It didn't just screw with your transmitters; it could screw up even implanted, artificial hardware and make it malfunction via feedback loops. It was worse than having a goddamned virus.

The chip went in and as soon as she came out the movement out of the corners of her eyes stopped—like that. She was cured. Not of depression, but of seeing things. The doc said he wanted her to come in for a checkup in a week to see if her symptoms were affected. He apologized for the inconvenience—the treatment was illegal but he wanted to report on the results anyway. His wife had killed herself years ago because of the disease. He'd had her uploaded onto the illegal retro network, and something surprising had happened—her depression had infected the network.

The wife had to be quarantined as a static file. Basically, she was for-real dead, at least until they could find a cure.

The idea scared her. She, Bernice, had been known to get into a black mood a time or two. What if she couldn't be uploaded when she died? What if she had to be quarantined?

She asked Dr. Wiltsey about it, and he said it was a possibility. Or she might be partially quarantined, allowed to "live" on the retro servers but kept separated by firewalls. "But it's research like this that's our best chance for a solution," he said. "And besides, if it works out it'll be worth billions."

"And it will save your wife," she said. "Of course I'll come in and you can poke me and prod me for a while. I donate millions every year to scientific research, I can donate a couple of hours of my time."

Dr. Wiltsey blinked a couple of times. "Thank you, Ms. Stimac."

"Call me Bernice, doc."

Bobby didn't appear to her again. She understood why—he'd taken a pretty big risk showing himself earlier, if he was trying to make sure nobody suspected anything—but it started her grieving all over again.

She hadn't really grieved when he died. She'd saved most of it up for when his chip was removed.

This time wasn't as bad, a couple of weeks of severe blues that never quite turned black, then faded into some dull grays for a month or two, then lightened up and let the sun peek through the clouds a month after that. At first the doc was worried about her, saying that the chip seemed to have caused a major depression, but then as she climbed out of the hole he looked happier and happier with her results.

She didn't have the heart to tell him it was all a fake. Cutting herself off champagne had probably had more to do with the results than anything else.

She'd been waiting for Bobby to come back for long enough. It was time to live.

"And then I started seeing things out of the corner of my eye again," the dame said. "Nothing head-on. Nothing I could ever be sure that I had actually *seen*. And not the same as before. More...solid. At first I got my hopes up. I thought it was Bobby spying on me."

Charlie had a breathing space and he took it, loading up the dishwasher with empties and wiping down the bar top. He raised an eyebrow at the dame—*want another one?*—and she shook her head. The glass was empty; even the ice had been chewed. He pulled a glass from behind the bar, loaded with nothing but ice.

She gave him a thin, pitiful smile and started crunching the ice.

"That doesn't sound like something to get your hopes up about," he said.

"It doesn't, does it? But it wasn't him. Just more shadows. I set up an appointment with my doc and told him all about it; he said that whatever it was, wasn't coming from the new chip. He didn't think it had anything to do with my depression, either."

Charlie leaned against the bar, relaxing. Like magic, Dolores appeared with an order for half a dozen different mixed drinks, no virtuals. He pushed off and started mixing. The peak of the night had passed. People were still drinking pretty steadily but it was without the urgency from earlier. The kitchen was almost ready to close down and he sent Mick, the head cook, a message with an order for a ham sandwich on rye with a lot of mustard. It wasn't fancy fare but he might be able to choke down a bite or two between orders.

The rendering was still off. Something was up.

The dame said, "In fact the doc didn't think there was anything wrong with me at all."

She picked up the glass, looked down into it, then picked out another piece of ice with her fingernails. They were painted with black and gold stripes, to match her dress.

"So what was it following you? The shadow?"

She shook her head. "That's skipping too far ahead."

The shadow started to appear more often and for longer periods. It would work its way into crowds, it would hide behind things—it knew she was looking for it. If she spotted it, it would try to hide.

It wasn't a regular blocked person. Blocked people looked like walking TV static patterns, not shadows, and they didn't float through pedestrians and parked cars.

Whoever or whatever it was, it never tried to communicate with her, either to threaten her or ask for her help. It never got closer to her than ten feet or so. Sometimes she could shake it by getting into a random cab and turning off her network—but it always found her again as soon as she turned her network on again.

She sent a couple of worried messages to Bobby, the first she'd ever sent him. She knew him; until she was uploaded onto the network he would be a stranger to her—he was living his other life now. But this was important. Someone might be trying to get at his chip.

I'm being followed.

She received a name and an address on a retro card via an anonymous message. She couldn't read the blurred letters. *If it gets bad, the info will become clear. Don't let anyone take the chip. Love, Bobby.*

He didn't have to tell her not to contact him again.

Then one day the skin over the new chip started to itch. The chip underneath was warm to the touch and the skin was tender and sore.

"Are you trying to tell me something, Bobby?" she asked it, leaning forward over the ivory pedestal sink in the master bathroom. She'd folded her ear over and was looking at the little knot of scar tissue there. It was a white lump surrounded by reddened skin.

Bobby didn't answer.

It had been a long day. She'd had a board meeting all afternoon for a pediatric brain tumor society and, during dull moments, had ordered all kinds of clothing online. *Shopping*. She should have thought of it before. The meeting had stretched all day long but she had come home to a veritable snowdrift of red and white Macy's bags just inside the front door.

Now she was trying on her new clothes. The dark shadow had peeped on her all day until she'd come home—then had stopped at the sidewalk of the house across the street and taken up watch there.

Which was almost as unnerving as having it follow her into the house.

"I really just want to scratch this thing until it pops out of the skin," she told her reflection. She dragged her fingernails across it—she'd just had them done today, a French manicure. She grimaced and forced herself to put her hands down.

She looked like a pretty young woman in her early twenties. She had diamond studs in her ears and her hair in a Marcel wave. She was trying on a black and gold striped flapper dress. Now that the retro clubs were becoming more known, designers were targeting the market. Some less discreetly than others.

Softly, the front door opened downstairs.

Bobby?

She wasn't living the kind of life at the moment where anyone but the maids had keys to the front door. And it wasn't their day to dust.

She tiptoed into the bedroom and slid open the drawer with the gun in it, then opened a connection to emergency services.

Emergency Services. How can I help you?

Bernice muttered, "Hello...I think I may have a home intruder downstairs."

The operator asked her to confirm her information and she did so. A police officer is on the way. Please stay calm and leave the line open. We need permission to access your household security system so I can send the relevant details to the officer.

Bernice switched the house systems over to *emergency—intruder* mode. The house asked her to confirm that she had already called emergency services and she did so; then it opened access to the operator.

All the lights went off.

Bernice cut the connection to emergency services without a second thought. The operator had to be a fake.

She froze for a few seconds, waiting for her eyes to adjust. The orange glow of streetlights came in through the window along the street. She picked her way across the room, slipping on the blue coat and picking up a pair of new shoes. She tucked the revolver into a pocket.

Someone was climbing the stairs. She tiptoed over to the window and looked down: there was a car parked along the street. The streetlight reflected off the front windshield. It was an electric car and she couldn't tell if the engine was running or if the car still held a driver.

At least with the connection cut they couldn't watch her from her own security cameras.

She retreated swiftly from the window into the walk-in closet. There was a small panel between the backs of the two bedroom closets, almost as though someone had planned for some hanky-panky.

She ducked through an armful of coats. The panel was already open; she must have forgotten to shut it the last time she'd shown it to someone. She slipped into the spare bedroom, the door of which was thankfully closed.

The spare bedroom faced the back of the house—and the black, wrought-iron fire escape original to the house. She slid open a window and looked out. The last ten feet or so would be a straight drop onto the grass. She slipped her feet into her new shoes and hoped they wouldn't raise blisters.

She called up the retro card, called a taxi using a neighbor's unprotected wireless network, and gave the driver a nearby address.

"So you were followed?"

The dame shrugged, the Marcel wave moving slightly against her head. The grain of her hair almost matched the swirling wood of the bar. She finished crunching the last piece of ice. Charlie shoved the last bite of his ham sandwich into his mouth and scanned over the room.

Dolores, despite being the biggest bitch of the bunch, was still working her tail off like a trooper. Yvette was AWOL, probably having a quiet joint out back with the dishwashers, and Marie had retreated to the back of the room.

She was watching him. Her mascara was smeared. Not tear streaks but like she'd reapplied it with a heavy hand. Almost raccoon eyes.

"Why did you come here?" he asked finally.

"It was the address on the card. What else was I going to do, call the cops?"

She flashed him another dimple.

"Why tell me?"

"You have a friendly face."

"What are you going to do next?"

"You tell me, Charlie. You tell me. I can't turn on my network or the bad guys will be able to find me. And dollars to donuts they're on my trail as it is. I've been here one too many times for them not to check it out. Just in case. I can't go to the cops and I can't contact Bobby without turning on my network connection. I don't know what else to do."

"So you're asking me?"

"Why not?"

By then he had caught on to the way that this dame saw the world. Either she didn't know or she wasn't ready to admit it to herself.

He said, "What do you think is in the chip? Have you tried to find out?"

She grimaced. "I'm no hacker. For all I know, trying to find out might cause it to self-destruct. That might even be why it was itching. The itching stopped since I disconnected the network. I think someone was trying to hack it."

Charlie gave the situation some thought. Not just the dame's story but the whole night. "The only advice I got for you is to drink another drink, listen to the music, and maybe dance the Charleston when they push back the tables."

"I can't pay for it. Not without getting on the network."

"Like I said, that's my advice."

She flashed her dimple. "Then give me another drink. Another gin rickey, and use the modern gin, not that bootlegger crap."

He mixed it as specified and she sipped at it.

Miss Alice and the rest of the band were setting up on stage. The drummer was rattling his traps and the saxophone was trying to tune to the piano—a heroic effort. Finally everything was ready and Alice gave the xylophone player a nod. Behind the tiny percussionist was an enormous gong: she picked up a mallet and drove it onto the huge brass plate.

As soon as the gong rang a dozen busboys leapt from behind the columns and folded the tables in the center of the room, lifting them overhead and making them disappear. The bottoms of the tables all had heavy plastic bags underneath; the leftover dishes and napkins and silverware slid inside with a rattle. The guests were used to it and rescued their drinks before they were snatched away.

The chairs were pushed back from the center of the room, the mortal guests doing most of the work. The gold-sequined waitresses came in with big push brooms and swept the floor.

And then the room went dark.

A spotlight irised open, focusing on Miss Alice.

She wore a purple sequined dress and a silver feather boa that sparkled against her skin. She had waved purple hair and diamond earrings, and long white gloves that went almost to the shoulder. She was a retro but you'd never know it, not even under a spotlight.

She inhaled, clasped her big silver microphone with both gloves, and started to croon.

The dame twisted around on her bar stool and watched the show. About a hundred guests got up from their seats and started to dance. The look on the dame's face was classic. She was missing her Bobby. He could tell.

A small red icon appeared on Charlie's retinal display. Another alert. He opened it.

Warning, intrusion into guest areas by several non-state agents. Do not evacuate at this time. Agents are armed with guns and knives and have injured several people upstairs. Agents include two mortals and one or more retros, were heard asking whether the front door guards had seen a woman in a black and gold dress. Report suspicious activity/persons immediately.

Charlie flagged the dame. She acquired a red halo that only he and the other staff could see.

A second later, Yvette came up to the bar with an order for a sidecar, an Old Fashioned, and a Hanky Panky. Dolores arrived a second later, sarcastically mentioning that if Charlie could mix up a pair of French 75s for her guests, that would be nice. Marie, her mascara now truly smeared, asked him if he'd ever made that G&T she'd ordered half an hour ago—which she hadn't.

He groused and started making the sidecar. It was just a show: the girls were waiting for orders.

Out of the corner of his eye he saw a shadow. And flagged it. It moved through the crowd, ignored by all of the guests—mortal and retro both.

The dame stiffened. "I didn't...my network...how..."

Charlie said, "I see it, miss. Act natural."

She didn't quite relax.

Out in the darkness, two other shapes popped up red as they were tagged by other staff members. The busboys began to move in, slim and short and easy to overlook—until they had your arms twisted behind your back and a stun gun at the base of your spine.

The shadow ducked behind a column and disappeared from view.

Another alert popped up. This one said, All outgoing network connections blocked. Beware hacking and viral activity.

Miss Alice kept singing as the jaws of the trap closed in. The shadow and the two goons crept toward the dame. It was almost comic, the way they tried to sneak up on her. All four of them were flagged bright red.

A countdown timer appeared, twelve seconds and decreasing. *Prepare for acquisition and suppression of main targets.* The girls stepped in close around the dame, trying to look casual instead of deadly.

Ten…nine…eight…seven…six…five…four…three…two…

The lights went out and Miss Alice disappeared. The sounds of scuffle filled the room. A gasp. A woman's scream, quickly smothered. A grunt of effort. The sound of shattering glass.

"What are you *doing*?" someone said.

Charlie turned to face the noise and requisitioned use of one of the night-vision cameras in the main hall. The world turned green and he saw a woman holding something with a long barrel leaning over the balcony, pointing the end toward the dame.

"Get down!"

In a second he was over the bar and standing in front of the dame. She dove to the floor.

A shot rang out, he felt a streak of what felt like fire run through his shoulder, and the wood of the bar crunched.

The shot hadn't come from the direction he'd expected it to come from.

Gritting his teeth, he sent a top-priority message back to the system. False information reported to cameras. Suspected virus. Also send medic, I'm hit.

More screams, more scuffles. "Get behind the bar," he growled at the dame, stripping off his apron and tying it around his arm. The girls already had their holdouts in hand, slim gold weapons that stayed tucked into their garters most of the time.

Marie said, Charlie something's wrong with the—

The network cut out.

Charlie slid open a panel in the side of the bar and swept a pair of stun guns onto the floor. Then he shoved the false floor open. "Ladder," he hissed at the dame. "Follow tunnel to ladder leading up. Don't take any turns. Opens onto alley. No lights but everything else runs on backup generators."

"Okay," she breathed. Then she turned onto her stomach and slid in. In a second she was gone. He closed the two panels, grabbed the two stun guns, and started to edge around the end of the bar.

And that's when Yvette smashed him over the head with a thick glass bottle of Prohibition-style hooch.

⸻ ◈ ⸻

Bernice fled through the dark to the other end of the tunnel. She'd just reached the ladder going upward when a voice hissed behind her. "Miss? Miss!"

She hesitated.

"Miss! Don't go that way, they're waiting for you in the alley! You have to follow me!"

A small penlight flashed on. It was one of the girls from the New Cotton Club, dressed in shimmering gold sequins and holding a tiny gold gun.

"Miss! Can you hear me? Are you all right?"

Bernice looked up the ladder. The girl was walking in her direction. She only had a few seconds to make her decision.

She took a step toward the girl...then hesitated.

Behind her was the shadow that had been following her for weeks…it seemed like forever. Infecting her life like it was a…

A virus.

She shuddered. Her *mind* had been hacked. It was starting to make sense now. Someone must really want Bobby's chip.

A deeper darkness lay off to the side of the ladder. A niche? Another tunnel?

She stepped inside. The niche was deeper than she'd hoped—it was a narrow corridor. She started backing away, trying to time her steps so they fell at the same time as the girl's. The floor underfoot felt like hard-packed dirt.

The girl reached the ladder and looked upward. Her face looked perfect, even cartoonish. *She looks like she's had the full youth treatment lately*, she thought.

A voice that seemed to come from directly behind her said, *Hey doll*.

She didn't dare breathe, let alone say his name. She checked her retinal display; there wasn't a single sign of a network connection.

The light in the tunnel brightened as the door opened from above. "Nothing," said a voice. The girl in the gold-sequined dress cursed, then turned around in a circle.

"This place is lousy with tunnels," she said.

"You think she's lost?"

"I think she's hiding."

The other voice cursed. "I'm going to pass the disruptor down to you. Don't drop it."

"I won't."

Bobby said, Hey doll. Come with me.

She was standing behind something square and metal, like a big air duct. The penlight swept over it.

"I see something."

A bullet pinged into the duct and Bernice stepped back from it.

"She's back there."

She looked behind her and saw Bobby standing in his pinstripe suit, still wearing his mustache. He held out a hand to her and she took it. It wasn't solid but she could feel the pressure of it.

Be brave for me, doll.

Footsteps came running down the narrow corridor toward her. It was pitch black. The penlight picked out the gold on her dress.

"I see her!"

The gun fired again.

Bernice stood in the middle of the corridor and shook. Her chest was burning. She put a hand to the gaping hole and caught the blood running out. Her cupped hand was filled in about a second.

She was going to die.

Bobby said, Come on, doll. If we hang around much longer they're going to be able to shoot you with a disruptor gun and scan your data as it recompiles.

"But..."

He waved a hand and the wound went away. It's all in your mind, doll. It's all in your mind.

She started to cry.

<hr>

A few twists and turns later through the narrow corridors and they'd lost the footsteps behind them—but not the shadow, which followed them both relentlessly. Finally they made it to a heavily bolted steel door in a blank cement wall, one with a speakeasy grill at eye level.

Bobby stepped up to it and said, "It's me. Let us in."

A deep voice on the other side said, "What's the password?"

Bobby said, "Stop kidding around, Monroe."

"What's the password?"

"Hanky-panky."

The door opened and a bright light shone in Bernice's face. She raised a hand to shade her eyes—but her whole arm had gone transparent.

Bobby pulled her inside and the door slammed behind them.

Just like that they were back in the dining room of the New Cotton Club. This time it was just the two of them, a single table with a rosebud in a tiny white vase, two champagne flutes, and a bottle with a bow on it.

She collapsed into the chair. Her body was flickering in and out, a shorted TV signal. She buried her face in her hands and tried to ignore the fact that she could see through them about half the time.

He poured, and touched the rim of her glass with his. "Welcome home," he said.

"How long have I been *dead*?" she asked. But as soon as she asked the question it came to her in a flash: ever since she'd put the gun in her mouth. The day his chip had been removed. She hadn't even lasted a day without him. She'd pulled the trigger and they'd brought her back...

...but wiped her memory of it.

She'd stopped taking lovers and her only human contact was board meetings—which were so impersonal that they might as well have been held over a video chat session anyway. And the places she went all catered to the wealthy—and thus to retros. People had been pandering to a rich retro trying to keep up appearances.

He started to explain but she waved a hand to cut him off. "Never mind, I figured out what happened. But why?"

He nodded at the champagne; she sipped.

It tasted just right—not perfect, not an ideal kind of champagne, but *right*. A little drier than she liked, yet addictively bubbly. Her tongue felt like it was drowning in dryness. She finished the flute and Bobby refilled it.

"Your depression kept shutting you down," he said. "You would collapse and it would start infecting the system. We had to keep you isolated...we thought we were going to have to quarantine you and leave you offline. But Mr. Codere—"

"The funeral director," she said.

"The funeral director. He had a suggestion: we would isolate you from the wider retro community and erase your memories of killing yourself. We would force the memory of you taking the gun out of your mouth, convince you that it was your idea to go on living, and...see what happened. It worked for a while. Then the depression started to come back. Because you're a retro you could see it—you could literally see your depression. We had it wiped from your native software but it had spread onto the network—it was trying to find a way back in."

The shadow that had been following her.

Was something that she had created herself.

"Okay," she said. "That's just wrong. But what about the chip?"

"There was no chip. No hardware. Just a software upgrade...Dr. Wiltsey had the idea for it. It's a fairly complicated algorithm for interrupting feedback routines without damaging the routine itself...the complication comes from all the coding necessary to keep the algorithm from being infected by the broken feedback mechanism in the first place, along with everything else."

"I...see..." she lied.

He grinned at her. "Don't worry. I can't follow how it works, either. But if it works—and it seems like it is, now that Dr. Wiltsey's made a few more tweaks—it's going to be revolutionary. We're going in business together. Subject number two is his wife."

"Doc Wiltsey deserves some happiness in his life."

"So does his wife."

"Speaking of wives," she said. "And sons."

She was pretty sure she knew who the attackers had been: the people who stood most to profit from Bobby's new business venture. Retro business wasn't supposed to cross over into the real world. If they managed to get the proof from her, they could sue to have all the assets turned over to them.

Bobby's shoulders sagged. "I should have known not to tell them I was going retro at all. I didn't tell them about the experimental treatment, but when they didn't inherit the house after your death...when I set it up so you could project yourself...when they drove past the house and saw you through the window...they knew something was up."

She sipped at her champagne. The bubbles felt *real. Everything* felt real. "They knew long before I did."

"And I never would have guessed that Mary would take a full fountain of youth treatment and get hired on at the club. Yvette...what a name. Sounds like a French maid or something. She must have found out that I was part-owner and decided to take a chance that it would pay off at some point."

Bernice shrugged. "I'm more concerned about the bartender. Why didn't you tell me they were all named Charlie?"

"Because it didn't matter which one you talked to. The system recorded every word you said once you walked in the door." He hesitated. "You don't know how many times I started to contact you to tell you..."

She put a finger on his lips. "I'm glad you didn't. I would have infected you."

He shrugged.

She looked around the New Cotton Club. "This isn't really the club, is it? It's a...a simulation? A virtual reality? What?"

"An instance," Bobby said. "And yes. It is."

"I'm really dead."

"You're really dead."

"I didn't even notice."

"That's how it goes when you're a natural. Which you are. Me? I struggled with it. I couldn't figure out how to have feet, let alone walk."

She shook her head.

"So what comes next?"

"Next...next we live it up. We travel. We party. We follow whatever interests us...we explore the universes inside the retro servers...we hitch a ride on a probe headed into space. We can do anything, doll."

She reached across the table. One hand went through the champagne bottle. *Oops.* Bobby didn't seem to mind.

"Okay, Bobby. Whatever you say."

The New Cotton Club faded out.

•◆•

Charlie blinked and turned off his retinal display. Getting shot with a disrupter canister and beat over the head with a bottle of rotgut *hurt* and he was already tired of lying around in a hospital bed. The dame had given him access to see the final scenes, though, which was something. When you get shot for someone, you should at least get to see how it all turns out.

Although he really couldn't complain.

The coin she'd rolled across the counter at him when she first arrived had at first held a couple of bucks; by the time he'd woken up it had also held her postdated will, including the deed to a Willow Street house and about eighty-five million bucks. He was supposed to split the money between him and the rest of the staff—except Yvette—but he could keep the house.

It was still a pretty good tip.

The Dame shook her head. "I don't know about you guys, but I gotta say, that was a lot of guesswork about what the future holds. I don't know where you get half the things you made up there, Madame Ixnay. It all just seem to come outta nowhere!"

Madame Ixnay blinked, then stared at the Dame, her face blank. I couldn't blame her. If the Dame was going to criticize me as harshly as she had Madame Ixnay, I wasn't sure I wanted to tell a story at all.

Sneering at the Dame, the Detective said, "I didn't hear any rules about not telling stories that predicted the future. Is that a new rule?"

The Vampire said, "It is not. It is merely a comment on the lady's part."

"Well, I say that it was uncalled for," the Detective snapped. "Especially by someone who's only been to the table once before at most."

The Dame muttered, "I been here more than that!"

Slowly, Madame Ixnay said, "How long have the rest of you been coming to this table? Who's been here the longest?"

The Dame giggled and said, "We all know who's been here the longest—that guy!" and pointed toward the Vampire.

The Vampire gave her a smile but didn't answer.

The Spy cleared his throat and said, "As far as one can determine, Madame, your statement is disingenuous at best."

The Dame lifted an eyebrow at him, her face hardening slightly. "Are you callin' me a liar?"

The Spy looked around the table. His eyes lingered on me—the new kid—and I could tell that he was wondering if I could handle what I was about to hear.

I half-started to get up, but Dom put his hand on my shoulder. "The kid stays," he said. "And nothing happens to him—unless he talks. We all know how to be discreet."

He glared at me, and I shrank into my shoulders, nodding my head.

The Spy cleared his throat. "I, myself, have attended these meetings since 1889, when I returned from India. You, sir," he nodded toward the Vampire, "were present. As was..." He bowed toward the Dame.

Her smile widened, and she flapped a hand at him. "Aw, you musta been mistaken," she said, but took her denial no further than that.

Just how old was she?

The Spy continued, "Other than the young gentleman here, Madame Ixnay and the gentleman formerly assisting the Pinkertons are our most recent appointees, having only previously joined us for one meeting, in 1919. Dom, our bartender, joined us in 1899, missed the 1909 meeting, and was present in 1919. My seatmate to the left—" He nodded toward the Actress— "was present in 1909, at a younger age than our most recent attendee, and so was the good doctor on my right, also a good deal younger than he is now. The gentleman we have been discussing was to attend for the first time tonight, having, er, pressured Dom for right of entrance."

It seemed impossible. Even if she had only been a baby when she first showed up at these meetings in 1889, the Dame wasn't no forty-year-old broad. In fact, the Spy had said that the Actress was the youngest person to join—not the Dame.

What was going on here?

The Vampire said, "The gentleman we have been discussing off and on this evening should be considered off the table. He has been, as it were, removed from the board. At any rate, the question has been answered. Let us proceed."

The Dame said, "Who's next?" She looked around until her eyes fastened on me. She pointed my direction. "You go next."

My stomach flip-flopped like I'd swallowed Mexican jumping beans. I said, eloquently, "Uh, wasn't it supposed to be..."

I looked toward the Detective.

He shrugged. "Go on. I can wait."

The last thing I wanted was to have my story followed up by one that was actually good! I looked toward Dom, silently begging him to get me out of it somehow.

Dom guffawed, leaning so far back in his chair that I thought he was going to flip it over. But he got a grip and stood up, saying, "My friend here needs a moment. Put in your orders. I'll be your dogsbody."

I stared at my notebook, my mind a complete blank.

❖

By the time Dom got everyone settled again, I was ready. I had found the story I wanted to tell. That is, I hadn't found it; it wasn't in my notebook. But it was in my heart, a hurt that had cut me down to the quick when it happened, that I had never been able to make right or find a way to understand.

They'd said it didn't matter if my story was bad. I decided that I would tell it and see what came of it, maybe write it down if anyone liked it.

I jotted a couple of notes down in case I blanked out while I was talk-ing—it's been known to happen—and waited until everyone was looking at me.

My Jack Rose had been replaced by a glass of ginger beer, which was probably a good thing. I'd finished all that applejack brandy without even knowing it, and the last thing I needed was to get drunk.

I took a sip of the ginger beer. My throat felt parched and raw even before I started talking.

"Here goes nothing..."

THE MYSTERIOUS ARTIFACT
THE KID'S TALE

My brother William and I often walked through the Mt. Vernon cemetery of the city of Philadelphia, to view the various gravestones and their inscriptions. From the fine marble archway of the front entrance, to the unnamed headstones whose names, dates, and symbols of faith had been eroded away by that fell godes *TIME*, we found it a fascinating place, worthy of reminisce and repeated meanderings.

I had been much devastated by the death of my husband, Henry Stowe, in the year we called 1910, when his ship had sunk during a treasure hunting expedition off San Salvador Island. My brother and his wife adopted me, as it were, and I became the beloved Aunt Mabel, and nearly a second mother to their seven children, especially after my brother William had left the family home. William had volunteered immediately upon the entry of the United States into the war in April 1917, and had only recently returned in January of 1919.

By 1921, William had not yet recovered from the horrors of war, and I still had not yet recovered from the death of my husband. Over a decade had passed, and I was no longer young or desirable, being thirty-five and a widow, and, although beloved, much unfitted to the role of aunt and children's nurse, for rather than encouraging the children to settle themselves, I was rather more responsible than not for encouraging dreams, impracticalities, and flights of fancies. I have ever been more a spirit of the air than a woman of the earth.

William and I were two lost souls, then, but it was a land filled with lost souls after the Great War, and when we were afoot in the cemetery, we were little remarked upon or even noticed.

On one particular night, a damp and flower-fragrant evening in early June while the children were all asleep after their milk-toast supper and William's wife Dorothy was contentedly at her knitting and purling at her soft wool in their cozy, wood-paneled townhouse on North 33rd Street, William and I walked the deep greenery of the cemetery, both of us restless and irritable. We had come to an agreement not to let our wandering souls disturb Dorothy's homey placidity on such nights, and Dorothy had come to view the click of the front door with rather more relief than worry.

The leaves rustled quietly in the breeze, and the air felt as though a storm were coming, but later rather than sooner: the air felt tense with static, ready to crackle, but with a sense that the rain was to come only early the following morning, if not the following day. I am sure that everyone is familiar with such irritating sorts of days, where one says all sorts of cross remarks that one doesn't mean, or doesn't mean to state aloud at any rate. It was the sort of evening to curl the hairs inside one's ears, an evening of broken pottery and lovers' quarrels.

The two of us, rather than walking sedately along the cemetery's pleasant paths, had come to walk faster and faster along them, arguing as we went: William took the position that the Negro race was not to be welcomed in Philadelphia, and that the moniker "The City of Brotherly Love" referred only to one's brothers in race, and not in one's brothers in humanity itself. I had thought little about the matter, but was in such a mood that I could do no other than insist upon the complete reverse of every position of William's. The Negroes were to be welcomed; they had suffered much in their travails through abduction from their homelands and under the institution of slavery itself; they had much to offer, especially if decency, camaraderie, and opportunity were offered to them with a hand of welcome rather than the hand of begrudging resentment; and because they had long been living with us, it was hardly truthful to call them such names as William hurled upon them: *strangers, immigrants, foreigners, invaders,* and worse. The more I spoke, the more passionately I felt upon the matter. Moreover, I argued that what William suggested as remedies for the "unfortunate situation of the Negro in Philadelphia," were worse than the situation itself: he suggested, in short, nothing less than the regulation of all native Philadelphians so that they were assigned legal identities, and those legal identities could only be established by race, birth, and explicit approval by the government. All others who arrived in our fair city, he said, were to be sterilized, so as not to impugn upon our fair city by requirements lasting more than a single generation only, for he much feared the effects of interbreeding, he claimed, for the degeneration of the race.

It was, he claimed, a fair compromise.

Our argument was fortunately interrupted by a singular event, or rather object. We had come to one of the more unusual monuments in the cemetery, a moss-grown granite sphere engraved with the name *MONROE* and commemorating the death of a woman named Leonora in 1882. The monument had long been a favorite of ours, to argue over. Neither of us had ever been able to determine whether it was to represent a baseball, a type of ball that might be used in a game: for the sphere was engraved with a sort of "seam" carved into the stone, and decorated to look like stitching. It was a point of pride between us that the sphere was not to be cleaned or touched, and that one must solve the puzzle by logic alone.

The singular object was not the sphere, with which we were familiar, but on top of it: it was a sort of gold, two-headed artifact, like a double bowling pin, with deep grooves cut along the sides, to reveal a thinner inner spindle. It was of a small size, such that it could be concealed in a large man's palm, or, in a smaller hand such as my own, would show only the two smooth knobs on the outer ends.

It seemed precariously balanced on top of the moment: the two of us broke off our argument to regard it with surprised interest.

"Is that some sort of memorial object?" asked William. "Like leaving a stone or a coin on top of a gravestone?"

"If so, I have never seen such a thing before. I wonder that it does not roll off."

William reached out to take the object. I put a hand on his shoulder to stop him. Suddenly our evening's irritations were instantly recalled. He tried to shake my hand off his shoulder, saying, "I'll put it right back—" while I grasped him all the harder, a sudden dread tightening my throat. "Wait—"

The instant that his hand touched the object, all our surroundings vanished—or, rather, we vanished from our surroundings.

———◄○►———

We were floating or falling in midair, and surrounded by darkness on all sides but one, which showed before us a sort of curtain made of shimmering color, like oil reflecting the sun. The patterns to be found in the curtain were something like those of the constellations, and something like those of ice crystals formed on a day when the temperature dropped quickly, leaving long and feathery ice trails across windows, puddles, and upon wrought-iron railings.

William clutched the artifact, and I clutched at William's shoulder, sure that I should be lost forever if I should release him.

I could see the side of William's mouth moving, as though he were trying to speak to me, but could hear nothing but the howling of wind, as if through an abandoned house. We seemed to fall toward the curtain at great speed—we approached it so quickly that there was barely time to suppose what would occur when we struck it—and then we were through, with a wet, tangled sort of creeping passing all over my skin, as if we had passed through a spiderweb stretched in the darkness between the stars.

We appeared—or landed—in an open park, with large trees stretching overhead, and a pleasant green lawn all around us. We had left just after twilight, and found ourselves in a similar evening: but the air was so fresh that I could not mistake it for that of Philadelphia, which carried a tang of industry that one never notices until its rusted, soot-flavored spice is removed from the tongue. Of any gravestones or memorials, there was no sign.

I looked upward, to see whether the stars above us were the stars that I knew: and saw only a smooth surface, far above us, that was dark, but dotted with stars—stars whose artificiality was as clearly defined as the straightness of the gridwork into which they had been set, like lights above a theater.

William said, "I'll be damned!" and dropped the artifact—which, upon striking the ground, vanished! I dropped to my knees and searched for it, thinking that it had rolled off into the grass, but never did find it. William tugged me to my feet, saying, "What's gone is gone."

"Where are we?" I asked.

He had no answer to that question, nor to what the artifact might be. What we ought to do next, in order to return home—whether that be to call for help or to lie down and attempt to sleep, hoping to wake in our own beds at home—he could not say either.

I turned around in a slow circle and found that the edges of the lawn were bounded by a high stone fence near us, topped with ironwork; however, a path led amongst some trees to another, broader path: "Let us go in that direction," I said, "and hope that we can see an exit in one direction or another from the other path."

William led the way to this other path, then to a white marble archway not unlike the one we had used to enter the cemetery, in Philadelphia.

Outside the walls of the lawn or park were pleasant, tree-lined lanes paved with cobblestones, between close-set townhouses of a whimsical, fairy-like architectural style, with sharply inclined rooves of silver metal, with long columns over an open garden, and a narrow, three- or four-story house rising from within a tangled rose-briar, or ivy patch, or sculpture garden, or other delight. The windows glowed dimly of a pale, blue light, which had in places been tinted by colored glass. The scent of jasmine hung in the air, from some garden which was just out of sight.

A few other figures walked along the lane, dressed in what seemed like old-fashioned clothing of my early childhood: bustles, squarish hats, jackets with puffed sleeves, tight collars with large lace bows; other figures wore suits with top-hats and somber, long tails: the ties were broad and made of silk, and one of them was nearly as big as a woman's, with a large rhinestone stud in the center. Several of the men carried ivory-tipped canes.

But there were also differences from the fashions I knew: glowing lights winked from the lengths of the canes, and nearly all the figures wore a sort of ear-piece that would occasionally throw a glowing light in front of one eye, as if it were a sort of monocle, into which they would peer intently.

And, most remarkably, many of the figures were not of the White race.

Few of the figures looked twice at us for more than a glance.

I said, "William, do you think that your house is still there? Is *that* Thirty-Third Street?"

"I'll be damned!" his whispered. "I think it is."

The two of us turned down an unmarked street, and walked to the approximate location of the townhouse where his family resided: the townhouse which was located there did not resemble his own, but was no less attractive for that.

"Ah!" said William, "Now I am worried, Mabel, about whether we shall find our way home or not. I miss my Dorothy, and my children."

I suggested that we return to the park and try to locate the strange artifact which had brought us here; he said that "we would never find it" and that we would "be trapped here forever," and grew quite despondent.

As for myself, I watched the figures walking along the street, and wondered whether I would not like to join them: they appeared human, but with a difference. Their faces were open, and friendly, and pleasant; their attitude seemed to show that they felt their leisurely pace to be time well spent; they seemed to live in a utopia without hurry, worry, or filth.

William grew increasingly agitated. I walked away from him, intending to return to the park to continue to search for the artifact, when I was interrupted by one of the figures, who stopped to lift his hat, and said something in a language which I felt I ought to have recognized, but didn't. I smiled pleasantly and excused myself with a murmur, returning to the park.

Just before I passed through the archway, I looked back to see my brother at the entrance of the second lane down which we had passed. I waved to him, and he looked away, striding in the other direction.

I passed into the park and began to search for the mysterious artifact where I thought I had lost it in the grass, but it was nowhere to be found. At last I sighed and seated myself upon a stone bench that sat near the outer wall, near where we had appeared. It had become quite late, with only faint lights at the gate of the park to illuminate the grass before me: no wonder, then, that the pedestrians' fashion was to illuminate themselves. Of my brother, there was no sign.

The night had been cool and somewhat damp, with pale moths fluttering over the grass. Overhead, the dome enclosed the city, providing a feeling of both comfort and limitation.

Then two figures in top hats walked through the gate of the park and looked about: with a start, I realized that they must be looking for me.

I rose to my feet and walked toward them, fearing that something had happened to my brother. Why I supposed that they had been sent to find me, I do not know—for I am sure that they could understand my brother no better than they could understand me myself.

"Hello?" I said to them. "Are you looking for me?"

One of them spoke to me in turn, his pale white gloves glowing dimly of their own accord, and tracing shapes in the air as he spoke to me animatedly, gesturing as animatedly as a Russian telling a story.

"I am sorry," I said. "I do not understand what it is that you are saying."

The man with the gloves seemed to try to redouble his efforts. Then the other of the two men, this one carrying a cane and seeming to be of a Native race, put his hand on the other's shoulder, and shook his head, saying something whose tone was in the negative.

The two men turned to look at me. The man with the cane held his hand out to me: I took it; he bowed over it, and kissed the air over the back of my hand, like a Victorian gentleman.

"I wish I could understand a word that you say," I said. The man with the can held out his arm to me, and I took it. The two of us walked out of the park, followed by the man with the white gloves.

We did not walk quickly, yet there was a sense of urgency to our progress. We passed the little lane where my brother's house would have been, if we had been on our Earth; we proceeded to a widening in the lane to a thoroughfare, along which were several carriages pulled by animals that were not the least bit horses, but a pair of elegant, single-hooved, antelope-like animals the size of a small elephant, with golden-brown fur dotted with rows of darker spots, a jaw or beak that was somewhere between the shape of a lizard's and a horse's, and a high, horned crest rising off the top of its head. It was four-legged and had the long, sinuous tail of a cat.

I was handed up into the carriage, which resembled the sort of carriage that one might find on a summer day giving rides to tourists across from Independence Hall, with the man with the cane climbing up with me, and the other lifting his top hat and bidding the other adieu. The driver was given instruction to depart immediately, and, I presume, directions to wherever it was that I was to be taken. I did not feel myself in any sort of danger, but instead feared for my brother.

The carriage and its strange beast took us through several neighborhoods, thick with trees and pleasantly interrupted by all sorts of parks, past what might have been an elevated railway line whose train passed in such a whirl that I could scarcely follow it with my eyes, and past what would have been Girard College, in my day. The great old buildings, clad in pale marble with their somber white columns, were silent.

We passed another train—this one moving at ground level, and much more slowly, at about the running speed of a fast horse—and then, quite an hour after we had begun our ride, we arrived at Old Town.

The lights of Old Town were dim and charming; the horse and carriage—which were nearly alone in passing along the streets, except for throngs, here and there, of pedestrians afoot—seemed to be able to navigate by instinct, in the dark.

I was handed down in front of the plain, practical red brick of Independence Hall, if that was what it was: for the bronze statue of Washington which had always stood in that place upon its marble base at Chestnut Street, was replaced by the statue of a beautiful woman in a dress from the Nineteenth century, a book in one hand, and her other hand reached toward me, as if to help me climb up to the pedestal with her. I was drawn past her, too quickly to read her name upon the base of the statue, for it was altogether dark.

We passed inside the building, and the man with the cane brought me quickly to the Assembly Room, with its wood paneling, small tables, marble fireplaces, and broad windows. Where the wood rail had been, to keep those overlooking the historic spot from wandering about and disturbing the preserved scene, there was nothing but bare floor: in fact, several of the seats were filled with people discussing matters of some importance—or at least, discussing matters with a tone of importance.

William was in the middle of the room, his hands locked before him in handcuffs, with a guard on either side of him. He looked up as I entered the room, and I saw that he had dark stains—blood?—on the front of his suit.

What had he done?

I ran past the others in the room and embraced him. "William! What happened?"

"These bastards have arrested me," he said.

"For what?"

He refused to answer. I plucked at the sleeves of his coat, and found them tacky and wet with a dark red liquid that was very like, but not quite like, blood.

"They aren't human," he said, when I demanded an answer directly of what he had done.

"Did you kill one of them?"

"He put his hands on me!"

I shook my head. "Oh, William."

"Where is the artifact?"

"I do not have it. I could not find it."

"You did not even look!" And here he added vile sentiments such that I could not comprehend that they came from my brother. I watched him closely, yet was unable to reply, I was so stunned. He accused me of leeching off his family—he called me a burden—he said that I was good for nothing—that he had taken me in only out of pity—that I had wasted every opportunity—that I had betrayed him, by making him drop the artifact, and then refusing to find it.

Every second that passed, seemed to see the William that I knew destroyed, until finally my brother had been completely replaced by a stranger and madman.

Was there some alien chemical in the air, which drove him mad? Was he under hypnosis? Either possibility seemed incredible.

"Our home has been taken over by these *monsters!*" he exclaimed finally.

"This is not our home," I said gently. "This is a foreign place to which we do not belong."

"That's a lie! This is our home, our home! Don't you recognize it? Can't you see what they've done?"

"What about the horses?" I asked. "The language? The dome overhead, with its artificial stars? The air itself smells different. This is some other place, or some far, distant future. It is not our home."

"They have perverted it!"

"William," I said, "If you are not careful, these people will do something—"

"They are not people!"

And with that, he grasped the sleeve of one of the guards standing next to us, and tore open the coat of the guard, then the shirt.

Underneath the old-fashioned clothing was a figure inhuman. It had smooth, pale flesh, and a second pair of thin arms, folded up in the fashion of some insects, which attempted to pull closed the white shirt that William had just torn open. It wore no undershirt, and I suddenly guessed that was because it had never seen one: only the outer fashion had been copied.

William gave the creature a push, and it stumbled backward, losing its top-hat, and revealing a face which had seemed *almost* human, but not quite—to be a face entirely alien. I cannot describe it, except to say that its face was human enough, but the top of its head was clearly out of the ordinary, hairless and covered in ridges.

I stepped between William and the other creatures, stretching my arms out. "Please don't hurt him!"

"Get out of my way!" he cried, and pushed past me, both hands still locked together in their handcuffs, which were, I noticed, of a *very* antique design, like something Dickens's Peelers might have used. They must have been recreations, not intended for general use.

Almost immediately this was proven to be the case, for, unlike the arm-draggingly heavy restraints of Dickens's time, these broke open easily, and fell to the floor with a clatter. William, finding himself free of them, wasted no time in putting his hands around one of the creatures' throats.

"William!" I screamed. "No!"

"Help me," he shouted.

The creatures, though slow to react in their surprise, were closing 'round William, looking at each other in puzzlement, a puzzlement that could soon turn to anger. I came up behind William, pressing my way through the small throng, picked up one of the silver candlesticks from a small table, and swung it against the back of his head.

With a grunt he fell limp, sliding onto the floor.

I dropped the candlestick and sat on the floor next to him, checking his skull for cuts, but finding only a swelling bruise. His eyes had rolled back in their sockets, showing only this hazel moons of his irises when I pulled one eyelid back.

"I am sorry, I am sorry," I told the not-quite-human creatures. "He didn't mean it."

Even though I was sure, however sorry *I* might be, that *he* had meant it.

⸻ ◆ ⸻

William was taken out of Independence Hall, and I went with him. The gentleman with the cane—although I knew then that he was not human, I could not think otherwise of him than by the appellation *gentleman*—gently tried to remove me from William's side several times. When William was taken out of the building, the gentleman tried to keep me back. When William was loaded into a paddy-wagon, the gentleman tried to escort me to a more decorous carriage, then accompanied the two of us when it was clear that I would go no other way than with my brother.

I sobbed. I regretted what I had done: but I still could think of no other alternative than to let him be killed while I watched. I feared what William would do, when he awoke. I feared what would be done to him.

The paddy-wagon was not drawn by horses, and although the conveyance seemed to fit within the general milieu that these people had adopted for themselves, it was quite sophisticated, being of a cool temperature, a neutral scent, and without the slightest upset whatsoever, even what one would have expected from driving over cobblestone streets. It seemed to float in the air. There was even a water-fountain to get a drink of water, and a medical kit with which the gentleman cleaned and inspected William's wounds.

I said, "I wish I could speak to you, sir, to thank you for what you have done for me and my brother."

The gentleman pursed his lips and tilted his head. Then an idea seemed to occur to him, and the strange monocle of light appeared before him. He held up a finger. *One moment*, he seemed to say.

William moaned, and I turned toward him. The gentleman had placed William's own tweed coat beneath his head, and William was tossing so that I worried his head might strike the hard Bakelite floor.

Suddenly, the gentleman said, haltingly, "What...did...you...say?"

I started, and looked at him. He had set his top-hat aside, and looked more alien than human. I reminded myself that, with regards to polite behavior, manners were of more importance than species.

Slowly, I said, "Thank you for helping my brother and myself."

The gentleman took this with a blank expression for a moment. Then an expression of enlightenment came to him. Then he frowned, and appeared to concentrate. Then, slowly, he said, "I did not help him."

I thought about that for a moment, then said, "What will happen?"

The same process occurred: finally, the gentleman said, "He will be taken to the judgment."

I nodded sadly. My brother would have to face a trial of some sort, for attacking others. I supposed that *that* was a universal truth: that one wasn't allowed to perform bodily harm on another at a whim.

Except it hadn't been on a whim—but because William had seemed to go mad. I wanted to ask whether there was something in the air which might have caused William to become enraged, but I thought that that line of inquiry might go nowhere: how would the gentleman know? How would *anyone* know?

"My name is Mabel," I said.

The gentleman's face lit up. "Please call me Carnehan."

The name immediately brought to mind the scallywag of Kipling's *The Man Who Would Be King*, which this gentleman did not resemble in the slightest.

"Thank you, Mr. Carnehan."

The gentleman seemed to glow with pleasure, as if it meant the world to be called a certain name.

"Where are we?" I asked.

"Phi-le-del-phia," he said, enunciating every syllable. "The Planet Philadelphia."

"We are not on Earth?"

His eyes widened. "No. Are you from Earth?"

"Yes."

Astonishment overtook him, and he spoke rapidly in his own language, which unfortunately meant nothing to me. When I did not answer him, he berated himself for a moment, looking frustrated, then laboriously worked out what he wished to say, with the help of his monocle: "Earth is dead."

"I supposed as much," I admitted. "Why do you look like a human from Earth?"

This occupied several moments' consideration. Then the gentleman said, "The last human asked us to be Earth that was not."

"The Earth that was not," I said, placing a hand upon my chest. My throat had tightened terribly, and my eyes filled with tears.

To say that humanity—as a whole, or as individuals—had not lived up to the possibilities promised by our abilities and awareness was more than a cliché, but a truth: and now it was an epithet, or a eulogy.

Here, then, was Philadelphia Planet, a place dedicated what some poor soul had seen as one of the best memories of Earth, and where my brother, one of the only two Earthlings upon it, had attacked a peaceable citizen, for the crime of touching him—or simply coming within arm's reach, for I would not have put it past my brother, as maddened as he was, to attack without warning or cause, then lie about the reason.

We *were* humanity, my brother and I: I wished to see the betterment of the world, but was useless at it; he wished to see the betterment of what was his, at the expense of all others. His love for me was the love of a possession: I was *his* sister. To allow me to fall into poverty was to belittle his bloodline, and to deny his family the advantages of a woman devoted to their care. I cost little, and aided his self-love and long-term prospects much.

I had no purpose, no use, but that of a tool which a husband or a brother might wield, or not. It was supposed to be that women were achieving their independence, but it was a sort of game that few might win, and seemingly at the expense of another. *One* woman might become a secretary, and win for herself a precious autonomy, but find herself employed for a man, in *his* office, in a position much desired by hundreds, if not thousands, of women. To become her own master was a sort of lottery with impossible odds. The banks would not loan to her, the laws would not support her, the vote would not be for anyone like her, and every man would inspect her, judge her, and hold himself the determiner of whether she was fit to take *his* place. No honor would accrue to her, and she would be able to take no credit: not unless she won at every turn of the game, a game in which everyone was allowed to cheat but herself. And I was of the white race, which meant that I had fewer cheats set against me than other women. No matter my desire to improve the lot of humanity: I had no time with which to do so, being forced to play at being an aunt, for my survival—one that would not outlast the last bit of my nieces' and nephews' childhoods.

I looked down at my brother, whom I had been taught to love with a fierce defensiveness, always to save him from his own worst impulses, to check every violent tendency, to put myself beneath him in every way, and I resolved that, if I were to return to Earth, I would flee him as I would a villain. What had I done to him, but allowed him the freedom to be the worst sort of man, ungovernable?

What had his madness revealed, except his own true nature?

I had mourned my husband long enough. Ten years was long enough: and he ought not have left me in the first place, to die on an adventure in solitude. I was a fool, it was certain; but at least I would not be the sort of fool who allowed, out of inertia, our species' potential to be remembered only by "the Earth that was not."

William stirred, and I held a finger to my lips, cautioning Mr. Carnehan to keep silent.

"Where are we?" William asked.

"They have apologized," I said. "There was a terrible misunderstanding, and we are being escorted to a place where we might, if we are lucky, be able to return to our Earth."

"Where are we?" he asked.

"In the far, far future," I said. "We are on a sort of planet where…alien folk come to enjoy themselves."

"Like tourists?" He laughed. "Well, get an eyeful of a real Earthling, why don't you? When will we get there? How are they going to do it?"

"I don't know how long it will take," I said, "It was a lot of hand gestures and making faces at each other."

William glanced at Mr. Carnehan's face; Mr. Carnehan assumed an expression profoundest sorrow, and bowed from the waist.

"*This* one seems all right," William said. "Okay, I guess this is as good as it's going to get. I just wish you hadn't lost that artifact."

"I am sorry, brother," I said. "It was so small that I could not find it. And it was round...it rolled away quickly."

"But it was bright gold," William said. "I don't see how you could have missed it."

"It was dark in the park, with no lights. I think," I leaned closer to him, lowering my voice, "that they can see in the dark."

"Well, no point in worrying about it now," he said. It was a game that I had had to play a thousand times with him: to give him the illusion of control over everything that surrounded him, so that he might graciously choose to control himself. He climbed off the floor of the paddy-wagon and onto one of the benches, unfolding his coat and feeling the back of his head. "Damn, the back of my head is sore! What happened there?"

He didn't sound as though he were testing me, but genuinely confused.

"They had some sort of energy weapon that they aimed at you in the Assembly Hall," I said. "An electrical shock, I think. You fell and hit your head. That was then they realized how mistaken they were."

"I'll say," William said. "What a place. You have an innocent complaint about being manhandled by an alien thug, and they beat the bejeesus out of you for it."

The story had once again changed, but the blood on my brother's coat, which he had unfolded and put on, had not.

⚬

After a time which we passed more or less in silence, which seemed only half as long as the journey that I had taken with Mr. Carnehan in the carriage and which was interrupted only by my brother's queries of whether we had yet arrived (a fact which he could just as easily discern for himself in the negative, and which were really demands for comfort from yours truly), the paddy-wagon finally slowed and came to a stop.

The doors in the back were opened, and Mr. Carnehan quickly spoke to the two who greeted us there, I think to tell them that they were to put a false face on the situation for my brother. The expressions on their faces changed, and became nearly obsequious in their over-obvious concern.

My brother assumed their courtesies as his natural right, but refused any assistance in climbing out of the back of the paddy-wagon. He swayed on his feet, then looked back to me to give me a foul look. "I'm falling down on my feet here."

I accepted Mr. Carnehan's assistance, and stepped out of the paddy-wagon, holding his hand rather too firmly in mine, for I was shaking with terror at where we had been brought: what lay in front of us was what seemed to be an ancient castle, stones blackened and worn with time, two great towers lying to the right and to the left of the brute-fashioned entrance, arrow slits peering down at us with suspicion, while a third tower overhead seemed to be ready to call out to the men-at-arms that we were invaders, to be repulsed at all costs.

Two gargoyles were perched over the entrance, and ivy crept two-thirds of the way up the walls. Within the entrance were severe iron gates, which now stood slightly ajar. Our reception committee had begun to escort us toward those gates.

We had arrived at no other location than the Eastern State Penitentiary, a place famed for its cruelty. Past the gates, the "castle" itself was built in a wheel-shaped fashion, and proposed to cure inmates of their anti-social desires by isolating each from the other, a technique which should have worked well on someone like *me*, but had served only to madden and enrage those men like my brother.

Surely he recognized it, I thought, but he said nothing, only allowed himself to be drawn forward with the two guards, thinking them his escort of honor.

I shivered. It seemed as though William was about to be imprisoned here.

Wings of the prison extended to the right and the left, at acute angles to our path. We were led through the courtyard and up some steps into the intake hall, at the central hub of the building, which was a room smaller than I expected, with eight doorways around us, each guarded by a steel door which split down the center, with a glass window on each side of the upper half. The doors were closed, but through them I could see only rows of cells and barred gates. Each door was numbered, one through eight, with the entrance door numbered as eight. If *this* was to be the Philadelphia that was not, then why had this building been brought here? Was *this* place part of the Philadelphia that should have been?

Was there no hope for humanity, that we should always be required to have a place of correction, of penance, of punishment? And *such* a place, designed by the cruelest sort of men themselves?

"Where...?" I said, then swallowed the rest of the sentence.

"Don't worry your pretty little head," my brother said. "It's all going to be fine."

Mr. Carnehan did not answer my question, and I was glad that he did not.

We were received at a simple oak desk in the octagonal hall, where a woman—or, rather, one who seemed to be human, a woman from Africa, perhaps, wearing a brushed wig and dressed in a severe gray tight-throated dress of human times past—listened to the brief explanation given by the guards, and then, nodding, by Mr. Carnehan. Her lips thinned. If the other aliens had been trained to keep to the expressions of humanity, then, I realized, *this* one had taken the craft to such an extent that I could sense no difference between her and any prim, small-mouthed woman of my own time.

In accented English—it almost sounded as though she were from Russia—she said, "Welcome to the museum, William. I would call you by your last name, but my friends do not know it. They do not speak your language, only their own."

"It is Wolfe," said William. "I am William, and this is Mabel, my sister. We are from Earth."

The woman's pressed lips thinned almost to a smile. "You must have suffered some confusion upon your arrival. For this is a sort of reconstruction of Earth."

"Not a very good one," William said. "I wasn't fooled for a moment. Those houses were all wrong!" He laughed.

"There are a few differences," the woman admitted. "Do you know why you are here?"

"To try to get the two of us home again," William said.

"Yes, that is true," said the woman.

I glanced at Mr. Carnehan, but his face was blank.

The woman continued, "There is an artifact which we house inside this museum. The museum is a replica of the Eastern State Penitentiary. Are you familiar with it?"

"I'm not a criminal!"

"In our time, we do not lock criminals up in prison; this place is merely a museum. Is it still being used as a prison in your time?"

"Yeah."

"My apologies. At any rate, the artifact is located within one of the prisoners' cells. Many consider the walk to the cell rather disturbing. I wished to warn you."

"Consider me warned. Look, I realize you must want to ask us a thousand questions—" He rolled his eyes— "but I just want to get back home. My wife and kids are waiting for me."

"I understand," said the woman. "Perhaps your sister would like to stay with us for a time longer to answer questions, if she is not needed."

William laughed. "You can keep her as long as you want."

He did not even look at me, as he said it.

A tear came to my eye, which I quickly blinked away. It was not sadness which I felt. The woman spoke to the guards, who gave her a bow. She backed away from the desk so smoothly that I realized that she was sitting in a chair that moved: there were no wheels, only a platform that slid smoothly along the floor, with a straight-backed oak chair on top of it. Her skirt was arranged to cover most of the platform, with only the toes of her shoes poking out the bottom.

William watched her with fascination. "Say, that's pretty advanced, your chair, that is. We're in the future, all right."

She gave him another smile, then led our group down hallway number 1. The doors of the cells were all closed but the first one. Each of the hardwood doors, much worn and held on sliding tracks like a cattle-gate, had a steel plate with a peephole in it, for spying on the prisoners within. William looked through the first few. The cell with the open door showed only the ruins of a prison cell, with a bed frame, a porcelain toilet seat, and a few pipes suggesting a radiator. Although my eyes seemed to have adjusted somewhat to the lower light used by the aliens in general, it was difficult to make anything else out in the darkness.

Further and further we proceeded along the corridor. The spaces between the cells were marked with plaques covered with images and writing, much the way that they would have been in a human museum, although I could not read a word of what was written.

Finally, at the last cell before the exit door—which was open and unlocked, much to my relief, opening onto the early-morning darkness of a long, mild night—the woman stopped, pulled a rusty-looking heavy iron key from a pocket in her dress, and used it to unlock the old-fashioned lock in the cell door. One of the guards slid the door open. The woman's platform entered the cell easily, despite the high, awkward threshold. The rest of us had to duck.

The interior of this place was little different than the rest of the cells in the corridor, except that the bed and toilet had been removed. The chipped paint fell from the walls and covered the floor, and was ground to dust as we walked noisily upon it. The smell was that of *TIME* itself, mildewed and dusty, full of lapsed spiderwebs and dead, hollow flies.

At the far end of the room, a little stand made of painted tin, a bed-table with a single drawer, and decayed rubber feet.

The woman opened its single drawer; something rattled within.

"Ah," she said. "Here it is."

She did not touch whatever it was in the drawer. William looked over her shoulder and laughed.

"It's that damned artifact Mabel picked up earlier!" he cried, and reached for it.

She caught his arm with an iron grip. He was so startled that he did not struggle against it.

"Consider," she said, "that your sister might wish to accompany you."

"She won't," he said. "She hates modern times. She's always whining about how she'd rather live in the past. This is close enough to heaven for her that she'll never notice the difference. And," he said, glancing at me with an unreadable expression, "it's not like we need her all that bad at home."

"Do you wish to stay?" the woman asked me.

"I...there's no place for me there," I said.

The woman lifted an eyebrow. "It may not always be pleasant here—some would treat you like a talking monkey in a zoo—but you would of course have a place here. A human scholar."

"I'm no scholar," I said.

The woman approached me on her platform, and took my hand. It was cold, but not strangely so, and the bones were thin and fine. "You are whatever you decide you must be."

My brother, left uncontrolled, grabbed the artifact and vanished. Everyone in the room started in surprise. I looked inside the drawer: it was empty.

The woman rolled over to the bed-table and closed the drawer. I looked at Mr. Carnehan, who had relit his monocle.

"Well," I said. "That—"

There was a bang and a rattle from the drawer. The woman opened it, looked inside, and clucked her tongue. "It's back already." She pulled a handkerchief out of her pocket and withdrew the artifact, wiping it with the handkerchief, careful not to touch the metal itself. I saw the glint of gold, the rounded shape, the deep grooves, the darkened stain upon it. Then the artifact went back into the drawer, which was closed. "I really ought to wash it," she said. She handed the handkerchief to one of the guards, who looked at it for a moment, then tossed it, disgusted, into the corner.

My throat tight, I said, "What...where did you...?"

"Back to Earth, my dear," said the woman. "That is all, I promise you. But to snatch it up so quickly..." She paused. "I am sorry, of course, for allowing your brother to take hold of it before I had sufficient time to warn him. And I offer you my sympathy at your leaving the Earth-that-was. Even when it is one's choice to abandon one's home, there is grief to be suffered. But I think you will find that the consolations of the present will more than make up for its loss. I, certainly, have found it so."

I clung to Mr. Carnehan's arm, numb, and followed her out of the wing of the prison, back to the central desk, and then to a carriage pulled by alien steeds, and was fitted with a monocle of my own, and had many adventures, and was sometimes tempted to return to Earth, but never for long—I had only to return to the Eastern State Penitentiary, and peer through the peep-holes into the cells, and to look at the handkerchief in the corner, falling into dust: even after many years, it was brown with old, stained blood.

The woman's name was Leonora, as it happened; and soon we were fast friends.

The Actress said, "That was well done."

My mouth was dry again and the ginger beer was long gone. I said, "Thank you." It came out in kind of a croak.

The Dame said, "I knew he'd be all right at telling a tale." She turned toward the Vampire. "Didn't I say so?"

To me, Dom said, "You thinking of your aunt?"

My Aunt Claire had done away with herself about a year before then. My family never had the money that Mabel's family did—we never lived in, or even near a townhouse—but nobody wants to hear about families so poor that they hafta turn a near relation out into the cold.

Aunt Claire was the one who got me to reading all those stories. I'd wanted to do her an honor. I hoped I had. But I shrugged, embarrassed that Dom knew.

The Detective said, "The gentleman in question had tonight's prize on him. Might I ask how he came to have it?"

"Where did he get it?" asked Dom. "Why, he was a thief. He stole it."

"Stole it from who, though?"

The Detective was leaning across the table toward the Actress. The jewelry box lay between them.

"From the previous winner," the Actress said, jerking her head toward the Vampire. "You know who I'm talking about."

The Vampire said, "The previous winner of this contest no longer needed it, and ought to have turned it over to one of us to safeguard until the time had come—but yes. That is where he got it."

Dom said, "I can't guard all of you all of the time."

My eyebrows must have made a noise as they rose, because Dom turned to face me, then went back to the rest of the table. "My first meeting here was not in 1899. I been coming to dese tings far longer than that."

The Spy said, trying to sound casual, "How long?"

"Since forever," Dom said. "Before this, I was in Karlovy Vary. I seen Vienna, I seen Rome, I seen Samarkand. I been sitting around fires and turning spits while people told their stories since the cave days. A long time."

And he looked at me again, and winked.

I think half my face must have been stretched over the top of my head, my eyebrows had risen so much.

"Don't worry, kid," Dom said. "I ain't gonna steal you away some night, and you don't gotta leave me out a dish of milk of a night."

The Spy murmured, "One of the fae."

"Something like that," Dom said. "Your kind domesticated mine about the time you started throwing bones to the dogs. What we always wanted was this—" He waved a hand around the table. "—the stories."

The Spy said, again in that careful way of his, "Did the object in the box come from your people?"

"Nah. What's in there was got during…the eighteenth century? Before that we had some Greek nectar of the gods in there. But it got used up. Before that, something else."

The Spy turned toward the Dame. "Have you used it?"

The Dame said, "Who, me? Why would I have needed to use it?"

Again, the Spy backed down. "My question was impertinent. Please, forgive me."

"Forgiven, and forgotten," the Dame announced. Then she licked her lips and said, "Playing twenty questions is fun and all, but who's next? Oh yeah, the Tec!"

I felt myself go limp with the relief of having the story over and everyone moving on to the next one. I barely even minded that it was the Detective who would go next. I put my elbows on the table and my head in my hands. Dom elbowed me and said, "Put on some coffee, kid. You're not the only one about to fall asleep."

I got up and did as I was told.

I still had no idea what was going on. But I'd passed the test, the one that mattered to me. I had told my story, and the Actress had said it was well done. I was glowing.

There's something in you that changes, when something like that happens. Something magic.

⸻◆⸻

A few more people asked for coffee, and the Spy asked for more tea, so I was kept hopping. In bits and pieces, I overheard them talking about what they would do if they won.

The Doctor said he wanted to help some people he knew escape some bad trouble they were in. The Actress said she wanted to do something she had not done, something she couldn't forgive herself for not doing. Dom never said anything, as far as I could tell, and neither did the Vampire. The Dame said she was going to use it to be rich and famous—but for some reason I thought she was lying. Madame Ixnay wanted to make a different life for herself. The Detective asked, "A respectable one?" and she said, "Maybe," and the Detective said she wouldn't need to win in order to do that, and she laughed and asked if that was a proposition, and the Detective started coughing and shaking his head. When he could talk again, the Detective said he was going to try to take an illusion away, and make people face the truth about something. The Vampire wished him good luck with that, in a snide tone.

The Spy was saying, as I returned with his tea, that he would "like to put his finger on the bow knot of history, and keep something dear to me from coming untied," although he also admitted that he didn't know if he could do it, even with the help of whatever was in the box.

At that, the Dame's face softened, and she gave him a look of pity that the Spy studiously ignored.

I tapped him on the shoulder, and, when he looked at me, smelling like tobacco and dusty leather, I pointed toward his steaming pot of hot tea.

"Thank you, my boy," he said, and I sat down.

The Detective had an ugly look on his face, and I wondered if I was about to watch one of my heroes fall right off his pedestal.

I hoped not.

He said,

MEMENTO TEMPORIS
THE DETECTIVE'S TALE

I drove carefully on my way to the hotel. The last thing I wanted to do get in a car accident.

In my pocket was a yellowed piece of paper. The thing had to be decades old. It had some instructions on it, and an address to a place called "The Crossroads Hotel." I had hired a car, a 1927 Moon Sedan manufactured in St. Louis, Missouri. It was a brand-new car, but I had some trouble adjusting to the old-timey controls.

In my pocket beside the yellowed piece of paper was a pocket watch. It looked like a Lalique piece, and about as delicate as a perfume bottle. The front was studded with moonstones and enameled with a design of bats and witches. The bats and the witches sort of faded into each other, so it took some investigation to tell where one started and the other ended. On top of the winding-stem, for the chain-loop, was a snake eating its own tail.

Inside, the watch face was more unusual than I care to explain. The watch had nothing to do with telling time, and everything to do with telling time what to do.

I had come from 1959, all the way back to 1929. Thirty years.

Science hadn't brought me here. Aliens hadn't crash-landed in the Nevada desert, bringing time-traveling technology down to mankind. A nuclear explosion hadn't knocked me for a time loop.

Instead, I had borrowed a pocket watch from a woman in 1959. Nancy Mattson was the wife of a junior colleague at Concordia University, in Portland. She had a wide brow and a cleft chin. You could just as easily imagine her in a suit and tie as a cocktail dress. She had that kind of mannish face. She was a good hostess—kept the vodka in the freezer box and was never afraid of putting out the sardines or Tabasco sauce.

I don't know how she knew to give me the watch, but she did.

It was that time of year again, July 16th. I wasn't teaching summer classes and I didn't have anything to get me out of bed in the mornings other than running out of cigarettes on my nightstand. It was the anniversary of *her* death—the woman who should have been my wife. I had lost Laina in Portland thirty years ago, to the day. Now instead of being a young writer with promise, I was a middle-aged professor with leather patches on his elbows to cover up the fabric getting worn through.

I had been invited to a faculty dinner-and-drinks party at Mike Mattson's house, and I had accepted on the grounds that being bored to death by faculty summer gossip would be less fatal than being home alone that night.

About eight o'clock, Nancy pulled me aside by the drinks table. "Jim, you look like death warmed over. Whatever is the matter? You didn't get fired, did you?"

"It's that date again," I said, swaying a little. I hadn't gone easy on the ice-cold vodka. Or the sardines. I must have been a real jewel. "Thirty years now. Christ, I shouldn't have come tonight."

"That date?" she asked. "What date?"

And, there and then, I was drunk enough to tell her what had happened.

Laina Jarvy and I had been sweethearts. She wasn't the most beautiful woman ever, unless you were me. Even I have to admit that she had started out sort of forgettable in appearance—until suddenly she was the most beautiful thing I'd ever seen. I had met her at the university's secretarial pool. She was reading *A Voyage to Arcturus* by David Lindsay. I had asked her if she hadn't bitten off more than she could chew—the book is a scientific and philosophical mouthful.

She said she liked it just fine and gave me the evil eye, then refused to speak another word to me.

In apology, I gave her a copy of the Gregory Zilborg translation of *We*, a Russian book by Yevgeny Zamyatin that I thought she might like. Then I took her on a date to a special showing of *Metropolis*. I didn't like to get caught out as being demeaning to a lady, and I figured I had to make it up to her.

She had blue eyes and a heavy brow, a broad face and thin lips. The expression she wore was generally flat, as if she had looked under the hood of your automobile and found the engine less than impressive. She wasn't a flirt. She had a solid figure, more sand at the bottom of her hourglass than on top, and calves like a football player. She didn't make the most of what she had, either. Most of the time, she dressed in old-fashioned clothes. She didn't have the figure of a flapper.

What she did have was a way of looking at you like you were the only person in the world. When she was angry with me, other men would give me looks of pity—even though she hadn't said a word. But when she was pleased with me, the whole world disappeared.

What she saw in me, I never knew. I'm no saint, no great beacon of intelligence or wisdom, and not much of a writer. A mediocre professor, and a poor cook.

Without her, not even much of a man.

She died crossing Broadway. She had quit the university secretarial pool and was working at a building across Burnside. A speeding drunk driver hit her as she walked to lunch, dragged her about half a block, pinned her up against a streetlight, and killed her. I'd only known her a year, a little less. A week or so before she died, I'd started walking around with a gold ring in my pocket, looking for the perfect opportunity. I'd just about worked myself up to the point where "perfect" was taking too long, and any opportunity would do. And then she was gone. I didn't even hear about it until the next day, the seventeenth.

July 16th. Nothing special about the date, except what it meant to me.

Nancy listened to the story. I didn't cry. I didn't tear up. It had been thirty years, after all.

She gave me a look. It wasn't one of Laina's *looks*, the kind that made the whole world go away. I had the feeling that Nancy had too many irons in the fire to give anyone, even her husband, that kind of look. But nevertheless it was a *look*, and it was directed at me.

"Let me get you something from upstairs," she said. "I think we might be able to do each other a favor."

I made a joke about anything something less painful than a shotgun or strychnine, but she had already left the room. It was the kind of party where the guests were wallowing in their lassitude. Even though the start of the fall term was half a summer away, there was a last-minute sort of feel to the night. A "Sunday night before Monday morning" sort of feel. There were thirty or so university professors and their wives both inside and outside of the house, and no one had the energy to get in a quarrel. None of the drinks were unpleasantly drunk. There was barely energy enough for gossip.

Nancy came back into the room, a cool breeze on a hot night, and people stirred around her. I had a brief thought that she was trying to get rid of me, because my mood had been dragging down everyone else's.

But she smiled with real warmth and handed me a jeweler's box, larger than you'd need for a ring or a pair of earrings, and heavier, too. "Be careful with this," she said. "It's irreplaceable."

"What is it?"

She put it in my open palm, wrapping my fingers around the edge of the box. "Don't open it here. Go home, Jim. Read the note."

"The note?"

"It doesn't explain much, but maybe it'll be enough. I got the box from my mother," she added. "She was a witch."

The handwritten note was on yellowed, brittle typing paper. It gave me instructions on how to set the watch to the fifteenth of July, 1929, and said that I was to hire a car from such-and-such a garage, then drive to a certain hotel along the coast, a place called "The Crossroads Hotel." I was to meet a woman, Rita Barkman, at the hotel. She would ask me to do her a favor, one that I wouldn't mind doing. Then I was to drive back to Portland, do the favor for Rita Barkman, then do whatever was necessary to stop the drunk driver from hitting my future wife.

The note said, "Don't shave, and wear a hat."

It was walking distance from Nancy's to my house, which was lucky, although by the time I read the note, I had sobered up a little. When I finished reading the note, I was tempted to start drinking again, but I didn't. Instead I found myself sitting in my favorite armchair with the cover of the watch open, playing with the little gears and dials inside until I had set the date: the fifteenth of July, nineteen hundred and twenty-nine.

There was a little button to push, when you were ready to travel. I held my thumb over it, both wanting and not wanting to press it, wondering what would happen if it worked—and knowing what I would do if it didn't.

I got up out of my chair and walked out onto the front porch of my little brick bachelor's bungalow. I looked overhead. The sun had set by then. I think it was about midnight. Moths swarmed around the streetlights and the air had a whiff of dew to it. I told myself there wasn't any rush. If you're traveling backward into the past by thirty years, you might as well make it thirty years and a few hours to spare, and I had. But nevertheless I found myself anxious.

"Now or never," I said, and pushed the button.

As soon as I did, I cursed at myself—I had completely forgotten to wear my hat.

Whatever drove the watch wasn't science, but magic—I think I mentioned that. I found myself in an alleyway with my hand cupped around a cigarette, lighting a smoke. It was afternoon, not midnight, and the weather was hot and a little dry. I got the cigarette going, shook out the match, then straightened up.

My clothes had changed: I was wearing a suit of a distinctly older style. It was in better condition than the clothes I had been wearing. Having read more than a few time-travel stories out of the magazines, I looked around for a piece of window glass. There was one right around the corner. I stepped around the building. I was on an unfamiliar sidewalk. On my side of the walk there was no glass, but across the street was a haircutting place. I crossed the street and gave myself a look.

I hadn't changed much. I hadn't returned to the questionable handsomeness of my youth, that was for sure. I was thinner in the face, and grayer around the hair and stubble. If I had to guess, I'd say that I'd aged five years or so.

There was a price to going backward in time that Nancy's mother the witch hadn't bothered to mention.

There was probably a price for returning, too.

I turned back to my side of the street and walked around to the front of the block. The name looked familiar. *Harvey & Sons – Garage & Repairs.* Just the place I was supposed to hire a car, according to the note.

I patted around my pockets, but my wallet was gone—in my other pants, I supposed, the ones still back in 1959 or wherever they were. The watch and the note, however, had made the trip. I shrugged and went into the garage, more to see what would happen than anything else.

In fact, the car had already been paid for—all I had to do was pick it up. In the back seat of the car was a leather suitcase with a second, clean suit, a wallet with cash and an Oregon driver's license made out to "John A. Barkman," and some toiletries. There wasn't a razor inside the suitcase, just a toothbrush, toothpaste, and some soap, and I remembered that I had been instructed not to shave.

The witch seemed to have thought of everything. I looked around for a hat, and didn't find it at first—but it had rolled underneath the seat.

I bought a map and some gas at a gas station with some of the money from the wallet, and asked where a good place to get supper might be. The attendant directed me to a café about ten miles down the road. I picked at my food but didn't eat it, and drank a lot of coffee. It was five o'clock.

The drive to the hotel took about three hours.

It was a Victorian-style place, away from any town, on top of a cliff overlooking the ocean, three stories, the kind of place halfway in style between a boarding house and a grand hotel but with a size leaning toward the former rather than the latter. I checked in under "John Barkman." I had a reservation. The man at the desk re-read the entry and said, "And your wife?"

Without missing a beat, I replied, "She'll be meeting me later. She's coming up from California with a girlfriend of hers. If she comes in late, don't let her talk you into giving her a different room. I won't sleep till she gets in anyhow. But if the girlfriend wants a room, she has to get her own. Don't let my wife pay for it."

The man nodded, and handed me the key for Room 1125. A high number, I thought, for such a small hotel.

The inside of the hotel looked cozy but was unsurprisingly a bit damp. The wind coming in from the coast hummed against the windows. My room had all sorts of gewgaws in it from the 1890s and earlier, a mishmash of styles and eras. The embroidered quilt was pure white and had crocheted lace around the edges. There was a bathroom at the end of the hall with running water, and also a pitcher and basin in the room, both filled with dust. The owner was a collector, I decided, but not a very particular one. A bookshelf half-filled with tchotchkes and half-filled with nice hardback editions with gold foil sat in the corner, and I promised myself I'd look at the titles later. I hung up the other suit and washed up, then went downstairs.

"Say," I said. "Where's a good place for a man to get some supper around here?" It was late, about eight thirty. I was prepared to accept a packet of dry crackers and a glass of water for the night.

Instead, I was directed a tavern a mile or so down the coast highway, a white clapboard two-story building, the kind where the owners live upstairs. Downstairs they served buttered salmon, roast turkey, or roast beef, with cream of pea soup for a starter—no choice on the soup. I wasn't expecting to be hungry but I was, then. I ate and went back to the Crossroads Hotel and asked if my wife had come in. "Not yet," said the owner. I wandered around the hotel, which was stuffed to the gills with those jumbled-up antiques everywhere I turned, and listened to the radio for a while. A plain-looking woman in a clean apron came out and asked me if I wanted a whiskey. I said I'd better not. She brought me some coffee instead—good coffee. I tried to remember whether coffee had been that good back then, or if it was just the hotel. Then I went upstairs and looked at the books on the shelves. The first Agatha Christie was there, and *Last and First Men*, by Olaf Stapledon. I picked that one up and took it back downstairs with me. The woman in the apron brought me more coffee, and time passed one second at a time. I had to force myself not to pace.

"I'm sure your wife will be fine," said the woman in the apron. Word must have gone around. A few other guests checked in, but none came down to socialize. I could see through the door of the parlor of sitting room into the entry hall, and watch the guests check in. While the guests seemed ordinary enough as people, each guest's face told of it being an unusual day. Some of them were wide-eyed and hopeful. Others' faces writhed with self-hate, or despair.

They all seemed to be waiting for something.

At eleven I went upstairs. The woman in the apron had been giving me concerned looks for the previous hour. I got the feeling she was staying up just to keep me company, and I decided to get out of her hair, reminding her that when my "wife" arrived, she should be sent up straight away.

Rita Barkman arrived at midnight, as scheduled, giving a soft tap on the doorway and calling, "John? Are you still awake?"

"Still awake," I called, getting up out of the armchair where I'd been reading.

She let herself in and closed the door softly behind her as she put a little powder-blue overnight case on the floor. "Keep your voice low," she cautioned me. "These walls are like paper."

I had been listening to some of the other guests for the past hour, arguing and laughing and making love—some of them all at the same time—and agreed with her. I showed her to an armchair, taking the one closest to the window for myself.

Rita was the spitting image of her daughter, that same wide brow and cleft chin, that same mannish face. The dark hair was longer, halfway down her back, and her eyebrows were plucked a little differently, but that was all. Otherwise they could have been twins.

"Your daughter Nancy sent me," I said. I took the note out of my pocket and handed it to her.

She read the note, nodding. "You still have the watch?"

I told her I did, but didn't offer to give it to her.

She said, "Make sure to keep it on you. If you don't, you won't be able to make it back."

"What if I want to stay here?" I asked.

"Your sweetheart won't recognize you, you know," she said. "And if everything goes as planned..."

I had been wondering what would happen. The sci-fi novels I'd read didn't bode well. "I'll disappear, vanish as though I had never been born?"

"Something like that," she said, looking away.

She was either lying or not telling me the whole truth, but I decided I didn't mind, as long as it kept Laina from getting hurt.

"What's the favor I need to do for you?" I asked, to change the subject.

Her eyes narrowed and her jaw tightened, making her look more mannish than ever. "I need to fool a demon."

I blinked. I had traveled thirty years backward in time in order to change the past, using a magic watch. Now was not the time to quibble over whether or not demons could exist.

"What's the story?" I asked.

"My soul in exchange for whatever I wanted," she said. "Up to the value of my soul, that is."

"The value of your soul?"

"Everyone's soul has a value," Rita Barkman said stiffly, her back fire-poker straight. "Yours, for example, isn't worth much."

I laughed. "I could have told you that."

"Mine is worth even less."

I raised my eyebrows. "It looks valuable enough, from where I'm looking."

Her lips thinned. "Looks can be deceiving. The problem is, I've already traded against the value of my own soul. So I have to rope in other souls."

"You can trade someone else's soul?" I asked.

"It happens all the time," she said.

I thought about it, and about a student's work that I'd cribbed from a few years ago for something to publish. The student got an "A" on his work. I got tenure. Fair trade, I'd thought at the time.

"Yeah, all right," I said. "You can trade off someone else's soul. I'm assuming that mine is one of the ones you're trading off. I get to save Laina, you get whatever you can get on my soul in trade." I blinked. A nasty thought occurred to me. "Unless you're really just trying to get hold of Laina's. I'll kill you if you touch her soul."

"Even if it means she dies?" Rita asked.

"Death probably isn't that big of a deal, with a soul like hers."

"Her soul won't be improved by spending a life with a soul like yours," Rita said. "You're only going to drag her down."

"That's my own look-out," I said.

Another thin smile. "As you say. Neither one of us is an angel, then. You have your price. You'll give up your soul in exchange for...?"

"For saving Laina's life, soul untouched," I said.

"What if she ends up with someone else? What if she takes one look at the person your past self used to be, you down on your knee and holding out a ring, laughs and says 'no'? You could include that in the price, too, you know. That she has to say 'yes.'"

In fact, that very scenario was a fear of mine—that Laina would never really love me if I didn't force her somehow. I shook my head. "Tempting. Are you sure you're the witch, and not the demon?"

"I've picked up on some skills here and there," she admitted.

"The answer is 'no,'" I said. "I don't want a guarantee. I just want a fair shot."

Rita tilted her head a little. "Why?"

"None of your business."

One side of her lips curled. "You wouldn't make a bad trader of souls yourself. The reason I ask is that, if you sacrifice your soul for someone else, that makes your soul more valuable. In your case, it almost doubles the value. Which means that what I'm offering you is a lowball offer. I don't want to owe you anything, afterwards. I want this to be a clean break."

"That's your problem," I said, settling back in my chair. "It sounds like I'm going to get everything I want out of this."

"You don't have any family you want to leave money to?"

"Just Laina."

Rita rolled her eyes. "You're a one-note tune, you know that?"

"I'm glad you're figuring that out." When she didn't have a reply to that, I added, "So what do you need my soul for, anyway?"

"I've been trading souls for life," she said. "Extra years of life. Magical power—that, too. But mostly life."

"Is death so bad, then? What are you so scared of?"

"Hell," she said.

I shook my head. "If you hadn't traded your soul to a demon in the first place, you wouldn't have that problem."

She showed me her teeth. "Oh, Mr. Barker. You've only known me for a short little while. I *do* beg to differ. I have always had a reason to fear Hell."

For a second I saw a vision of a woman in a tall, powdered wig and a ruff around her throat, her face dusted so white it almost looked like a corpse's, a black beauty-mark pasted on her cheek. Then I blinked, and the vision was gone.

I said, "Set up a scheme to trade off someone else's soul, get some life, set up another scheme. Sounds like a real job."

She shrugged. "It's a life. All right, Mr. Barker. Let's get down to brass tacks. Do you agree to give me your soul, in exchange for the chance to save Laina's life, soul untouched?"

She *really* wasn't going to like what I had to say. But I'd been thinking.

"No," I said. "It seems to me that I'm already back in the past, and I can take the chance to save Laina's life, whether I trade my soul to you or not. The favor I was supposed to do for you wasn't exactly specified in the note, so I think I'm justified in saying that I've already done it for you."

"What?" she asked, incredulously and a little too loudly.

"I heard you out," I said. "After which you made me an offer that I declined."

She gritted her teeth. I heard them groaning in her jaw.

"Then what do you *want*?" she asked.

I closed my eyes. The world was my oyster. Thirty extra years of life might do me a treat. I could save Laina, get my youth back, and replace my previous self. *How* was a detail that Rita would have to take care of. Not my problem.

Or I could take the place of a renowned writer. Maybe that kid Hemingway. Back in my time, he was well along the road of drinking himself to death. But in 1929, he was imbibing his first few heady drops of success.

Or I could make investments, play some numbers—work my future knowledge of the world for all it was worth, which could be a considerable amount.

Love—fame—fortune. If I played my cards right, I could have all three.

Of course it was a trap.

I said, "I want you to owe me a favor. Of the equivalent value of my soul."

She didn't care for the idea, but I stood firm. She argued that the value of my soul would fluctuate. And what if I died before I called in that favor? She'd be stuck with a soul due and none to give the demon. She threatened to have Laina killed. Then she threatened to go to Laina and make her the same deal she was trying to make me: Laina's soul, in order to save my own.

I laughed at her and told her that I'd kill myself before that happened, not that Laina would be dumb enough to take her up on a deal like that in the first place. I had her right where I wanted her.

Finally she agreed.

She *had* to agree. I had what she wanted, and she'd already given me what I needed.

I asked her when she was supposed to meet her demon, to turn over the goods. She explained that her deadline was noon on the seventeenth of July. I remarked that she was cutting it close.

She waved a hand and said, "I have a pocket watch that takes me through time."

"I have the pocket watch, you mean," I said.

She smiled and took the exact same watch out of her pocket and showed it to me. "No, I still have it."

I patted my pocket. The watch was still there. I shook my head. "Time is stranger than I thought." I was having trouble making heads or tails of it, magic or no magic. There seemed to be no logic to it. "Why don't you just go back in the past and escape that way?"

"I will, if I have to," she said. "But there's a cost. If you'll look in the mirror, you'll see that you've paid a price for traveling into the past already. You've lost about five years."

I'd noticed, of course, but I'd been wondering if she'd say something about it.

"You could stand to lose five years, easy," I said. "Wouldn't hardly take the shine off."

"Thanks," she said sarcastically. "But I'd rather have your soul and be done with it. Looping back around—" She cut herself off. "It thins out your soul. And mine is already pretty thin." She stood up from the chair. "Fine. I'll owe you a favor, Mr. Barkman. For whatever the going rate is of your soul at the time."

She walked over to the door and picked up the powdered-blue overnight case.

"Just make sure you call it in on time."

⸺❖⸺

I didn't sleep a wink that night, just lay in bed and smoked with the window cracked open and the wind from the ocean skirling around the room. I was making plans, and thinking about the nature of time.

If I succeeded, what would happen to me? The younger me wouldn't have a reason to go back in time, if he had Laina by his side. Or would events conspire so that he would lose her again, be confronted by Nancy Mattson again—if that was her real name—and travel back in time again, losing little slices of our soul until there was nothing left to promise her, no reason for her to call us back? Would I be layered on top of myself, shaving down ever-thinner slices of soul between us, a dozen Jims, a hundred, until I popped like a bubble?

And how could the value of my soul go up or down, like shares on the stock exchange?

And what was this demon, anyhow? A creature from Hell, bat-winged and carrying a pitchfork? Or something different?

I spent the night staring at the ceiling, then reading for a while, then staring at the ceiling again.

In the morning I bathed and changed into the second suit. I checked out. The woman in the apron from the night before was there, yawning, and bid me good morning. She didn't say anything about my wife, just offered to pour me some more of that magnificent coffee, which I accepted, and to drop everything and make me some breakfast, which I declined.

I checked the pocket-watch against the clock above the checkout desk. Right on time. But the second hand was ticking ever onward, so I closed the cover and put the watch in my pocket. I carried my own luggage out to my car. I didn't like the thought of that woman wasting any more of her time on me than she had to.

Before I turned off the coastal highway to Portland, I stopped by the ocean. It churned and frothed and crashed against giant-like basalt rocks standing and squatting in the shallows, surrounded by spray and mist. I would have hated to try to sail there, or run a motorboat. For a moment I imagined that I was seeing entire worlds in that churn and spray, different possible histories, different timelines, different universes, brought about by a miniscule change from *this* to *that*, crashing against the rocks.

Popping like bubbles.

It was only eleven a.m. by the time I arrived in Portland and found a place to park near the intersection where Laina would be hit by the car. I had some time to kill, not enough to actually accomplish something useful, but enough to make my presence suspicious if I lingered on the sidewalk.

I went to the café that Laina had been trying to get to, when she'd been hit by the drunk.

I wasn't just being morbid; it was a good place to eat lunch at. The small tables were covered with pristine white tablecloths and pressed up against the wall, with a glass-topped counter holding a row of stools for the single men, like me, who wanted a bite to eat. Under the glass were about a million bucks of pies and cakes. I ordered a roast turkey sandwich with mashed potatoes. The waitress, who was dressed in a starched white dress with a little black jacket and a ruffled cap—I'd forgotten how cute the bobbed haircuts looked on the girls back then—lifted an eyebrow at me; I was a little early for the lunch crowd, and a little late for breakfast. I told her I'd been on the road all morning, and that seemed to cover the situation. I asked for coffee and was disappointed to find that not *all* coffee in the past was as good as the hotel's.

After the waitress walked off to polish the other end of the countertop, I took out the watch, the one that had taken me thirty years back into the past, and taken five years off my life. In order to travel back in time, I had used half the dials. When I had first used it, I had wondered what the other half of the dials were for.

After my talk with Rita the previous night, the answer had become obvious. The *other* dials were set to the seventeenth of July, 1929. The date that Rita's traded years expired.

What would happen if the time passed without Rita's getting my soul? Would the demon come and take her?

When I had refused to hand over my soul the night before, I had done it instinctively, more out of a sense of getting railroaded and not liking it than anything else. On the drive from the coast, I'd realized that if I held back the price of my soul, then if something went wrong with trying to save Laina, I'd still have an opportunity to rectify the situation. What if I pushed Laina out of the way and *another* car hit her? What if I were hit by a car, before I had a chance to save her? Holding back the promise of a soul wasn't perfect insurance, but it was better than the deal that Rita had tried to push me into.

I tapped my fingers on the glass countertop, thinking. If everything went well and I saved Laina, what would happen next?

I was pretty sure that Rita Barkman would arrange for things to go badly. *Real* badly.

Most likely, I'd be hit by the car that was meant to hit Laina. I'd be in terrible pain, unable to die until I'd called in my favor. At that point, I might be irrational enough to say something like "Kill me" or "Put me out of my misery." Wouldn't that be a laugh! Death, as the final price of my soul.

What I ought to do was come up with a plan, something like, "Send me back to 1959, in the same condition that I left." Only that might leave me in that bad old world of mine, the one where Laina had died in 1929. On second thought, I decided not to ask for that.

I could wish for Laina's happiness, but that would probably mean that she wouldn't end up with *me*, and I wasn't sure there was enough juice in my soul to provide more than five minutes of genuine happiness to anybody anyhow.

As previously mentioned, I was no saint. Rita had already stiffed me once—by making me pay five years of my life without warning me—and would have stiffed me again, if I hadn't refused to give in to her "deal" the previous night.

A plan was starting to come to me, one that no saint would have come up with, but one that might solve at least a few of my problems…and shove the bill onto Rita, to boot.

⁌◦⁍

By the time I left the café, at 11:40, my plan was in place. I stood on the corner outside the café and paced back and forth, checking my watch as if I were waiting for someone. I had told the waitress that I was waiting for a business partner to meet me when I paid the bill, and said that I had expected him at 11:30. If anyone asked any questions about what I was doing out front of the café, she would no doubt answer them for me.

The midday air was heavy with car exhaust and humidity, along with a tang of factory smoke. The cars rolled past me along Broadway. Streetcars, too. Pedestrians walked carefully when they crossed the street. The electric streetlights seemed ineffective, with cars pushing through intersections against the light, then getting whistled down by the police. Most of the people out and about were men in dark suits, a few women here and there in shapeless day-dresses. A few Klaxon car-horns sounded along the street, echoing between the buildings.

I spotted Laina right away.

She was walking down the street toward me, wearing a gray knit skirt and cardigan, a striped blouse, and a cloche hat. She walked briskly, no nonsense allowed.

As she approached the corner, her eyes swept along the street, then fastened on mine.

Her mouth opened a little, and she stumbled as she approached the curb.

I ran forward across the street. This was the one part of my plan that I wasn't sure of. I heard shouts and the sound of a roaring engine.

"Hey, mister, watch out!"

I ignored whoever had shouted to me. I only had eyes for Laina. I dashed straight into her, knocking her backward into the men waiting at the end of the sidewalk.

She stumbled, then grabbed onto my suitcoat, and swung me around so that we both stumbled, but didn't fall. My hat, which I'd put back onto my head after leaving the café, took a tumble. The men around us caught hold of us and pulled us away from the curb—as the car that should have killed Laina swept behind us, with a monster's roar.

Instead of turning onto Broadway, dragging Laina along with it until it hit a light pole, the car carried onward along Burnside, clipping a parked car, then disappeared out of sight. It must have taken my hat alongside, because there was no sign of it anywhere.

Laina was still clutching my suitcoat. This was the part I wasn't sure of: would she recognize me, or not?

"Mister," she said. "I believed you saved my life."

I was shaking, as was she. I said, "My pleasure, miss."

"You all right?" she asked.

"I should be asking you."

She laughed. "I'm shaking. But is that because I haven't eaten, or because I just had the bejeesus scared out of me? I can't tell which, pardon my French."

I said, "I just ate, but I'll drink a cup of coffee with you just to be courteous—and to have an excuse to sit down. How about that café over there? They just made me a good turkey sandwich."

She said that would be just the place.

Looking both ways, we crossed the street and to the café that I'd just left. The waitress said, "What happened, mister? Where's your partner? You look like you've seen a ghost!"

I had her seat us at a table. Then I told her what had happened. Everyone agreed that it was a bit of luck, me running across the street like that, and nobody getting hurt. Laina ordered a sandwich and coffee. I just had the coffee. When the waitress brought it, I reached out to pick it up and my hands were still shaking.

Laina leaned forward and whispered, "It's like something out of a science fiction novel. You look about fifty years old, Jim. I'm not sure how you did it, but it's you, and you're older. Time travel? Is that it? I was *supposed* to get hit by that car, wasn't I? And you came back to save me."

She'd recognized me, all right.

I murmured, "You weren't supposed to recognize me."

She said, "But I did, and here we are." She reached across the table to slip her hand into mine. "What did it cost you to get here?"

The bell above the door of the café tinkled, and I turned to look over my shoulder.

It was Rita Barkman, come to collect her bill. Her face brightened with artificial friendliness as she spotted us and waved. The waitress headed in her direction.

My hand tightened on Laina's as I turned back toward her.

Her mouth was a straight line and her eyebrows were beetled together. "I think I see the price coming in through the door," she said. "Tell her she can't have you."

"Don't worry about me," I said. "I'm just a piece of leftover time that's served its purpose. If you want to do me a favor, let the younger me spend the rest of his life trying to make you happy."

"I can't let you—"

But whatever it was that she couldn't let me do got lost as Rita Barkman walked over to our table, and seated herself next to Laina. The waitress brought Rita a cup of coffee, and Rita smiled gratefully up at her. The waitress said, "He didn't mention that his business partner was a lady!"

Rita said, "You know how some people are about women in business."

"What kinda business?" the waitress asked.

Rita's eyes flashed, looking a little less friendly all of a sudden. I said, "Life insurance. She runs things. I just sell the policies." I held a finger up to my lips. "You know how some people are about women in business."

The waitress gave us a wink and walked off.

As Rita sat down, Laina let one of her blank looks settle over her face. The waitress brought Laina's sandwich, and Laina started eating it calmly, as if she hadn't almost just been killed.

Rita said, "So, John. Everything seems to have worked out for you."

"Sure," I said agreeably.

"Have you thought about that favor?" she asked.

"I have," I said. "I'm going to have to decline."

Rita's eyes widened, and her nostrils flared.

As if I hadn't noticed, I continued: "I don't really need anything from you, you see. As far as the price of my ticket goes," I waved at my face, "I already paid. So we're square."

She shook her head, but I could tell that she hadn't give up on me yet. "I should have seen it coming. So what will you do now? Go back to where you came from? Or stay here?"

"I don't see how that's any of your business," I said.

"I'm just curious."

I shrugged. "Lots of people don't get their curiosity satisfied."

Rita's eyes slid over to Laina, who was still calmly eating her lunch. "People who are curious have been known to cause accidents."

I leaned toward her and grinned. "Or stop them. You know you're not the only one who can make deals around here, doll."

Rita gasped, and her hand dipped into her pocket. She pulled out her watch and flipped open the cover.

Laina looked at it curiously. "Hey, miss. Nice watch you got there. Looks expensive." She stretched out her neck a little, to get a glimpse of the mechanism inside the case. "Lotta dials inside, too. You have it custom-built for you?"

Rita ignored her, staring into the watch face. Her face had gone pale. "But—"

I said, "Like you said, I already got everything I wanted. I had to stop and ask myself, *What's left for a guy to want, in that situation*? Why, insurance that he won't lose what he has."

I reached into my own pocket and took out the watch that was there. Laina looked back and forth between them.

"Mister," she said, "you must have gone shopping at the same watch-maker's as this friend of yours did."

"I did," I said. "Bought and paid for."

Rita looked up at me.

"You—"

Although it had seemed like a week had passed since the accident, it had only been a few minutes. In fact, it was just coming up on noon. Outside, church bells started to ring.

It was the damnedest thing.

The watch dropped straight through Rita's hand and onto the table. Laina's face followed it as it fell, like a cat keeping an eye on a mouse. Rita had gone pale and flickering, like film from a movie theater that had been threaded in wrong. She opened her mouth in terror, but nothing came out.

Then, as fast as it takes to take a big, gulping breath, the watch sucked her in, every particle of her, down to the last little wisps.

The lid of the watch closed shut with a satisfied little *click*.

Laina reached for the watch, but froze when I shook my head. I wasn't sure how this part was going to go, but I didn't want her touching the thing—not yet.

I lay my watch on the table next to Rita's copy of it. The two shuddered a little, then slid into each other, like two strong magnets. When they came together, there was only one watch left.

I nodded at Laina. She picked up the watch and looked it over, then opened the cover.

"Two sets of dials," she said. "But they both show the same time—no, wait—" There was an almost silent *tick*— "The lower one says it's twelve-oh-one now."

Laina looked at me, then over her shoulder at the waitress, who smiled at her and lifted an eyebrow, to see if Laina needed anything.

The third cup of coffee had vanished, while neither of us was looking.

Laina frowned, and in a low voice said, "If this is a proper time-travel story, I'm going to forget all this, aren't I?"

"I suppose you might," I said.

"What did you do?"

"Rita had a bill coming in on her soul, one that wasn't supposed to come due until noon tomorrow. I paid a little time for the bill to come due a day earlier, that's all."

"A soul?" Laina said. "Souls exist? What about Heaven? Or Hell?"

"I don't know about any of that," I said, taking the watch from her and closing the lid, then putting it into my pocket. "But time exists. Maybe that's all a soul is: what time you have left, and what you do with it."

I didn't say anything about what Rita had said, about the values of souls fluctuating, about the thinness that came about, if you traveled in time too much. Or about the fact that I had lied about what I had had to pay. I just hoped that the extra value of time lost would spill over to my previous self. He needed all the help he could get.

"What will you do now?" Laina asked.

"I don't want to stick around and interfere," I said. "I wish the best of luck to the both of you, but I think I'm going to do something I've always wanted to do."

"What's that?"

I patted my pocket. "See the future. It'll cost me some—but I'll be happy there. I know it."

Her face lit up. Before she could ask me any questions, I took five dollars out of the wallet Rita had given me, and set it on the counter. Then I leaned over and kissed Laina on the cheek.

"Good luck, kid," I said. "And don't forget the time. You don't want to be late to work."

"Wait—Jim—"

The bell above the café door tinkled, and then I was gone. Let Laina believe what she wanted to. I trotted to the corner and turned around it, feeling Laina's eyes on my back, until I was out of sight.

But the bell didn't tinkle again. She hadn't followed.

I handed the watch to a man waiting on the corner to cross, feeling my steps slow, like I was walking ever deeper into a raging river, about to be swept downstream.

My hands were already a little translucent.

⸺◆⸺

I stared down at the backs of my hands, asking myself if I would have done that, if there was anything I wanted so bad that I would have erased who I was to get it.

There wasn't, I realized. They called me the Kid, and they were right. I hadn't really lived yet. I felt ashamed of the story I'd told. I had mostly stolen it from someone else. I hadn't lived enough to write my own stories. I was a fraud.

"Regrets?" the Dame asked coyly. "Feelin' a little guilty about some a what you done?"

The question was directed toward the Detective, but it made me jump, too.

The Detective glared at her, then looked away, his face slack.

The Dame said, "Tell me the truth. Did you have him killed, or didn't you? You knew he had the treasure."

"I...did not," the Detective said. "But there is nothing I can say that will prove that to you, is there?"

Madame Ixnay snorted. "We don't need to make this complicated. The gentleman in question was a thug and a gangster and a blackmailer. We just need to work out who he had blackmail material on, and the money to hire a hitman. And we all know who had the money around here."

She looked at the Vampire.

The Vampire said, "I did not have him killed, nor cause anyone else to do so, either directly or indirectly. My hands are clean in this matter."

He lifted up his hands, and I noticed that though they were colorless and pale, they weren't as wrinkled as they should have been.

I said, "What if it wasn't that someone didn't want his story to be told—it wasn't the story itself that was important—I mean—I'm saying this all wrong. What if someone didn't want him to tell any story? What if telling a story, uh, kind of protected him?"

The Detective said, "You're a good guesser, kid. Telling a story at the table does protect you...specifically, Dom protects you. But only once you've told a story."

I turned toward Dom, remembering that he'd said something about not being able to protect everyone all the time.

And that even though nobody supposedly knew that the Boss had been killed, there hadn't been enough chairs set out. Dom had had to give me an extra one.

He'd known the Boss was going to get killed. It was like reading a mystery tale where nothing makes sense but there's one clue you can't deny.

"You?" I asked him incredulously. "You had him killed?"

Everyone turned toward Dom.

Dom raised his hands and said, "All right, all right. The kid has it straight. I was the one who had the gentleman in question killed. But if anyone had the right to do so, I did."

Everyone else at the table appeared to consider that point. Nobody disagreed with him.

Dom turned to me. "The gentleman in question was the Boss. But you should know dat he was working for me, not de other way around. And he did something dot reflected bad on me."

I goggled at him.

"I can't own property," Dom explained, although he didn't explain why he couldn't. "And while I don't mind cracking a couple of skulls now and then, I didn't want to get involved in the day-to-day management of the business. It's a real pain in the ass."

I unlocked my jaw. "But...why? Why have him killed?"

Dom shook his head. "I found out he done something that couldn't be forgiven. And I took care of it."

I goggled. "What?"

Dom spread his hands and chewed on the words through his heavy accent. "Not my tale to tell."

The Good Doctor asked, "What did I see, earlier? A car? A monster?"

"Some friends of mine," Dom told him. "From the old country. The very old country. I'd leave it at that."

The Good Doctor did so.

The Vampire said, "Very well. If we have satisfied ourselves on the matter, let us return to the stories. Unless there is another delay...?" When no one responded, he turned to the Actress. "Young lady. You may begin."

The Actress bowed her head for a second, and I was shocked to see a drop of sweat roll down the side of her face. She was just as nervous as I had been—if not more so. But hadn't she been here before?

"I mentioned earlier that there was a thing I had not done, which I wished to have done," she said, "And that was why I wanted to take the prize tonight. I—"

The Spy reached to take her hand, and squeezed it. She lowered her head again, and for a moment I thought she would break out in sobs.

Instead, she said, "The first two times I came to this table, I didn't know the sort of world that we lived in. I was naïve. I was not innocent—but I was naïve. You all must have been laughing at the stars in my eyes. I thought I could escape the world I came from and create a new one on the movie screen, shining and silver, where the world was fair and everyone was beautiful and kind and strong. But that world never existed, and it was already under the control of awful, awful people. And recently I—ignored a plea for help. I don't know what to do now. I feel like I'll never be able to forgive myself."

The Spy said, "One must remember that there is hope."

The Actress wiped her face. "There is. That's true, sir. But in the shadow of hope, there is regret."

Still holding the Spy's hand, the Actress began to speak:

THE PAGE-TURNERS
THE ACTRESS'S TALE

The hypnotic sound of the train wheels against the iron rails has lulled you into a half-slumber. The half of you that isn't asleep is having trouble remembering that the soft thumping sound comes from the wheels hitting the rail joints isn't really a heartbeat. The other half is dreaming of someone calling your name, trying to wake you up.

The velvet seat underneath you is polished smooth in places; the air smells of carpet-dust and distant rain from an open window. You can't get comfortable. Voices murmur. Your head sinks—then jerks upright. Sinks again.

You're going to see your dying mother in Chinatown. Your mother has a tumor growing on her left ovary, one that is so large that she struggles to breathe. In his letters, your father tells you that your mother is in good spirits and confident that the tumor is shrinking. She wants you to know, you father says, that it would ease her mind considerably to know that you're getting married. Your mother has been having prophetic dreams about it.

You have been sick to your stomach this entire journey. You have ridden on three different trains so far; it's midnight in the middle of nowhere past Omaha. You're not in a sleeping car; you don't have that kind of money, although you did put on your new traveling suit, a black jacket and a smart black skirt, with a cloche hat tilted over one eye. You're wedged against the back of the seat, your feet against the feet of the seat in front of you. The train sways gently as it passes around a bend in the rails. You'd been trying to read a book earlier in the day but the letters seemed to blur and reverse themselves, as if trying to turn into hànzì characters but not quite succeeding. Your mother would have said it was a message from the spirits.

An older gentleman, white, in a gray traveling suit with a blue wool jacket over his shoulders, is crossing from one end of the carriage to the other.

Trip him.

Your foot slips off the bronze bench leg and catches against his shoe. It was an accident. He's carrying a stack of old, leather-bound books. He stumbles and the books slide into your seat.

He apologizes as you sit up straight, rub your eyes, and beg his forgiveness. You hand him the books, one by one. He takes them and continues down the car. His coat is crooked on his thin old shoulders and you have to repress the urge to straighten it for him. He had a look in his eye as the two of you were apologizing to each other that was pure mockery. Treating you as human was a game to him. Some whites are like that, especially in the South. Act without humility and subservience—in any way at all—and the teeth come out.

It's a test. It's always a test.

The train sways again. Something slides under the seat, a hiss like snakeskin. Your handbag with your cigarette case is wedged between your hip and the window, perfectly safe. You bend over to look.

It's a book.

You look around. "Hey, mister—"

But he's gone.

———— ◄○► ————

The book is large, very large. You don't remember seeing the man carrying it. Surely you would have remembered a book like this. When you drag it off the floor, you let out a little grunt. It covers your entire lap. It's covered in leather, very smooth, dyed red and covered with gold leaf in swirling designs. Not the kind of book that could be missed. Maybe it's not the old man's book after all. You turn around—there's no one in the seat behind you. Yours now. The pages have gold edges to them. No letters on the cover or the spine. Nothing to indicate what's inside.

Open the cover.

You turn to the first pages, which are parchment, like some of your mother's old books. There's no title—no. There *was* a title, but the letters have been scraped away. You riffle through the pages. The pages have been written on, but there are traces that other words have been scraped off. You can't remember the word for that, paper that's been reused.

Palimpsest.

The word comes to you out of nowhere. It's always a relief to remember something on the tip of your tongue—it closes a door that was standing open, letting in the winter breeze, summer mosquitos, and men, spring and autumn, with amusingly pleading eyes.

After letting the edges of the pages purr pleasantly through your fingers several times, you turn back to the front cover. A name, you can barely pick out the letters that have been scraped away.

Jimmy O'Toole.

A boy's name, you recognize *Jimmy,* but working out where O'Toole comes from is beyond you.

Irish. European.

That's right. There was a fiercely frowning woman, Bridget O'Connor, who kept house for William Carlisle who would bring the laundry to the general store to have it done when there were too many guests for her to keep up with. She had red hair and freckles and a terrible squint, and John had said that she was Irish, and therefore must be a drunk, but she never smelled of alcohol, only vinegar and soap. She had lost an eye and wore an eyepatch that always seemed to be sprinkled with dust or some other stain that faded into the skin of her face.

You had lusted after that eyepatch. You mean to be an actress someday.

But what was the boy's name doing in the book? And why had it been scraped out?

You turn the pages. You can read in Cantonese and a little Korean, and of course now in English. You think you could recognize Latin, and maybe Russian—all those backward letters.

The characters that were scraped off—at least, the ones you can see—are all in English. The rest of the characters make no sense whatsoever. They are full of swoops and slashes. You're not even sure whether the letters go from right to left or left to right. Sometimes they go up and down, sometimes they're tucked into circular spaces. Someone has inserted sketches throughout the text. A bowl, a spoon, a corked jar, a small animal that seems to have no eyes and a very long nose, a candleholder that looks like a lobster, a tree branch with a fruit like a raspberry that also grows feathers, a curved dagger, symbols that are clearly not text of the language that the book is written in, but something else altogether.

The last third of the book is blank. No way to tell whether it's finished—or if the book that was copied into it was simply shorter than the book it occupies.

You run your hands over the blank pages. Touching the inked-in letters feels wrong. Your throat tightens when you move your fingers toward them. But the blank pages are fine. It feels like touching a young man's cheek.

Close the cover. Now!

You close the cover and tuck the book behind you, under your handbag, not that it's large enough to conceal such a book.

The old man in the gray suit walks past your seat, glaring from side to side. He has a cane now, ivory-topped, and has left the other books behind, as well as his wool coat.

He looks at you. He looks right at you, and you shrink into your seat, giving him your widest, most frightened look. He is *angry.*

Don't give him the book.

You couldn't force yourself to move or speak, even if you wanted to. His eyes linger on you for a moment, and the toe of his leather shoe taps on the floor of the train car.

With the tip of his cane, he scrapes the floor under your seat.

"You haven't seen a book lying about, have you?" he asks.

You shake your head. It's as though he's released you from a spell—but only a little bit. The entire train car is hushed now. It feels as though cotton has been stuffed into your ears, muffling all sounds. None of the other passengers are talking or making a sound. You all feel it, the menace radiating from this man.

Why doesn't he see the book?

For the same reason that he didn't know that he had dropped it earlier, you suppose.

"Don't lie to me," he says. "You're the one who made me drop my books."

"I didn't mean to, sir," you say. "It was an accident. I was sleeping..."

He raises a hand and your throat closes on itself. "Tell me the truth."

"I was sleeping, sir, I'm so sorry."

You have a long history of saying things which, if technically true, aren't anything that your mother would approve of. Or actually believe.

His lips twitch. Above them is long mustache that must be his pride and joy, and eyebrows that have been carefully combed. Suddenly he looks elsewhere. The door of the car has opened, and a man in a dark suit has entered, a newspaper tucked under one arm and his circle-lensed glasses flashing in the carriage lights overhead.

The man in the gray suit draws back, glances at you again. His eyes slide over you. You are nobody, no one, nothing.

He turns around and leaves.

You reach over and touch the book: it is still there. But when you first glance at it, for a moment even you can't see it.

After a few moments you take your cigarette case out of your purse and withdraw one of the cigarettes. You spent some of your extra money buying them at the train station. In Atlanta, you roll your own unless someone buys them for you. You've tried to stay out of the habit entirely, but...sometimes temptation is too much to resist.

The man in the dark suit is squinting his way through the car, tilting his head this way and that as if he were wearing bifocals. The round glasses do seem to distort his face oddly through the lower halves.

You pull a matchbook out of your purse, tug one of the matches off, and close the cover on it. The snap and puff of flame draws the man's eyes toward you. They widen.

He's only a few steps away. You take out another cigarette with your fingertips, hold it to your lips, and light it on a second match. He sits next to you, and you pass him the cigarette. He takes it.

"So. What's a nice girl like you doing with a book like that?" he asks.

You lift an eyebrow. So this guy can see the book when the supposed owner of the book cannot.

"Why, is your name Jimmy O'Toole?"

His mouth opens. Then it closes again. "Where did you hear that name?"

"It's written in the book, that's all."

In the dim light of the train car he looks sick, sick to his stomach as the train sways around another corner.

"You read it?"

"Just the parts that had been scraped off, mister. I don't think anybody could read the rest of it. It isn't in any language that I ever heard of, anyway. So tell me, do you normally take cigarettes from strange women before you investigate their reading habits?"

You're trying to flirt, that's all. He's a cute guy, and you could use some amusement. You've been staring out into space, talking to yourself, and smoking too much, and you're not even halfway there yet. By the time you get to San Francisco, you'll go crazy.

"Where'd you find it?" he says, completely ignoring your questions and insinuations.

"Who are you, that you need to know?" you ask. You're not used to being completely ignored on a S.A. level. People generally at least acknowledge your efforts.

The guy pulls out a leather wallet and shows you a pot-metal badge inside: PINKERTON NATIONAL DETECTIVE AGENCY.

"Name's Soland," he says. "Marvin Soland."

"Shouldn't you be wearing that badge on your jacket?" you say.

"I'm not with the cops," he says.

"I didn't say you were, Mister Soland. So what do you need to know about this book for?"

A minute ago you wanted his company. Now you don't. His questions are getting under your skin. Too personal yet impersonal at the same time. If he doesn't start learning to treat you with some respect, you're going to dig your heels in. See if you don't.

"I need to know about it because it was stolen."

"Stolen, hah?" You take a drag on the cigarette. The tobacco's usually better if you roll your own but it isn't considered ladylike in public. "By the gentleman in the suit? Who is he?"

"His name is Henry Russell. The third."

You grunt.

"You've heard of him?"

The name is not unfamiliar to you. He comes from a plantation family, one that managed to hold onto its wealth, and one that would definitely find a way to make your life difficult if you turned this book over to anyone but him and he found out about it.

"So what if I have?"

Soland leaned back against the seat, blowing smoke upward. "Lady, I get that you're being cautious. But if he finds you with that book, he's gonna kill you."

"So just trust you and you'll take care of everything."

"Basically, yes."

You shake your head. Where could you hide a book like this? You could throw it out the window, that's about it.

You decide to take a risk. If it goes south, you could just give him the book. But it's starting to feel like you need to protect the book. It's like protecting a little kid. You do it without question.

Not so little.

"So why couldn't he see the book?"

Soland straightens up. "What?"

"You saw him. He was standing next to me when you came into the car. He stumbled when he was coming through here earlier and dropped the book, then came back to look for it. He looked right at it. Why couldn't he see it?"

"I don't know."

You raise an eyebrow and exhale smoke toward the ceiling. That's not a statement you can believe, not at all. You say, "I think the book is magic. And I think you know all about that."

"Magic? It doesn't exist."

"Don't lie to me. I've seen some strange things in my life."

That's more or less a lie, although there have been a couple of times when your mother's superstitions got to you.

"You seem...perceptive."

He says it like it has a special meaning. You smirk at him. "I seem perceptive...but not perceptive enough to see through your excuses, right? Tell me one more thing. Why did Russell leave the train car when he saw you?"

"Because he knows I'm with the Pinkertons."

"And why would the Pinkertons send out one of their agents after a stolen book? Aren't you busy with real crimes?"

"This is a real crime, lady."

"It's just a book." You run a hand across the cover. "I might keep it myself."

Soland hesitates. "If you knew what that book really was, lady, you wouldn't. You'd throw it at me and tell me to burn it."

"Black magic?"

"The blackest." He seems to have no problem admitting it now.

"What, summoning demons? Blood rituals? Sacrificing virgins at midnight, just like in the pulps? Creatures from other dimensions?"

"Stock market."

You tip your head back and laugh. "The *stock market*?"

"That one. Jimmy was good with numbers."

You feel icicles running over your skin. He can't be saying what it sounds like he's saying.

"Jimmy O'Toole disappeared from Staten Island three years ago, when he was thirteen. His mother worked at a laundry and his father was dead. A vulnerable kid, you could say. He was a math genius, though. Working far and above what most adults could do. Or so they tell me. He had a hobby of playing the stock market with the papers. No money to put in it but what people gave him, and he'd already built it up to a thousand bucks. You see?"

"No."

"He disappeared. Then someone starts playing the market the same way Jimmy did. Again, I'm no math whiz, I couldn't tell you how anybody worked that out. But they assure me that it was so. They tracked the player down and found Russell, working behind a couple of intermediaries. It took a while. Three years."

"So?"

"So they didn't find Jimmy. They just found that book."

Your hand's still touching the cover. It gives a little shiver.

"So? It's just a book."

He exhales again. "It's a book with Jimmy's name scraped out of it."

"It was Jimmy's book?"

"Look, lady. I know you're not dense. They kidnapped Jimmy, turned him into a book, scraped out the parts that were *him*, and turned him into a slave with the spells inside."

"You're crazy."

"Yeah. Crazy. Now give me the book."

He pulls a gun out of his pocket. You can't run. He's got you pinned in against the seat...and even if you did manage to climb out over the top, you couldn't drag that book with you. It's too heavy. Heavy enough that you'd struggle to carry it in both hands.

And you know you can't leave it behind.

He's just a kid, after all.

※

You turn the page, then lift up your hand to look at it, turning it from front to back. It's older than you remember, a bit papery across the back of your hand, with several liver spots. The nails are clipped neatly. White clouds float across the pink nailbeds. The skin around them is wrinkled but smooth.

This is not how you remember yourself. A moment ago you were a young Chinese woman in the 1920s. Now you're someone else.

But who?

You dimly remember leaning your head back against the window. You've always had trouble staying awake at two o'clock. The older you get, the more inclined you are to just lean back and take a nap. Your granddaughters were chattering at each other and looking at their phones like you didn't exist.

Oh well, only their last trip with their only living grandparent…you were reading something just before you fell asleep.

Ah.

You were reading the story and you fell asleep, and then you started dreaming it. You have to wonder what the main character, the Chinese woman, would think about being dreamed by an old man. Probably she'd think about it with a smirk on her face. That's how she strikes you, as shouldering the vicissitudes of life with a half-turn of the lips.

There were worse ways to live.

But now you're not in the dream, you're back on the train. But you're not quite awake, either. Either that or your granddaughters have gone missing and everyone's clothing has gone back a century. The men are all wearing old-fashioned suits. The women aren't wearing jeans and tee-shirts, but skirts and hats.

You'd like to feel nostalgia for times gone past, but you can't. Those were bad times, too; it's just that nobody says so.

You're still in the story—or the dream, maybe. Wouldn't it be funny, though, if this were a book? And you were being read by a reader, who is being read by another reader? Some might say the final reader is God, but you like the idea of an infinite chain of readers better. At least, right now you do.

Your back is stiff and you set the book aside and stretch, then get up and shuffle toward the dining car. If this is an old-fashioned train, then there should be a dining car and you mean to take advantage of it, dream or not. You find it and sit at one of the tables. The white tablecloth in front of you is spotless. A black man comes to ask whether you have coffee, and you're staring at the tablecloth, thinking, that's going to stain. The black man is in a white jacket and you feel your face sink as you tell him that yes, you'd like coffee, coffee and a rugelach, if they're available.

These were not good times, not for anybody. Sooner or later you will wake up next to your granddaughters playing games on their phones and you'll take a moment to embrace them both. And then you'll tell them to get off their phones for a minute and appreciate the scenery outside the car, because you won't be able to help yourself.

A few moments later, the black man returns with coffee and a Danish. It's good coffee, although of course not the best. But for a train in the middle of a dream, it's pretty good.

Is this the same train as in the story? No, no, it couldn't be. Even if your dream were describing the train in the story, it wouldn't be the same train. The thought of a unicorn might be a real thought, but the thought of a thought of a unicorn isn't the same thought as the thought of a unicorn, last time you checked.

It's important to keep these things straight.

◆

If only Jimmy's book were smaller, you could stuff it in your purse and make a run for it. As it is, with a gun aimed at you in a train car after midnight and a massive tome by your side that appears and reappears by some will of its own—

Soland the Pinkerton says, "What happened to the book?"

Your hand is on the book; it's still right there. You glance at it. Apparently it's gone invisible for Soland. If there are sides to be chosen, then it's chosen yours, whatever that is.

You can't help but wonder if that's the right choice, but then you remember Soland talking about destroying the book. Which you already know that you could never do.

There has to be a way to change the book back.

Your first instinct is to ask Soland if it's possible, but you already know that he's just going to tell you know, given his attitude from earlier. He sees the book as the monstrosity that needs to be destroyed, not the magicians who made a kid into one. He'd probably deny it—but you know how that works. When someone with power does something monstrous, it's easier to shift the blame onto the victim. It's easier to find someone safe to hurt—and a victim is, by definition, just the right type.

"I don't know," you say disingenuously. "It vanished."

You pat around on the seat.

"Where did it go? Did it fall off the seat?"

Soland's face goes stiff with anger. "Give me the book," he says.

"It's gone."

And it *is* gone. Either the book has decided against you as well as Soland—or it has some other plan.

"Stop playing with me."

You roll your eyes and stand up, clasping your purse to your side. "Go on, switch seats with me. Try to find it yourself."

You're taking a risk, but what else can you do?

Soland switches seats with you and starts patting around, looking for the book. He doesn't find it. He twists around and pats around with his hands on the floor around your seat. The few people who are still awake look at the two of you. Obviously you've lost something. Fortunately the seats next to yours hold sleepers, or nobody.

The door opens at the far end of the car and, even before you see who it is, you duck into one of the empty seats and put your head down, pulling your hat over your face and staring out the window.

The car has acquired that particular hush that you heard last when Henry Russell III was trying to convince you to give up the book. You keep your head down and pretend to sleep.

Footsteps approach. Soland seems oblivious; he's still half-under the seat, searching for the book. And not finding it.

The footsteps hesitate when they approach your seat. Russell has come to pressure you again, you can tell. He hasn't given up on the idea that you know something.

But then he hears Soland moving around in the seat in front of you. Soland, who earlier seemed to make Russell turn and flee. Soland, who now can't see anything other than the dusky dust under the seat. His hand brushes your shoe, then grabs it. He must think the leather belongs to the book.

You let your foot slide forward, and Soland grunts with disgust.

Russell begins to mutter under his breath.

The train car shakes.

You open your eyes but try not to move otherwise. You're looking down at your legs, the velvet of the seat in front of you, the edge of your purse, a little bit of the train car wall. Maybe an inch of darkness that makes up the window.

They all seem to ripple.

In the seat in front of you, Soland freezes, then slowly twists around on the cloth, sitting up straight.

"Russell," he says, an angry, challenging tone to his voice.

Russell is still muttering to himself, in a language that you don't understand but that sounds wrong.

Soland starts muttering in what might be the same language too.

And then the train really starts to shake.

The light flicker, glass crackles, fragile things fall on the floor.

The sleepers wake. "What's going on?"

You decide that you'd bring more attention to yourself by pretending to be asleep at this point, and you straighten up slowly.

The two men are staring at each other, muttering under their breaths. Suddenly Russell makes a small sweeping motion with one hand. Almost a flick. The train gives a terrible jolt as he does it, as if it had come off its rails and fallen back again.

And Soland flickers.

The backs of Soland's shoulders tense, then move. You suspect that he's making the same gesture that Russell just did, too.

The train lurches again—not as much—and Russell flickers. His face goes paler than before, his cheeks slack, as if he has received a serious blow but refuses to be distracted by it. He makes another flicking gesture.

Again the train jolts.

And this time, when Soland flickers, he comes back just a little different. You wouldn't have noticed—

—except that you can see a light shining through his hat.

His muttering falters. The deadly silence in the train car breaks. Someone is sobbing. Others are demanding, over and over again, to know what is going on.

The two men are trying to kill each other, that's what. Or something worse, from the looks on their faces. A long hatred is coming to fruition. The train car shuddered again, but nobody screams. Nobody so much as whispers a protest.

Over and over again the two men flick their fingers. But what happens to them isn't the same.

Russell stays the same, to the increasing rage, panic, and dismay of Soland.

Soland...disappears.

One flick at a time, he gets more and more translucent, until you can see completely through him.

And then he's gone.

Russell takes a deep, shuddering breath. He looks right at you, but his eyes are glazed over from the effort of what he's done.

"I know you're here, Jimmy," he says. "Come out, come out, wherever you are..."

You catch movement out of the corner of your eye. The other passengers are slumping down in their seats, as if suddenly oppressed by sleep.

You do, too, just letting yourself go completely slack, until you *do* feel the weight pressing down on you, and it turns the world black around you.

It feels sweet, like the best slumber you've ever had—like sleeping in on a weekday morning under the best, fluffiest quilt, a stolen holiday.

You sigh. The train rocks you to sleep.

<hr>

You wake up a few hours later. It's still dark. Your body resents the fact that you've forced it out of what was the best sleep it's ever had, outside your mother's ever-complaining womb. Before you come all the way out of slumber, you remember a fragment of a dream—you're talking to a scrawny red-headed boy named Jimmy. The one who got turned into a book. He tries to explain something that it's vital that you remember. But of course you don't.

A look around under your heavily-lidded eyes reveals nothing unusual, and your purse tucked under your elbow. You sit up and look around: no Russell. And, in the seat in front of yours, definitely no Soland.

Did you dream it all? The book, talking to Soland, Soland's disappearance?

You snort to yourself. It sounds like one of the ghost stories that your father tells. He's fond of those stupid tales about ghosts and cats and the railroad traveler who wakes up to discover that it's all been a dream.

Which means that you're not easily fooled. Anybody can argue whatever they like, but you know what you saw, and there's nobody who can convince you otherwise—not even *you*.

You hold your hands in front of you and make the flicking gesture. It reminded you of something...what?

Nobody else is awake, it seems. After a while you decide to take a walk around the car. When you stand up, your watch slides off your wrist and into your lap. Your hat is askew—even though you had it firmly pinned.

You've been searched but not robbed while you were asleep. You put yourself back together and start wandering the car. The other passengers are solidly asleep. You shake their shoulders but there's no returning from where they've gone, not yet.

When you're done, you return to your seat—not your original seat, but the new one—and search your handbag. Inside is a small notebook with a leather cover, the parchment pages folded across the seam and sewed with sinew. You flip it open—Jimmy O'Toole remains in scraped, faded letters on the first page.

"That's where you've been hiding," you say. You riffle through the pages. The arcane and occult writing stares back at you, practically blotting out the other letters underneath.

Sad. But what to do about it?

"Are you just trying to escape? What do you need me to do?" you ask. Of everyone on the train, you're the one that he picked, and rightly so: you've always had a soft spot for those in need. You're not stupid, though. You keep your ears pricked for the tall tale...the kind that people tell to others in order to gain sympathy, and the kind that people tell to themselves, in order to keep their self-respect. Both can be deadly to anyone trying to help.

Help me.

You recognize that inner voice as something that doesn't belong to you, now. You had your suspicions earlier, but it was too busy to satisfy your curiosity at the time.

You wonder whether Jimmy knows what's going on around him...how conscious is he, as a book? What can he do?

You keep wondering.

"How can I help you?" you whisper.

Hide me until we reach San Francisco. Then take me to one of the magicians there. She can bring me back to life. I just know it! Russell talked about her all the time.

"Who?"

He tells you the name, and you nod. Of course it's your mother.

On the one hand, everything should go smoothly; Russell has already overlooked the book more than once. On the other hand, "should" is not a word that you've learned to rely upon. The unforgiveable mistakes of this life almost always start out with that word.

"What else can I do to help you? What should I do, for example, if Russell returns and sees you?"

He won't.

"What is he doing on this train anyway?"

He heard that the magician was dying. He wanted to see her one last time, to try to convince her to give up her books.

"And he was going to use you to convince her?"

He and—

The book goes quiet. *Too* quiet.

"Yes?"

Nothing.

You make a face. "If you don't tell me what's going on, I'll drop you on the floor and leave you for some Iowa farmer to pick up. See how well you do with *him* for a while. I think he'll buckle. He'll give you right back to Russell of his own free will. He has too much to lose. Me? I can afford to take a few risks."

There's another magician on the train. With another book.

The door of the train car behind you opens.

⸻ ◈ ⸻

You close the cover of the book. Now you're somewhere else, not on the 1920s train, not on the old-fashioned train car from the 1880s. It feels more like a modern metro train, the kind that runs along the backsides of city streets, underneath buildings, and over bridges. The seats are hard plastic.

You don't have granddaughters—you're only thirty-four.

This time.

You remember being a grandfather, a white guy, possibly Jewish. Was that you, or was that in the book you were reading just now? You look at the book and it's a Judith Krantz, which is not a book that you would have been reading in the first place. You momentarily suspect that you drifted off and some joker swapped out the book you had been reading with this one. But what that book would have been, you can't recall.

You've always had a soft spot for books, whether they're waterlogged fifty-cent second-hand paperbacks or fifteenth-century manuscripts, but it's rare that you find one that truly catches your interest. It's like the difference between people-watching and falling in love. Some books stay with you forever.

Judith Krantz? You set it aside.

Most of the people around you, if they read at all, read on their phones, either slumped in a C-shape against the back of the plastic seats, leaning forward with their elbows on their knees, or turned sideways with their feet sticking out into the aisle, which they pull up onto the seat with them when someone tries to pass—without even seeming to notice. When the cars fill up, the readers straighten up, tuck their elbows in, and lean away from everyone around them. They tend to take the window seats. And they never seem to miss their stations.

You read real, paper books, sitting up straight and with your ankles crossed. Where most of the people around you are slovenly, your clothes are ironed. A rarity in this day and age. It's the little things.

Now that you've set the Judith Krantz aside like an awkward seatmate, you need something to read. You dig through the handbag on your lap. Inside is a small leather journal and you get a flash of the 1920s train, and you think, I wonder if this is Jimmy's book. *You open the front cover. The pages feel softer than you expected, not paper but parchment, and yes, there's a ghostly name on the inside front cover.*

But, unlike the story you were reading, you can make out the other words, the ones that were printed in red ink. You can read them but they don't make sense:

The hypnotic sound of the train wheels against the iron rails has lulled you into a half-slumber. The half of you that isn't asleep is having trouble remembering that the soft thumping sound comes from the wheels hitting the rail joints isn't really a heartbeat. The other half is dreaming of someone calling your name, trying to wake you up.

Wasn't that the beginning of the other book? What would happen if you kept reading this one—would you pop in and out of the different levels of the story until you looped back around to here, and had to keep reading the same story over and over again?

It almost makes you want to pick up the Judith Krantz instead. You might not be an escapist reader but you certainly don't read in order to make your head hurt.

———◆———

Don't turn around, don't turn around.

You don't turn around. Instead you tuck the little notebook back in your purse. You have to trust that Jimmy will do whatever he can to defend himself. You're just there to play stupid.

It's still dark.

Footsteps come toward you down the train car, and a person settles himself into the seat across from you. Someone is already sitting there, as a matter of fact, a small old white woman with large eyes, a ridiculous broad-brimmed straw hat, and a fluffy white scarf wrapped around her shoulders and throat in a way that looks almost like a drift of snow. She's awake and staring at the man who's just settled himself in the seat.

A pair of black-and-white wing-tipped shoes, a gray suit two shades darker than Russell's that he tugs up at the knees as he sits, and a razor-sharp face. He looks Japanese, one of the new class of businessmen who work for international firms and leave their families behind without a glance back. He has a gold watch on a chain in his waistcoat pocket, and a longish haircut, sleek with Brilliantine.

You give him the broad kind of smile that any pretty girl would give upon seeing a handsome man: not quite predatory, but not exactly disinterested either, should there be drinks and supper provided.

"Hiya, Handsome."

He clucks his tongue, as if you had just made a mistake. "What your mother would say if she could see you now."

"I know my mother. She'd say, 'Ask him if he's married.'"

He chuckles. "I think you know why I'm here."

"I'm flattered." You cross, then recross your ankles.

He holds out his hand. "The book?"

You try not to do anything stupid, like say, "What book?" Too many choices flash through your head at the same time for you to sort through them. You grab one out of thin air.

"What's in it for me?" you say.

He grins, showing off perfectly white, perfectly spaced teeth. "Fame. Riches. Anything."

"I want a Hollywood career," you say. "And none of this maids-and-seductresses who die in the second reel business. I want to be a star. A real star."

"And you'll give us the book?'

"Yeah, after my first major picture comes out and I'm rich."

"So wealth *and* fame."

"No good being wealthy without fame, or vice versa."

"Why didn't you give the book to Mr. Russell, my compatriot?"

"The white-haired guy? Because he was rude. And he didn't offer me anything. Not a red cent. He just loomed over me and looked angry...I don't work so well with threats."

The man across from you nods as though he were taking you seriously.

"Hey, what's your name?" you ask.

His smile goes a little flat. "It's not important for you to know. The deal would be concluded through Mr. Russell, not myself."

"I guessed that," you admit. "But...him I'm not so sure of. You seem a lot nicer and more trustworthy. I'd rather make a deal with you."

You hold out your hand and he shakes it without hesitation. "Aragaki Hideo."

That's a lucky break...we have both their names now. But don't tell him your name.

Aragaki reminds you of one of your father's old stories, the bottle of scorpions who kill each other off until only one is left—leaving only the king of the scorpions, which turns into a demon when the bottle is opened.

"Pleased to meetcha." You lean back, letting your hand slip out of his.

He's looking you over through half-lidded eyes. What is he up to, you want to know.

Trying to think what kind of book you would make.

You shudder. In that instant, you make up your mind: you're going to get this book back to your mother and see if she can do anything about the way Jimmy has been treated. Maybe he'll stop planting ideas in the back of your head. Maybe your mother can even work out a way to get him free.

You've always been good at making things up as you go along; why stop now?

You can't get off the train now; maybe later, you could lose yourself in a train station and go weeping to the conductor that the train to San Francisco has left you behind, and oh oh oh...

You're pretty good with tears. It would work. Then take the next train and head straight home. Avoid temptation and be a good girl for once.

It's a plan that has never really worked for you before, however.

Aragaki says, "And your name is?"

"I could tell you, but I'd be lying."

He insists; you tell him the name you've got picked out as your stage name. He accepts it and you feel a tug on your heart, as though Aragaki were weaving a spiderweb around you and one of the strands had brushed your chest.

But the name that you gave him wasn't the one your family gave you; it wasn't the one that you grew up with, that was mocked by your classmates and shouted in disappointment by your mother. This name might contain all your hopes and dreams—but the other one is stronger.

He knows that he's caught *something* of your spirit with the name, though, and that's good enough for him. He gives you a satisfied smile, says that he'll be back soon with Russell's counteroffer, and leaves the car.

You take out the notebook and a pencil. Pencil can be erased—you might be literally writing on someone's soul but you have to be able to communicate with perfect clarity right now, no mistakes. In the margins, you write, *That was the other magician, right?*

Words swim up out of the unintelligible red ink.

Right.

You write, *Brrr.*

I told you not to give him your name. They have a private car...they're going to hold the ritual.

What ritual?

The one that turns you into a book. They can do a lot of things to you, with a name.

I didn't give them my real name. Just my stage name. And I don't even use that very often.

It's probably still enough.

You make a face. *No, it's just a stage name.*

You're the expert, then?

You snort. *What do you suggest?*

Either stopping the ritual or killing yourself.

Is it so bad, being a book?

In answer, the page turned blood red, erasing every word on the page—leaving only the faint pencil marks from your half of the conversation.

After a few minutes you're pretty sure that Aragaki's not coming back to "negotiate." Whatever it was he wanted from you he got—and the only thing he got from you was your stage name.

You curse under your breath. Jimmy's little leather notebook is still covered in red ink. Fine. You're on your own. You quickly take an eraser to your pencil marks. It might not make a difference, but seeing them on Jimmy's pages makes you feel a little ill.

You stand up just as the train starts going around a corner, so you pause to hold the back of the seat as everything sways. It's still solid darkness, and almost everyone has gone back to sleep, even with all the running in and out of train cars so late at night. Few eyes would meet yours even if they were awake, not for longer than a second or two. You tell yourself that you're used to it but that's a lie; you'll never be used to feeling like you're somehow taboo.

The train comes out of the curve and you start walking toward the back of the train. You wonder what it would be like, being a book. Maybe Jimmy's making a bigger deal out of it than it really is. You get to do the thing that you're good at. And it would be a kind of immortality.

Then again, maybe the process of becoming a book is so traumatic that you never get over it. Maybe that's Jimmy's problem. He's a soldier constantly reliving the war.

The train gives a lurch, and dizziness hits you.

Without thinking, you look down at your hand to make sure it's not going transparent the way that Pinkerton agent did. But you're still all there.

How do I stop them? You try to focus the answer toward Jimmy. There's no answer. That's gratitude for you. You're only trying to save his life or something.

You try to remember if your mother ever said anything about books, magic books. You don't think so. Whatever involvement she has in that world, she hasn't shared it with you.

The compartment door sounds too loud when you open it. You step through the short passage between cars. The night plucks at you. You reach across to the handhold on the far side, then step across the swaying platform to the next train car. You jerk open the other car door, step through, then close it behind you.

This is a better class of car, where the seats are further apart and have been folded down to make beds. Everyone here is asleep, too. A pair of cute girls lean against each other, snoring. A prim colored woman eyes you briefly, then looks back down at her book. It looks almost like—but no. Jimmy's book is in your purse.

You keep moving through the train, headed the same direction that Russell and Aragaki went.

The dining car is next. An old man looks up at you, opens his mouth as if to speak—then moves on. And then a first-class type of car, in which there are private compartments. The blinds have been drawn behind the glass. Most of them are dark. One of them is still lit.

You hesitate in front of the door, then tap softly at it. "Hello? Mr. Aragaki? Is that you?"

You half-hope that nobody answers, or an angry stranger's voice does.

Aragaki says, "My dear! I was about to return to you, but—" The door slides open, and his carefully bland, handsome face appears. Behind him you can see Mr. Russell, sitting on the edge of the lower bed. His fists are clenched in his lap and his eyes are bloodshot. A large book sits across from him. The color of the leather is different but it's the same kind of book as Jimmy O'Connor. A blood-red ribbon marks a page.

"Come in, come in," Aragaki says.

You give them your most winning smile and step inside.

The door slides closed behind you. The train sways again, another turn in the tracks. You're glad that it didn't do that while you were crossing from car to car. Rolling along so quickly through the night in the middle of nowhere, it almost feels as though if you had stumbled, you wouldn't have fallen from the train.

You would have disappeared in the darkness.

"Have you decided about the deal?" you ask, peremptorily. "Will you give me what I want or not?"

You're playing things a little too brashly. But on purpose. Which doesn't make it less of a risk.

"Of course, of course," Aragaki says.

But Russell isn't having it. "Why should that little chink get something out of this? All she did was find my damn book. I wouldn't be surprised if she didn't trip me in the first place. Thief, that's what she is. She gets *nothing*."

You're shocked by the epithet; it feels almost like a physical blow. Negotiations haven't been going very well. You sit down across from Russell and lift the other book onto your lap. As you touch the leather you feel another presence. One that is staying silent—for now. There are two books to be saved here, not just one, and everything just got harder.

"One takes one's opportunities where one may," you say reprovingly. "I stole nothing. I found something...something that may or may not belong to you. You might take a little effort to convince me. Otherwise I might just find another Pinkerton agent..."

You let your voice trail off.

The old white man finally looks up at you and acknowledges your existence. "*What* Pinkerton agent? He doesn't exist!"

And then he chortles to himself, as if he's told the world's most amusing joke. One that you're too stupid and ignorant and Chinese to get.

You smile.

You have put yourself inside the dragon's mouth, you have entered the lion's den.

"Oh, I remember him quite well," you say. "I know where he went...*and* I might have a way to bring him back."

You make a plucking gesture in the air, showing off your red-nailed manicure, as if picking a peach from a tree.

The old man chortles again. "You know nothing."

You hate to drag your mother into this, but it seems as though nothing else would do. You give them your mother's name and ask them if *she* would know.

Russell's eyes narrow and you see Aragaki shift at his position, now blocking the door. You run your fingers along the spine of the book, then along the top of the pages, where the red ribbon marks a page. It is toward the back of the book—an appendix.

You open the book to the marked page.

Inside are words that you can't read, and a drawing of a book with its pages open. You're not sure how to bluff your way forward from here.

Probably, though...neither one of them knows Chinese.

In a soft yet terrible voice, you start chanting one of your father's old stories, about Yu the Great turning into a dragon in order to battle the monsters causing the land to flood.

Aragaki tries to snatch the book out of your hands, but the book refuses to move. It presses down on your legs, grinding your heels into the floor—it's as though you were supporting a book made of stone.

Help me. Please, miss. Help me!

A little girl's voice. Your nostrils flare and you begin to chant more loudly.

How many hours until you will arrive at the next station? How much longer will you have to keep up your bluffing, until you have a chance to escape?

"Enough!" Aragaki shouts. He says your stage name and makes a gesture—the same one that Russell made before, the page-turning gesture—and you feel the book sinking into your legs.

Contemptuously, you flick your fingers back at him. *Skip to the end of the book, Aragaki Hideo,* you think viciously. *This one's not holding my interest.*

Aragaki turns pale, almost white, and his eyes roll back in his head. He's going to faint.

Russell inhales, and you turn toward him. Slowly, you lick one fingertip and start getting ready to turn to the next page...

You're bluffing. But Russell isn't. He shouts your stage name, starts chanting gibberish, and makes the page-turning gesture quickly, over and over again. The invisible pages blur as they are turned...you feel as though you are sliding out of your own skin.

One moment you are there, and the next you hear the thump of the book falling onto the sleeping car floor as you disappear. You have been turned out of your world and into a different one.

But where?

⚬

You're sitting in a train next to the window. Your hands are lying palm-up in your lap, as if in supplication or you were wearing handcuffs. You know what your mother would say: you got yourself into this mess. You have to get yourself out.

The girl next to you is eleven. You're sixteen. There are another four of you in this train car, all of you trying not to cry. It's been a long day. You're being moved away from a prairie reservation to somewhere in California. The boss keeps trying to convince you that this is a good thing. You'll be able to make a lot more money there and pay off your debts. You owe the boss a lot of money for getting you out of a bad situation. The only thing is, from the way he keeps reminding you about it, you're starting to wonder if you don't really and you could get out of it. How much are train tickets worth, anyway? One man's sweaty back grinding at you? Ten men's?

The girl next to you, who is eleven, says, "Don't cry. You just dropped your book. I'll get it."

She bends over and picks it up for you. You say thank you and try to read some more, but it's kind of pointless. Reading lets you escape from your situation for a little while—but it always brings you right back to where you started. You've always liked books but they don't change anything.

If you thought it would help to stand up and shout, "Get me out of here, I'm being kidnapped by my pimp!" you would. But what's the best that could happen?

They could take you back to your mom and your stepdad, that's what.

And the stories that the girl next to you says are even worse than yours. If you say something now, she goes back "home" too.

This can't go on forever. It can't.

It can, says the book in your lap. If you just let stories happen to you. Then they stay the same forever.

Yeah, whatever, book. Like you know about changing the words on your own pages.

You feel like you've read too many books lately. You're too many people, all of them trapped inside the depressed shell of a dispossessed Sioux, and none of them tell you what to do or how to escape. Tell the boss that you have to pee and jump off the side of the train, that's about it. You'll hit the ground at a hundred and fifty miles an hour and every bone in your body will shatter. They'll ram into your internal organs like spears.

Help me. Help me.

At first you think the voice is coming from the girl beside you. But she's the one looking at you with concern.

"Are you okay?"

You shake your head. Not like "no," but like "not now, don't talk now." The girl looks over her shoulder at the boss.

The boss is watching you.

You look back down at your book and try to start reading again. That story about the pretty Chinese woman, she reminds you of Anna May Wong, the Chinese film star from the Twenties and Thirties. You hope that the heroine of the story gets to become an actress. Someone with such an attitude, such reckless bravery, should get what she wants.

You wouldn't mind being her for a while.

In fact of all the people you've read about, it's yourself that you want to be the least. You're just a lame runaway who's sleeping her way to freedom, and you're so bad at it that you're not going to be able to pay off a tenth of your debt before you end up dead in a gutter.

The book in your lap has a leather cover. All right, that's cool. Just like in the story. So what about it? What if this is one of those magic books, made out of someone's soul and flesh?

It's not. You know it's not because the ink is black and you can read the words and it was published in 1993. So much for ancient magics.

You still raise your hand as if to turn a page in the air, though. What the hell, you know? Why not. What's the boss going to do, beat you for making a secret gesture to the back of the train seat in front of you?

Probably. He's that kind of boss.

You say your own name and swipe your finger across the air and nothing happens. The boss raises an eyebrow at you and the girl next to you pokes you in the side with her elbow.

"Knock it off."

Hah, your fingers are too dry. So dry that they're chapped. You lick your finger and try again. No hope, just the perversity of the doomed.

You turn the page.

You flip yourself back into the private train car with Russell and Aragaki. Aragaki has fainted. Russell is struggling to his feet—he's clutching the other book in his hands.

"What are you—where did you—"

Wherever you went, you brought something back with you. *Look at that Japanese dude on the floor again.*

It doesn't sound like Jimmy O'Connor; it doesn't even sound like Aragaki's book, which called you "miss."

Aragaki is sitting in a pool of blood. You push back the lapels of his jacket and see a knife still stuck into his chest. Sloppy. Russell thinks he can page himself somewhere else and leave a mysterious murder behind for the attendants.

He's killed Aragaki and stolen the book made out of human skin and soul. You think that makes him a bad man.

"Put it down," you say.

"I don't know how you made it back here but—"

Put it down, says the new voice. *Or I will slit your throat.*

Russell puts the book down. You think that this should be harder, defeating a magician who plays with reality the way that screenwriters play with a script. And if you hadn't scared the man so badly, maybe it would be. He wasn't expecting you to come back.

Help me, you say to the books. *I can't do this without you.*

You say his name, raise your hand, and start turning pages. You have his number. Russell flickers. He raises his hand to start turning your pages—you slap him across the face. He blinks. You keep turning the pages, making mysterious random statements to keep him distracted: "I am stronger than you can even dream, little man. I have read *such lives* that you cannot even imagine. What are you? A slaver. A slaver of men and a slaver...of...books."

The last three pages were like turning brick walls but you do it.

Russell is gone. Where the books have put him is anyone's guess.

———◆———

Later, you discuss the situation with your mother. She tries to change the subject and wants to know when you're getting married. But you remember about being a grandfather and know that she's only nagging at you—she'll still love you, even if you didn't drag a fiancé home with you.

"It'll happen when it happens," you say.

"When are you going back to Georgia?"

"Who knows? Maybe I'll finally get lucky out here."

"As an actress?"

You shake your head. "I might try writing."

She gives you an approving look. "What about the man who died when you were in his train car?"

"I didn't kill him."

"Were you sleeping with him?"

You don't tell your mother that you think he might have been Japanese, with a name like Aragaki. She might not take it well.

"Tell me about the books," you insist. You can keep coming back to this all night, even if your mother *is* dying of cancer.

"They're dead. Nothing you can do about it to bring them back."

"But Jimmy said..."

"Those books will say anything. They still think they're alive half the time. They don't remember getting skinned alive."

"Was that what they were going to do to me?"

"Oh, sure."

The two of you are drinking tea at a tea shop; your mother looks wasted and pale, as if the doctors had been leeching out her blood. Her flesh has melted off her bones. Not that she was ever very large. You believe her when she says the tumor is shrinking: all she would have had to do was name it, and turn a few pages. But the hole left behind? That you're not sure about.

"Where did I go, Mother? When Russell turned me out of the page?"

"Somewhere else."

"Where?"

Your mother gestures at the tea set, and you fill your mother's cup from the fair cup. "Up," she says.

"Up?"

"If a person in a story reads a story, then where does that go? Down. You went up."

"To the person reading the book."

"More than one person can read a book," your mother says. She's so stubborn. She never tells you what you want to know; she wants you to learn things the hard way instead. It's maddening.

"And when I came back?"

"You brought a little of them back with you."

You nod seriously, as if you understand the implications of what your mother says. That's about all there is that you can do: pretend to understand, and she might let a secret or two fall. A hint. A clue.

"Are you a sorcerer, too?" you ask. "Have you ever made one of those books?"

"Me? No!" Your mother seems offended, which is something of a relief. "I know how to read them, that is all. I try to keep them safe."

"If they can't be brought back to life, what do you do with them? Destroy them?"

Your mother shudders theatrically. This weak woman, whose life is as thin and frail as if she were half-turned out of reality already.

"No. I just read them," your mother says. She sinks in her chair and your heart skips a beat. You didn't want to come here with her; she's too fragile. "I read them out loud so that their stories don't disappear. Someone is always upwards from us. Someone is always reading. No one is ever lost forever, as long as someone is reading."

"But they're dead," you say.

"Yes. But everyone likes to know that their story isn't over. That they are still remembered. That their spirits are honored."

Your mother flicks her fingers in the air, and the tea shop flickers, and becomes her bedroom, thick with the smell of herbs and medicines.

"I'm tired now," she says. "Help me into bed."

You help her out of her chair. It seems perfectly natural, what she has just done. You tuck her in, and kiss her on the forehead.

"I don't normally like to skip ahead to the good parts," she says. "But I'm tired."

You take the Jimmy O'Connor book out of your purse. It grows from a small notebook to something more easily read, with larger pages and letters.

"Would you like me to read one of the new ones to you?"

"Yes."

The letters in the book have changed. The ones you couldn't read—they're faded and scraped down to ghosts. The real letters, the ones with Jimmy's story, have grown stronger. They're bright and clear and you're not sure what language they're written in. Truth, you hope.

Those are the ones that you begin to read.

⸻⬦⸻

The Actress had clutched the Spy's hand throughout her tale. The young woman and the old man seemed a mismatched pair, and strangers who had met only twice previously, I think. But he was truly kind to her, and that's not something you see every day.

When she was done telling her tale, she said, "Of course it didn't happen exactly like that, and now it's too late. But..." She looked around the room at the rest of us. Her shoulder sank. "You don't believe me. Nobody believes me."

The Vampire cleared his throat, cutting off a callous comment from the Dame. "My dear, perhaps it is different where you came from, but at this table, we are not concerned with questions of belief or unbelief. We are here to evaluate your skill as a teller of tales—as a liar."

She accepted a kerchief from the Spy and used it to dab her face. "But I told you the truth. Mostly."

The Vampire nodded. "Exactly. 'Mostly.' In some way, each of us has told a tale that contains a great deal of the truth. More truth than most people could stand to tell, if it were not couched in lies."

She frowned at him. "I don't understand."

The Vampire looked at the Detective, who shrugged carelessly, then at me.

I didn't know what to say, but I felt like I had to say something.

I chewed on the inside of my cheek, trying to sort my thoughts out, then blurted, "There's this tradition down in the South a-among l-l-landowners. They would get together on certain days every once in a while and catch up on all the local news and gossip. Always at the same place, that would set up a big table for them to meet at. They would call the table a 'liar's table,' because it had heard so many lies."

My voice was hoarse, either because I'd been talking too much, or because it had been a long night, or because I was coming down with something.

"This isn't a storyteller's contest, not really. It's a b-bunch of...I don't know? Special, uh, people...anyway, they get together to catch up on the news? But they've been around so long that they don't know how to tell news anymore, only stories. A-and sometimes they let people like us come to the table so they can remember what it's like? To be people?"

I looked around the room, my shoulders pulled in tight.

The Vampire, he was a rich man, but he was also—literally, I believed—a Vampire. The Dame, well, if someone told me she had been dancing in temples since Babylon, I would have believed it. Or at least not disbelieved it. Dom had said he came from the fae—sort of. The three of them had told the first three stories, too.

Whether Madame Ixnay, the Detective, the Spy, or the Good Doctor were something...odd...I didn't know. I didn't think so. I think the rest of us were all more or less regular folks who had got caught up in something strange, and found—or been brought to—the liar's table because we wouldn't squeal, and could still believe in stories, at least mostly. I did wonder whether Madame Ixnay came from the future, or if the Detective had come back from there.

The Vampire looked at me without blinking, and I blushed.

Dom was nodding. "Yes, dot's it. Some of the old ones, dey are gone now, because they forgot what it was like. I cannot say how many of my brudders are turned to stone, because they did not remember the hot blood of life."

A smile flashed across the Vampire's lips. "Just so."

The Dame gave me a sweet, stupid, wide-eyed smile followed by a sudden wink. "Okay, okay. Just this once, I'll admit to my real age. But never bring this up again, toots."

I shook my head vigorously.

The rest of us looked at each other. But no one else spoke up. I decided that meant I was right, or at least close enough.

I turned back to the Actress. "One of us will win that prize and do something with it that...that's magic. And that person will move on. The rest of us will keep coming back, keep trying to figure out how to talk about the strangest thing that happened to us since the last time, and knowing that it's better to lie a little, than to never be able to tell the story at all."

The Actress pulled into herself, her eyes flooding with tears. She covered her face with the Spy's handkerchief for a moment, then dabbed her eyes and sat up. "So the world my mother told me about was always true. The world behind the screen, the ordinary world, the dull world where they're nasty to you because you come from across the ocean, that's the false world. The illusion? Is that what you're trying to say?"

The Spy patted her hand. "Alas, my dear girl, just because there is magic in the world does not mean, not in the slightest, that injustice and evil do not exist. The things that have happened to you in that terribly ordinary world, they have happened, and they have happened to you, and they will happen to others, too. Even magic might not have saved whomever you lost."

She threw her arms around him and buried her face against his shoulder. Muffled by his suitcoat, she said, "Thank you."

She said other things, too, but he drowned them out by saying "there, there" and petting the top of her head, as if she were a child. He was old enough to be her grandfather, it was true.

———◆———

After a bit of refreshment that gave the Actress enough time to gather herself, we all returned to the table. Only two tales left: the Good Doctor's, and the Spy's.

Dom had gone upstairs to check on a few things. It made me wonder about the time. There was no clock in the Honeybee's Sting, and I didn't have a watch. The Detective had a plain silver pocket watch. He took it out and checked it, then snapped it shut and tucked it back away.

"Damn thing's not working," he said.

The Spy cleared his throat softly to get his attention. "It will not. Not until the final tale is told. And then it will be dawn. This night will last as long as is necessary, so that all the stories may be told."

The Vampire said, "You are observant, sir."

The Spy gave him a sitting bow, not mocking at all. "Shall I go next?"

I said, "What I want to know is, is why? Why the Boss got killed."

Dom had just come into the room. He heaved a sigh as he lowered himself into the seat at the bottom of the table. "It's a long story."

The Good Doctor said, "It isn't. Truly it is not."

He had a strange tone to his voice, and I looked over to him. He was shaking.

In a bitter voice, he said, "I'll tell you why he was killed. My tale has not a single fantastic element to it...except for the fact that a white colleague of mine told it to me. If you don't mind, sir?" he added, directed toward the Spy.

The Spy bowed again. "I am in no hurry."

The Good Doctor breathed deep for several long seconds, then began by reciting a list of ingredients.

The Last Word Cocktail
The Good Doctor's Tale

*T*he Last Word Cocktail

    3/4 ounce gin

3/4 ounce green Chartreuse

3/4 ounce Maraschino liqueur

3/4 ounce fresh lime juice

Shake all ingredients together with crushed ice and strain into a chilled coupe glass. The liquid should seem light in color, almost milky, as if the outside of the glass were about to come all over with frost.

Garnish with a lemon twist.

It was the sort of cocktail that Victor always felt left a lingering taste in his soul. The exact taste varied. Upon one occasion, one might savor the taste of high summer and feel sun-warmed, flower-bedecked mountain breezes upon one's face. At another, an unpleasant bitterness might present itself. A third occurrence might allow for a complex, almost horrifying sweetness, the bitterness present but faded to a mere afterthought.

It was a cocktail of nostalgia, of regret—for what else is bitterness but the flavor of regret, which has aged in its cold, dark cask?—and, at times, of some emotion which Victor felt but rarely, and so had no name for: it was not love, nor joy, nor even simple pleasure. When this unnamable emotion found him, it left him eyes closed, one hand to cover his face, and rocking gently, as though to soothe himself.

If despair could taste of sweetness—if untimely death could have a flavor—perhaps it would taste like that.

But it was a rare occasion for Victor to drink a last word cocktail—just as it was rare for him, with his sister, to have the literal last word. To have both Chartreuse—and one must use green Chartreuse, and not the yellow—and maraschino liqueur at the same moment was unusual. To simultaneously obtain both a lemon and a lime at one and the same time was a piece of luck beyond the odds easily contemplated by a seasoned gambler. The year was 1926, and America had been wallowing in its pretense of purity, the Noble Experiment of Prohibition, for some years.

It was not an era for *luck*.

"Well? You haven't said a word since you returned," said Lucy, his sister.

This was, in essence if not quite in fact, true. Upon his return, he had showed her the bottles that he had obtained, then, drawing out the anticipation, had ignored her when she had commented upon her recent acquisition of some drinkable gin and asked whether he happened to have brought with him a lemon, a lime, or—if the fates so coincided—both. Instead he had gone to wash his face in the porcelain sink in the white-tiled bathroom.

To the left of the faucet was the porcelain niche holding his water-glass. To the right was Lucy's. The little tooth-brush shelf held two brushes, both boar-bristle brushes with steel handles, one facing to the right—the other facing to the left. The water smelled clean and fresh, although the unspeakable scent still clinging to Victor's hands somewhat spoiled its effect. He rolled up the sleeves of his shirt and scrubbed his hands and arms vigorously with red carbolic soap, which lay in its own porcelain dish—everything with a place, and everything in its place, a sort of joke between them—using a boar's bristle brush that could be applied with some force without stripping the skin from his hands. The scent lingered, but less forcefully than before.

Lucy had found him still standing at the sink. She ordered him to change his shirt and trousers, and tutted at him for the condition of his shoes, which were wet through, with ice clinging to the soles.

"If you take a chill, who will see to your patients?"

He had not answered her.

With a sigh, she said, "I'll make them without the lime juice," she said. To tease him she added, "With luck, I might be able to buy an orange out on the street."

He finished rinsing his arms, then reached into his pockets. Suddenly his anticipation had lost its savor. Into Lucy's outstretched hands he placed one lime and one lemon, saying, in a strained voice, "Only the one lime."

"I'll make do," she said, rolling her eyes.

He was fifty years old and she was a spinster, both of them with unsmiling and humorless faces, gray hair, and flat gray eyes. They were not the merry, stout sort of German. And yet, as with many things, appearances could be deceiving: they seemed so plain and stern because their lives were so rich with amusement. They had no need to advertise their inner selves with loud laughter, bright colors, or sparkling wit: they each were known by the other, and how many can say that of themselves? To be known at all?

Victor went into his bedroom and changed his clothing, donning evening dress. The jacket was the old-fashioned sort of satin lapels. One might wear it to the most formal occasions: the opera or a seven-course dinner with mignardise, attended by poets or emperors. The trousers had a narrow stripe of satin down the sides as well, in case of musicians; one liked to feel capable of a march. His shirt and waistcoat were ivory, as were his cuffs. He did not put on white gloves, which were no longer in fashion, nor the ridiculously high, stiff collar which had been purchased at the same time as the suit. He was not the sort of man to require such assistances to remain aware of his dignity.

"Oh, Victor," said Lucy, with a womanish sort of laugh as he entered their parlor, the kind of soft amusement that can't help itself. She handed him the lovely old silver-plated shaker. He shook it with practiced vigor, then filled the chilled coupe glasses generously and solemnly, as if they were drinking the last alcohol in existence.

They both sipped.

Victor said, "Today, I was called in to give my opinion on the circumstances of a certain death."

"Oh? Was it of any interest?"

"A banker's wife, Mrs. Hoffmann by name. The banker's name is Helmut, and her name was Leonie. Did you know her?"

"No, although I am sure that I know a dozen women who will claim, tomorrow, to have known her all their lives."

"She had been poisoned after drinking at the Cotton Club last night with Mr. Hoffmann."

"Poisoned how?"

"That was the question. Mr. Hoffmann insisted that her death was due to denatured alcohol being added to the drinks at the Cotton Club."

Lucy frowned so that her faint silver eyebrows came together like two opposing waves crashing against the same shore, but said nothing.

"I thought the same thing," Victor said. "The Cotton Club is not in the habit of allowing their guests to be poisoned. But that was what was said. Mr. Hoffmann was distraught. Word spread—" He stretched out the fingers of his right hand— "and Lucky Luciano heard of it."

"He's the Italian smuggler who supplies the club?"

"If he is not, he knows the supplier well enough to have taken the accusation personally," Victor said.

"You are German," Lucy pointed out. "So is Hoffmann."

"And yet I was the only doctor who could be agreed upon."

"You have a reputation for fairness," she said, as if it were ridiculous that it should be so. "*Probity.*"

He flicked his fingers at her. "Would you like another?"

A half-shrug: *you decide.* "There isn't the lime juice for it."

"Let us sip slowly, then," he decided. "I examined the dead woman in an unheated warehouse. She was still warm. I believe she expired on Christmas Eve, but so close to midnight as to make little difference. It was clear that she had not died in the warehouse, but had been brought there. From the patterns of lividity, it was clear that she had lain upon a sofa cushion at the time of her death: there was a white line across her cheek, like so."

He drew the trail of it across his right cheek.

"Her ear?"

"The lower half was white as well."

Lucy said, "So likely she had been moved, lividity had occurred, and yet she was still warm in an unheated warehouse, which, I note, you have not described or identified its location. I assume that absence of fact relates to the extreme lateness of the hour."

"It does, but no matter."

"Rigor?"

"In progress, but only just: it was cold."

"And yet the body, as you say, was still warm."

"And the pupils were only just becoming hazy."

"Six or seven hours since the death?"

"Perhaps. If I had to make a guess. I first saw her at eight this morning."

"And are you sure the woman was Mrs. Hoffmann?"

He flicked his fingers. "I am uninterested in that aspect of the case. I did not note any element inconsistent with her being so. She was a woman of Germanic descent, red hair, downturned lips, blue eyes, you know the type, good teeth, no callouses except on her feet. She wore a wedding band that was too small for her, and had a little bread dough around the setting of the stone. And no one claimed she was not."

"Very well: she was Mrs. Hoffmann, or so close as to make no difference, and she had been brought to the unheated warehouse."

"She was wearing a flesh-colored dress with jet beads, the type where the pattern reminds one of the Pharaohs of Egypt."

Lucy said, "'Worship, if you dare, at the goddess's temple.'"

"Just so. One shoe was on, the other off; the one that was present was buckled and strapped and thick-heeled for dancing; she wore silk stockings which were torn but not laddered. I was not allowed to remove the dress in order to check for contusions. Fortunately, it was a short dress, just below the knee, and quite close-fitting."

"Did you check the hairline?"

"No ligature marks: there were scratches about the throat, but no sign of her throat having been gripped."

"The eyes?"

"No stippling," he admitted. "You see what I am about to tell you."

"I suspected that you would."

Every doctor in New York City—as well as every doctor's assistant—was familiar with the signs of wood-alcohol poisoning, which did not occur among those who could afford to go to the Cotton Club, and would not have occurred so suddenly as to have left its victim in an expensive, beaded dress. No contusions, no blood, no strangling: a different poison had been used.

"There was black vomitus present," he said. "Her tongue was black, her teeth chalky and white. I prodded one with the small pick and the outer surface flaked."

"Burns?"

"Yes, about the mouth, and the skin around her lips and following the trail of vomitus down her cheek."

Lucy pursed her lips.

Victor said, "Her throat was marked with scratches."

"Her throat would have swollen, but she would have died before she could suffocate."

"Just so," he said. "The hands were a little reddened."

"From the vomitus."

"I think so, yes."

"Oil of vitriol?" she asked.

Dishonest bootleggers were known to make use of the technique of *beading*, which involved mixing sulfuric acid, also known as oil of vitriol, with sweet almond oil, and adding the mixture to watered, and therefore lower-proof, liquor to make it act as though it were of a much higher alcoholic content. It was as common a practice as taking government-ordered denatured alcohol and renaturing it again, and just as looked down upon by the customers of the Cotton Club, who insisted on properly smuggled liquor. And for the amount of money they paid for it, well they should.

"Was that the true accusation, then?" asked Lucy. "That Luciano had beaded his alcohol so severely that it had done this to Mrs. Hoffmann?"

"I may have misspoken myself earlier," Victor said.

"Oh?"

"The warehouse contained more than myself, Mr. and Mrs. Hoffman, and Mr. Luciano, but a much larger number of people. Owney Madden was present, for example."

"The owner of the Cotton Club?"

"None other."

"Which implies that more than one reputation was impugned. Go on."

"I went over the body thoroughly, more thoroughly than was necessary. I wished to observe Mr. Hoffmann."

"What did you observe?"

"That his hands were a little reddened."

"As if he had been assisting his wife, who had just swallowed a great deal of oil of vitriol?" asked Lucy.

Victor shrugged. "His hands were a little reddened. He blustered a great deal. He could not restrain himself for a single moment's silence. He paced, he swung his arms as he spoke, he smoked a cigar, he frowned continually."

"And the others?"

"Mr. Luciano was angry, the sort of anger that keeps hold of itself, all the better to spring out later, unlooked-for."

"How old is Mr. Luciano?"

"Twenty-nine or thirty. He kept his head."

"He kept it *then*," said Lucy. "From what I have heard, I do not think he is wise as a man is wise. He has an animal's wisdom."

"He is young."

"The Italians, they are animals."

Victor shook his head. It was an old argument. The women of Harlem came to him as they would a practical witch: lotions for head lice; salves for chilblains; cures for freckles, lighteners; abortifacients; formulations for flypaper and label glue; treatments for coughs. None of them were animals, or very few. He said no prayers and cast no spells, but they came to him all the same.

Lucy had other opinions; she had forgotten—or had *not* forgotten—that Germans, too, had been called animals, and not so long ago.

"What did you do then?" she asked.

"I told them that Mrs. Hoffmann did not show signs of having drunk wood alcohol but had likely expired from the ingestion of some other substance."

"You could not say anything else," Lucy said. "It would not have been wise."

"They wished to know what other substance she might have ingested. I spoke of various substances: of cyanide, of arsenic, of strychnine..."

"You were delaying for time."

"I was delaying for time."

"Was she pregnant?"

He tilted his head to acknowledge her astuteness on a key point. "Perhaps in the early stages. I think so."

Lucie's eyes narrowed to an eager sharpness. "Who *else*, Victor, was at the warehouse?"

"I do not like to say his name. It would not be politic."

"You can always," Lucy said, "take comfort in the fact that no matter how politically you must present yourself to others, I would always rather hear your rough-hewn truth."

"The truth, no matter how roughly hewn, is always too smooth for your tastes," he said.

She accepted the statement as a compliment. "But you have not said his name."

"He was a Negro, one of the performers. That should give you enough information, if you are so curious as to all that. But it is unimportant."

"Or it is very important, and you try to disguise the fact. You're like a puppy on tile, Victor."

"As you say. I asked Mr. Hoffmann what had occurred before the death of his wife. Why did I need to know, he asked. Could I not determine the cause of death from the symptoms alone?"

"'You are, after all, Dr. Lyon,'" said Lucy.

"That was his implication. But finally he was persuaded to speak, which he did so with great reluctance, many delays, much pacing, and more than a few misleading statements, self-interruptions, and other indirection."

"Or misdirection."

Victor said, "In short, Mr. Hoffmann and his wife had gone to the Cotton Club at nine o'clock that evening, and she had begun to feel ill soon afterwards. By ten they had left to return to their home, taking a cab so that she would not have to walk. Her symptoms worsened. She lay down upon the sofa, and began to vomit: just before midnight, her husband claimed, she was dead."

"There is no oddness about any dates with regards to inheritance?" Lucy asked.

"Not that I know of. There is money, but not that much money."

"You inquired as to their families before you came home?"

"I made some inquiries," he admitted.

"Were you satisfied?"

He did not answer her question; he could not. "I asked what had happened before nine o'clock. The resistance to answering the question became even more severe. Threats were made by Mr. Luciano. Then Mr. Madden stated he would cut Mr. Hoffmann off from use of the club."

"And that convinced him?"

"It seemed to. In the event, Mr. and Mrs. Hoffmann had gone to a speakeasy before their trip to the Cotton Club."

"Why on earth would they do that? If only these fools would *think*, Victor."

He had no answer to that statement, either. "Mr. Luciano seemed on the edge of violence, when the fact of the speakeasy visit came to light."

"I should think so!"

"But Mr. Madden had a cooler head."

"I have heard that he is a killer," Lucy said casually. "And that his birthday is Christmas."

"I have heard that, too. But I think he is the sort of man who would rather not have his birthday known."

"Superstitious?"

"He doesn't like give anyone a handle, I suspect. I thought well of him."

"If only the Cotton Club weren't so *loud*," Lucy complained.

Victor restrained himself from pointing out that it was, after all, a club. "The owner of the speakeasy was a Jew. He had invited the Hoffmanns in order to show off his nephew, who was a comedian."

Lucy shook her head. "And?"

"And there was some delay, then, so the Jew could be brought to the warehouse. A few guards were left with Mrs. Hoffmann, and the rest of us excused ourselves in order to eat. We went to an apartment belonging to Mr. Luciano or some member of his family, where several women served us."

"What did you eat?"

"There were several dishes: courgette fritters, grilled sardines, fregola pasta. Then baked chicken with olives, and finally some roasted leeks."

She nodded in approval. To her, it would not have been romantic to travel the world—only an annoyance—but she liked to try new dishes. But for the case of the Hoffmanns, she would have demanded he describe every detail of the meal. She herself was an exacting cook, an artist for an audience of one.

"And when you returned?"

"The Jew was present. He said that he had seen the woman and the man before and identified them as Mr. and Mrs. Hoffmann, and was sorry to see that she had died. Did he bead his alcohol? That was the question. Sometimes he did, he admitted. But he beaded his alcohol, he said. He didn't add alcohol to his vitriol to conceal that it was poison."

"Well said."

"I thought so, too. Then who had done it? asked Mr. Hoffmann. Who had killed his wife?"

"He should not have asked that," said Lucy.

"He should not have asked that. The question was soon answered, via the torture of Mr. Hoffmann to extract the truth."

"Did you cause him to answer it?"

"Not I," Victor said, amused. "There were men there for that sort of thing. It was quickly accomplished. Then they executed Mr. Hoffmann, and both bodies were removed."

"Then—what delayed you?" Lucy asked. It was almost ten o'clock in the evening.

Victor grimaced. "There was some unpleasantness."

"The Negro man," said Lucy. "And the wife newly pregnant."

"He was given a warning but was not executed, due to his impressive talents."

"Did they establish that their suspicions were correct?"

"No," said Victor. "For them, it was enough that he had been accused. The mob treats such men as though they were Caesar's wife: the shame came from having been suspected in the first place."

Lucy shrugged. "And then?"

"And then?"

"You still have not fully accounted for the time."

Victor said, "It is true, I have not."

"The true art of establishing what exists is defined by noticing that which is missing," Lucy said. "What one does not see is often the picture of the thing itself."

"That is true," he admitted.

"Then what is it that you have left out?"

"You tell me, sister, what I left out, for what grim tasks they yet had need of a doctor for." He leaned back in the chair. It was an old leather chair, one that his father had used to sit in, which Victor had been tempted to sell many times over the past year. The old man was gone, yet Victor was forced to choose what parts of him remained.

"Why must I tell you?" she said. Then: "Ah. You took his virility."

Victor put his hand over his face. "He will live. Afterwards, I walked along the streets for a time. I was troubled."

"It had to be done," she said. "Otherwise—"

He flicked his fingers at her, at the world, at the barrier he had crossed: it could not be described, what he had felt at the moment he had had to perform the terrible deed, the man frozen in silence and terror, lest any movement change his punishment to an execution.

They were, all of them, instruments or tools—or obstacles—to such men, the men who always—*always*—had the last word.

What Victor felt—so insignificant, so trivial, so indelible—could only be tasted.

The cocktail, whose ingredients had been so graciously provided by Owney Madden as payment for Victor's services, now reminded him, subtly, bitterly, of blood.

The Good Doctor finished his tale, and we all sat quietly, lost in thought.

In a low voice, he said, "I was told this story, almost entirely as I have repeated it to you. I found that I had to change a few of the names and locations. I hope that does not strike anyone here as unacceptable. The gentleman in question…I hope it is obvious what sort of man he was, what sort of monster."

He took a deep breath.

"I happened to repeat this tale to one of the musicians while attending a patient upstairs. Shortly afterward, the man in question died in my arms. I cannot say that it strikes me as justice, except as the most primitive sort. It is not what I wanted. If I had the right of punishing those who had hurt my people, the earth would be entirely barren of white men—and I would have lost my soul."

He looked down at his hands like a man imagining them still covered with blood.

"I am sorry to have come here tonight. I will go."

He stood up, and Dom stood up, too, putting a hand on his shoulder. "Do not go. Not before the end of the last story."

"Why?"

Dom looked almost embarrassed. "The police have come. They are upstairs."

Madame Ixnay got up so fast that her chair scraped on the floor. "I have to help the girls."

Dom spread his hands. "I hid them. They will be all right…a little confused in the morning, yah. But you—" He turned back toward the Good Doctor— "would surely have some trouble, a colored doctor attempting to leave here in the early hours of the morning…with bloodstained clothes."

The Good Doctor cursed. He walked away from the table and out into the other room, his footsteps making good time as he paced back and forth. His coat rustled as he picked it up and shook it out. He cursed again, then dropped the coat on the floor, the buttons rattling as they hit the cement.

I rose out of my chair. Dom gave me a look, then nodded.

The Good Doctor had opened the heavy oak door. He stood at the foot of the stairs, his chin in his hand, looking upward.

I picked up his coat and laid it on top of one of the tables. It was damp but not bloody; it was too cold in the basement room to have dried much while we were talking, but at least I'd done a good job getting the blood out.

"I should go," the Good Doctor told me. "I should risk it."

"Why?" I asked. "Why not stay until it's safe?"

"Safe?" The Good Doctor laughed. "When are my people ever safe? But I cannot stay here. Not when a man was murdered for my sake."

"Well," I pondered over what would be the least terrible thing to say. "Are you even sure there's an outside up there?"

"What do you mean?"

I took a breath. I wasn't sure what I meant, other than to stop the Good Doctor from going upstairs and maybe getting himself killed. "I mean, what time is it on your watch?"

He did have a watch, a plain steel one, in his pocket. He took it out and checked it. "It's stopped at seven." He tried winding it, then held it to his ear. "One more loss."

I shook my head. "It's stopped because time has stopped. How long have we been here, telling stories? Aren't you hungry? Tired? Haven't you noticed that the only time you get thirsty is between stories? Haven't you noticed how long all of this has taken?"

He frowned at me. "You're pulling my leg."

I pointed upstairs. "Are you sure *there's anything out there? Or that you can leave?"*

He lifted a foot and put it on the first step. "You're just a boy. What do you know?"

"I know better than to talk myself into thinking that whatever you seen earlier tonight was just a car." I paused. "Maybe you'll even win. And then you can help those folks escape whatever it was you were talking about earlier."

His nostrils flared. He lifted himself onto the second stair. "Men like me don't win. All we have is our pride, and if I stay here tonight, I won't even have that."

I turned my back on him and walked away. "Suit yourself," I said. "But I'd think hard about the folks I could save, before I opened the door at the top of the stairs."

"You're just making up stories! There is no magic!"

I didn't answer him, just walked into the back room and sat down in my chair. Dom said, "He will not come? Dot is a shame. But we have one more story to tell, I tink."

The Spy startled, coming out of his thoughts.

Then he sighed. "Yes. One more, though I mislike to tell it. It does not reflect well upon the world of men. And I have been trying to have more faith lately, because...because I must."

The Vampire had gone completely still, closing his eyes and steepling his fingers in front of him, looking like a statue of himself. Barely moving his lips, he said, "Faith in humanity? That would *be foolish. But have faith in yourself. You have always been a decent man."*

"I have done things I have regretted."

"It is your regrets that make you decent," the Vampire said. "You ruminate on what you might have done...when you had already done what little you could. But you have wasted enough of our time. Proceed."

He opened his eyes and stared coldly at the Spy; I think he didn't know how to look anything other than cold. He had the kind of face where smiling might have killed him.

The Spy had lowered his head to look at his hands. "And yet..."

Out in the other room, the oak door closed. Two seconds later, the Good Doctor entered and seated himself.

The Spy paid him no mind; either he was too discreet to remark on the Good Doctor's return, or he had retreated so far inside himself that he was no longer aware of the rest of us.

He said:

The Man Who Would Sell Fear

The Spy's Tale

The oldest and strongest emotion of mankind is fear, and the oldest and strongest kind of fear is fear of the unknown. —H.P. Lovecraft

...

It was the year of 1920 when I met the man who would sell fear.

We sailed aboard the cargo steam-ship the *SS Flammarion* from Perth to the Île de Nachtegal, which is an island quite far to the south of the Indian Ocean. Nachtegal is the sort of place which gives one the clearest possible aspect of the southern sky, and which serves as a sort of early-warning system of events occurring over the horizon in the Antarctic. Nachtegal has its mountains, its sheltered ports, and its high vantages from which to aim a telescope at any direction across the sea, or into the night sky. It is a chill place but not a frigid one, although the southern faces of the island are covered very nearly year-round with frost and snow, for the sun melts too little that which the storms which buffet the island deposit upon it from the south-west.

The *Flammarion* carried supplies from Perth to Port-au-Morbihan: fuel, foodstuffs, drink, machinery, clothing, household goods, spare parts, medicines, books, and other amusements. I was a paid passenger who had found a spare berth in the officers' quarters. French cargo-captains were always looking for a few extra sous here and there in those days, and were quite willing to accommodate that which their owners new little about, but generally tolerated. I was in a hurry to travel from Indonesia to Cape Town for reasons which were not solely my own, and the *Flammarion* promised a faster trip than any other ship prepared to leave within the next fortnight, even including the stopover at Nachtegal.

Of especial note was another paying passenger, a man named Métier who was an amateur astrologer and journalist. He had been sent on the improbable route of traveling from New York City, to Nuuk in Greenland, to London, to Cape Town, to Jakarta, to Dutch Batavia, in the East Indies, to Perth. He was to crown the glory of his trip with a visit to Nachtegal during the solar eclipse predicted for May 18th, where it was best to be viewed.

Métier was tall, but not remarkably so; thin, but not waiflike; and possessed of a long, stretched sort of visage, unpleasant to regard in and of itself, but also for the blankness of the eyes which stared from it, and the complete lack of lines upon its surface: neither laughter, nor tears, seemed to have spoiled that unblemished hide. He was full of mysterious claims and pronouncements, and spoke continuously of his dreams, in a way that made me wonder at his claims of being a trusted reporter for the *Herald*, for no editor of a newspaper—even one founded in the youth of a nation such as might be found on the American continent—would have tolerated the inexactitude of Métier's statements. He was a dreamer, of the type that makes little distinction between dreams and realities.

Being the only two passengers upon the ship, we spoke frequently together; he seemed anxious for my approval, for I have been known to put tales to the page, and even to be paid for them, and I felt the sort of curiosity that one feels upon viewing a Russian dancing bear the first time—but I speak with unnecessary cruelty. Métier was young, and uncouth, and wished to have fame, and wealth, and respect from those who had come before him, without having to make the slightest effort to obtain those things.

But then, who does not hope for the world to bless him, without him having to give her recompense?

We exchanged stories from noon to sunset. During the evenings, Métier would seal himself in his room for a short nap, then arise well after midnight, to watch the skies from the captain's telescope, or to sit in his cabin and type, until very nearly dawn, at which point he would nap again. We also played cards at first with the captain or whatever officers wished to vary their company and try out their tricks upon new victims, but that practice soon came to a halt. Métier was uncanny, and would predict with awful accuracy the cards that others held in their hands. His play was abysmal; it was not *he* that a player would be wary of, but the man who sat to his left, and to his right, who had heard, and would make better use of, Métier's prognostications.

We proceeded, as I said, to Nachtegal, to deliver our supplies and to take on whatever materials that were determined to be of interest to the French government. We would travel with only the barest supplies from Nachtegal to Cape Town, then refuel and resupply, before returning, in fits and starts, to France, where Métier would take a passenger-steamer to the Americas.

I myself had little idea what to expect from Nachtegal. I supposed it to be dull, isolated, and full of gossip; perhaps there would be a movie-projector, a card-shark or two, and a small heated bar where one could drink French brandy and experience the depths of that delicate emotion which the French have mastered far in excess of the English, called *ennui*. One might stand upon a windswept, treeless cliff, thought I, and glory in the absence of all civilization as one faced toward Antarctica—then watched the partial eclipse pass over the sun, giving the world that odd, shuddering sort of light that only sees during such celestial events—then shiver, and return to the more than physical warmth of the presence of one's fellow men.

I wondered, too, what Métier would make of it. He had shown me some of the tales he had written, full of mystical tomes, dread gods, dreams, and the occult. Of astronomy he had written little, but made many notes for future articles. I fully expected him to write of fell presences which had been invoked by the eclipse, or at least of an attack by sea-monsters.

When we arrived, there were hushed conferences between the captain and the governor of the island. The supplies the *Flammarion* had brought were moved off her and taken to warehouses, but she was not afterwards reloaded. Métier and the other officers and I visited the officers' mess at Port-au-Morbihan, where we were toasted with brandy—which Métier refused—and welcomed into card games with over-heartiness. The officers of Port-au-Morbihan did not suffer any sort of reluctance in playing cards with Métier, but only laughed at his accuracy, accusing him of hiding cards up his sleeve, of counting cards, of using small mirrors; in short, of every sort of trickery possible.

Every accusation seemed to be a direct hit, and Métier grew more and more cross, until it was *he* who removed himself from the table, complaining that the others were set against him. No, the French officers assured him, he was such an ill player that they adored his presence at the table...

Métier disappeared, and I had not the strength of character—not that night, at least—to follow him from the room. He was thirty years of age; high time for the boy within him to be tried and tested, and to become Man.

When I discovered that he had not returned to our room in the officers' quarters that evening, I regretted the lazy, unthinking words that I had said to myself: not all boys are given the test of an Antarctic island for their blooding, for not all of them would survive.

I went in search of him, asking here and there: "Have you seen the tall American with the long face?"

If they *had* seen him, they immediately knew of whom I spoke; if they had not, they shook their heads, but offered to help me look. I accepted the offer of one of the men, a Lieutenant de Grainville, to help me search.

We looked about the officers' quarters, then the men's, all public areas, and then back to the *Flammarion* to see if Métier had ended his upset on board the ship.

He was nowhere to be found.

De Grainville became more and more agitated, until finally he declared that he was forced to report the matter to the Port Governor and our captain.

I did not hear the discussion that ensued—I, an Englishman, was not welcome to their councils—but I soon learned of its aftermath: Port-au-Morbihan must be searched from one end of to the other, by all hands, without delay. I joined in the search, as did the members of our crew, staying close to the side of Lieutenant de Grainville.

He seemed eager to get rid of me—or, rather, to turn me aside from certain areas. After the third time we had turned from a certain path that led deeper into the island, I managed to remove myself from his presence, saying that I would meet him in the officers' mess when Métier had been found, then doubled back to take the path.

The day, May 17th, was a chill one, being the equivalent of November in the Northern hemisphere. The land was barren, with a thin, brown lichen being its most plentiful crop, accompanied by desiccated grass. I had been told that in spring, the colors would brighten, some few cabbages would sprout, and that I might see penguins, whales, and seals of all sorts. Upon the island were wild rabbits, feral housecats, reindeer, and wild sheep as well. Although I did not see any, I spotted their spoor here and there, in the frozen mud and snow. The wind was stiff but not unkind, and the sky overhead was blue and bright. The rocks seemed to be made of basalt and cement, with tall columns of dark rock along the coast, and pebbles agglutinated into severe masses further inland.

Upon the path, which was little more than sand and gravel put down to help one keep one's footing on the slippery rocks, I saw the traces of several men's boots.

I followed the trail for about a half-mile, ascending to the top of a low ridge, then overlooking it.

What I saw along the bottom of next ridge, in a valley so rounded that it might have been scooped out of the ground by a child's cup, was an immense citadel or fortress.

It is not ordinary for fortresses to be built at the bottoms of valleys, rather than at the tops of them, but this one had been. It rose far enough that the top of the fortress rose above my eye level, but it was not so tall that it would have been visible from the port along the coast.

The walls were perfectly smoothed, and bowed slightly along the walls, which were not made of rock, but of some sort of bluish metal that, although dull, was untarnished. The walls seemed perfectly smooth, although they were stained with the signs of a fire, or perhaps a massive lightning strike, for the walls had been blackened in patches and streaks.

Along the lowermost edge of the fortress wall, rocks had been thrown up here and there along the edge of the city. The trail I followed led into a shadowed pile of rock.

I began to descend the ridge. Before I reached the fortress, I had to cross a small, half-frozen river, on an ordinary, if worn, bridge of stone. The stream was no moat, and the bridge was no drawbridge, but a permanent fixture. I stumbled as I walked, for I could not even blink; I must stare at the strange fortress. I descended, I crossed the rough-hewn bridge with barely a thought, then stepped into the shadow of the fortress.

The presence of the fortress, with the bulk of it rising a thousand feet or more above me from its base, felt almost holy in nature. I felt awe and wonder, such that one feels in the greatest of temples and cathedrals. If you have ever been to Notre Dame or the Ramanathaswamy Temple, you would recognize my emotions, although what I felt then dwarfed anything I have felt within, or before, walls of stone.

The air was chill in the fortress's shadow, and seemed to hum with music. It was not music that I recognized, for it had no melody or tune or key. It was more akin to the sound of a beehive that lays near a field of flowers, or the soft murmur that one finds in a museum. It was a contented sort of sound.

The path led me among the rocks, and, upon rounding a series of tumbled, chaotic rocks that were devoid of even the island's usual faint greenery, I saw a rent in the wall of the fortress—or, rather, in the hull of the ship.

For that was what it was, a ship. In the absence of better berth or harbor, the immense structure that loomed above me had been plowed into the earth itself, and with such force that it had created for itself the valley in which it was now located.

It was a terrible sight.

The walls were stained and warped from a heat so immense that I could not imagine it, not even in the hottest part of a foundry, not even in the depths of a volcano. In the sunlight, the hull showed different colors, from the warping and the destruction come from the impact.

The rent itself had been created along an invisible seam in the wall of the ship, for one edge of the tear in the metal plate was more or less straight. The other edge of the tear showed that the metal had been peeled back, folded over upon itself like a curl of apple-peel. The peel on the ship, however, was ten feet thick if it was an inch, and had been cruelly marked with every sign of heat, and warp, and burn.

Whatever had landed that ship, had done so while in terror of its life, and of every soul aboard that ship.

The trail led to the rent in the hull. My feet carried me toward it, whether I willed it or no.

Within the ship was more than mere darkness, although I could not say that it was well-light. What was inside was a shimmering, half-reflected world of oily glistenings that moved and shifted as I watched.

I suffered a moment of abject terror, either unwilling or unable to flee from that which approached.

Then the shimmering colors solidified, and Métier appeared at the entrance, coming out.

His eyes were wide, horrified—triumphant.

"I have seen much of that which man was not meant to comprehend," said he.

I said, "Who hasn't?" and made to walk inside the entrance.

He lifted an arm to bar my way. "Do not go where only madness follows."

I said, "Métier, damn you, do you think I came this far to let another man's lack of curiosity send me away? They're looking for you back at the port. The least you could do is walk back there and say you saw me going the other way. I have no doubt that they will charge us with murder and throw away the key, but first I intend to see what's in this damned ship before they lock us away."

Métier shrugged, and said, "I'll go back inside with you, then."

And we walked inside together, side by side.

⬥

As it happened, we were neither arrested, nor imprisoned, but rushed off the island and onto the boat. Métier wished to stay, so that he could see the eclipse on the following day, but such a plan was no longer to be considered. A rumor had gone 'round the soldiers, sailors, and scientists stationed upon the island that Métier and myself had been lured to the ship by some supernatural force, and that we had been murdered, and replaced with doubles. To see us in person, even to clasp our hands and speak to us, gave no comfort. Everyone who had seen Métier seemed to be of the opinion that he had been inhuman, even before his arrival on the island.

On the ship we were loaded, as roughly as if we had been cargo, and with the first tide we fled.

As soon as the ship had settled itself (inasmuch as it *might*), the captain called us into his personal quarters, to consult with us on the truth of the matter. He offered us brandy, which I accepted, and Métier, once again, did not.

This time, however, his refusal seemed to carry more significance.

"The two of you are not inhuman sailors from beyond Heavens and beyond, then?" the captain jested.

I said, "I heard the rumor that we had been stolen away and replaced, as if by the fairies. How strange people are. It was nothing more severe than the force of curiosity which summoned me to that ship, or led me to go inside it."

Métier added, "And yet, if such a thing had happened, how would we know?"

I snorted. "You saw what lay inside the ship. I do not think that, if pricked, those forms would bleed red blood, such as you or I would, but in some other color."

Métier snatched up a fine-nibbed pen from the captain's table, and stabbed the back of his hand with it. A red bead of blood flowed. He handed me the pen and said, "Now, you."

I pushed the pen away, but Métier shoved it at me again. "How is anyone to know whether you would not murder one of us in the night, if you don't prove your humanity now?"

I sighed. "If you think you can stir up men's fears and make use of them—"

Without warning, Métier stabbed me with the pen, catching me in the webbing between thumb and forefinger; blood welled up, and it stung like blazes. I snatched the pen away from the man and tossed it back onto the captain's table, calling Métier ten different types of fool.

The captain said, "Never mind all that. What did the two of you *see*?"

The description that Métier gave was one of awe and terror: although he had seemed perfectly cool as he had accompanied me into the ship, and directed my attention to this or that, when it came time to describe what he had seen, he used the words of a man who had been in fear of his life, albeit in the same cool tones as ever. He seemed to invite the captain to find repulsive and full of dread mystery the pitiable things which we had seen.

As for myself, I had seen only tragedy: the alien dead which lay about the ship, the chaos and disorder of the crash, the agony of the motionless, ancient, desiccated, twisted, crystalline bodies.

I had wept to see the inside of the ship, and I said as much to the captain.

The captain shook his head. "That's as the case may be, gentlemen. But I must ask you to keep silent on these matters until we land in Cape Town, and then only speak as your best judgment guides you."

We both agreed to stay silent, although Métier had a look in his eye that told me, and, no doubt, the captain, that he would break his promise as soon as he wished to impress upon someone a feeling of fear, of loathing, or of terror.

I prayed that he would hold his tongue until we reached Cape Town, but knew that he would not.

―•―

The following day was May 18th, with the greatest amount of shadow—a little over half—of the visible eclipse to occur in the late morning. Métier gnashed his teeth with every nautical mile that passed, as we moved to the north-west.

The air carried a feeling of tension, not merely brought about by the rumors that had been spread around the ship. In one of the stories, Métier and I had been supplanted by reproductions of ourselves. In another, the hold of the *Flammarion* had been stuffed with crates full of the dead, brought out from the alien ship to our own when we had first debarked on the island. In a third story, one of the aliens had "risen," and was stalking its way about the ship. In yet another story, a few of the crew members had been eating the flesh of the dead, and now were possessed of immortality and other powers. But even rumors such as those—and I heard of them because the crew members came to me to ask whether they were true—could not explain all the tension on board the ship.

The feeling of tension mounted as the eclipse approached.

The captain ignored it, having his own concerns, but the rest of us lingered on the deck, waiting for the eclipse to begin.

If one has not seen an eclipse, even a partial one, it must be described as strange. One hears legends of those who believed in ancient times—although many did not—that the sun was about to be snuffed out, as a giant might pinch out a candle. Until one experiences an eclipse, the sensation cannot be described.

It is not the thought of the sun being put out that is so terrible; it is the *light* itself, which seems to vibrate and hum, to be itself so distorted that one's eyes cannot comprehend it.

If such a thing can happen, and can happen within the bounds of nature itself, then nature is not what it seems: that is what a solar eclipse seems to say.

On board the *Flammarion* were a number of hands who had seen an eclipse before, but many of them had not.

The moon began to slide over the sun. The older hands cautioned the younger not to stare at the sun, lest they burn out their sight. (Which is no unusual matter, when one considers that one can burn out one's sight at any time—but it is only during an eclipse that the temptation to *look* becomes so great.) The younger ones laughed and mocked their elders, saying that no one was such a fool as to stare at the sun—then had to be shaken, for they *did* look, they *must*.

As the eclipse increased, so did the agitation of the crew. The light changed, and bent, so that it seemed as though all the world began to shudder and shimmer. The light that reflected off the waves had changed its shape, reflecting light in colors that were not ordinarily seen at midday:

deep purples mixed with orange, bright greens in the midst of rosy pinks. The change in colors was rapid, nearly flickering.

The amount of the solar disk covered by the moon increased steadily. The laughing and joking had ceased when half of the sun had vanished. The feeling that we had crossed into some kind of uncanny half-existence touched on every soul, even those of us who had felt such a thing before.

Then one of the men screamed, pointing at another, accusing him of being "one of those creatures that came on the alien ship!"

As soon as the terrible words were said, I wished them to be retracted. But the second man, the one who stood accused, only screamed back at him that it was *he* who was other than human.

The two men were both seized, and sea-knives were taken from their sheaths. Each man was pricked with a knife. The blood did not merely bead up on the skin, but ran down their naked forearms, onto the deck.

Here I must admit, that, in the weird light of the eclipse, it did not seem as though the blood of *either* man were quite red.

Métier watched the events closely, but said nothing until the moment when he had seen both men's blood.

"Neither one of them is human. Throw them overboard, before the infection spreads." As all hands turned toward him in horror, in his cool tone, he added, "It spreads by the blood, you know."

And the men began to do it. I believe that at any other moment, the men would have laughed, and gone about their business.

But with the light as strange as it was, and the rumors as terrifying as they were, and with a hold full of who-knew-what on its way to distant Cape Town—for we were another thirteen days, at least, until we reached our destination—I believed in an instant that they were about to do it.

I shouted and ran forward, snatching the sea-knife away from one of the sailors, and stabbed Métier in the arm.

Blood ran from him as easily as it would have from anyone, and of the same color as the two men who had just been themselves pricked.

I shouted, "Should we throw *him* over the side, too? We must check *all* men's blood, before we condemn these two!"

It was as near to anything as I have ever seen, that sudden flash of mutiny and madness. Then I turned to the man closest beside me, and pricked him. He shouted in surprise, then drew his knife and demanded a chance at *my* arm.

I provided it, and the dark blood flowed.

Man challenged man, until the captain himself was forced to come out on the deck and stab himself, holding up his arm in that uncanny light, and shout, "What idiots! It's just the damned eclipse. Anyone who participates in throwing a man over gets thrown over himself—and I'll not rescue the culprit! Come inside and get something to drink, and play cards by lamplight, if you can't control yourselves on deck!"

The disgusted tone with which he spoke did much to soothe tempers; every man looked at his brother, and saw that each had paid for his foolishness in blood.

Métier had done and said nothing, after his first fatal announcement. As the men shuffled off belowdecks—for the eclipse was to last for some time yet, and the offer of an extra ration of ship's brandy was not to be declined—I rounded upon Métier.

"What did you hope to accomplish with *that* madness?" I demanded.

"The truth," said he, as naïvely as one might please.

"Murder, you mean," said I, and removed myself from his presence, lest I hurl him from the ship myself.

———◆———

The final two weeks of the voyage passed slowly. The captain left word to the men that Métier was to be watched constantly, and kept from getting at the crates down in the hold, or stirring up the men to fear with his stories, or even playing cards.

Métier barely seemed to notice. He wrote, typing away in his room at all hours.

When we arrived in Cape Town, he said to me, "I intend to report the owner of this ship for smuggling illegal material. That should get those crates opened up finally—but no matter. I have written my reports."

"I know," I said. "I have heard you all night. Were you able to sleep?"

"A little while ago," he said. "But they are finished. What have you accomplished? Have you written your reports?"

"I haven't done much of anything but play cards," I said. "I have only myself to please, after all, and neither write reports nor many tales, these days."

Métier gave me a long look, as though to say that *he* knew better than that. But after a few moments, he looked away, toward Table Mountain. "Does that mountain not remind you of the ship?"

"I suppose it must do," said I.

We circled around Mouille Point, and came in to dock. Métier found himself an official to declare the captain's dishonesty to; the official, who knew the captain long of yore, asked the captain whether he might inspect the cargo in the hold; the captain assured him that there were only geological samples to be found; the official asked to open a few of the crates and was allowed to do so, with Métier and myself—at Métier's smug insistence—watching; and several, seemingly random crates of rock were opened, revealed, and nailed shut.

Métier was stiff with outrage as we were escorted from the boat.

On the pier, waiting for our luggage, we stood and listened to the sound of the sea.

I said, "Métier, you must listen to me."

"Must I?" said he.

"There is a thing that men such as you and I must know, down to the bottoms of our souls."

"That some truths must never be spoken?" Métier asked bitterly. "That the world is set against us, always and forever? You seem to have worked out how to swindle your way through it."

"No," I said. "That we are men who walk along the borderland between the ordinary and the monstrous."

"I like that," he said.

"You mistake my meaning," I said. "*We* are the monsters, Métier, or at least have one foot solidly planted in a monstrous country. We have but to shift our balance a little, and fall all the way in. You must lean away from shock, and awe, and turmoil, and horror—or else you will fall all the way in. Men are not meant to take on the powers of the gods, lest we become tainted with them."

"What would you know?" he sneered.

"I leaned too far the wrong way once," I said. "And I pray God that I never do so again. I feel it in my soul at times, calling me."

"You're a fool," Métier sneered.

"With grace, I am an ordinary man," I said.

"A *very* ordinary one," said Métier.

Our luggage arrived, and I hired a man to take mine to my hotel.

I said, "What will you do, if your astrological journals will not publish your reports?"

"I will sell them to the magazines," Métier said. "I will do as you have done before, and call them fiction—call them lies."

"God save us all," said I, cursing him, "from men such as you, who would sell not cautions, not warnings, not conscientiousness—who would sell nothing but fear."

THE LIAR'S TABLE, PART 2

As the Spy finished his tale, he leaned back in his chair and exhaled as if he were releasing a ghost.

The Dame rubbed her hands over her shoulders. "Brr! Did it get cold in here, or was it just me? That fella, he sounds like a real character."

The Spy rested silently for a moment before he inhaled again. When he did, his words came out in a rush. "I feel relief at having released that tale into your care. After all these years, what I have learned that when I cannot turn these odd occurrences into fiction for the public, I must still tell them *somewhere*. And I worry that I will not be able to tell such a tale again, and have to carry such a thing with me to my grave."

The Dame flashed a smile at him. "Do ya wanna live forever, then?"

The Spy shuddered, took off his glasses, and cleaned them. "Heaven forbid. Please do not tempt me."

The Dame cackled uproariously, slapping the table with glee. Quietly, the Actress slipped her hand into the Spy's, and he squeezed it.

I thought back to the story I'd told, trying to give a life to my Aunt Claire, the one she never got to have. *I feel relief at having released that tale into your care*, the Spy had said. That was it exactly. Just so.

Everyone else at the table was talking to each other, nodding, shaking their heads, whispering, murmuring softly, talking about the Boss.

The Vampire cleared his throat and the table went silent. He said, "All the stories have been told. Now they must be judged, and the best selected, so that its teller may benefit and the rest of us may return to our beds for some well-deserved rest. As the Host, I will monitor the proceedings, and shall not vote unless called upon to break a tie, nor allow that my story be voted for."

The Dame said, "You just don't think you can win, sweetie. So you don't want to play."

"As the case may be," the Vampire said. "Nevertheless, you know that this is how it is done." Then he looked at me. "We will begin with your vote."

I could just about feel my eyes pop out of my head. "Me? I just got here. I wasn't even invited."

The Vampire lifted one eyebrow. There was a lot of threat behind that eyebrow. I swallowed.

"Do I just say my vote aloud?" I asked. "Or can I write it down or something?"

Dom said, "Just say it, kid."

I swallowed again. Nobody could vote for the Vampire's story, and you could have pulled my teeth and fingernails out, but I wouldn't have voted for my own story. Neither Dom's story about the pigs nor the Dame's story about the starlet tricking the witch had caught my ear, and the Good Doctor's tale was too dark for me. The Actress's story about the grimoire was about the same: I couldn't stand to think about the poor kid's soul being trapped as a grimoire for too long. For all that it was a strange story, it felt all too real, especially because the ending of the real story—whatever it was—must be even darker still.

But I'd liked the one Madame Ixnay had told, about the mistress with the mechanical ghost or whatever it was in her head, the Detective's pock-et-watch story, and the Spy's story about the two storytellers on the ship.

I said, "My vote is for the Spy's story. Do I have to say why?"

Dom said, "No, unless you want."

"Good, because I don't know why I liked it best. I just did."

The Spy made a disgusted sort of face, then flushed and lowered his head.

The Vampire said, "Your vote is noted." Then he turned to Madame Ixnay to me. "And yours?"

She voted for the Detective's time-traveling pocket-watch story. Next, the Detective voted for the Good Doctor's story, which surprised me—for some reason, I thought he'd vote for his own. The Dame voted for the story about the grimoire, saying that it had brought a tear to her eye. The Vampire abstained. The Actress—I have to admit that I hoped she would vote for my story, but she didn't—voted for the Spy's story, which gave him two votes, more than anyone else.

The Spy considered the matter, and said that he would vote for the Good Doctor's story, as he did not wish to vote for his own.

Which made it a tie: The Good Doctor's story against the Spy's.

The Good Doctor said, "I suppose I could vote for my own story, but I won't. I vote for the boy's story, because it makes me remember my mother's sister. She couldn't walk. And I like to think that somewhere, somewhen, someone had the pure decency to create a world where the only thing holding her back from her gifts was she herself. One damned world where things were fair—even if it was a world that never existed. Yes, I like that very much."

I wanted to burst into tears like a little boy. Someone had voted for my very first story! From that day to this, I have not forgotten that moment. If I had won that day, I could not have asked for a finer gift.

Dom drummed his fingers on the table. I just had time to wonder if he was deliberately drawing out the suspense—then he made a cutting gesture with one hand. "I vote for the tale of the house-fae who were freed. It pleases me. Let the old vampire across the table from me cast the deciding vote. It is what he wants to do anyway."

The Vampire said, "What I want is immaterial."

Madame Ixnay, who might have just been sore because nobody had voted for her story, said, "You have the deciding vote. I wouldn't say that what you want is immaterial."

The Vampire ignored her. He closed his eyes. It seemed like the bones of his face shone through his skin, he was so thin, and so frail, and so old. He put one hand on the box in front of him, then, strangely, picked it up and held it against one ear. After a moment, he sighed and put it back down again.

"Of the Good Doctor's story and the one regarding the two men on the ship, I must say that I am in favor of the tale of the Good Doctor." He raised a hand to forestall protests that weren't actually coming—everyone was silent—and added, "It was, after all, the shortest."

The Dame snorted. "What a maroon!"

Ignoring her, the Vampire reached one long, spiderlike arm to the center of the table, and pushed the jeweled box over to the Good Doctor, who reached one shaking arm out and opened it.

Inside the box lay an expensive pocket watch with an enameled cover in a bat pattern and tiny moonstones—the watch from the Detective's story.

The Good Doctor's hand closed over the watch. Then he said, "What do I do now? How does it work?"

The Vampire waved a hand lazily. "This one, you need only whisper your wish to it. Mind your phrasing—there will be only one wish."

The Good Doctor lifted the watch up to his mouth, closed his eyes, and wished. His lips moved, but he did not voice it aloud, whatever he wished for.

I never found out exactly what it was he wanted, nor whether he got it: I don't read lips.

When he was done wishing, he put the watch down on the table. "It is done. I feel it."

In the silence that followed his statement, I heard something crying, from inside the watch.

The hair stood up at the back of my neck. There was something *inside* the watch!

The Dame was looking around the room, staring at each of our faces in turn.

Then she said to the Good Doctor, "I thought I had ya pegged. I thought I knew what you were gonna ask for. I guess I was wrong, because our colors ain't different! You didn't make us all the same color, and we ain't had our colors reversed, neither."

The Good Doctor shook his head. "The Haves would always have a way to identify us Have-Nots, madame. You know how it is."

"Do I ever," she agreed.

The Detective grabbed the watch off the table and inspected it. "This is my client's watch! I wasn't even going to come here, except to get this damned watch!"

The Vampire said, "I believe that that is what my agent hired you to do, yes. You may take the watch to him, of course, although you should not be surprised when he commends you on your excellent work, pays you well for your time and trouble, and gives you the watch as a memento of your service. Guard it well; in ten years' time, bring it with you to the table, and you may attempt to win it again, and have your wish. By then...it should be ready."

The Detective stood up and lifted the watch above his head, as if to hurl it to the floor. "Bullshit! I didn't want to win it this time, except I was hired!"

Beside him, Madame Ixnay had gone pale. She put a hand on his arm. "Wait, Dash. If you break that..."

He lowered his hand slowly, then held the watch out to her. "You take it. I don't want to see this thing again as long as I live."

She took the watch, her jaw working as she swallowed several times in a row. If it *was* a time-traveling watch...

But I never found out about that either.

The Vampire looked around the table. "In ten years' time, then? Domovoi shall ensure that all of us are notified in the proper time, and summoned to the proper location, whether here or otherwise, and shall take care to invite others so we reach a full complement." He sniffed loudly, then flicked his fingers toward us. "You may go. You will find, my Good Doctor, that the police have left."

And then, sooner than I expected, it was over. Everyone got up and left. I stood in the corner, waiting to clear the table and clean the room. Dom was out in the main room, giving out coats. The Actress and the Spy left together, he holding her hand tenderly.

As the Good Doctor stumbled from the room, stunned by the turn of events, he thrust a wad of cash at me. "Here," he said. "I won't need it." It was something like a hundred dollars; I used it to buy a typewriter and to help some other folks out.

Madame Ixnay stood frozen for a few moments, staring at the watch in her hand, then threw her head back and carried herself out of the room with her spine as stiff as a poker. The Detective followed her, scowling at me, at the Vampire, at the empty chairs.

The Dame lingered for a moment, reaching out to pat the Vampire on the hand.

"It's almost dawn," she said. "You better get a move on, Davidson."

"I'll just be a moment," he said.

"Don't take too long," she said, then left the room in such a way that I had to force myself not to stare at her as she went.

Finally it was just the two of us, me and the Vampire. I found his cane tucked back against the wall next to the wine bottles, and handed it to him, ready to help him up.

He said, "Boy, you did well. Remember that, later. You belonged at the table this night. Also of import is to note that you did not win."

"I'll remember that, sir."

He reached into his pocket, pulled out an envelope, and said, "Make sure Domovoi receives this."

"I will, sir."

He nodded. "And now, please allow me the privacy of the room for a moment. You can take your rag to the table later."

"Yes, sir," I said, wondering what he meant, but closing the door behind me as I went.

———◦———

Dom was standing in the main room, watching the last view of the Dame as she disappeared up the stairwell. He looked at me, then looked at the door to the back room, then looked at me again and winked. He opened the door to the back room with a flourish.

The Vampire was no longer inside.

How had the old man, who needed a cane to walk, made it up the old coal chute by himself—without making a sound?

Maybe, I decided, I didn't want to know.

After I gave him the envelope, Dom went upstairs, saying he needed to help Madame Ixnay with the girls—I wondered where he'd hidden them, and hoped they were all right.

I hoped that the Good Doctor had made it out safely. I hoped that whatever he'd wished for had gone all right.

I cleaned up the back room, washed out the bowls of bloody water from the Good Doctor's coat, wiped out the tea pot—already stained dark on the inside from all the tea that had gone through it that long night—and washed the glasses.

Then I looked around, wondered once more where the gas furnace could be hiding, and shut off the lights, wondering what would happen next.

It turned out that the Boss had named me his heir as a favor to an old mistress of his who had been my aunt—meaning my Aunt Claire, who hadn't been any man's mistress, as far as I knew—and I inherited the whole business, at least in name.

Dom ran the place for a while and taught me the ropes, then faded into the shadows again. I kept the place as decent as I could and typed my stories early in the morning, when everyone was asleep but the Chinese ladies at the laundry. (I might have stolen a tale or two from them.) I sent my stories to the rags under a different name. I was never famous, never picked as one of the best, and my tales faded from most folks' memories.

But there were always a few who sent me letters through the publishers, saying how much one or another particular tale meant to them, so I kept at it.

Shortly after that night, the Good Doctor disappeared, along with about a hundred other colored folks who were never seen again. They had been just ordinary folks, as far as I knew—not imprisoned, per se, but I could see how the Good Doctor might not have seen it that way.

The Good Doctor sent a note Dom in November of 1939 with a note saying, "Everyone that could be saved, has been." Madame Ixnay won in 1939, made her wish on the watch, and retired, leaving the watch behind and moving to the West Coast. I lost track of her. If she used that watch to travel in time, I never found out. The Spy never returned, and neither did the Actress. The Detective died in '61 of lung cancer without having won.

I stayed with the Honeybee's Sting until late 1949, when it closed. By then I'd been the owner of record for almost twenty years, with rumors flying that I'd been the illegitimate son of the Boss, and that's why I'd inherited the place. I just kept my mouth shut and tried to make sure nobody got hurt.

I still see the Dame around, under different names. Today she doesn't seem any older, or less pretty. I was hoping to see her tonight, but she couldn't make it.

New folks joined, won, lost, disappeared, died, went broke, made it big on Broadway, gone on to become rich and famous, or rich and not so famous.

I have so far resisted winning. I've never wanted more money or fame. Selling the old Honeybee's Sting building has kept me in funds to this day, and I make a modest amount from my storytelling. And I am cautious of trying to change the world, at least by means of magic.

But tonight I ask a favor of you. Tonight, if I win, I will release the creature inside the watch. For there *is* a creature inside that watch, one that has been there longer than I would like to think. If you hold the watch up to your ear, as I have, you can hear it pleading from within.

The old ones, they will find other treasures to pass amongst us to tempt us to tell them our stories. But the rest of us, we are human beings, and not meant to be so heartless.

I have thought long and hard upon the matter. The creature within the watch should be freed, if we are to keep hold of our souls.

At least, if I am to keep hold of mine.

Every time men create a slave, every time we force a soul to conceal its true nature, every time we lay our burdens on the shoulders of another, we lose something vital about ourselves. We turn toward our fears, and use them to justify the most monstrous of acts.

We forget who we are.

We are not the old ones. We are born to strut upon the stage and die when our hour is over, to have lived with gusto and tragedy, to have our brief flames spent upon the stories of our lives.

We are not meant to be immortal, nor meant to hold the power of one. We are not meant to restore that which could have been, nor to rewrite reality as we wish it. We are meant to dream of such things—but never to do them.

I would like to free that which is inside the watch, and restore my own humanity.

I would like to tell it not to think too badly of us, as the dawn comes and it decides what to do about those who have trapped it there for so long. In all of the cold black night of the universe, those of us with a little decency are but faint stars glimmering in the distance, very cold, and very far away. But sometimes we join hands, and glimmer a little brighter for a while, and provide a little warmth and meaning in the world.

Think about that as you vote on my story, at the end of this long, cold night.

· · · THE END· · ·

Author Checkin!

H i all,

As I write this, we are waiting for Tropical Storm Elsa to do whatever it's about to do to Florida. This will be the first tropical storm I've been through, but probably not the last. I'm post-divorce and living at an AirBnB in St. Pete with my daughter, Ray, who's nineteen-going-on-twenty. Yesterday I made her eggs benedict with lime juice and curry powder. I think she has become part Shaggy from Scooby-Doo.

Hello! In case we haven't met before, my name is DeAnna Knippling, and I'm the author of this collection of short stories. I recently got divorced, moved across the country from Colorado to Florida, went from being a freelance writer and stay-at-home-mom to full-time employed, and brought my adult daughter with me so she can get residency to go to school in Florida. I feel like my personality right now is mostly "tired."

This is the first author check-in that I've written, and I'm already liking it!

But onward...

The story behind this collection is that it was inspired by the book, by David W. Mauer. Mauer was a linguist who got interested in the slang that con artists used in the 1930s and 1940s, but who ended up learning a *lot* about how cons worked in the process and wrote a (non-scholarly) book in the process. It's a fun, witty read that impressed me so much that I decided to write a bunch of stories about cons. The collection is set in the

1920s, though, because I like the 1920s more as a historical period. (Why? I dunno. *The Great Gatsby* isn't my favorite book or anything.)

In an earlier short story collection, *A Murder of Crows*, I wrote a frame story similar to "The Liar's Table" in this collection to stick together a series of horror stories. It went well, so I decided to do it again here. It's a lot of work, though:

- Write all the stories.

- Figure out what order you want the stories in.

- Figure out a story that somehow means that the stories (which you didn't really write with any logical connection other than "something something cons, 1920s?!?") have to be in exactly that order for the connective story to make sense.

- Make sure that the whole thing flows together.

I had forgotten how hard it was to write the frame story the *first* time. I remembered.

"When Pigs Fly" is a non-magical con story, à la *The Sting*, the Robert Redford movie. This was as close as I ever got to writing a story about a traditional con.

"Myrna and the Thirteen-Year Witch" was written for a collection about immigration—and about slavery, and how we might be participating in an evil act with neutral or good intentions. I'm still not sure about this story. Does it say what I want it to say? Or did the racism and other biases that I grew up in wreck the story? Hard for me to say.

"The Magician's Grift" came about because...I thought the Foshay Tower was a pretty nifty piece of Art Deco architecture! All the characters have major secrets (except Robert). I tried to hide them in plain sight.

"All the Retros at the New Cotton Club" is set in the future; I've had more people ask me to write more stories set in this world than anything else I've written. I've decided at the very least to write some short stories there—"Be Careful What You Steal," the bonus story, is set in the same world. I don't actually remember why I wrote "All the Retros"! I think I just said, "I want to write a sci-fi con story this time" and went from there. I do remember that the main plot twist wasn't something I consciously decided. I got to the same point where the main character finds out—and the big reveal came to me at the same moment. I had something completely different planned out, but kept going, "Something funny is going on here." In "Be Careful What You Steal," I sort of planned for the same thing. I said, "This needs to be set in a future 1920s world where retros are a thing, and I need a big plot twist." I picked out the setting (Tribune Tower!) and just started writing. Okay, first I overthought what I might do for plots, but I threw them out and decided to trust myself instead. And it worked!

"The Mysterious Artifact" is another sci-fi tale, this one inspired by Francis Stevens's book *The Heads of Cerebus,* which I read because it sounded like a Gene Wolfe title. I liked it! She's been called "the woman who invented dark fantasy."

"Memento Temporis" was written for a side project, . I did a bunch of short time-travel stories in a row for some reason around then, trying to answer the question, "If you could have a do-over, what would happen to the person you are now?" I feel like it needs to be said that making healthy choices for yourself sometimes makes your unhealthy self feel like you're getting left behind.

"The Page-Turners"...look, sometimes you just write the story that you want to write, the story that you believe in. I had been thinking about how real life is never as organized as fiction, and usually not as happily-ending, either. Why is that? Because it's fiction—under the control of the reader, as it were. This one's in second person because of the second-person movie Europa/Zentropa by Lars von Trier, which I liked. The main character is based on Anna May Wong, the Chinese-American actress.

"The Last Word Cocktail" was written after going to the Mob Museum in Las Vegas, where I picked up a book on Prohibition-era mixology, reconstructed from a doctor's notes. After I wrote it, I realized the sister was inspired by a "friend" on Facebook who had showed her ass as a racist asshole. I felt ill having been around someone who was that much of a piece of poison the entire time I knew her. How could I not have known? Probably because I needed to work on myself, but that's another story.

"The Man Who Would Sell Fear" was inspired by two men: Rudyard Kipling and H.P. Lovecraft. By pretty much any account, Lovecraft was a racist asshole who had no ambition in life but to prove that he was better than everyone else. He took people's fear of the unknown and preyed on it for attention.—That's not to say I don't like a lot of his fiction. I really do. But all he really has to say about the universe, etc., is "The universe is scary...*be scared!* And possibly disgusted by fish genitals." I read his entire collected works of fiction.

Kipling, on the other hand, is a colonialist but at least humane piece of cheese whose message is, "Dear Britain, fuck around and find out." The part that he missed was that Britain, while indeed fucking around, never really did find out, and hasn't paid for it yet and probably never will, and it was naïve to think they ever would. (I think where Britain is now has more to say about its internal predators than about payback.) I can relate, given that I'm white and Amercian. But Kipling also has other emotions to convey—a lot of friendship and wonder at how big the world is.

The two men *could* have met. I checked. Also, I'm permanently going to think of Kipling as a part of British espionage services until I die, due to comments left in "The Man Who Would Be King" and other tales. Or maybe technically he wasn't a member of any service because that hadn't been formalized yet, but did espionage work for them nonetheless.

The frame story, "The Liar's Table," is a tale to stick the rest together. When I went to put the collection together, I knew I wanted to have a bunch of cons involved, trying to con each other out of the treasure on the table, each story more outrageous than the last. The frame story wasn't intended to have magic in it. The end was supposed to be a twist somehow in which the thing in the middle of the table was worthless all along, and had been stolen before the night had even started.

But I didn't like the original plan, so I changed it.

Magic crept in, first with the object on the table (the watch), and then into a few of the characters. I've been writing a lot of stories about powerful characters mixed in with the rest of us lately, and it felt natural to include some here—I didn't discover which ones were powerful until about three-quarters of the way through the collection, though. Sometimes writers surprise themselves.

I still intended to make the ending a con or swindle somehow, but I just couldn't make myself do it. I wasn't feeling it. I came to realize that there was a sentient being in that watch, and I just couldn't leave it there.

But I also didn't feel quite right letting it out, either, to derail the end of the story—so I'll leave the decision up to you.

Love, De

St. Petersburg, FL

July 6, 2021

More to Read! - The House Without a Summer

If you enjoyed this story, please consider checking out *The House Without a Summer.*

Nobody builds dread—or dark wonder—like DeAnna Knippling, veteran author of 80+ books.

England, 1816. The Industrial Revolution. Penderbrook. The grandest estate in Northamptonshire chews through human souls like water turning a water-wheel. Younger son Marcus Sewell knows this. He bought a military commission at seventeen to escape Penderbrook—and his father.

Now death calls him back.

The Tambora volcanic eruption cast red dust across the globe. The sky burns red at dawn. Wheat freezes in the fields, bread tastes of must and rot, and the hungry stream toward London in their thousands.

Marcus's dead brother lies in the wine cellar, unburied. His father the Earl sits in the nursery, mad and waiting for his dead son to return. And Lucy Abbott—dark, sharp, entirely too sensible—hands Marcus a glass of off-tasting whisky and starts to explain how his brother ended up in the wine cellar.

He doesn't want to be here. Penderbrook doesn't care what he wants.

A gothic horror novel about inheriting a world you don't want—and the cost of trying to outrun the consequences of those who came before you.

You can find it on my website, WonderlandPress.com.

THE HOUSE WITHOUT A SUMMER

It wasn't until Miss Lucy Abbott had attended the Great Exhibition of 1851 several times that she began to truly understand what had happened in the year of 1816.

Decades had passed; the unendurable, mad year of 1816 had come to a close; those who had died had faded from memory for the most part, either disappearing as if they had never lived, or taking on the aspect of the people they ought to have been, rather than the blackguards they were. In particular, the reputation of the Earl of Penderbrook had been much ameliorated.

In Lucy's secret heart of hearts, she suspected that she herself had been changed little by what had happened, although at the time she had felt herself to have been transformed entire. What she had lost seemed the world to her. But, both before the tragedy and after, she was as dark of mind and eye as ever; her heart still dwelled upon the injustices that she saw everywhere. But who might she have been, if events had occurred otherwise? A wife, a mother, and a fine addition to society—if somewhat macabre of humor and a little too interested in novels.

Until the Great Exhibition, she had supposed herself entirely recovered of her peace of mind. And indeed, the first several times she visited the Crystal Palace, home to the exhibition, she felt only wonder, sore feet, and delight.

But as the Great Exhibition progressed, her heart began to leap uncomfortably about in her chest: at the sight of certain too-familiar, yet altogether featureless faces; the smell of mildew and unwashed bodies; even the sound of a laugh, shrill yet commanding, that reminded her of the Earl's.

As she wound her way through the endless exhibits collected by Prince Albert and his committees, she was forced to remind herself more and more often that she was not walking through the halls of Penderbrook.

Penderbrook was gone as though it had never existed.

Thank God.

———— ◦◦◦ ————

When first the Great Exhibition had opened, she had gone to see it like everyone else: it was a marvel, a wonder, the gathering of all that was brightest and best in the world, the promise of increase and prosperity to all mankind. She went because she had been invited by friends. She went because she had always had more curiosity than sense. She went because she had an idea that she would like to set one of her stories there, or at least to gather the flavor of a hundred different countries around the world, so that she might set her stories anywhere, and at least have some hope of getting something right.

She was always in despair that a reader would catch her out in some hideous inaccuracy, although they seldom did, or cared.

The Crystal Palace was a shining edifice, grand and impressive, a hall made of steel and glass. She could see inside it as the carriage approached, the sea of humanity that entered it, and, through the glass, the bustle upstairs, and an endless row of booths. She was handed out her carriage, escorted inside, and treated with all civility. She was not so overwhelmed that she did not understand that she was being treated as visiting royalty in the hopes that she would write something favorable about the exhibition for the Press.

It was everything that she had hoped for, and she promised herself that she would return again and again, and the next time she would attend with a notebook and more comfortable shoes. Later, she remembered little of her first visit but a blur.

She continued to visit the exhibition, to take copious notes, to study, to dream.

This continued into October of 1851, when the exhibition was about to close. The sense of wonder still remained, but it was a frantic sort of emotion now, the kind of feeling that one gets when one stays up past one's bedtime and had drunk just enough brandy to feel a certain amount of strain underneath one's own merriment.

It was a twilight sort of mood.

The exhibits, over the course of the exhibition, became less and less well maintained. The upper tiers of British society began to absent themselves, and the exhibition put on specials for the lower classes to attend more cheaply. The halls were more packed than ever. Little things began to disappear, either stolen by thieves or preventatively removed by the owners, wary of thievery.

She began to feel a certain familiarity, not of the exhibition itself, but of some other place, which she could hardly remember.

Then one day she turned in the hallway around one booth to the next and did not recognize where she was. She was surrounded by pale figures rushing past her, not quite ghosts, but men and women with all the color washed out of their faces, as though they were illustrations printed on onionskin paper. They grimaced at her and at each other, baring their teeth. Her skin rose up in instant gooseflesh, and her teeth chattered against each other several times, shivering, before she clenched them together.

When she glanced back over her shoulder, the hall seemed familiar again. There was the new steam engine; there was the new type of lock that everyone had been so certain of no-one ever being able to pick! But of course it had been defeated by an American locksmith in a matter of days... In other words, she knew her ground. The phantoms had vanished, or rather been subsumed back into the people surrounding her, who seemed as perfectly ordinary as always.

But upon walking forwards a few steps, she shuddered again.

Penderbrook.

As the word came to her, she jumped back from a pale-faced gentleman who had come forwards to shake her hand. She had no wish to startle the man—he wished only to tell her that he enjoyed her stories—so she forced a laugh and quipped, "You made me think of my editor for a moment!" He laughed, and they chatted briefly.

She hoped that she had concealed her true emotions from appearing on her face.

At any moment, she expected to be snatched from behind, a cold limb twining itself about her shoulders.

Lucy...

You know you must leave, Lucy, before it is too late.

After her admirer had excused himself, she had been solicitously asked by her secretary if she wished him to find her a seat; she had gone quite pale. She clutched his arm, saying that she felt a bit dizzy and did not wish him to leave her side, lest she fall.

Do not let me vanish.

It had long seemed to her that she owed a debt to Penderbrook. Or perhaps debt was not the right word. But there was a part of her which belonged to Penderbrook, which she had always suspected would someday be reclaimed as its own.

Her secretary held his arm stiffly at his side, and she clung to it, near to weeping. The halls seemed to spiral about her, wrapping her tighter and tighter until her breath became painful in her chest. The sense of being pulled or called increased. The faces spinning past her seemed to leer at each other, every face turned into a kind of translucent, bloodless clay.

This place is dying, she realized.

The Crystal Palace was clinging to life as a drowning man might cling over-tightly to his would-be savior, causing them both to sink.

As Penderbrook had done.

And she, of all who were present, was perhaps the only one to understand the sensation, because she had felt it before.

She must not let it take her; she must not let it take her secretary. She would linger no longer.

Slowly, carefully, deliberately, she took a step forwards. The Crystal Palace pulled at her. Oh, how it pulled! Like softness, like warmth, like the stupor after lovemaking, like candlelight. But she knew what it was now, knew that it was only winding up its cocoon, tighter and tighter, seeking a place of safety and finding only self-destruction.

Lucy...

You must leave, Lucy, before it is too late...

Her secretary stopped her to ask, "Miss Abbott? Are you quite all right?"

"I have a desperate need of air," she told him, and he led her outside of the Crystal Palace, to which she never again returned.

The building was pulled down soon after. They said it was to be rebuilt on the top of Sydenham Hill, to hold permanent exhibits.

But it was not the same place, and she ever after felt herself having very narrowly escaped indeed.

⸻◆⸻

You can find The House Without a Summer via my website:
WonderlandPress.com

About the Author

Nobody delights—or devastates—readers quite like DeAnna Knipling, veteran author of 80+ strange stories for interesting people.

DeAnna collects new systems the way crows collect shiny things. She makes cocktails to understand flavor logic, reads tarot cards to study psychology, plays a number of musical instruments badly, loves museums, explores via kayak whenever possible, and picks up a new hobby four times a year...because that's just how her brain (over) works.

She lives in Las Vegas, Nevada. Find her at WonderlandPress.com.